**George Gr**

C000000282

# History of Greece
## Volume 2

George Grote

# History of Greece
## Volume 2

1st Edition | ISBN: 978-3-75235-391-4

Place of Publication: Frankfurt am Main, Germany

Year of Publication: 2020

Outlook Verlag GmbH, Germany.

# HISTORY OF GREECE

BY

GEORGE GROTE

VOL. II.

.

PART I.

## CONTINUATION OF LEGENDARY GREECE.

# CHAPTER XVIII.

## CLOSING EVENTS OF LEGENDARY GREECE.—PERIOD OF INTERMEDIATE DARKNESS, BEFORE THE DAWN OF HISTORICAL GREECE.

### SECTION I.—RETURN OF THE HERAKLEIDS INTO PELOPONNESUS.

In one of the preceding chapters, we have traced the descending series of the two most distinguished mythical families in Peloponnêsus,—the Perseids and the Pelopids: we have followed the former down to Hêraklês and his son Hyllus, and the latter down to Orestês son of Agamemnôn, who is left in possession of that ascendancy in the peninsula which had procured for his father the chief command in the Trojan war. The Herakleids, or sons of Hêraklês, on the other hand, are expelled fugitives, dependent upon foreign aid or protection: Hyllus had perished in single combat with Echemus of Tegea, (connected with the Pelopids by marriage with Timandra sister of Klytæmnêstra,[1]) and a solemn compact had been made, as the preliminary condition of this duel, that no similar attempt at an invasion of the peninsula should be undertaken by his family for the space of one hundred years. At the end of the stipulated period the attempt was renewed, and with complete success; but its success was owing, not so much to the valor of the invaders as to a powerful body of new allies. The Herakleids reappear as leaders and companions of the Dorians,—a northerly section of the Greek name, who now first come into importance,—poor, indeed, in mythical renown, since they are never noticed in the Iliad, and only once casually mentioned in the Odyssey, as a fraction among the many-tongued inhabitants of Krête,—but destined to form one of the grand and predominant elements throughout all the career of historical Hellas.

The son of Hyllus—Kleodæus—as well as his grandson Aristomachus, were now dead, and the lineage of Hêraklês was represented by the three sons of the latter,—Têmenus, Kresphontês, and Aristodêmus, and under their conduct the Dorians penetrated into the peninsula. The mythical account traced back this intimate union between the Herakleids and the Dorians to a prior war, in which Hêraklês himself had rendered inestimable aid to the

2

Dorian king Ægimius, when the latter was hard pressed in a contest with the Lapithæ. Hêraklês defeated the Lapithæ, and slew their king Korônus; in return for which Ægimius assigned to his deliverer one third part of his whole territory, and adopted Hyllus as his son. Hêraklês desired that the territory thus made over might be held in reserve until a time should come when his descendants might stand in need of it; and that time did come, after the death of Hyllus, (see Chap. V.) Some of the Herakleids then found shelter at Trikorythus in Attica, but the remainder, turning their steps towards Ægimius, solicited from him the allotment of land which had been promised to their valiant progenitor. Ægimius received them according to his engagement, and assigned to them the stipulated third portion of his territory:[2] and from this moment the Herakleids and Dorians became intimately united together into one social communion. Pamphylus and Dymas, sons of Ægimius, accompanied Têmenus and his two brothers in their invasion of Peloponnêsus.

Such is the mythical incident which professes to explain the origin of those three tribes into which all the Dorian communities were usually divided, —the Hyllêis, the Pamphyli, and the Dymanes,—the first of the three including certain particular families, such as that of the kings of Sparta, who bore the special name of Herakleids. Hyllus, Pamphylus, and Dymas are the eponymous heroes of the three Dorian tribes.

Têmenus and his two brothers resolved to attack Peloponnêsus, not by a land-march along the Isthmus, such as that in which Hyllus had been previously slain, but by sea, across the narrow inlet between the promontories of Rhium and Antirrhium, with which the Gulf of Corinth commences. According to one story, indeed,—which, however, does not seem to have been known to Herodotus,—they are said to have selected this line of march by the express direction of the Delphian god, who vouchsafed to expound to them an oracle which had been delivered to Hyllus in the ordinary equivocal phraseology. Both the Ozolian Lokrians, and the Ætolians, inhabitants of the northern coast of the Gulf of Corinth, were favorable to the enterprise, and the former granted to them a port for building their ships, from which memorable circumstance the port ever afterwards bore the name of Naupaktus. Aristodêmus was here struck with lightning and died, leaving twin sons, Eurysthenês and Proklês; but his remaining brothers continued to press the expedition with alacrity.

At this juncture, an Akarnanian prophet named Karnus presented himself in the camp[3] under the inspiration of Apollo, and uttered various predictions: he was, however, so much suspected of treacherous collusion with the Peloponnesians, that Hippotês, great-grandson of Hêraklês through Phylas and Antiochus, slew him. His death drew upon the army the wrath of Apollo, who destroyed their vessels and punished them with famine. Têmenus, in his distress, again applying to the Delphian god for succor and counsel, was made acquainted with the cause of so much suffering, and was directed to banish Hippotês for ten years, to offer expiatory sacrifice for the death of Karnus, and to seek as the guide of the army a man with three eyes.[4] On coming back to Naupaktus, he met the Ætolian Oxylus, son of Andræmôn, returning to his country, after a temporary exile in Elis, incurred for homicide: Oxylus had lost one eye, but as he was seated on a horse, the man and the horse together made up the three eyes required, and he was adopted as the guide prescribed by the oracle.[5] Conducted by him, they refitted their ships, landed on the opposite coast of Achaia, and marched to attack Tisamenus son of Orestês, then the great potentate of the peninsula. A decisive battle was fought, in which the latter was vanquished and slain, and in which Pamphylus and Dymas also perished. This battle made the Dorians so completely masters of the Peloponnêsus, that they proceeded to distribute the territory among themselves. The fertile land of Elis had been by previous stipulation reserved for Oxylus, as a recompense for his services as conductor: and it was agreed that the three Herakleids,—Têmenus, Kresphontês, and the infant sons of Aristodêmus,—should draw lots for Argos, Sparta, and Messênê. Argos fell to Têmenus, Sparta to the sons of Aristodêmus, and Messênê to Kresphontês; the latter having secured for himself this prize, the most fertile territory of the three, by the fraud of putting into the vessel out of which the lots were drawn, a lump of clay instead of a stone, whereby the lots of his brothers were drawn out while his own remained inside. Solemn sacrifices were offered by each upon this partition: but as they proceeded to the ceremony, a miraculous sign was seen upon the altar of each of the brothers,—a toad corresponding to Argos, a serpent to Sparta, and a fox to Messênê. The prophets, on being consulted, delivered the import of these mysterious indications: the toad, as an animal slow and stationary, was an evidence that the possessor of Argos would not succeed in enterprises beyond the limits of his own city; the serpent denoted the aggressive and formidable future reserved to Sparta; the fox prognosticated a career of wile and deceit to the Messenian.

Such is the brief account given by Apollodôrus of the Return of the Herakleids, at which point we pass, as if touched by the wand of a magician, from mythical to historical Greece. The story bears on the face of it the stamp, not of history, but of legend,—abridged from one or more of the genealogical poets,[6] and presenting such an account as they thought satisfactory, of the first formation of the great Dorian establishments in Peloponnêsus, as well as of the semi-Ætolian Elis. Its incidents are so conceived as to have an explanatory bearing on Dorian institutions,—upon the triple division of tribes, characteristic of the Dorians,—upon the origin of the great festival of the Karneia at Sparta, alleged to be celebrated in expiation of the murder of Karnus,—upon the different temper and character of the Dorian states among themselves,—upon the early alliance of the Dorians with Elis, which contributed to give ascendency and vogue to the Olympic games,—upon the reverential dependence of Dorians towards the Delphian oracle,—and, lastly, upon the etymology of the name Naupaktus. If we possessed the narrative more in detail, we should probably find many more examples of coloring of the legendary past suitable to the circumstances of the historical present.

Above all, this legend makes out in favor of the Dorians and their kings a mythical title to their Peloponnesian establishments; Argos, Sparta, and Messênê are presented as rightfully belonging, and restored by just retribution, to the children of Hêraklês. It was to them that Zeus had specially given the territory of Sparta; the Dorians came in as their subjects and auxiliaries.[7] Plato gives a very different version of the legend, but we find that he, too, turns the story in such a manner as to embody a claim of right on the part of the conquerors. According to him, the Achæans, who returned from the capture of Troy, found among their fellow-citizens at home—the race which had grown up during their absence—an aversion to readmit them: after a fruitless endeavor to make good their rights, they were at last expelled, but not without much contest and bloodshed. A leader named Dorieus, collected all these exiles into one body, and from him they received the name of Dorians instead of Achæans; then marching back, under the conduct of the Herakleids into Peloponnêsus, they recovered by force the possessions from which they had been shut out, and constituted the three Dorian establishments under the separate Herakleid brothers, at Argos, Sparta, and Messênê. These three fraternal dynasties were founded upon a scheme of intimate union and sworn alliance one with the other, for the purpose of resisting any attack which might be made upon them from Asia,[8] either by the remaining Trojans or by their allies. Such is the story as Plato believed it; materially different in the incidents related, yet analogous in mythical feeling, and embodying alike the idea of a rightful reconquest. Moreover, the two accounts agree in representing both the entire conquest and the triple division of Dorian Peloponnêsus as begun and completed in one and the same enterprise,—so as to constitute one single event, which Plato would probably have called the Return of the Achæans, but which was commonly known as the Return of the Herakleids. Though this is both inadmissible and inconsistent with other statements which approach close to the historical times, yet it bears every mark of being the primitive view originally presented by the genealogical poets: the broad way in which the incidents are grouped together, was at once easy for the imagination to follow, and impressive to the feelings.

The existence of one legendary account must never be understood as excluding the probability of other accounts, current at the same time, but inconsistent with it: and many such there were as to the first establishment of the Peloponnesian Dorians. In the narrative which I have given from Apollodôrus, conceived apparently under the influence of Dorian feelings, Tisamenus is stated to have been slain in the invasion. But according to another narrative, which seems to have found favor with the historical Achæans on the north coast of Peloponnêsus, Tisamenus, though expelled by the invaders from his kingdom of Sparta or Argos, was not slain: he was allowed to retire under agreement, together with a certain portion of his subjects, and he directed his steps towards the coast of Peloponnêsus south of the Corinthian Gulf, then occupied by the Ionians. As there were relations, not only of friendship, but of kindred origin, between Ionians and Achæans, (the eponymous heroes Iôn and Achæus pass for brothers, both sons of Xuthus), Tisamenus solicited from the Ionians admission for himself and his fellow-fugitives into their territory. The leading Ionians declining this request, under the apprehension that Tisamenus might be chosen as sovereign over the whole, the latter accomplished his object by force. After a vehement struggle, the Ionians were vanquished and put to flight, and Tisamenus thus acquired possession of Helikê, as well as of the northern coast of the peninsula, westward from Sikyôn; which coast continued to be occupied by the Achæans, and received its name from them, throughout all the historical times. The Ionians retired to Attica, many of them taking part in what is called the Ionic emigration to the coast of Asia Minor, which followed shortly after. Pausanias, indeed, tells us that Tisamenus, having gained a decisive victory over the Ionians, fell in the engagement,[9] and did not himself live to occupy the country of which his troops remained masters. But this story of the death of Tisamenus seems to arise from a desire, on the part of Pausanias, to blend together into one narrative two discrepant legends; at least the historical Achæans in later times continued to regard Tisamenus himself as having lived and reigned in their territory, and as having left a regal dynasty which lasted down to Ogygês,[10] after whom it was exchanged for a popular government. [11]

The conquest of Têmenus, the eldest of the three Herakleids, originally comprehended only Argos and its neighborhood; it was from thence that Trœzen, Epidaurus, Ægina, Sikyôn, and Phlius were successfully occupied by Dorians, the sons and son-in-law of Têmenus—Deiphontês, Phalkês, and Keisus—being the leaders under whom this was accomplished.[12] At Sparta, the success of the Dorians was furthered by the treason of a man named Philonomus, who received as recompense the neighboring town and territory of Amyklæ.[13] Messênia is said to have submitted without resistance to the dominion of the Herakleid Kresphontês, who established his residence at

Stenyklêrus: the Pylian Melanthus, then ruler of the country, and representative of the great mythical lineage of Nêleus and Nestôr, withdrew with his household gods and with a portion of his subjects to Attica.[14]

The only Dorian establishment in the peninsula not directly connected with the triple partition is Corinth, which is said to have been Dorized somewhat later and under another leader, though still a Herakleid. Hippotês—descendant of Hêraklês in the fourth generation, but not through Hyllus,—had been guilty (as already mentioned) of the murder of Karnus the prophet at the camp of Naupaktus, for which he had been banished and remained in exile for ten years; his son deriving the name of Alêtês from the long wanderings endured by the father. At the head of a body of Dorians, Alêtês attacked Corinth: he pitched his camp on the Solygeian eminence near the city, and harassed the inhabitants with constant warfare until he compelled them to surrender. Even in the time of the Peloponnesian war, the Corinthians professed to identify the hill on which the camp of these assailants had been placed. The great mythical dynasty of the Sisyphids was expelled, and Alêtês became ruler and Œkist of the Dorian city; many of the inhabitants, however, Æolic or Ionic, departed.[15]

The settlement of Oxylus and his Ætolians in Elis is said by some to have been accomplished with very little opposition; the leader professing himself to be descended from Ætolus, who had been in a previous age banished from Elis into Ætôlia, and the two people, Epeians and Ætolians, acknowledging a kindred origin one with the other.[16] At first, indeed, according to Ephorus, the Epeians appeared in arms, determined to repel the intruders, but at length it was agreed on both sides to abide the issue of a single combat. Degmenus, the champion of the Epeians, confided in the long shot of his bow and arrow; but the Ætolian Pyræchmês came provided with his sling,—a weapon then unknown and recently invented by the Ætolians,—the range of which was yet longer than that of the bow of his enemy: he thus killed Degmenus, and secured the victory to Oxylus and his followers. According to one statement, the Epeians were expelled; according to another, they fraternized amicably with the new-comers: whatever may be the truth as to this matter, it is certain that their name is from this moment lost, and that they never reappear among the historical elements of Greece:[17] we hear from this time forward only of Eleians, said to be of Ætolian descent.[18]

One most important privilege was connected with the possession of the Eleian territory by Oxylus, coupled with his claim on the gratitude of the Dorian kings. The Eleians acquired the administration of the temple at Olympia, which the Achæans are said to have possessed before them; and in consideration of this sacred function, which subsequently ripened into the celebration of the great Olympic games, their territory was solemnly pronounced to be inviolable. Such was the statement of Ephorus:[19] we find, in this case as in so many others, that the Return of the Herakleids is made to supply a legendary basis for the historical state of things in Peloponnêsus.

It was the practice of the great Attic tragedians, with rare exceptions, to select the subjects of their composition from the heroic or legendary world, and Euripidês had composed three dramas, now lost, on the adventures of Têmenus with his daughter Hyrnethô and his son-in-law Dêiphontês,—on the family misfortunes of Kresphontês and Meropê,—and on the successful valor of Archelaus the son of Têmenus in Macedonia, where he was alleged to have first begun the dynasty of the Temenid kings. Of these subjects the first and second were eminently tragical, and the third, relating to Archelaus, appears to have been undertaken by Euripidês in compliment to his contemporary sovereign and patron, Archelaus king of Macedonia: we are even told that those exploits which the usual version of the legend ascribed to Têmenus, were reported in the drama of Euripidês to have been performed by Archelaus his son.[20] Of all the heroes, touched upon by the three Attic tragedians, these Dorian Herakleids stand lowest in the descending genealogical series,—one mark amongst others that we are approaching the ground of genuine history.

Though the name Achæans, as denoting a people, is henceforward confined to the North-Peloponnesian territory specially called Achaia, and to the inhabitants of Achæa, Phthiôtis, north of Mount Œta,—and though the great Peloponnesian states always seem to have prided themselves on the title of Dorians,—yet we find the kings of Sparta, even in the historical age, taking pains to appropriate to themselves the mythical glories of the Achæans, and to set themselves forth as the representatives of Agamemnôn and Orestês. The Spartan king Kleomenês even went so far as to disavow formally any Dorian parentage; for when the priestess at Athens refused to permit him to sacrifice in the temple of Athênê, on the plea that it was peremptorily closed to all Dorians, he replied: "I am no Dorian, but an Achæan."[21] Not only did the Spartan envoy, before Gelôn of Syracuse, connect the indefeasible title of his country to the supreme command of the Grecian military force, with the ancient name and lofty prerogatives of Agamemnôn,[22]—but, in farther pursuance of the same feeling, the Spartans are said to have carried to Sparta both the bones of Orestês from Tegea, and those of Tisamenus from Helikê, [23] at the injunction of the Delphian oracle. There is also a story that Oxylus in Elis was directed by the same oracle to invite into his country an Achæan, as Œkist conjointly with himself; and that he called in Agorius, the great-grandson of Orestês, from Helikê, with a small number of Achæans who joined him.[24] The Dorians themselves, being singularly poor in native legends, endeavored, not unnaturally, to decorate themselves with those legendary ornaments which the Achæans possessed in abundance.

As a consequence of the Dorian establishments in Peloponnêsus, several migrations of the preëxisting inhabitants are represented as taking place. 1. The Epeians of Elis are either expelled, or merged in the new-comers under Oxylus, and lose their separate name. 2. The Pylians, together with the great heroic family of Nêleus and his son Nestôr, who preside over them, give place to the Dorian establishment of Messênia, and retire to Athens, where their leader, Melanthus, becomes king: a large portion of them take part in the subsequent Ionic emigration. 3. A portion of the Achæans, under Penthilus and other descendants of Orestês, leave Peloponnêsus, and form what is called the Æolic emigration, to Lesbos, the Trôad, and the Gulf of Adramyttium: the name *Æolians*, unknown to Homer, and seemingly never applied to any separate tribe at all, being introduced to designate a large section of the Hellenic name, partly in Greece Proper, and partly in Asia. 4. Another portion of Achæans expel the Ionians from Achaia, properly so called, in the north of Peloponnêsus; the Ionians retiring to Attica.

The Homeric poems describe Achæans, Pylians, and Epeians, in Peloponnêsus, but take no notice of Ionians in the northern district of Achaia: on the contrary, the Catalogue in the Iliad distinctly includes this territory under the dominions of Agamemnôn. Though the Catalogue of Homer is not to be regarded as an historical document, fit to be called as evidence for the actual state of Peloponnêsus at any prior time, it certainly seems a better authority than the statements advanced by Herodotus and others respecting the occupation of northern Peloponnêsus by the Ionians, and their expulsion from it by Tisamenus. In so far as the Catalogue is to be trusted, it negatives the idea of Ionians at Helikê, and countenances what seems in itself a more natural supposition,—that the historical Achæans in the north part of Peloponnêsus are a small undisturbed remnant of the powerful Achæan population once distributed throughout the peninsula, until it was broken up and partially expelled by the Dorians.

The Homeric legends, unquestionably the oldest which we possess, are adapted to a population of Achæans, Danaans, and Argeians, seemingly without any special and recognized names, either aggregate or divisional, other than the name of each separate tribe or kingdom. The post-Homeric legends are adapted to a population classified quite differently,—Hellens, distributed into Dorians, Ionians, and Æolians. If we knew more of the time and circumstances in which these different legends grew up, we should probably be able to explain their discrepancy; but in our present ignorance we can only note the fact.

Whatever difficulty modern criticism may find in regard to the event

9

called "The Return of the Herakleids," no doubt is expressed about it even by the best historians of antiquity. Thucydidês accepts it as a single and literal event, having its assignable date, and carrying at one blow the acquisition of Peloponnêsus. The date of it he fixes as eighty years after the capture of Troy. Whether he was the original determiner of this epoch, or copied it from some previous author, we do not know. It must have been fixed according to some computation of generations, for there were no other means accessible,— probably by means of the lineage of the Herakleids, which, as belonging to the kings of Sparta, constituted the most public and conspicuous thread of connection between the Grecian real and mythical world, and measured the interval between the Siege of Troy itself and the first recorded Olympiad. Hêraklês himself represents the generation before the siege, and his son Tlepolemus fights in the besieging army. If we suppose the first generation after Hêraklês to commence with the beginning of the siege, the fourth generation after him will coincide with the ninetieth year after the same epoch; and therefore, deducting ten years for the duration of the struggle, it will coincide with the eightieth year after the capture of the city;[25] thirty years being reckoned for a generation. The date assigned by Thucydidês will thus agree with the distance in which Têmenus, Kresphontês, and Aristodêmus, stand removed from Hêraklês. The interval of eighty years, between the capture of Troy and the Return of the Herakleids, appears to have been admitted by Apollodôrus and Eratosthenês, and some other professed chronologists of antiquity: but there were different reckonings which also found more or less of support.

# SECTION II.—MIGRATION OF THESSALIANS AND BŒOTIANS.

In the same passage in which Thucydidês speaks of the Return of the Herakleids, he also marks out the date of another event a little antecedent, which is alleged to have powerfully affected the condition of Northern Greece. "Sixty years after the capture of Troy (he tells us) the Bœotians were driven by the Thessalians from Arnê, and migrated into the land then called Kadmêïs, but now Bœotia, wherein there had previously dwelt a section of their race, who had contributed the contingent to the Trojan war."

The expulsion here mentioned, of the Bœotians from Arnê "by the Thessalians," has been construed, with probability, to allude to the immigration of the Thessalians, properly so called, from the Thesprôtid in Epirus into Thessaly. That the Thessalians had migrated into Thessaly from the Thesprôtid territory, is stated by Herodotus,[26] though he says nothing about time or circumstances. Antiphus and Pheidippus appear in the Homeric Catalogue as commanders of the Grecian contingent from the islands of Kôs and Karpathus, on the south-east coast of Asia Minor: they are sons of Thessalus, who is himself the son of Hêraklês. A legend ran that these two chiefs, in the dispersion which ensued after the victory, had been driven by storms into the Ionian Gulf, and cast upon the coast of Epirus, where they landed and settled at Ephyrê in the Thesprôtid.[27] It was Thessalus, grandson of Pheidippus, who was reported to have conducted the Thesprotians across the passes of Pindus into Thessaly, to have conquered the fertile central plain of that country, and to have imposed upon it his own name instead of its previous denomination Æolis.[28]

Whatever we may think of this legend as it stands, the state of Thessaly during the historical ages renders it highly probable that the Thessalians, properly so called, were a body of immigrant conquerors. They appear always as a rude, warlike, violent, and uncivilized race, distinct from their neighbors the Achæans, the Magnetes, and the Perrhæbians, and holding all the three in tributary dependence: these three tribes stand to them in a relation analogous to that of the Lacedæmonian Periœki towards Sparta, while the Penestæ, who cultivated their lands, are almost an exact parallel of the Helots. Moreover, the low level of taste and intelligence among the Thessalians, as well as certain points of their costume, assimilates them more to Macedonians or Epirots than to Hellens.[29] Their position in Thessaly is in many respects analogous to that of the Spartan Dorians in Peloponnêsus, and there seems good reason for concluding that the former, as well as the latter, were originally victorious invaders, though we cannot pretend to determine the time at which the invasion took place. The great family of the Aleuads,[30] and probably other Thessalian families besides, were descendants of Hêraklês, like the kings of Sparta.

There are no similar historical grounds, in the case of the alleged migration of the Bœotians from Thessaly to Bœotia, to justify a belief in the main fact of the legend, nor were the different legendary stories in harmony one with the other. While the Homeric Epic recognizes the Bœotians in Bœotia, but not in Thessaly, Thucydidês records a statement which he had found of their migration from the latter into the former; but in order to escape the necessity of flatly contradicting Homer, he inserts the parenthesis that there had been previously an outlying fraction of Bœotians in Bœotia at the time of the Trojan war,[31] from whom the troops who served with Agamemnôn were drawn. Nevertheless, the discrepancy with the Iliad, though less strikingly obvious, is not removed, inasmuch as the Catalogue is unusually copious in enumerating the contingents from Thessaly, without once mentioning Bœotians. Homer distinguishes Orchomenus from Bœotia, and he does not specially notice Thêbes in the Catalogue: in other respects his enumeration of the towns coincides pretty well with the ground historically known afterwards under the name of Bœotia.

Pausanias gives us a short sketch of the events which he supposes to have intervened in this section of Greece between the Siege of Troy and the Return of the Herakleids. Peneleôs, the leader of the Bœotians at the siege, having been slain by Eurypylus the son of Telephus, Tisamenus, son of Thersander and grandson of Polynikês, acted as their commander, both during the remainder of the siege and after their return. Autesiôn, his son and successor, became subject to the wrath of the avenging Erinnyes of Laius and Œdipus: the oracle directed him to expatriate, and he joined the Dorians. In his place, Damasichthôn, son of Opheltas and grandson of Peneleôs, became king of the Bœotians: he was succeeded by Ptolemæus, who was himself followed by Xanthus. A war having broken out at that time between the Athenians and Bœotians, Xanthus engaged in single combat with Melanthus son of Andropompus, the champion of Attica, and perished by the cunning of his opponent. After the death of Xanthus, the Bœotians passed from kingship to popular government.[32] As Melanthus was of the lineage of the Neleids, and had migrated from Pylus to Athens in consequence of the successful establishment of the Dorians in Messênia, the duel with Xanthus must have been of course subsequent to the Return of the Herakleids.

Here, then, we have a summary of alleged Bœotian history between the

Siege of Troy and the Return of the Herakleids, in which no mention is made of the immigration of the mass of Bœotians from Thessaly, and seemingly no possibility left of fitting in so great and capital an incident. The legends followed by Pausanias are at variance with those adopted by Thucydidês, but they harmonize much better with Homer.

So deservedly high is the authority of Thucydidês, that the migration here distinctly announced by him is commonly set down as an ascertained datum, historically as well as chronologically. But on this occasion it can be shown that he only followed one amongst a variety of discrepant legends, none of which there were any means of verifying.

Pausanias recognized a migration of the Bœotians from Thessaly, in early times anterior to the Trojan war;[33] and the account of Ephorus, as given by Strabo, professed to record a series of changes in the occupants of the country: First, the non-Hellenic Aones and Temmikes, Leleges and Hyantes; next, the Kadmeians, who, after the second siege of Thêbes by the Epigoni, were expelled by the Thracians and Pelasgians, and retired into Thessaly, where they joined in communion with the inhabitants of Arnê,—the whole aggregate being called Bœotians. After the Trojan war, and about the time of the Æolic emigration, these Bœotians returned from Thessaly and reconquered Bœotia, driving out the Thracians and Pelasgians,—the former retiring to Parnassus, the latter to Attica. It was on this occasion (he says) that the Minyæ of Orchomenus were subdued, and forcibly incorporated with the Bœotians. Ephorus seems to have followed, in the main, the same narrative as Thucydidês, about the movement of the Bœotians out of Thessaly; coupling it, however, with several details current as explanatory of proverbs and customs.[34]

The only fact which we make out, independent of these legends, is, that there existed certain homonymies and certain affinities of religious worship, between parts of Bœotia and parts of Thessaly, which appear to indicate a kindred race. A town named Arne,[35] similar in name to the Thessalian, was enumerated in the Bœotian Catalogue of Homer, and antiquaries identified it sometimes with the historical town Chæroneia,[36] sometimes with Akræphium. Moreover, there was near the Bœotian Korôneia a river named Kuarius, or Koralius, and a venerable temple dedicated to the Itonian Athênê, in the sacred ground of which the Pambœotia, or public council of the Bœotian name, was held; there was also a temple and a river of similar denomination in Thessaly, near to a town called Iton, or Itônus.[37] We may from these circumstances presume a certain ancient kindred between the population of these regions, and such a circumstance is sufficient to explain the generation of legends describing migrations backward and forward,

13

whether true or not in point of fact.

What is most important to remark is, that the stories of Thucydidês and Ephorus bring us out of the mythical into the historical Bœotia. Orchomenus is Bœotized, and we hear no more of the once-powerful Minyæ: there are no more Kadmeians at Thêbes, nor Bœotians in Thessaly. The Minyæ and the Kadmeians disappear in the Ionic emigration, which will be presently adverted to. Historical Bœotia is now constituted, apparently in its federative league, under the presidency of Thêbes, just as we find it in the time of the Persian and Peloponnesian wars.

# SECTION III.—EMIGRATIONS FROM GREECE TO ASIA AND THE ISLANDS OF THE ÆGÆAN.

### 1. ÆOLIC.—2. IONIC.—3. DORIC.

To complete the transition of Greece from its mythical to its historical condition, the secession of the races belonging to the former must follow upon the introduction of those belonging to the latter. This is accomplished by means of the Æolic and Ionic migrations.

The presiding chiefs of the Æolic emigration are the representatives of the heroic lineage of the Pelopids: those of the Ionic emigration belong to the Neleids: and even in what is called the Doric emigration to Thêra, the Œkist Thêras is not a Dorian but a Kadmeian, the legitimate descendant of Œdipus and Kadmus.

The Æolic, Ionic, and Doric colonies were planted along the western coast of Asia Minor, from the coasts of the Propontis southward down to Lykia (I shall in a future chapter speak more exactly of their boundaries); the Æolic occupying the northern portion, together with the islands of Lesbos and Tenedos; the Doric occupying the southernmost, together with the neighboring islands of Rhodes and Kôs; and the Ionic being planted between them, comprehending Chios, Samos, and the Cycladês islands.

### 1. ÆOLIC EMIGRATION.

The Æolic emigration was conducted by the Pelopids: the original story seems to have been, that Orestês himself was at the head of the first batch of colonists, and this version of the event is still preserved by Pindar and by Hellanikus.[38] But the more current narratives represented the descendants of Orestês as chiefs of the expeditions to Æolis,—his illegitimate son Penthilus, by Erigonê daughter of Ægisthus,[39] together with Echelatus and Gras, the son and grandson of Penthilus, together with Kleuês and Malaus, descendants of Agamemnôn through another lineage. According to the account given by Strabo, Orestês began the emigration, but died on his route in Arcadia; his son Penthilus, taking the guidance of the emigrants, conducted them by the long land-journey through Bœotia and Thessaly to Thrace;[40] from whence Archelaus, son of Penthilus, led them across the Hellespont, and settled at Daskylium on the Propontis. Gras, son of Archelaus, crossed over to Lesbos and possessed himself of the island. Kleuês and Malaus, conducting another body of Achæans, were longer on their journey, and lingered a considerable time near Mount Phrikium, in the territory of Lokris; ultimately, however,

15

they passed over by sea to Asia and took possession of Kymê, south of the Gulf of Adramyttium, the most considerable of all the Æolic cities on the continent.[41] From Lesbos and Kymê, the other less considerable Æolic towns, spreading over the region of Ida as well as the Trôad, and comprehending the island of Tenedos, are said to have derived their origin.

Though there are many differences in the details, the accounts agree in representing these Æolic settlements as formed by the Achæans expatriated from Lacônia under the guidance of the dispossessed Pelopids.[42] We are told that in their journey through Bœotia they received considerable reinforcements, and Strabo adds that the emigrants started from Aulis, the port from whence Agamemnôn departed in the expedition against Troy.[43] He also informs us that they missed their course and experienced many losses from nautical ignorance, but we do not know to what particular incidents he alludes.[44]

### 2. IONIC EMIGRATION.

The Ionic emigration is described as emanating from and directed by the Athenians, and connects itself with the previous legendary history of Athens, which must therefore be here briefly recapitulated.

The great mythical hero Thêseus, of whose military prowess and errant exploits we have spoken in a previous chapter, was still more memorable in the eyes of the Athenians as an internal political reformer. He was supposed to have performed for them the inestimable service of transforming Attica out of many states into one. Each dême, or at least a great many out of the whole number, had before his time enjoyed political independence under its own magistrates and assemblies, acknowledging only a federal union with the rest under the presidency of Athens: by a mixture of conciliation and force, Thêseus succeeded in putting down all these separate governments, and bringing them to unite in one political system, centralized at Athens. He is said to have established a constitutional government, retaining for himself a defined power as king, or president, and distributing the people into three classes: Eupatridæ, a sort of sacerdotal noblesse; Geômori and Demiurgi, husbandmen and artisans.[45] Having brought these important changes into efficient working, he commemorated them for his posterity by introducing solemn and appropriate festivals. In confirmation of the dominion of Athens over the Megarid territory, he is said farther to have erected a pillar at the extremity of the latter towards the Isthmus, marking the boundary between Peloponnêsus and Iônia.

But a revolution so extensive was not consummated without creating much discontent; and Menestheus, the rival of Thêseus,—the first specimen, as we are told, of an artful demagogue,—took advantage of this feeling to assail and undermine him. Thêseus had quitted Attica, to accompany and assist his friend Peirithöus, in his journey down to the under-world, in order to carry off the goddess Persephonê,—or (as those who were critical in legendary story preferred recounting) in a journey to the residence of Aidôneus, king of the Molossians in Epirus, to carry off his daughter. In this enterprise, Peirithöus perished, while Thêseus was cast into prison, from whence he was only liberated by the intercession of Hêraklês. It was during his temporary absence, that the Tyndarids Castôr and Pollux invaded Attica for the purpose of recovering their sister Helen, whom Thêseus had at a former period taken away from Sparta and deposited at Aphidnæ; and the partisans of Menestheus took advantage both of the absence of Thêseus and of the calamity which his licentiousness had brought upon the country, to ruin his popularity with the people. When he returned, he found them no longer disposed to endure his dominion, or to continue to him the honors which their previous feelings of gratitude had conferred. Having, therefore, placed his sons under the protection of Elephenôr, in Eubœa, he sought an asylum with Lykomêdês, prince of Scyros, from whom, however, he received nothing but an insidious welcome and a traitorous death.[46]

Menestheus, succeeding to the honors of the expatriated hero, commanded the Athenian troops at the Siege of Troy. But though he survived the capture, he never returned to Athens,—different stories being related of the place where he and his companions settled. During this interval, the feelings of the Athenians having changed, they restored the sons of Thêseus, who had served at Troy under Elephenôr, and had returned unhurt, to the station and functions of their father. The Theseids Demophoôn, Oxyntas, Apheidas, and Thymœtês had successively filled this post for the space of about sixty years,[47] when the Dorian invaders of Peloponnêsus (as has been before related) compelled Melanthus and the Neleid family to abandon their kingdom of Pylus. The refugees found shelter at Athens, where a fortunate adventure soon raised Melanthus to the throne. A war breaking out between the Athenians and Bœotians, respecting the boundary tract of Œnoê, the Bœotian king Xanthus challenged Thymœtês to single combat: the latter declining to accept it, Melanthus not only stood forward in his place, but practised a cunning stratagem with such success as to kill his adversary. He was forthwith chosen king, Thymœtês being constrained to resign.[48]

Melanthus and his son Kodrus reigned for nearly sixty years, during which time large bodies of fugitives, escaping from the recent invaders throughout Greece, were harbored by the Athenians: so that Attica became populous enough to excite the alarm and jealousy of the Peloponnesian Dorians. A powerful Dorian force, under the command of Alêtês from Corinth and Althæmenês from Argos, were accordingly despatched to invade the

Athenian territory, in which the Delphian oracle promised them success, provided they abstained from injuring the person of Kodrus. Strict orders were given to the Dorian army that Kodrus should be preserved unhurt; but the oracle had become known among the Athenians,[49] and the generous prince determined to bring death upon himself as a means of salvation to his country. Assuming the disguise of a peasant, he intentionally provoked a quarrel with some of the Dorian troops, who slew him without suspecting his real character. No sooner was this event known, than the Dorian leaders, despairing of success, abandoned their enterprise and evacuated the country. [50] In retiring, however, they retained possession of Megara, where they established permanent settlers, and which became from this moment Dorian, —seemingly at first a dependency of Corinth, though it afterwards acquired its freedom and became an autonomous community.[51] This memorable act of devoted patriotism, analogous to that of the daughters of Erechtheus at Athens, and of Menœkeus at Thêbes, entitled Kodrus to be ranked among the most splendid characters in Grecian legend.

Kodrus is numbered as the last king of Athens: his descendants were styled Archons, but they held that dignity for life,—a practice which prevailed during a long course of years afterwards. Medon and Neileus, his two sons, having quarrelled about the succession, the Delphian oracle decided in favor of the former; upon which the latter, affronted at the preference, resolved upon seeking a new home.[52] There were at this moment many dispossessed sections of Greeks, and an adventitious population accumulated in Attica, who were anxious for settlements beyond sea. The expeditions which now set forth to cross the Ægean, chiefly under the conduct of members of the Kodrid family, composed collectively the memorable Ionic Emigration, of which the Ionians, recently expelled from Peloponnêsus, formed a part, but, as it would seem, only a small part; for we hear of many quite distinct races, some renowned in legend, who withdraw from Greece amidst this assemblage of colonists. The Kadmeians, the Minyæ of Orchomenus, the Abantês of Eubœa, the Dryopes; the Molossi, the Phokians, the Bœotians, the Arcadian Pelasgians, and even the Dorians of Epidaurus,—are represented as furnishing each a proportion of the crews of these emigrant vessels.[53] Nor were the results unworthy of so mighty a confluence of different races. Not only the Cyclades islands in the Ægean, but the great islands of Samos and Chios, near the Asiatic coast, and ten different cities on the coast of Asia Minor, from Milêtus in the south to Phokæa in the north, were founded, and all adopted the Ionic name. Athens was the metropolis or mother city of all of them: Androklus and Neileus, the Œkists of Ephesus and Milêtus, and probably other Œkists also, started from the Prytaneium at Athens,[54] with those solemnities, religious and political, which usually marked the departure of a swarm of Grecian colonists.

Other mythical families, besides the heroic lineage of Nêleus and Nestôr, as represented by the sons of Kodrus, took a leading part in the expedition. Herodotus mentions Lykian chiefs, descendants from Glaukus son of Hippolochus, and Pausanias tells us of Philôtas descendant of Peneleôs, who went at the head of a body of Thebans: both Glaukus and Peneleôs are commemorated in the Iliad.[55] And it is a remarkable fact mentioned by Pausanias (though we do not know on what authority), that the inhabitants of Phokæa,—which was the northernmost city of Iônia on the borders of Æolis, and one of the last founded,—consisting mostly of Phokian colonists under the conduct of the Athenians Philogenês and Dæmôn, were not admitted into the Pan-Ionic Amphiktyony until they consented to choose for themselves chiefs of the Kodrid family.[56] Proklês, the chief who conducted the Ionic emigrants from Epidaurus to Samos, was said to be of the lineage of Iôn, son of Xuthus.[57]

Of the twelve Ionic states constituting the Pan-Ionic Amphiktyony—some of them among the greatest cities in Hellas—I shall say no more at present, as I have to treat of them again when I come upon historical ground.

### 3. DORIC EMIGRATIONS.

The Æolic and Ionic emigrations are thus both presented to us as direct consequences of the event called the Return of the Herakleids: and in like manner the formation of the Dorian Hexapolis in the south-western corner of Asia Minor: Kôs, Knidus, Halikarnassus, and Rhodes, with its three separate cities, as well as the Dorian establishments in Krête, Melos, and Thêra, are all traced more or less directly to the same great revolution.

Thêra, more especially, has its root in the legendary world. Its Œkist was Thêras, a descendant of the heroic lineage of Œdipus and Kadmus, and maternal uncle of the young kings of Sparta, Eurysthenês and Proklês, during whose minority he had exercised the regency. On their coming of age, his functions were at an end: but being unable to endure a private station, he determined to put himself at the head of a body of emigrants: many came forward to join him, and the expedition was farther reinforced by a body of interlopers, belonging to the Minyæ, of whom the Lacedæmonians were anxious to get rid. These Minyæ had arrived in Laconia, not long before, from the island of Lemnos, out of which they had been expelled by the Pelasgian fugitives from Attica. They landed without asking permission, took up their abode and began to "light their fires" on Mount Taygetus. When the Lacedæmonians sent to ask who they were, and wherefore they had come, the Minyæ replied that they were sons of the Argonauts who had landed at Lemnos, and that, being expelled from their own homes, they thought themselves entitled to solicit an asylum in the territory of their fathers: they asked, withal, to be admitted to share both the lands and the honors of the state. The Lacedæmonians granted the request, chiefly on the ground of a common ancestry,—their own great heroes, the Tyndarids, having been enrolled in the crew of the Argô: the Minyæ were then introduced as citizens into the tribes, received lots of land, and began to intermarry with the preëxisting families. It was not long, however, before they became insolent: they demanded a share in the kingdom (which was the venerated privilege of the Herakleids), and so grossly misconducted themselves in other ways, that the Lacedæmonians resolved to put them to death, and began by casting them into prison. While the Minyæ were thus confined, their wives, Spartans by birth, and many of them daughters of the principal men, solicited permission to go in and see them: leave being granted, they made use of the interview to change clothes with their husbands, who thus escaped and fled again to Mount Taygetus. The greater number of them quitted Laconia, and marched to Triphylia, in the western regions of Peloponnêsus, from whence they expelled the Paroreatæ and the Kaukones, and founded six towns of their own, of which Lepreum was the chief. A certain proportion, however, by permission of the Lacedæmonians, joined Thêras, and departed with him to the island of Kallistê, then possessed by Phœnician inhabitants, who were descended from the kinsmen and companions of Kadmus, and who had been left there by that prince, when he came forth in search of Eurôpa, eight generations preceding. Arriving thus among men of kindred lineage with himself, Thêras met with a fraternal reception, and the island derived from him the name, under which it is historically known, of Thêra.[58]

Such is the foundation-legend of Thêra, believed both by the Lacedæmonians and by the Theræans, and interesting as it brings before us, characteristically as well as vividly, the persons and feelings of the mythical world,—the Argonauts, with the Tyndarids as their companions and Minyæ as their children. In Lepreum, as in the other towns of Triphylia, the descent from the Minyæ of old seems to have been believed in the historical times, and the mention of the river Minyëius in those regions by Homer tended to confirm it.[59] But people were not unanimous as to the legend by which that descent should be made out; while some adopted the story just cited from Herodotus, others imagined that Chlôris, who had come from the Minyeian town of Orchomenus as the wife of Nêleus to Pylus, had brought with her a body of her countrymen.[60]

These Minyæ from Lemnos and Imbros appear again as portions of another narrative respecting the settlement of the colony of Mêlos. It has already been mentioned, that when the Herakleids and the Dorians invaded Lacônia, Philonomus, an Achæan, treacherously betrayed to them the country, for which he received as his recompense the territory of Amyklæ. He is said to have peopled this territory by introducing detachments of Minyæ from Lemnos and Imbros, who, in the third generation after the return of the Herakleids, became so discontented and mutinous, that the Lacedæmonians resolved to send them out of the country as emigrants, under their chiefs Polis and Delphus. Taking the direction of Krête, they stopped in their way to land a portion of their colonists on the island of Mêlos, which remained throughout the historical times a faithful and attached colony of Lacedæmôn.[61] On arriving in Krête, they are said to have settled at the town of Gortyn. We find, moreover, that other Dorian establishments, either from Lacedæmôn or Argos, were formed in Krête; and Lyktos in particular, is noticed, not only as a colony of Sparta, but as distinguished for the analogy of its laws and customs.[62] It is even said that Krête, immediately after the Trojan war, had been visited by the wrath of the gods, and depopulated by famine and pestilence; and that, in the third generation afterwards, so great was the influx of emigrants, the entire population of the island was renewed, with the exception of the Eteokrêtes at Polichnæ and Præsus.[63]

There were Dorians in Krête in the time of the Odyssey: Homer mentions different languages and different races of men, Eteokrêtes, Kydônes, Dorians, Achæans, and Pelasgians, as all coexisting in the island, which he describes to be populous, and to contain ninety cities. A legend given by Andrôn, based seemingly upon the statement of Herodotus, that Dôrus the son of Hellen had settled in Histiæôtis, ascribed the first introduction of the three last races to Tektaphus son of Dôrus,—who had led forth from that country a colony of Dorians, Achæans, and Pelasgians, and had landed in Krête during the reign of the indigenous king Krês.[64] This story of Andrôn so exactly fits on to the Homeric Catalogue of Kretan inhabitants, that we may reasonably presume it to have been designedly arranged with reference to that Catalogue, so as to afford some plausible account, consistently with the received legendary chronology, how there came to be Dorians in Krête before the Trojan war,— the Dorian colonies after the return of the Herakleids being of course long posterior in supposed order of time. To find a leader sufficiently early for his hypothesis, Andrôn ascends to the primitive Eponymus Dôrus, to whose son Tektaphus he ascribes the introduction of a mixed colony of Dorians, Achæans, and Pelasgians into Krête: these are the exact three races enumerated in the Odyssey, and the king Krês, whom Andrôn affirms to have been then reigning in the island, represents the Eteokrêtes and Kydônes in the list of Homer. The story seems to have found favor among native Kretan historians, as it doubtless serves to obviate what would otherwise be a contradiction in the legendary chronology.[65]

Another Dorian emigration from Peloponnêsus to Krête, which extended also to Rhodes and Kôs, is farther said to have been conducted by Althæmenês, who had been one of the chiefs in the expedition against Attica, in which Krodus perished. This prince, a Herakleid, and third in descent from Têmenus, was induced to expatriate by a family quarrel, and conducted a body of Dorian colonists from Argos first to Krête, where some of them remained; but the greater number accompanied him to Rhodes, in which island, after expelling the Karian possessors, he founded the three cities of Lindus, Ialysus, and Kameirus.[66]

It is proper here to add, that the legend of the Rhodian archæologists respecting their œkist Althæmenês, who was worshipped in the island with heroic honors, was something totally different from the preceding. Althæmenês was a Kretan, son of the king Katreus, and grandson of Minos. An oracle predicted to him that he would one day kill his father: eager to escape so terrible a destiny, he quitted Krête, and conducted a colony to Rhodes, where the famous temple of the Atabyrian Zeus, on the lofty summit of Mount Atabyrum, was ascribed to his foundation, built so as to command a view of Krête. He had been settled on the island for some time, when his father Katreus, anxious again to embrace his only son, followed him from Krête: he landed in Rhodes during the night without being known, and a casual collision took place between his attendants and the islanders. Althæmenês hastened to the shore to assist in repelling the supposed enemies, and in the fray had the misfortune to kill his aged father.[67]

Either the emigrants who accompanied Althæmenês, or some other Dorian colonists afterwards, are reported to have settled at Kôs, Knidus, Karpathus, and Halikarnassus. To the last mentioned city, however, Anthês of Trœzên is assigned as the œkist: the emigrants who accompanied him were said to have belonged to the Dymanian tribe, one of the three tribes always found in a Doric state: and the city seems to have been characterized as a colony sometimes of Trœzên, sometimes of Argos.[68]

We thus have the Æolic, the Ionic, and the Doric colonial establishments in Asia, all springing out of the legendary age, and all set forth as consequences, direct or indirect, of what is called the Return of the Herakleids, or the Dorian conquest of Peloponnêsus. According to the received chronology, they are succeeded by a period, supposed to comprise nearly three centuries, which is almost an entire blank, before we reach authentic chronology and the first recorded Olympiad,—and they thus form the concluding events of the mythical world, out of which we now pass into historical Greece, such as it stands at the last-mentioned epoch. It is by these migrations that the parts of the Hellenic aggregate are distributed into the places which they occupy at the dawn of historical daylight,—Dorians,

Arcadians, Ætolo-Eleians, and Achæans, sharing Peloponnêsus unequally among them,—Æolians, Ionians, and Dorians, settled both in the islands of the Ægean and the coast of Asia Minor. The Return of the Herakleids, as well as the three emigrations, Æolic, Ionic, and Doric, present the legendary explanation, suitable to the feelings and belief of the people, showing how Greece passed from the heroic races who besieged Troy and Thêbes, piloted the adventurous Argô, and slew the monstrous boar of Kalydôn, to the historical races, differently named and classified, who furnished victors to the Olympic and Pythian games.

A patient and learned French writer, M. Raoul Rochette,—who construes all the events of the heroic age, generally speaking, as so much real history, only making allowance for the mistakes and exaggerations of poets,—is greatly perplexed by the blank and interruption which this supposed continuous series of history presents, from the Return of the Herakleids down to the beginning of the Olympiads. He cannot explain to himself so long a period of absolute quiescence, after the important incidents and striking adventures of the heroic age; and if there happened nothing worthy of record during this long period,—as he presumes, from the fact that nothing has been transmitted,—he concludes that this must have arisen from the state of suffering and exhaustion in which previous wars and revolution had left the Greeks: a long interval of complete inaction being required to heal such wounds.[69]

Assuming M. Rochette's view of the heroic ages to be correct, and reasoning upon the supposition that the adventures ascribed to the Grecian heroes are matters of historical reality, transmitted by tradition from a period of time four centuries before the recorded Olympiads, and only embellished by describing poets,—the blank which he here dwells upon is, to say the least of it, embarrassing and unaccountable. It is strange that the stream of tradition, if it had once begun to flow, should (like several of the rivers in Greece) be submerged for two or three centuries and then reappear. But when we make what appears to me the proper distinction between legend and history, it will be seen that a period of blank time between the two is perfectly conformable to the conditions under which the former is generated. It is not the immediate past, but a supposed remote past, which forms the suitable atmosphere of mythical narrative,—a past originally quite undetermined in respect to distance from the present, as we see in the Iliad and Odyssey. And even when we come down to the genealogical poets, who affect to give a certain measure of bygone time, and a succession of persons as well as of events, still, the names whom they most delight to honor and upon whose exploits they chiefly expatiate, are those of the ancestral gods and heroes of the tribe and their supposed contemporaries; ancestors separated by a long lineage from the present hearer. The gods and heroes were conceived as removed from him by several generations, and the legendary matter which was grouped around them appeared only the more imposing when exhibited at a respectful distance, beyond the days of father and grandfather, and of all known predecessors. The Odes of Pindar strikingly illustrate this tendency. We thus see how it happened that, between the times assigned to heroic adventure and those of historical record, there existed an intermediate blank, filled with inglorious names; and how, amongst the same society which cared not to remember proceedings of fathers and grandfathers, there circulated much popular and accredited narrative respecting real or supposed ancestors long past and gone The obscure and barren centuries which immediately precede the first recorded Olympiad, form the natural separation between the legendary return of the Herakleids and the historical wars of Sparta against Messênê,—between the province of legend, wherein matter of fact (if any there be) is so intimately combined with its accompaniments of fiction, as to be undistinguishable without the aid of extrinsic evidence,—and that of history where some matters of fact can be ascertained, and where a sagacious criticism may be usefully employed in trying to add to their number.

# CHAPTER XIX.

## APPLICATION OF CHRONOLOGY TO GRECIAN LEGEND.

I NEED not repeat, what has already been sufficiently set forth in the preceding pages, that the mass of Grecian incident anterior to 776 B. C. appears to me not reducible either to history or to chronology, and that any chronological system which may be applied to it must be essentially uncertified and illusory. It was, however, chronologized in ancient times, and has continued to be so in modern; and the various schemes employed for this purpose may be found stated and compared in the first volume (the last published) of Mr. Fynes Clinton's Fasti Hellenici. There were among the Greeks, and there still are among modern scholars, important differences as to the dates of the principal events:[70] Eratosthenês dissented both from Herodotus and from Phanias and Kallimachus, while Larcher and Raoul Rochette (who follow Herodotus) stand opposed to O. Müller and to Mr. Clinton. That the reader may have a general conception of the order in which these legendary events were disposed, I transcribe from the Fasti Hellenica a double chronological table, contained in p. 139, in which the dates are placed in series, from Phorôneus to the Olympiad of Corœbus in B. C. 776,—in the first column according to the system of Eratosthenês, in the second according to that of Kallimachus.

"The following Table (says Mr. Clinton) offers a summary view of the leading periods from Phorôneus to the Olympiad of Corœbus, and exhibits a double series of dates; the one proceeding from the date of Eratosthenês, the other from a date founded on the reduced calculations of Phanias and Kallimachus, which strike out fifty-six years from the amount of Eratosthenês. Phanias, as we have seen, omitted fifty-five years between the Return and the registered Olympiads; for so we may understand the account: Kallimachus, fifty-six years between the Olympiad of Iphitus and the Olympiad in which Corœbus won.[71]

"The first column of this Table exhibits the *current* years before and after the fall of Troy: in the second column of dates the *complete* intervals are expressed."

| Years before the Fall of Troy. | | Years intervening between the different events. | B. C. Eratosth. | B. C. Kallimach. |
|---|---|---|---|---|

| | | | | |
|---|---|---|---|---|
| (570)[72] | *Phoroneus*, p. 19 | 287 | (1753) | (1697) |
| (283) | *Daneus*, p. 73 <br> *Pelasgus V.* p. 13, 88 | 33 | (1466) | (1410) |
| (250) | *Deukalion*, p. 42 | 50 | (1433) | (1377) |
| (200) | *Erechtheus* <br> *Dardanus*, p. 88 | 50 | (1383) | (1327) |
| (150) | *Azan, Aphida, Elatus* | 20 | (1333) | (1277) |
| 130 | *Kadmus*, p. 85 | 30 | 1313 | 1257 |
| (100) | *Pelops* | 22 | (1283) | (1227) |
| 78 | Birth of *Hercules* | 36 | 1261 | 1205 |
| (42) | Argonauts | 12 | (1225) | (1169) |
| 30 | First Theban war, p. 51, h. | 4 | 1213 | 1157 |
| 26 | Death of *Hercules* | 2 | 1209 | 1153 |
| 24 | Death of *Eurystheus*, p. 106, x. | 4 | 1207 | 1151 |
| 20 | Death of *Hyllus* | $2^y 9^m$ | 1203 | 1147 |
| 18 | Accession of *Agamemnon* | 2 | 1200 | 1144 |
| 16 | Second Theban war, p. 87, 1 | 6 | 1198 | 1142 |
| 10 | Trojan expedition ($9^y 1^m$) | 9 | 1192 | 1136 |

Years
after
the Fall
of Troy.

| | | | | |
|---|---|---|---|---|
| | Troy taken | 7 | 1183 | 1127 |
| 8 | *Orestes* reigns at Argos in the 8th year | 52 | 1176 | 1120 |
| 60 | The *Thessali* occupy Thessaly <br> The *Bœoti* return to Bœotia in the 60th yr. <br> Æolic migration under *Penthilus* | 20 | 1124 | 1068 |
| 80 | Return of the *Heraclidæ* in the 80th year | 29 | 1104 | 1048 |
| 109 | *Aletes* reigns at Corinth, p. 130, m. | 1 | 1075 | 1019 |
| 110 | Migration of *Theras* | 21 | 1074 | 1018 |
| 131 | Lesbos occupied 130 years after the æra | 8 | 1053 | 997 |
| 139 | Death of *Codrus* | 1 | 1045 | 989 |
| 140 | Ionic migration 60 years after the Return | 11 | 1044 | 988 |
| 151 | Cymê founded 150 years after the æra | 18 | 1033 | 977 |
| 169 | Smyrna, 168 years after the æra, p. 105, t. | 131 | 1015 | 959 |
| | | 299 | | |
| 300 | Olympiad of *Iphitus* | 108 <br> 52 | 884 | 828 |
| 408 <br> 352 | Olympiad of *Corœbus* | .. | 776 | 776 |

Wherever chronology is possible, researches such as those of Mr. Clinton, which have conduced so much to the better understanding of the later times of Greece, deserve respectful attention. But the ablest chronologist can accomplish nothing, unless he is supplied with a certain basis of matters of fact, pure and distinguishable from fiction, and authenticated by witnesses both knowing the truth and willing to declare it. Possessing this preliminary stock, he may reason from it to refute distinct falsehoods and to correct partial mistakes: but if all the original statements submitted to him contain truth (at least wherever there is truth) in a sort of chemical combination with fiction, which he has no means of decomposing,—he is in the condition of one who tries to solve a problem without data: he is first obliged to construct his own data, and from them to extract his conclusions. The statements of the epic poets, our only original witnesses in this case, correspond to the description here given. Whether the proportion of truth contained in them be smaller or greater, it is at all events unassignable,—and the constant and intimate admixture of fiction is both indisputable in itself, and, indeed, essential to the purpose and profession of those from whom the tales proceed. Of such a character are all the deposing witnesses, even where their tales agree; and it is out of a heap of such tales, not agreeing, but discrepant in a thousand ways, and without a morsel of pure authenticated truth,—that the critic is called upon to draw out a methodical series of historical events adorned with chronological dates.

If we could imagine a modern critical scholar transported into Greece at the time of the Persian war,—endued with his present habits of appreciating historical evidence, without sharing in the religious or patriotic feelings of the country,—and invited to prepare, out of the great body of Grecian epic which then existed, a History and Chronology of Greece anterior to 776 B. C., assigning reasons as well for what he admitted as for what he rejected,—I feel persuaded that he would have judged the undertaking to be little better than a process of guesswork. But the modern critic finds that not only Pherekydês and Hellanikus, but also Herodotus and Thucydidês, have either attempted the task or sanctioned the belief that it was practicable,—a matter not at all surprising, when we consider both their narrow experience of historical evidence and the powerful ascendency of religion and patriotism in predisposing them to antiquarian belief,—and he therefore accepts the problem as they have bequeathed it, adding his own efforts to bring it to a satisfactory solution. Nevertheless, he not only follows them with some degree of reserve and uneasiness, but even admits important distinctions quite foreign to their habits of thought. Thucydidês talks of the deeds of Hellên and his sons with as much confidence as we now speak of William the Conqueror: Mr. Clinton recognizes Hellên, with his sons Dôrus, Æolus, and Xuthus, as fictitious persons. Herodotus recites the great heroic genealogies down from Kadmus and Danaus, with a belief not less complete in the higher members of the series than in the lower: but Mr. Clinton admits a radical distinction in the evidence of events before and after the first recorded Olympiad, or 776 B. C., —"the first date in Grecian chronology (he remarks, p. 123) which can be fixed upon *authentic evidence*,"—the highest point to which Grecian chronology, *reckoning upward*, can be carried. Of this important epoch in Grecian development,—the commencement of authentic chronological life,—

Herodotus and Thucydidês had no knowledge or took no account: the later chronologists, from Timæus downwards, noted it, and made it serve as the basis of their chronological comparisons, so far as it went: but neither Eratosthenês nor Apollodôrus seem to have recognized (though Varro and Africanus did recognize) a marked difference in respect of certainty or authenticity between the period before and the period after.

In farther illustration of Mr. Clinton's opinion that the first recorded Olympiad is the earliest date which can be fixed upon authentic evidence, we have, in p. 138, the following just remarks in reference to the dissentient views of Eratosthenês, Phanias, and Kallimachus, about the date of the Trojan war: "The chronology of Eratosthenês (he says), founded on a careful comparison of circumstances, and approved by those to whom the same stores of information were open, is entitled to our respect. But we must remember that a conjectural date can never rise to the authority of evidence; that what is accepted as a substitute for testimony is not an equivalent: witnesses only can prove a date, and in the want of these, the knowledge of it is plainly beyond our reach. If in the absence of a better light we seek for what is probable, we are not to forget the distinction between conjecture and proof; between what is probable and what is certain. The computation, then, of Eratosthenês for the war of Troy is open to inquiry; and if we find it adverse to the opinions of many preceding writers, who fixed a lower date, and adverse to the acknowledged length of generation in the most authentic dynasties, we are allowed to follow other guides, who give us a lower epoch."

Here Mr. Clinton again plainly acknowledges the want of evidence, and the irremediable uncertainty of Grecian chronology before the Olympiads; and the reasonable conclusion from his argument is, not simply, that "the computation of Eratosthenês was open to inquiry," (which few would be found to deny,) but that both Eratosthenês and Phanias had delivered positive opinions upon a point on which no sufficient evidence was accessible, and therefore that neither the one nor the other was a guide to be followed.[73] Mr. Clinton does, indeed, speak of authentic dynasties prior to the first recorded Olympiad, but if there be any such, reaching up from that period to a supposed point coeval with or anterior to the war of Troy,—I see no good reason for the marked distinction which he draws between chronology before and chronology after the Olympiad of Korœbus, or for the necessity which he feels of suspending his upward reckoning at the last-mentioned epoch, and beginning a different process, called "a downward reckoning," from the higher epoch (supposed to be somehow ascertained without any upward reckoning) of the first patriarch from whom such authentic dynasty emanates. [74] Herodotus and Thucydidês might well, upon this supposition, ask of Mr. Clinton, why he called upon them to alter their method of proceeding at the year 776 B. C., and why they might not be allowed to pursue their "upward chronological reckoning," without interruption, from Leonidas up to Danaus, or from Peisistratus up to Hellên and Deukalion, without any alteration in the point of view. Authentic dynasties from the Olympiads, up to an epoch above the Trojan war, would enable us to obtain chronological proof for the latter date, instead of being reduced (as Mr. Clinton affirms that we are) to "conjecture" instead of proof.

The whole question, as to the value of the reckoning from the Olympiads up to Phorôneus, does in truth turn upon this point: Are those genealogies, which profess to cover the space between the two, authentic and trustworthy, or not? Mr. Clinton appears to feel that they are not so, when he admits the essential difference in the character of the evidence and the necessity of altering the method of computation, before and after the first recorded Olympiad; yet, in his Preface, he labors to prove that they possess historical worth and are in the main correctly set forth: moreover, that the fictitious persons, wherever any such are intermingled, may be detected and eliminated. The evidences upon which he relies, are: 1. Inscriptions; 2. The early poets.

1. An inscription, being nothing but a piece of writing on marble, carries evidentiary value under the same conditions as a published writing on paper. If the inscriber reports a contemporary fact which he had the means of knowing, and if there be no reason to suspect misrepresentation, we believe his assertion: if, on the other hand, he records facts belonging to a long period before his own time, his authority counts for little, except in so far as we can verify and appreciate his means of knowledge.

In estimating, therefore, the probative force of any inscription, the first and most indispensable point is to assure ourselves of its date. Amongst all the public registers and inscriptions alluded to by Mr. Clinton, there is not one which can be positively referred to a date anterior to 776 B. C. The quoit of Iphitus,—the public registers at Sparta, Corinth, and Elis,—the list of the priestesses of Juno at Argos,—are all of a date completely uncertified. O. Müller does, indeed, agree with Mr. Clinton (though in my opinion without any sufficient proof) in assigning the quoit of Iphitus to the age ascribed to that prince: and if we even grant thus much, we shall have an inscription as old (adopting Mr. Clinton's determination of the age of Iphitus) as 828 B. C. But when Mr. Clinton quotes O. Müller as admitting the registers of Sparta, Corinth, and Elis, it is right to add that the latter does not profess to guarantee the authenticity of these documents, or the age at which such registers began to be kept. It is not to be doubted that there were registers of the kings of Sparta carrying them up to Hêraklês, and of the kings of Elis from Oxylus to Iphitus; but the question is, at what time did these lists begin to be kept continuously? This is a point which we have no means of deciding, nor can we accept Mr. Clinton's unsupported conjecture, when he tells us: *"Perhaps these were begun to be written as early as* B. C. 1048, the probable time of the Dorian conquest." Again, he tells us: "At Argos, a register was preserved of the priestesses of Juno, which *might* be more ancient than the catalogues of the kings of Sparta or Corinth. That register, from which Hellanikus composed his work, contained the priestesses from the earliest times down to the age of Hellanikus himself.... But this catalogue *might have* been commenced as early as the Trojan war itself, and even at a still earlier date." (pp. x. xi.) Again, respecting the inscriptions quoted by Herodotus from the temple of the Ismenian Apollo at Thêbes, in which Amphitryo and Laodamas are named, Mr. Clinton says, "They were ancient in the time of Herodotus, which *may* perhaps carry them back 400 years before his time: and in that case they *might* approach within 300 years of Laodamas and within 400 years of the probable time of Kadmus himself."—"It is granted (he adds, in a note,) that these inscriptions were *not genuine*, that is, not of the date to which they were assigned by Herodotus himself. But that they were ancient, cannot be doubted," &c.

The time when Herodotus saw the temple of the Ismenian Apollo at Thêbes can hardly have been earlier than 450 B. C. reckoning upwards from hence to 776 B. C., we have an interval of 326 years: the inscriptions which Herodotus saw may well therefore have been *ancient*, without being earlier than the first recorded Olympiad. Mr. Clinton does, indeed, tell us that *ancient* "may perhaps" be construed as 400 years earlier than Herodotus. But no careful reader can permit himself to convert such bare possibility into a ground of inference, and to make it available, in conjunction with other similar possibilities before enumerated, for the purpose of showing that there really existed inscriptions in Greece of a date anterior to 776 B. C. Unless Mr. Clinton can make out this, he can derive no benefit from inscriptions, in his attempt to substantiate the reality of the mythical persons or of the mythical events.

The truth is, that the Herakleid pedigree of the Spartan kings (as has been observed in a former chapter) is only one out of the numerous divine and heroic genealogies with which the Hellenic world abounded,[75]—a class of documents which become historical evidence only so high in the ascending series as the names composing them are authenticated by contemporary, or nearly contemporary, enrolment. At what period this practice of enrolment began, we have no information. Two remarks, however, may be made, in reference to any approximative guess as to the time when actual registration commenced: First, that the number of names in the pedigree, or the length of past time which it professes to embrace, affords no presumption of any superior antiquity in the time of registration: Secondly, that, looking to the acknowledged paucity and rudeness of Grecian writing, even down to the 60th Olympiad (540 B. C.), and to the absence of the habit of writing, as well as the low estimate of its value, which such a state of things argues, the presumption is, that written enrolment of family genealogies, did not commence until a long time after 776 B. C., and the obligation of proof falls upon him who maintains that it commenced earlier. And this second remark is farther borne out, when we observe that there is no registered list, except that of the Olympic victors, which goes up even so high as 776 B. C. The next list which O. Müller and Mr. Clinton produce, is that of the Karneonicæ, or victors at the Karneian festival, which reaches only up to 676 B.C.

If Mr. Clinton then makes little out of inscriptions to sustain his view of Grecian history and chronology anterior to the recorded Olympiads, let us examine the inferences which he draws from his ether source of evidence,— the early poets. And here it will be found, First, that in order to maintain the credibility of these witnesses, he lays down positions respecting historical evidence both indefensible in themselves, and especially inapplicable to the early times of Greece: Secondly, that his reasoning is at the same time inconsistent,—inasmuch as it includes admissions, which, if properly understood and followed out, exhibit these very witnesses as habitually, indiscriminately, and unconsciously mingling truth and fiction; and therefore little fit to be believed upon their solitary and unsupported testimony.

To take the second point first, he says, Introduction, p. ii-iii: "The authority even of the genealogies has been called in question by many able and learned persons, who reject Danaus, Kadmus, Hercules, Thêseus, and many others, as fictitious persons. It is evident that any fact would come from the hands of the poets embellished with many fabulous additions: and fictitious genealogies were undoubtedly composed. Because, however, some genealogies were fictitious, we are not justified in concluding that all were fabulous…. In estimating, then, the historical value of the genealogies transmitted by the early poets, we may take a middle course; not rejecting them as wholly false, nor yet implicitly receiving all as true. The genealogies *contain many real persons*, but these are *incorporated with many fictitious names*. The fictions, however, will have a basis of truth: the genealogical expression may be false, but the connection which it describes is real. Even to those who reject the whole as fabulous, the exhibition of the early times which is presented in this volume may still be not unacceptable: because it is necessary to the right understanding of antiquity that the opinions of the Greeks concerning their own origin should be set before us, even if these are erroneous opinions, and that their story should be told as they have told it themselves. The names preserved by the ancient genealogies may be considered of three kinds; either they were the name of a race or clan converted into the name of an individual, or they were altogether fictitious, or lastly, they were real historical names. An attempt is made, in the four genealogical tables inserted below, to distinguish these three classes of names.... Of those who are left in the third class (*i. e.* the real) all are not entitled to remain there. But I have only placed in the third class those names concerning which there seemed to be little doubt. The rest are left to the judgment of the reader."

Pursuant to this principle of division, Mr. Clinton furnishes four genealogical tables,[76] in which the names of persons representing races are printed in capital letters, and those of purely fictitious persons in italics. And these tables exhibit a curious sample of the intimate commixture of fiction with that which he calls truth: real son and mythical father, real husband and mythical wife, or *vice versâ.*

Upon Mr. Clinton's tables we may remark:—

1. The names singled out as fictitious are distinguished by no common character, nor any mark either assignable or defensible, from those which are left as real. To take an example (p. 40), why is Itônus the first pointed out as a fiction, while Itônus the second, together with Physcus, Cynus, Salmôneus, Ormenus, etc., in the same page, are preserved as real, all of them being eponyms of towns just as much as Itônus?

2. If we are to discard Hellên, Dôrus, Æolus, Iôn, etc., as not being real individual persons, but expressions for personified races, why are we to retain Kadmus, Danaus, Hyllus, and several others, who are just as much eponyms of races and tribes as the four above mentioned? Hyllus, Pamphylus, and Dymas are the eponyms of the three Dorian tribes,[77] just as Hoplês and the other three sons of Iôn were of the four Attic tribes: Kadmus and Danaus stand in the same relation to the Kadmeians and Danaans, as Argus and Achæus to the Argeians and Achæans. Besides, there are many other names really eponymous, which we cannot now recognize to be so, in consequence of our imperfect acquaintance with the subdivisions of the Hellenic population, each of which, speaking generally, had its god or hero, to whom the original of the name was referred. If, then, eponymous names are to be excluded from the category of reality, we shall find that the ranks of the real men will be thinned to a far greater extent than is indicated by Mr. Clinton's tables.

3. Though Mr. Clinton does not carry out consistently either of his disfranchising qualifications among the names and persons of the old mythes, he nevertheless presses them far enough to strike out a sensible proportion of the whole. By conceding thus much to modern scepticism, he has departed

from the point of view of Hellanikus and Herodotus, and the ancient historians generally; and it is singular that the names, which he has been the most forward to sacrifice, are exactly those to which they were most attached, and which it would have been most painful to their faith to part with,—I mean the eponymous heroes. Neither Herodotus, nor Hellanikus, nor Eratosthenês, nor any one of the chronological reckoners of antiquity, would have admitted the distinction which Mr. Clinton draws between persons real and persons fictitious in the old mythical world, though they might perhaps occasionally, on special grounds, call in question the existence of some individual characters amongst the mythical ancestry of Greece; but they never dreamed of that general severance into real and fictitious persons, which forms the principle of Mr. Clinton's "middle course." Their chronological computations for Grecian antiquity assumed that the mythical characters, in their full and entire sequence, were all real persons. Setting up the entire list as real, they calculated so many generations to a century, and thus determined the number of centuries which separated themselves from the gods, the heroes, or the autochthonous men who formed in their view the historical starting point. But as soon as it is admitted that the personages in the mythical world are divisible into two classes, partly real and partly fictitious, the integrity of the series is broken up, and it can be no longer employed as a basis for chronological calculation. In the estimate of the ancient chronologers, three succeeding persons of the same lineage—grandfather, father, and son,— counted for a century; and this may pass in a rough way, so long as you are thoroughly satisfied that they are all real persons: but if, in the succession of persons A, B, C, you strike out B as a fiction, the continuity of data necessary for chronological computation disappears. Now Mr. Clinton is inconsistent with himself in this,—that, while he abandons the unsuspecting historical faith of the Grecian chronologers, he nevertheless continues his chronological computations upon the data of that ancient faith,—upon the assumed reality of all the persons constituting his ante-historical generations. What becomes, for example, of the Herakleid genealogy of the Spartan kings, when it is admitted that eponymous persons are to be cancelled as fictions; seeing that Hyllus, through whom those kings traced their origin to Hêraklês comes in the most distinct manner under that category, as much so as Hoplês the son of Iôn? It will be found that, when we once cease to believe in the mythical world as an uninterrupted and unalloyed succession of real individuals, it becomes unfit to serve as a basis for chronological computations, and that Mr. Clinton, when he mutilated the data of the ancient chronologists, ought at the same time to have abandoned their problems as insoluble. Genealogies of real persons, such as Herodotus and Eratosthenês believed in, afford a tolerable basis for calculations of time, within certain limits of error: "genealogies containing many real persons, but incorporated with many fictitious names," (to use the language just cited from Mr. Clinton,) are essentially unavailable for such a purpose.

It is right here to add, that I agree in Mr. Clinton's view of these eponymous persons: I admit, with him, that "the genealogical expression may often be false, when the connection which it describes is real." Thus, for example, the adoption of Hyllus by Ægimius, the father of Pamphylus and Dymas, to the privileges of a son and to a third fraction of his territories, may reasonably be construed as a mythical expression of the fraternal union of the three Dorian tribes, Hyllêis, Pamphyli, and Dymanes: so about the relationship of Iôn and Achæus, of Dôrus and Æolus. But if we put this construction on the name of Hyllus, or Iôn, or Achæus, we cannot at the same time employ either of these persons as units in chronological reckoning: nor is it consistent to recognize them in the lump as members of a distinct class, and yet to enlist them as real individuals in measuring the duration of past time.

4. Mr. Clinton, while professing a wish to tell the story of the Greeks as they have told it themselves, seems unconscious how capitally his point of view differs from theirs. The distinction which he draws between real and fictitious persons would have appeared unreasonable, not to say offensive, to Herodotus or Eratosthenês. It is undoubtedly right that the early history (if so it is to be called) of the Greeks should be told as they have told it themselves, and with that view I have endeavored in the previous narrative, as far as I could, to present the primitive legends in their original color and character,— pointing out at the same time the manner in which they were transformed and distilled into history by passing through the retort of later annalists. It is the legend, as thus transformed, which Mr. Clinton seems to understand as the story told by the Greeks themselves,—which cannot be admitted to be true, unless the meaning of the expression be specially explained. In his general distinction, however, between the real and fictitious persons of the mythical world, he departs essentially from the point of view even of the later Greeks. And if he had consistently followed out that distinction in his particular criticisms, he would have found the ground slipping under his feet in his upward march even to Troy,—not to mention the series of eighteen generations farther up, to Phorôneus; but he does *not* consistently follow it out, and therefore, in practice, he deviates little from the footsteps of the ancients.

Enough has been said to show that the witnesses upon whom Mr. Clinton relies, blend truth and fiction habitually, indiscriminately, and unconsciously, even upon his own admission. Let us now consider the positions which he lays down respecting historical evidence. He says (Introduct. pp. vi-vii):—

"We may acknowledge as real persons all those whom there is no reason

34

for rejecting. The presumption is in favor of the early tradition, if no argument can be brought to overthrow it. The persons may be considered real, when the description of them is consonant with the state of the country at that time: when no national prejudice or vanity could be concerned in inventing them: when the tradition is consistent and general: when rival or hostile tribes concur in the leading facts: when the acts ascribed to the person (divested of their poetical ornament) enter into the political system of the age, or form the basis of other transactions which fall within known historical times. Kadmus and Danaus appear to be real persons: for it is conformable to the state of mankind, and perfectly credible, that Phœnician and Egyptian adventurers, in the ages to which these persons are ascribed, should have found their way to the coasts of Greece: and the Greeks (as already observed) had no motive from any national vanity to feign these settlements. Hercules was a real person. His acts were recorded by those who were not friendly to the Dorians; by Achæans and Æolians, and Ionians, who had no vanity to gratify in celebrating the hero of a hostile and rival people. His descendants in many branches remained in many states down to the historical times. His son Tlepolemus, and his grandson and great-grandson Cleodæus and Aristomachus, are acknowledged (*i. e.* by O. Müller) to be real persons: and there is no reason that can be assigned for receiving these, which will not be equally valid for establishing the reality both of Hercules and Hyllus. Above all, Hercules is authenticated by the testimonies both of the Iliad and Odyssey."

These positions appear to me inconsistent with any sound views of the conditions of historical testimony. According to what is here laid down, we are bound to accept as real all the persons mentioned by Homer, Arktinus, Leschês, the Hesiodic poets, Eumêlus, Asius, etc., unless we can adduce some positive ground in each particular case to prove the contrary. If this position be a true one, the greater part of the history of England, from Brute the Trojan down to Julius Cæsar, ought at once to be admitted as valid and worthy of credence. What Mr. Clinton here calls the *early tradition*, is in point of fact, the narrative of these early poets. The word *tradition* is an equivocal word, and begs the whole question; for while in its obvious and literal meaning it implies only something handed down, whether truth or fiction,—it is tacitly understood to imply a tale descriptive of some real matter of fact, taking its rise at the time when that fact happened, and originally accurate, but corrupted by subsequent oral transmission. Understanding, therefore, by Mr. Clinton's words *early tradition*, the tales of the old poets, we shall find his position totally inadmissible,—that we are bound to admit the persons or statements of Homer and Hesiod as real unless where we can produce reasons to the contrary. To allow this, would be to put them upon a par with good

35

contemporary witnesses; for no greater privilege can be claimed in favor even of Thucydidês, than the title of his testimony to be believed unless where it can be contradicted on special grounds. The presumption in favor of an asserting witness is either strong or weak, or positively nothing, according to the compound ratio of his means of knowledge, his moral and intellectual habits, and his motive to speak the truth. Thus, for instance, when Hesiod tells us that his father quitted the Æolic Kymê, and came to Askra in Bœôtia, we may fully believe him; but when he describes to us the battles between the Olympic gods and the Titans, or between Hêraklês and Cycnus,—or when Homer depicts the efforts of Hectôr, aided by Apollo, for the defence of Troy, and the struggles of Achilles and Odysseus, with the assistance of Hêrê and Poseidôn, for the destruction of that city, events professedly long past and gone,—we cannot presume either of them to be in any way worthy of belief. It cannot be shown that they possessed any means of knowledge, while it is certain that they could have no motive to consider historical truth: their object was to satisfy an uncritical appetite for narrative, and to interest the emotions of their hearers. Mr. Clinton says, that "the persons may be considered real when the description of them is consistent with the state of the country at that time." But he has forgotten, first, that we know nothing of the state of the country except what these very poets tell us; next, that fictitious persons may be just as consonant to the state of the country as real persons. While, therefore, on the one hand, we have no independent evidence either to affirm or to deny that Achilles or Agamemnôn are consistent with the state of Greece or Asia Minor, at a certain supposed date 1183 B. C., so, on the other hand, even assuming such consistency to be made out, this of itself would not prove them to be real persons.

Mr. Clinton's reasoning altogether overlooks the existence of *plausible fiction*,—fictitious stories which harmonize perfectly well with the general course of facts, and which are distinguished from matters of fact not by any internal character, but by the circumstance that matter of fact has some competent and well-informed witness to authenticate it, either directly or through legitimate inference. Fiction may be, and often is, extravagant and incredible; but it may also be plausible and specious, and in that case there is nothing but the want of an attesting certificate to distinguish it from truth. Now all the tests, which Mr. Clinton proposes as guarantees of the reality of the Homeric persons, will be just as well satisfied by plausible fiction as by actual matter of fact: the plausibility of the fiction consists in its satisfying those and other similar conditions. In most cases, the tales of the poets *did* fall in with the existing current of feelings in their audience: "prejudice and vanity" are not the only feelings, but doubtless prejudice and vanity were often appealed to, and it was from such harmony of sentiment that they acquired their hold on men's belief. Without any doubt, the Iliad appealed most powerfully to the reverence for ancestral gods and heroes among the Asiatic colonists who first heard it: the temptation of putting forth an interesting tale is quite a sufficient stimulus to the invention of the poet, and the plausibility of the tale a sufficient passport to the belief of the hearers. Mr. Clinton talks of "consistent and general tradition." But that the tale of a poet, when once told with effect and beauty, acquired general belief,—is no proof that it was founded on fact: otherwise, what are we to say to the divine legends, and to the large portion of the Homeric narrative which Mr. Clinton himself sets aside as untrue, under the designation of "poetical ornament?" When a mythical incident is recorded as "forming the basis" of some known historical fact or institution,—as, for instance, the successful stratagem by which Melanthus killed Xanthus, in the battle on the boundary, as recounted in my last chapter,—we may adopt one of two views; we may either treat the incident as real, and as having actually given occasion to what is described as its effect,—or we may treat the incident as a legend imagined in order to assign some plausible origin of the reality,—"Aut ex re nomen, aut ex vocabulo fabula."[78] In cases where the legendary incident is referred to a time long anterior to any records,—as it commonly is,—the second mode of proceeding appears to me far more consonant to reason and probability than the first. It is to be recollected that all the persons and facts, here defended as matter of real history, by Mr. Clinton, are referred to an age long preceding the first beginning of records.

I have already remarked that Mr. Clinton shrinks from his own rule in treating Kadmus and Danaus as real persons, since they are as much eponyms of tribes or races as Dôrus and Hellên. And if he can admit Hêraklês to be a real man, I cannot see upon what reason he can consistently disallow any one of the mythical personages, for there is not one whose exploits are more strikingly at variance with the standard of historical probability. Mr. Clinton reasons upon the supposition that "Herculês was a *Dorian* hero:" but he was Achæan and Kadmeian as well as Dorian, though the legends respecting him are different in all the three characters. Whether his son Tlepolemus and his grandson Cleodæus belong to the category of historical men, I will not take upon me to say, though O. Müller (in my opinion without any warranty) appears to admit it; but Hyllus certainly is not a real man, if the canon of Mr. Clinton himself respecting the eponyms is to be trusted. "The descendants of Herculês (observes Mr. Clinton) remained in many states down to the historical times." So did those of Zeus and Apollo, and of that god whom the historian Hekatæus recognized as his progenitor in the sixteenth generation; the titular kings of Ephesus, in the historical times, as well as Peisistratus, the despot of Athens, traced their origin up to Æolus and Hellên, yet Mr. Clinton does not hesitate to reject Æolus and Hellên as fictitious persons. I dispute the propriety of quoting the Iliad and Odyssey (as Mr. Clinton does) in evidence of the historic personality of Herculês. For, even with regard to the ordinary men who figure in those poems, we have no means of discriminating the real from the fictitious; while the Homeric Hêraklês is unquestionably more than an ordinary man,—he is the favorite son of Zeus, from his birth predestined to a life of labor and servitude, as preparation for a glorious immortality. Without doubt, the poet himself believed in the reality of Herculês, but it was a reality clothed with superhuman attributes.

Mr. Clinton observes (Introd. p. ii.), that "because some genealogies were fictitious, we are not justified in concluding that all were fabulous." It is no way necessary that we should maintain so extensive a position: it is sufficient that all are fabulous so far as concerns gods and heroes,—*some* fabulous throughout,—and none ascertainably true, for the period anterior to the recorded Olympiads. How much, or what particular portions, may be true, no one can pronounce. The gods and heroes are, from our point of view, essentially fictitious; but from the Grecian point of view they were the most real (if the expression may be permitted, *i. e.* clung to with the strongest faith) of all the members of the series. They not only formed parts of the genealogy as originally conceived, but were in themselves the grand reason why it was conceived,—as a golden chain to connect the living man with a divine ancestor. The genealogy, therefore, taken as a whole, (and its value consists in its being taken as a whole,) was from the beginning a fiction; but the names of the father and grandfather of the living man, in whose day it first came forth, were doubtless those of real men. Wherever, therefore, we can verify the date of a genealogy, as applied to some living person, we may reasonably presume the two lowest members of it to be also those of real persons: but this has no application to the time anterior to the Olympiads,—still less to the pretended times of the Trojan war, the Kalydônian boar-hunt, or the deluge of Deukalion. To reason (as Mr. Clinton does, Introd. p. vi.),—"Because Aristomachus was a real man, therefore his father Cleodæus, his grandfather Hyllus, and so farther upwards, etc., must have been real men,"—is an inadmissible conclusion. The historian Hekatæus was a real man, and doubtless his father Hegesander, also,—but it would be unsafe to march up his genealogical ladder fifteen steps, to the presence of the ancestorial god of whom he boasted: the upper steps of the ladder will be found broken and unreal. Not to mention that the inference, from real son to real father, is inconsistent with the admissions in Mr. Clinton's own genealogical tables; for he there inserts the names of several mythical fathers as having begotten real historical sons.

The general authority of Mr. Clinton's book, and the sincere respect which

I entertain for his elucidations of the later chronology, have imposed upon me the duty of assigning those grounds on which I dissent from his conclusions prior to the first recorded Olympiad. The reader who desires to see the numerous and contradictory guesses (they deserve no better name) of the Greeks themselves in the attempt to chronologize their mythical narratives, will find them in the copious notes annexed to the first half of his first volume. As I consider all such researches not merely as fruitless, in regard to any trustworthy result, but as serving to divert attention from the genuine form and really illustrative character of Grecian legend, I have not thought it right to go over the same ground in the present work. Differing as I do, however, from Mr. Clinton's views on this subject, I concur with him in deprecating the application of etymology (Intr. pp. xi-xii.) as a general scheme of explanation to the characters and events of Greek legend. Amongst the many causes which operated as suggestives and stimulants to Greek fancy in the creation of these interesting tales, doubtless etymology has had its share; but it cannot be applied (as Hermann, above all others, has sought to apply it) for the purpose of imparting supposed sense and system to the general body of mythical narrative. I have already remarked on this topic in a former chapter.

It would be curious to ascertain at what time, or by whom, the earliest continuous genealogies, connecting existing persons with the supposed antecedent age of legend, were formed and preserved. Neither Homer nor Hesiod mentioned any verifiable *present* persons or circumstances: had they done so, the age of one or other of them could have been determined upon good evidence, which we may fairly presume to have been impossible, from the endless controversies upon this topic among ancient writers. In the Hesiodic Works and Days, the heroes of Troy and Thêbes are even presented as an extinct race,[79] radically different from the poet's own contemporaries, who are a new race, far too depraved to be conceived as sprung from the loins of the heroes; so that we can hardly suppose Hesiod (though his father was a native of the Æolic Kymê) to have admitted the pedigree of the Æolic chiefs, as reputed descendants of Agamemnôn. Certain it is, that the earliest poets did not attempt to measure or bridge over the supposed interval, between their own age and the war of Troy, by any definite series of fathers and sons: whether Eumêlus or Asius made any such attempt, we cannot tell, but the earliest continuous backward genealogies which we find mentioned are those of Pherekydês, Hellanikus, and Herodotus. It is well known that Herodotus, in his manner of computing the upward genealogy of the Spartan kings, assigns the date of the Trojan war to a period 800 years earlier than himself, equivalent about to B. C. 1270-1250; while the subsequent Alexandrine chronologists, Eratosthenês and Apollodôrus, place that event in 1184 and

1183 B. C.; and the Parian marble refers it to an intermediate date, different from either,—1209 B. C. Ephorus, Phanias, Timæus, Kleitarchus, and Duris, had each his own conjectural date; but the computations of the Alexandrine chronologists was the most generally followed by those who succeeded them, and seems to have passed to modern times as the received date of this great legendary event,—though some distinguished inquirers have adopted the epoch of Herodotus, which Larcher has attempted to vindicate in an elaborate but feeble dissertation.[80] It is unnecessary to state that, in my view, the inquiry has no other value except to illustrate the ideas which guided the Greek mind, and to exhibit its progress from the days of Homer to those of Herodotus. For it argues a considerable mental progress when men begin to methodize the past, even though they do so on fictitious principles, being as yet unprovided with those records which alone could put them on a better course. The Homeric man was satisfied with feeling, imagining, and believing particular incidents of a supposed past, without any attempt to graduate the line of connection between them and himself: to introduce fictitious hypotheses and media of connection is the business of a succeeding age, when the stimulus of rational curiosity is first felt, without any authentic materials to supply it. We have, then, the form of history operating upon the matter of legend,—the transition-state between legend and history; less interesting, indeed, than either separately, yet necessary as a step between the two.

# CHAPTER XX.

## STATE OF SOCIETY AND MANNERS AS EXHIBITED IN GRECIAN LEGEND.

THOUGH the particular persons and events, chronicled in the legendary poems of Greece, are not to be regarded as belonging to the province of real history, those poems are, nevertheless, full of instruction as pictures of life and manners; and the very same circumstances, which divest their composers of all credibility as historians, render them so much the more valuable as unconscious expositors of their own contemporary society. While professedly describing an uncertified past, their combinations are involuntarily borrowed from the surrounding present: for among communities, such as those of the primitive Greeks, without books, without means of extended travel, without acquaintance with foreign languages and habits, the imagination, even of highly gifted men, was naturally enslaved by the circumstances around them to a far greater degree than in the later days of Solôn or Herodotus; insomuch that the characters which they conceived and the scenes which they described would for that reason bear a stronger generic resemblance to the realities of their own time and locality. Nor was the poetry of that age addressed to lettered and critical authors, watchful to detect plagiarism, sated with simple imagery, and requiring something of novelty or peculiarity in every fresh production. To captivate their emotions, it was sufficient to depict, with genius and fervor, the more obvious manifestations of human adventure or suffering, and to idealize that type of society, both private and public, with which the hearers around were familiar. Even in describing the gods, where a great degree of latitude and deviation might have been expected,[81] we see that Homer introduces into Olympus the passions, the caprices, the love of power and patronage, the alternation of dignity and weakness, which animated the bosom of an ordinary Grecian chief; and this tendency, to reproduce in substance the social relations to which he had been accustomed, would operate still more powerfully when he had to describe simply human characters,—the chief and his people, the warrior and his comrades, the husband, wife, father, and son,—or the imperfect rudiments of judicial and administrative proceeding. That his narrative on all these points, even with fictitious characters and events, presents a close approximation to general reality, there can be no reason to doubt.[82] The necessity under which he lay of drawing from a store, then happily unexhausted, of personal experience and observation, is one of the causes of that freshness and vivacity of description for which he stands unrivalled, and which constituted the imperishable charm of the Iliad and Odyssey from the beginning to the end of Grecian literature.

While, therefore, we renounce the idea of chronologizing or historicizing the events of Grecian legend, we may turn them to profit as valuable memorials of that state of society, feeling, and intelligence, which must be to us the starting-point of the history of the people. Of course, the legendary age, like all those which succeeded it, had its antecedent causes and determining conditions; but of these we know nothing, and we are compelled to assume it as a primary fact, for the purpose of following out its subsequent changes. To conceive absolute beginning or origin (as Niebuhr has justly remarked) is beyond the reach of our faculties: we can neither apprehend nor verify anything beyond progress, or development, or decay,[83]—change from one set of circumstances to another, operated by some definite combination of physical or moral laws. In the case of the Greeks, the legendary age, as the earliest in any way known to us, must be taken as the initial state from which this series of changes commences. We must depict its prominent characteristics as well as we can, and show,—partly how it serves to prepare, partly how it forms a contrast to set off,—the subsequent ages of Solôn, of Periklês, and of Demosthenês.

1. The political condition, which Grecian legend everywhere presents to us, is in its principal features strikingly different from that which had become universally prevalent among the Greeks in the time of the Peloponnêsian war. Historical oligarchy, as well as democracy, agreed in requiring a certain established system of government, comprising the three elements of specialized functions, temporary functionaries, and ultimate responsibility (under some forms or other) to the mass of qualified citizens—either a Senate or an Ecclesia, or both. There were, of course, many and capital distinctions between one government and another, in respect to the qualification of the citizen, the attributes and efficiency of the general assembly, the admissibility to power, etc.; and men might often be dissatisfied with the way in which these questions were determined in their own city. But in the mind of every man, some determining rule or system—something like what in modern times is called a *constitution*—was indispensable to any government entitled to be called legitimate, or capable of creating in the mind of a Greek a feeling of moral obligation to obey it. The functionaries who exercised authority under it might be more or less competent or popular; but his personal feelings towards them were commonly lost in his attachment or aversion to the general system. If any energetic man could by audacity or craft break down the constitution, and render himself permanent ruler according to his own will and pleasure,—even though he might govern well, he could never inspire the

people with any sentiment of duty towards him. His sceptre was illegitimate from the beginning, and even the taking of his life, far from being interdicted by that moral feeling which condemned the shedding of blood in other cases, was considered meritorious. Nor could he be mentioned in the language except by a name[84] (τύραννος, *despot*,) which branded him as an object of mingled fear and dislike.

If we carry our eyes back from historical to legendary Greece, we find a picture the reverse of what has been here sketched. We discern a government in which there is little or no scheme or system,—still less any idea of responsibility to the governed,—but in which the mainspring of obedience on the part of the people consists in their personal feeling and reverence towards the chief. We remark, first and foremost, the king: next, a limited number of subordinate kings or chiefs; afterwards, the mass of armed freemen, husbandmen, artisans, freebooters, etc.; lowest of all, the free laborers for hire, and the bought slaves. The king is not distinguished by any broad or impassable boundary from the other chiefs, to each of whom the title *basileus* is applicable as well as to himself: his supremacy has been inherited from his ancestors, and passes by descent, as a general rule, to his eldest son, having been conferred upon the family as a privilege by the favor of Zeus.[85] In war, he is the leader, foremost in personal prowess, and directing all military movements; in peace, he is the general protector of the injured and oppressed; he farther offers up those public prayers and sacrifices which are intended to obtain for the whole people the favor of the gods. An ample domain is assigned to him as an appurtenance of his lofty position, while the produce of his fields and his cattle is consecrated in part to an abundant, though rude hospitality. Moreover, he receives frequent presents, to avert his enmity, to conciliate his favor,[86] or to buy off his exactions; and when plunder is taken from the enemy, a large previous share, comprising probably the most alluring female captive, is reserved for him, apart from the general distribution.[87]

Such is the position of the king, in the heroic times of Greece,—the only person (if we except the heralds and priests, each both special and subordinate,) who is then presented to us as clothed with any individual authority,—the person by whom all the executive functions, then few in number, which the society requires, are either performed or directed. His personal ascendency—derived from divine countenance, bestowed both upon himself individually and upon his race, and probably from accredited divine descent—is the salient feature in the picture. The people hearken to his voice, embrace his propositions, and obey his orders: not merely resistance, but even criticism upon his acts, is generally exhibited in an odious point of view, and is, indeed, never heard of except from some one or more of the subordinate princes. To keep alive and justify such feelings in the public mind, however, the king must himself possess various accomplishments, bodily and mental, and that too in a superior degree.[88] He must be brave in the field, wise in the council, and eloquent in the agora; he must be endued with bodily strength and activity above other men, and must be an adept, not only in the use of his arms, but also in those athletic exercises which the crowd delight to witness. Even the more homely varieties of manual acquirements are an addition to his character,—such as the craft of the carpenter or shipwright, the straight furrowing of the ploughman, or the indefatigable persistence of the mower without repose or refreshment throughout the longest day.[89] The conditions of voluntary obedience, during the Grecian heroic times, are family descent with personal force and superiority mental as well as bodily, in the chief, coupled with the favor of the gods: an old chief, such as Pêleus and Laërtes, cannot retain his position.[90] But, on the other hand, where these elements of force are present, a good deal of violence, caprice, and rapacity is tolerated: the ethical judgment is not exact in scrutinizing the conduct of individuals so preëminently endowed. As in the case of the gods, the general epithets of *good*, *just*, etc., are applied to them as euphemisms arising from submission and fear, being not only not suggested, but often pointedly belied, by their particular acts. These words signify[91] the man of birth, wealth, influence, and daring, whose arm is strong to destroy or to protect, whatever may be the turn of his moral sentiments; while the opposite epithet, *bad*, designates the poor, lowly, and weak; from whose dispositions, be they ever so virtuous, society has little either to hope or to fear.

Aristotle, in his general theory of government,[92] lays down the position, that the earliest sources of obedience and authority among mankind are personal, exhibiting themselves most perfectly in the type of paternal supremacy; and that therefore the kingly government, as most conformable to this stage of social sentiment, became probably the first established everywhere. And in fact it still continued in his time to be generally prevalent among the non-Hellenic nations, immediately around; though the Phœnician cities and Carthage, the most civilized of all non-Hellenic states, were republics. Nevertheless, so completely were the feelings about kingship reversed among his contemporary Greeks, that he finds it difficult to enter into the voluntary obedience paid by his ancestors to their early heroic chiefs. He cannot explain to his own satisfaction how any one man should have been so much superior to the companions around him as to maintain such immense personal ascendency: he suspects that in such small communities great merit was very rare, so that the chief had few competitors.[93] Such remarks illustrate strongly the revolution which the Greek mind had undergone during the preceding centuries, in regard to the internal grounds of political submission. But the connecting link, between the Homeric and the republican schemes of government, is to be found in two adjuncts of the Homeric royalty, which are now to be mentioned,—the boulê, or council of chiefs, and the agora, or general assembly of freemen.

These two meetings, more or less frequently convoked, and interwoven with the earliest habits of the primitive Grecian communities, are exhibited in the monuments of the legendary age as opportunities for advising the king, and media for promulgating his intentions to the people, rather than as restraints upon his authority. Unquestionably, they must have conduced in practice to the latter result as well as to the former; but this is not the light in which the Homeric poems describe them. The chiefs, kings, princes, or gerontes—for the same word in Greek designates both an old man and a man of conspicuous rank and position—compose the council,[94] in which, according to the representations in the Iliad, the resolutions of Agamemnôn on the one side, and of Hectôr on the other, appear uniformly to prevail. The harshness and even contempt with which Hectôr treats respectful opposition from his ancient companion Polydamas,—the desponding tone and conscious inferiority of the latter, and the unanimous assent which the former obtains, even when quite in the wrong—all this is clearly set forth in the poem:[95] while in the Grecian camp we see Nestôr tendering his advice in the most submissive and delicate manner to Agamemnôn, to be adopted or rejected, as "the king of men" might determine.[96] The council is a purely consultative body, assembled, not with any power of peremptorily arresting mischievous resolves of the king, but solely for his information and guidance. He himself is the presiding (boulephŏrus, or) member[97] of council; the rest, collectively as well as individually, are his subordinates.

We proceed from the council to the agora: according to what seems the received custom, the king, after having talked over his intentions with the former, proceeds to announce them to the people. The heralds make the crowd sit down in order,[98] and enforce silence: any one of the chiefs or councillors —but as it seems, no one else[99]—is allowed to address them: the king first promulgates his intentions, which are then open to be commented upon by others. But in the Homeric agora, no division of affirmative or negative voices ever takes place, nor is any formal resolution ever adopted. The nullity of positive function strikes us even more in the agora than in the council. It is an assembly for talk, communication, and discussion, to a certain extent, by the chiefs, in presence of the people as listeners and sympathizers,—often for eloquence, and sometimes for quarrel,—but here its ostensible purposes end.

The agora in Ithaka, in the second book of the Odyssey, is convened by the youthful Telemachus, at the instigation of Athênê, not for the purpose of submitting any proposition, but in order to give formal and public notice to the suitors to desist from their iniquitous intrusion and pillage of his substance, and to absolve himself farther, before gods and men, from all obligations towards them, if they refuse to comply. For the slaughter of the suitors, in all the security of the festive hall and banquet (which forms the catastrophe of the Odyssey), was a proceeding involving much that was shocking to Grecian feeling,[100] and therefore required to be preceded by such ample formalities, as would leave both the delinquents themselves without the shadow of excuse, and their surviving relatives without any claim to the customary satisfaction. For this special purpose, Telemachus directs the heralds to summon an agora: but what seems most of all surprising is, that none had ever been summoned or held since the departure of Odysseus himself,—an interval of twenty years. "No agora or session has taken place amongst us (says the gray-headed Ægyptius, who opens the proceedings) since Odysseus went on shipboard: and now, who is he that has called us together? what man, young or old, has felt such a strong necessity? Has he received intelligence from our absent warriors, or has he other public news to communicate? He is our good friend for doing this: whatever his projects may be, I pray Zeus to grant him success."[101] Telemachus, answering the appeal forthwith, proceeds to tell the assembled Ithakans that he has no public news to communicate, but that he has convoked them upon his own private necessities. Next, he sets forth, pathetically, the wickedness of the suitors, calls upon them personally to desist, and upon the people to restrain them, and concludes by solemnly warning them, that, being henceforward free from all obligation towards them, he will invoke the avenging aid of Zeus, so "that they may be slain in the interior of his own house, without bringing upon him any subsequent penalty."[102]

We are not of course to construe the Homeric description as anything more than an *idéal*, approximating to actual reality. But, allowing all that can be required for such a limitation, it exhibits the agora more as a special medium of publicity and intercommunication,[103] from the king to the body of the people, than as including any idea of responsibility on the part of the former or restraining force on the part of the latter, however such consequences may indirectly grow out of it. The primitive Grecian government is essentially monarchical, reposing on personal feeling and divine right: the memorable dictum in the Iliad is borne out by all that we hear of the actual practice; "The ruler of many is not a good thing: let us have one ruler only,—one king,—him to whom Zeus has given the sceptre and the tutelary sanctions."[104]

The second book of the Iliad, full as it is of beauty and vivacity, not only confirms our idea of the passive, recipient, and listening character of the agora, but even presents a repulsive picture of the degradation of the mass of the people before the chiefs. Agamemnôn convokes the agora for the purpose of immediately arming the Grecian host, under a full impression that the gods have at last determined forthwith to crown his arms with complete victory. Such impression has been created by a special visit of Oneirus (the Dream-god), sent by Zeus during his sleep,—being, indeed, an intentional fraud on the part of Zeus, though Agamemnôn does not suspect its deceitful character. At this precise moment, when he may be conceived to be more than usually anxious to get his army into the field and snatch the prize, an unaccountable fancy seizes him, that, instead of inviting the troops to do what he really wishes, and encouraging their spirits for this one last effort, he will adopt a course directly contrary: he will try their courage by professing to believe that the siege had become desperate, and that there was no choice except to go on shipboard and flee. Announcing to Nestôr and Odysseus, in preliminary council, his intention to hold this strange language, he at the same time tells them that he relies upon them to oppose it and counterwork its effect upon the multitude.[105] The agora is presently assembled, and the king of men pours forth a speech full of dismay and despair, concluding by a distinct exhortation to all present to go aboard and return home at once. Immediately the whole army, chiefs as well as people, break up and proceed to execute his orders: every one rushes off to get his ship afloat, except Odysseus, who looks on in mournful silence and astonishment. The army would have been quickly on its voyage home, had not the goddesses Hêrê and Athênê stimulated Odysseus to an instantaneous interference. He hastens among the dispersing crowd and diverts them from their purpose of retreat: to the chiefs he addresses flattering words, trying to shame them by gentle expostulation: but the people he visits with harsh reprimand and blows from his sceptre,[106] thus driving them back to their seats in the agora.

Amidst the dissatisfied crowd thus unwillingly brought back, the voice of Thersitês is heard the longest and the loudest,—a man ugly, deformed, and unwarlike, but fluent in speech, and especially severe and unsparing in his censure of the chiefs, Agamemnôn, Achilles, and Odysseus. Upon this occasion, he addresses to the people a speech denouncing Agamemnôn for selfish and greedy exaction generally, but particularly for his recent ill-treatment of Achilles,—and he endeavors, moreover, to induce them to persist in their scheme of departure. In reply, Odysseus not only rebukes Thersitês sharply for his impudence in abusing the commander-in-chief, but threatens that, if ever such behavior is repeated, he will strip him naked, and thrash him out of the assembly with disgraceful blows; as an earnest of which, he administers to him at once a smart stroke with the studded sceptre, imprinting its painful mark in a bloody weal across his back. Thersitês, terrified and subdued, sits down weeping; while the surrounding crowd deride him, and express the warmest approbation of Odysseus for having thus by force put the reviler to silence.[107]

Both Odysseus and Nestôr then address the agora, sympathizing with Agamemnôn for the shame which the retreat of the Greeks is about to inflict upon him, and urging emphatically upon every one present the obligation of persevering until the siege shall be successfully consummated. Neither of them animadverts at all upon Agamemnôn, either for his conduct towards Achilles, or for his childish freak of trying the temper of the army.[108]

There cannot be a clearer indication than this description—so graphic in the original poem—of the true character of the Homeric agora. The multitude who compose it are listening and acquiescent, not often hesitating, and never refractory[109] to the chief. The fate which awaits a presumptuous critic, even where his virulent reproaches are substantially well-founded, is plainly set forth in the treatment of Thersitês; while the unpopularity of such a character is attested even more by the excessive pains which Homer takes to heap upon him repulsive personal deformities, than by the chastisement of Odysseus;— he is lame, bald, crook-backed, of misshapen head, and squinting vision.

But we cease to wonder at the submissive character of the agora, when we read the proceedings of Odysseus towards the people themselves;—his fine words and flattery addressed to the chiefs, and his contemptuous reproof and manual violence towards the common men, at a moment when both were doing exactly the same thing,—fulfilling the express bidding of Agamemnôn, upon whom Odysseus does not offer a single comment. This scene, which excited a sentiment of strong displeasure among the democrats of historical Athens,[110] affords a proof that the feeling of personal dignity, of which philosophic observers in Greece—Herodotus, Xenophôn, Hippocratês, and Aristotle—boasted, as distinguishing the free Greek citizen from the slavish Asiatic, was yet undeveloped in the time of Homer.[111] The ancient epic is commonly so filled with the personal adventures of the chiefs, and the people are so constantly depicted as simple appendages attached to them, that we rarely obtain a glimpse of the treatment of the one apart from the other, such as this memorable Homeric agora affords.

There remains one other point of view in which we are to regard the agora of primitive Greece,—as the scene in which justice was administered. The king is spoken of as constituted by Zeus the great judge of society: he has received from Zeus the sceptre, and along with it the powers of command and sanction: the people obey these commands and enforce these sanctions, under him, enriching him at the same time with lucrative presents and payments.[112] Sometimes the king separately, sometimes the kings or chiefs or gerontes in the plural number, are named as deciding disputes and awarding satisfaction to complainants; always, however, in public, in the midst of the assembled agora.[113] In one of the compartments of the shield of Achilles, the details of a judicial scene are described. While the agora is full of an eager and excited crowd, two men are disputing about the fine of satisfaction for the death of a murdered man,—one averring, the other denying, that the fine had already been paid, and both demanding an inquest. The gerontes are ranged on stone seats,[114] in the holy circle, with two talents of gold lying before them, to be awarded to such of the litigants as shall make out his case to their satisfaction. The heralds with their sceptres, repressing the warm sympathies of the crowd in favor of one or other of the parties, secure an alternate hearing to both.[115] This interesting picture completely harmonizes with the brief allusion of Hesiod to the judicial trial—doubtless a real trial—between himself and his brother Persês. The two brothers disputed about their paternal inheritance, and the cause was carried to be tried by the chiefs in agora; but Persês bribed them, and obtained an unjust verdict for the whole.[116] So at least Hesiod affirms, in the bitterness of his heart; earnestly exhorting his brother not to waste a precious time, required for necessary labors, in the unprofitable occupation of witnessing and abetting litigants in the agora,—for which (he adds) no man has proper leisure, unless his subsistence for the year beforehand be safely treasured up in his garners.[117] He repeats, more than once, his complaints of the crooked and corrupt judgments of which the kings were habitually guilty; dwelling upon abuse of justice as the crying evil of his day, and predicting as well as invoking the vengeance of Zeus to repress it. And Homer ascribes the tremendous violence of the autumnal storms to the wrath of Zeus against those judges who disgrace the agora with their wicked verdicts.[118]

Though it is certain that, in every state of society, the feelings of men when assembled in multitude will command a certain measure of attention, yet we thus find the agora, in judicial matters still more than in political, serving merely the purpose of publicity. It is the king who is the grand personal mover of Grecian heroic society.[119] He is on earth, the equivalent of Zeus in the agora of the gods: the supreme god of Olympus is in the habit of carrying on his government with frequent publicity, of hearing some dissentient opinions, and of allowing himself occasionally to be wheedled by Aphroditê, or worried into compliance by Hêrê: but his determination is at last conclusive, subject only to the overruling interference of the Mœræ, or Fates.[120] Both the society of gods, and the various societies of men, are, according to the conceptions of Grecian legend, carried on by the personal rule of a legitimate sovereign, who does not derive his title from the special appointment of his subjects, though he governs with their full consent. In fact, Grecian legend presents to us hardly anything else, except these great individual personalities. The race, or nation, is as it were absorbed into the prince: eponymous persons, especially, are not merely princes, but fathers and representative unities, each the equivalent of that greater or less aggregate to which he gives name.

But though, in the primitive Grecian government, the king is the legitimate as well as the real sovereign, he is always conceived as acting through the council and agora. Both the one and the other are established and essential media through which his ascendency is brought to bear upon the society: the absence of such assemblies is the test and mark of savage men, as in the case of the Cyclôpes.[121] Accordingly, he must possess qualities fit to act with effect upon these two assemblies: wise reason for the council, unctuous eloquence for the agora.[122] Such is the *idéal* of the heroic government: a king, not merely full of valor and resource as a soldier, but also sufficiently superior to those around him to insure both the deliberate concurrence of the chiefs, and the hearty adhesion of the masses.[123] That this picture is not, in all individual cases, realized, is unquestionable; but the endowments so often predicated of good kings show it to have been the type present to the mind of the describer.[124] Xenophôn, in his Cyropædia, depicts Cyrus as an improved edition of the Homeric Agamemnôn,—"a good king and a powerful soldier," thus idealizing the perfection of personal government.

It is important to point out these fundamental conceptions of government, discernible even before the dawn of Grecian history, and identified with the social life of the people. It shows us that the Greeks, in their subsequent revolutions, and in the political experiments which their countless autonomous communities presented, worked upon preëxisting materials,— developing and exalting elements which had been at first subordinate, and suppressing, or remodelling on a totally new principle, that which had been originally predominant. When we approach historical Greece, we find that (with the exception of Sparta) the primitive hereditary, unresponsible monarch, uniting in himself all the functions of government, has ceased to reign,—while the feeling of legitimacy, which originally induced his people to obey him willingly, has been exchanged for one of aversion towards the character and title generally. The multifarious functions which he once exercised, have been parcelled out among temporary nominees. On the other hand, the council, or senate, and the agora, originally simple media through which the king acted, are elevated into standing and independent sources of authority, controlling and holding in responsibility the various special officers to whom executive duties of one kind or another are confided. The general principle here indicated is common both to the oligarchies and the democracies which grew up in historical Greece: much as these two governments differed from each other, and many as were the varieties even between one oligarchy or democracy and another, they all stood in equal contrast with the principle of the heroic government. Even in Sparta, where the hereditary kingship lasted, it was preserved with lustre and influence exceedingly diminished,[125] and such timely diminution of its power seems to have been one of the essential conditions of its preservation.[126] Though the Spartan kings had the hereditary command of the military forces, yet, even in all foreign expeditions, they habitually acted in obedience to orders from home; while in affairs of the interior, the superior power of the ephors sensibly overshadowed them. So that, unless possessed of more than ordinary force of character, they seem to have exercised their chief influence as presiding members of the senate.

There is yet another point of view in which it behoves us to take notice of the council and the agora as integral portions of the legendary government of the Grecian communities. We are thus enabled to trace the employment of public speaking, as the standing engine of government and the proximate cause of obedience, to the social infancy of the nation. The power of speech in the direction of public affairs becomes more and more obvious, developed, and irresistible, as we advance towards the culminating period of Grecian history, the century preceding the battle of Chæroneia. That its development was greatest among the most enlightened sections of the Grecian name, and smallest among the more obtuse and stationary, is matter of notorious fact; nor is it less true, that the prevalence of this habit was one of the chief causes of the intellectual eminence of the nation generally. At a time when all the countries around were plunged comparatively in mental torpor, there was no motive sufficiently present and powerful to multiply so wonderfully the productive minds of Greece, except such as arose from the rewards of public speaking. The susceptibility of the multitude to this sort of guidance, their habit of requiring and enjoying the stimulus which it supplied, and the open discussion, combining regular forms with free opposition, of practical matters, political as well as judicial,—are the creative causes which formed such conspicuous adepts in the art of persuasion. Nor was it only professed orators who were thus produced; didactic aptitude was formed in the background, and the speculative tendencies were supplied with interesting phenomena for observation and combination, at a time when the truths of physical science were almost inaccessible. If the primary effect was to quicken the powers of expression, the secondary, but not less certain result, was to develop the habits of scientific thought. Not only the oratory of Demosthenês and Periklês, and the colloquial magic of Socratês, but also the philosophical speculations of Plato, and the systematic politics, rhetoric, and logic of Aristotle, are traceable to the same general tendencies in the minds of the Grecian people: and we find the germ of these expansive forces in the senate and agora of their legendary government. The poets, first epic and then lyric, were the precursors of the orators, in their power of moving the feelings of an assembled crowd; whilst the Homeric poems—the general training-book of educated Greeks—constituted a treasury of direct and animated expression, full of concrete forms, and rare in the use of abstractions, and thence better suited to the workings of oratory. The subsequent critics had no difficulty in selecting from the Iliad and Odyssey, samples of eloquence in all its phases and varieties.

On the whole, then, the society depicted in the old Greek poems is loose and unsettled, presenting very little of legal restraint, and still less of legal protection,—but concentrating such political power as does exist in the hands of a legitimate hereditary king, whose ascendency over the other chiefs is more or less complete according to his personal force and character. Whether that ascendency be greater or less, however, the mass of the people is in either case politically passive and of little account. Though the Grecian freeman of the heroic age is above the degraded level of the Gallic *plebs*, as described by Cæsar,[127] he is far from rivalling the fierce independence and sense of dignity, combined with individual force, which characterize the Germanic tribes before their establishment in the Roman empire. Still less does his condition, or the society in which he moves, correspond to those pleasing dreams of spontaneous rectitude and innocence, in which Tacitus and Seneca indulge with regard to primitive man.[128]

2. The state of moral and social feeling, prevalent in legendary Greece, exhibits a scene in harmony with the rudimentary political fabrics just described. Throughout the long stream of legendary narrative on which the Greeks looked back as their past history, the larger social motives hardly ever come into play: either individual valor and cruelty, or the personal attachments and quarrels of relatives and war-companions, or the feuds of private enemies, are ever before us. There is no sense of obligation then existing, between man and man as such,—and very little between each man and the entire community of which he is a member; such sentiments are neither operative in the real world, nor present to the imaginations of the poets. Personal feelings, either towards the gods, the king, or some near and known individual, fill the whole of a man's bosom: out of them arise all the motives to beneficence, and all the internal restraints upon violence, antipathy, or rapacity: and special communion, as well as special solemnities, are essential to their existence. The ceremony of an oath, so imposing, so paramount, and so indispensable in those days, illustrates strikingly this principle. And even in the case of the stranger suppliant,—in which an apparently spontaneous sympathy manifests itself,—the succor and kindness

shown to him arise mainly from his having gone through the consecrated formalities of supplication, such as that of sitting down in the ashes by the sacred hearth, thus obtaining a sort of privilege of sanctuary.[129] That ceremony exalts him into something more than a mere suffering man,—it places him in express fellowship with the master of the house, under the tutelary sanctions of Zeus Hiketêsios. There is great difference between one form of supplication and another; the suppliant, however, in any form, becomes more or less the object of a particular sympathy.

The sense of obligation towards the gods manifests itself separately in habitual acts of worship, sacrifice, and libations, or by votive presents, such as that of the hair of Achilles, which he has pledged to the river-god Spercheius,[130] and such as the constant dedicated offerings which men who stand in urgent need of the divine aid first promise and afterwards fulfil. But the feeling towards the gods also appears, and that not less frequently, as mingling itself with and enforcing obligations towards some particular human person. The tie which binds a man to his father, his kinsman, his guest, or any special promisee towards whom he has taken the engagement of an oath, is conceived in conjunction with the idea of Zeus, as witness and guarantee; and the intimacy of the association is attested by some surname or special appellation of the god.[131] Such personal feelings composed all the moral influences of which a Greek of that day was susceptible,—a state of mind which we can best appreciate by contrasting it with that of the subsequent citizen of historical Athens. In the view of the latter, the great impersonal authority, called "The Laws," stood out separately, both as guide and sanction, distinct from religious duty or private sympathies: but of this discriminated conception of positive law and positive morality,[132] the germ only can be detected in the Homeric poems. The appropriate Greek word for human laws never occurs. Amidst a very wavering phraseology,[133] we can detect a gradual transition from the primitive idea of a personal goddess Themis, attached to Zeus, first to his sentences or orders called Themistes, and next by a still farther remove to various established customs, which those sentences were believed to sanctify,—the authority of religion and that of custom coalescing into one indivisible obligation.

The family relations, as we might expect, are set forth in our pictures of the legendary world as the grand sources of lasting union and devoted attachment. The paternal authority is highly reverenced: the son who lives to years of maturity, repays by affection to his parents the charge of his maintenance in infancy, which the language notes by a special word; whilst on the other hand, the Erinnys, whose avenging hand is put in motion by the curse of a father or mother, is an object of deep dread.[134]

In regard to marriage, we find the wife occupying a station of great dignity and influence, though it was the practice for the husband to purchase her by valuable presents to her parents,—a practice extensively prevalent among early communities, and treated by Aristotle as an evidence of barbarism. She even seems to live less secluded and to enjoy a wider sphere of action than was allotted to her in historical Greece.[135] Concubines are frequent with the chiefs, and occasionally the jealousy of the wife breaks out in reckless excess against her husband, as may be seen in the tragical history of Phœnix. The continence of Laërtês, from fear of displeasing his wife Antikleia, is especially noticed.[136] A large portion of the romantic interest which Grecian legend inspires is derived from the women: Penelopê, Andromachê, Helen, Klytæmnêstra, Eriphylê, Iokasta, Hekabê, etc., all stand in the foreground of the picture, either from their virtues, their beauty, their crimes, or their sufferings.

Not only brothers, but also cousins, and the more distant blood-relations and clansmen, appear connected together by a strong feeling of attachment, sharing among them universally the obligation of mutual self-defence and revenge, in the event of injury to any individual of the race. The legitimate brothers divide between them by lot the paternal inheritance,—a bastard brother receiving only a small share; he is, however, commonly very well treated,[137] though the murder of Phokus, by Telamon and Pêleus, constitutes a flagrant exception. The furtive pregnancy of young women, often by a god, is one of the most frequently recurring incidents in the legendary narratives; and the severity with which such a fact, when discovered, is visited by the father, is generally extreme. As an extension of the family connection, we read of larger unions, called the phratry and the tribe, which are respectfully, but not frequently, mentioned.[138]

The generous readiness with which hospitality is afforded to the stranger who asks for it,[139] the facility with which he is allowed to contract the peculiar connection of guest with his host, and the permanence with which that connection, when created by partaking of the same food and exchanging presents, is maintained even through a long period of separation, and even transmitted from father to son—these are among the most captivating features of the heroic society. The Homeric chief welcomes the stranger who comes to ask shelter in his house, first gives him refreshment, and then inquires his name and the purpose of his voyage.[140] Though not inclined to invite strangers to his house, he cannot repel them when they spontaneously enter it craving a lodging.[141] The suppliant is also commonly a stranger, but a stranger under peculiar circumstances; who proclaims his own calamitous and abject condition, and seeks to place himself in a relation to the chief whom he solicits, something like that in which men stand to the gods. Onerous as such special tie may become to him, the chief cannot decline it, if solicited in the proper form: the ceremony of supplication has a binding effect, and the Erinnys punish the hardhearted person who disallows it. A conquered enemy may sometimes throw himself at the feet of his conqueror, and solicit mercy, but he cannot by doing so acquire the character and claims of a suppliant properly so called: the conqueror has free discretion either to kill him, or to spare him and accept a ransom.[142]

There are in the legendary narratives abundant examples of individuals who transgress in particular acts even the holiest of these personal ties, but the savage Cyclops is the only person described as professedly indifferent to them, and careless of that sanction of the gods which in Grecian belief accompanied them all.[143] In fact, the tragical horror which pervades the lineage of Athamas or Kadmus, and which attaches to many of the acts of Hêraklês, of Pêleus and Telamon, of Jasôn and Mêdea, of Atreus and Thyestês, etc., is founded upon a deep feeling and sympathy with those special obligations, which conspicuous individuals, under the temporary stimulus of the maddening Atê, are driven to violate. In such conflict of sentiments, between the obligation generally reverenced and the exceptional deviation in an individual otherwise admired, consists the pathos of the story.

These feelings—of mutual devotion between kinsmen and companions in arms—of generous hospitality to the stranger, and of helping protection to the suppliant,—constitute the bright spots in a dark age. We find them very generally prevalent amongst communities essentially rude and barbarous,— amongst the ancient Germans as described by Tacitus, the Druses in Lebanon, [144] the Arabian tribes in the desert, and even the North American Indians.

They are the instinctive manifestations of human sociality, standing at first alone, and for that reason appearing to possess a greater tutelary force than really belongs to them,—beneficent, indeed, in a high degree, with reference to their own appropriate period, but serving as a very imperfect compensation for the impotence of the magistrate, and for the absence of any all-pervading sympathy or sense of obligation between man and man. We best appreciate their importance when we compare the Homeric society with that of barbarians like the Thracians, who tattooed their bodies, as the mark of a generous lineage,—sold their children for export as slaves,—considered robbery, not merely as one admissible occupation among others, but as the only honorable mode of life; agriculture being held contemptible,—and above all, delighted in the shedding of blood as a luxury. Such were the Thracians in the days of Herodotus and Thucydidês: and the Homeric society forms a mean term between that which these two historians yet saw in Thrace, and that which they witnessed among their own civilized countrymen.[145]

55

When, however, among the Homeric men we pass beyond the influence of the private ties above enumerated, we find scarcely any other moralizing forces in operation. The acts and adventures commemorated imply a community wherein neither the protection nor the restraints of law are practically felt, and wherein ferocity, rapine, and the aggressive propensities generally, seem restrained by no internal counterbalancing scruples. Homicide, especially, is of frequent occurrence, sometimes by open violence, sometimes by fraud: expatriation for homicide is among the most constantly recurring acts of the Homeric poems: and savage brutalities are often ascribed, even to admired heroes, with apparent indifference. Achilles sacrifices twelve Trojan prisoners on the tomb of Patroklus, while his son Neoptolemus not only slaughters the aged Priam, but also seizes by the leg the child Astyanax (son of the slain Hector) and hurls him from one of the lofty towers of Troy.[146] Moreover, the celebrity of Autolykus, the maternal grandfather of Odysseus, in the career of wholesale robbery and perjury, and the wealth which it enabled him to acquire, are described with the same unaffected admiration as the wisdom of Nestôr or the strength of Ajax.[147] Achilles, Menelaus, Odysseus, pillage in person, wherever they can find an opportunity, employing both force and stratagem to surmount resistance.[148] The vocation of a pirate is recognized and honorable, so that a host, when he asks his guest what is the purpose of his voyage, enumerates enrichment by indiscriminate maritime plunder as among those projects which may naturally enter into his contemplation.[149] Abduction of cattle, and expeditions for unprovoked ravage as well as for retaliation, between neighboring tribes, appear ordinary phenomena;[150] and the established inviolability of heralds seems the only evidence of any settled feeling of obligation between one community and another. While the house and property of Odysseus, during his long absence, enjoys no public protection,[151] those unprincipled chiefs, who consume his substance, find sympathy rather than disapprobation among the people of Ithaka. As a general rule, he who cannot protect himself finds no protection from society: his own kinsmen and immediate companions are the only parties to whom he can look with confidence for support. And in this respect, the representation given by Hesiod makes the picture even worse. In his emphatic denunciation of the fifth age, that poet deplores not only the absence of all social justice and sense of obligation among his contemporaries, but also the relaxation of the ties of family and hospitality. [152] There are marks of querulous exaggeration in the poem of the Works and Days; yet the author professes to describe the real state of things around him, and the features of his picture, soften them as we may, will still appear dark and calamitous. It is, however, to be remarked, that he contemplates a state of peace,—thus forming a contrast with the Homeric poems. His copious catalogue of social evils scarcely mentions liability to plunder by a foreign enemy, nor does he compute the chances of predatory aggression as a source of profit.

There are two special veins of estimable sentiment, on which it may be interesting to contrast heroic and historical Greece, and which exhibit the latter as an improvement on the former, not less in the affections than in the intellect.

The law of Athens was peculiarly watchful and provident with respect both to the persons and the property of orphan minors; but the description given in the Iliad of the utter and hopeless destitution of the orphan boy, despoiled of his paternal inheritance, and abandoned by all the friends of his father, whom he urgently supplicates, and who all harshly cast him off, is one of the most pathetic morsels in the whole poem.[153] In reference again to the treatment of the dead body of an enemy we find all the Greek chiefs who come near (not to mention the conduct of Achilles himself) piercing with their spears the corpse of the slain Hectôr, while some of them even pass disgusting taunts upon it. We may add, from the lost epics, the mutilation of the dead bodies of Paris and Deiphobus by the hand of Menelaus.[154] But at the time of the Persian invasion, it was regarded as unworthy of a right-minded Greek to maltreat in any way the dead body of an enemy, even where such a deed might seem to be justified on the plea of retaliation. After the battle of Platæa, a proposition was made to the Spartan king Pausanias, to retaliate upon the dead body of Mardonius the indignities which Xerxês had heaped upon that of Leonidas at Thermopylæ. He indignantly spurned the suggestion, not without a severe rebuke, or rather a half-suppressed menace, towards the proposer: and the feeling of Herodotus himself goes heartily along with him. [155]

The different manner of dealing with homicide presents a third test, perhaps more striking yet, of the change in Grecian feelings and manners during the three centuries preceding the Persian invasion. That which the murderer in the Homeric times had to dread, was, not public prosecution and punishment, but the personal vengeance of the kinsmen and friends of the deceased, who were stimulated by the keenest impulses of honor and obligation to avenge the deed, and were considered by the public as specially privileged to do so.[156] To escape from this danger, he is obliged to flee the country, unless he can prevail upon the incensed kinsmen to accept of a valuable payment (we must not speak of coined money, in the days of Homer) as satisfaction for their slain comrade. They may, if they please, decline the offer, and persist in their right of revenge; but if they accept, they are bound to leave the offender unmolested, and he accordingly remains at home without farther consequences. The chiefs in agora do not seem to interfere, except to insure payment of the stipulated sum.

Here we recognize once more the characteristic attribute of the Grecian heroic age,—the omnipotence of private force, tempered and guided by family sympathies, and the practical nullity of that collective sovereign afterwards called *The City*,—who in historical Greece becomes the central and paramount source of obligation, but who appears yet only in the background, as a germ of promise for the future. And the manner in which, in the case of homicide, that germ was developed into a powerful reality, presents an interesting field of comparison with other nations.

For the practice, here designated, of leaving the party guilty of homicide to compromise by valuable payment with the relatives of the deceased, and also of allowing to the latter a free choice whether they would accept such compromise or enforce their right of personal revenge,—has been remarked in many rude communities, but is particularly memorable among the early German tribes.[157] Among the many separate Teutonic establishments which rose upon the ruins of the Western Empire of Rome, the right as well as duty of private revenge, for personal injury or insult offered to any member of a family,—and the endeavor to avert its effects by means of a pecuniary composition levied upon the offender, chiefly as satisfaction to the party injured, but partly also as perquisite to the king,—was adopted as the basis of their legislation. This fundamental idea was worked out in elaborate detail as to the valuation of the injury inflicted, wherein one main circumstance was the rank, condition, and power of the sufferer. The object of the legislator was to preserve the society from standing feuds, but at the same time to accord such full satisfaction as would induce the injured person to waive his acknowledged right of personal revenge,—the full luxury of which, as it presented itself to the mind of an Homeric Greek, may be read in more than one passage of the Iliad.[158] The German codes begin by trying to bring about the acceptance of a fixed pecuniary composition as a constant voluntary custom, and proceed ultimately to enforce it as a peremptory necessity: the idea of society is at first altogether subordinate, and its influence passes only by slow degrees from amicable arbitration into imperative control.

The Homeric society, in regard to this capital point in human progression, is on a level with that of the German tribes as described by Tacitus. But the subsequent course of Grecian legislation takes a direction completely different from that of the German codes: the primitive and acknowledged right of private revenge (unless where bought off by pecuniary payment), instead of being developed into practical working, is superseded by more comprehensive views of a public wrong requiring public intervention, or by religious fears respecting the posthumous wrath of the murdered person. In historical Athens, this right of private revenge was discountenanced and put out of sight, even so early as the Drakonian legislation,[159] and at last restricted to a few extreme and special cases; while the murderer came to be considered, first as having sinned against the gods, next as having deeply injured the society, and thus at once as requiring absolution and deserving punishment. On the first of these two grounds, he is interdicted from the agora and from all holy places, as well as from public functions, even while yet untried and simply a suspected person; for if this were not done, the wrath of the gods would manifest itself in bad crops and other national calamities. On the second ground, he is tried before the council of Areiopagus, and if found guilty, is condemned to death, or perhaps to disfranchisement and banishment. [160] The idea of a propitiatory payment to the relatives of the deceased has ceased altogether to be admitted: it is the protection of society which dictates, and the force of society which inflicts, a measure of punishment calculated to deter for the future.

3. The society of legendary Greece includes, besides the chiefs, the general mass of freemen (λαοί), among whom stand out by special names certain professional men, such as the carpenter, the smith, the leather-dresser, the leech, the prophet, the bard, and the fisherman.[161] We have no means of appreciating their condition. Though lots of arable land were assigned in special property to individuals, with boundaries both carefully marked and jealously watched,[162] yet the larger proportion of surface was devoted to pasture. Cattle formed both the chief item in the substance of a wealthy man, the chief means of making payments, and the common ground of quarrels,— bread and meat, in large quantities, being the constant food of every one.[163] The estates of the owners were tilled, and their cattle tended, mostly by bought slaves, but to a certain degree also by poor freemen called Thêtes, working for hire and for stated periods. The principal slaves, who were intrusted with the care of large herds of oxen, swine, or goats, were of necessity men worthy of confidence, their duties placing them away from their master's immediate eye.[164] They had other slaves subordinate to them, and appear to have been well-treated: the deep and unshaken attachment of Eumæus the swineherd and Philœtius the neatherd to the family and affairs of the absent Odysseus, is among the most interesting points in the ancient epic. Slavery was a calamity, which in that period of insecurity might befall any one: the chief who conducted a freebooting expedition, if he succeeded, brought back with him a numerous troop of slaves, as many as he could seize, [165]—if he failed, became very likely a slave himself: so that the slave was often by birth of equal dignity with his master: Eumæus was himself the son of a chief, conveyed away when a child by his nurse, and sold by Phœnician kidnappers to Laërtês. A slave of this character, if he conducted himself well, might often expect to be enfranchised by his master and placed in an independent holding.[166]

On the whole, the slavery of legendary Greece does not present itself as existing under a peculiarly harsh form, especially if we consider that all the classes of society were then very much upon a level in point of taste, sentiment, and instruction.[167] In the absence of legal security or an effective social sanction, it is probable that the condition of a slave under an average master, may have been as good as that of the free Thête. The class of slaves whose lot appears to have been the most pitiable were the females,—more numerous than the males, and performing the principal work in the interior of the house. Not only do they seem to have been more harshly treated than the males, but they were charged with the hardest and most exhausting labor which the establishment of a Greek chief required: they brought in water from the spring, and turned by hand the house-mills, which ground the large quantity of flour consumed in his family.[168] This oppressive task was performed generally by female slaves, in historical as well as legendary Greece.[169] Spinning and weaving was the constant occupation of women, whether free or slave, of every rank and station: all the garments worn both by men and women were fashioned at home, and Helen as well as Penelopê is expert and assiduous at the occupation.[170] The daughters of Keleos at Eleusis go to the well with their basins for water, and Nausikaa, daughter of Alkinous,[171] joins her female slaves in the business of washing her garments in the river. If we are obliged to point out the fierceness and insecurity of an early society, we may at the same time note with pleasure its characteristic simplicity of manners: Rebecca, Rachel, and the daughters of Jethro, in the early Mosaic narrative, as well as the wife of the native Macedonian chief (with whom the Temenid Perdiccas, ancestor of Philip and Alexander, first took service on retiring from Argos), baking her own cakes on the hearth,[172] exhibit a parallel in this respect to the Homeric pictures.

We obtain no particulars respecting either the common freemen generally, or the particular class of them called Thêtes. These latter, engaged for special jobs, or at the harvest and other busy seasons of field labor, seem to have given their labor in exchange for board and clothing: they are mentioned in the same line with the slaves,[173] and were (as has been just observed) probably on the whole little better off. The condition of a poor freeman in those days, without a lot of land of his own, going about from one temporary job to another, and having no powerful family and no social authority to look up to for protection, must have been sufficiently miserable. When Eumæus indulged his expectation of being manumitted by his masters, he thought at the same time that they would give him a wife, a house, and a lot of land near to themselves;[174] without which collateral advantages, simple manumission might perhaps have been no improvement in his condition. To be Thête in the service of a very poor farmer is selected by Achilles as the maximum of human hardship: such a person could not give to his Thête the same ample food, and good shoes and clothing, as the wealthy chief Eurymachus, while he would exact more severe labor.[175] It was probably among such smaller occupants, who could not advance the price necessary to purchase slaves, and were glad to save the cost of keep when they did not need service, that the Thêtes found employment: though we may conclude that the brave and strong amongst these poor freemen found it preferable to accompany some freebooting chief and to live by the plunder acquired.[176] The exact Hesiod advises his farmer, whose work is chiefly performed by slaves, to employ and maintain the Thête during summer-time, but to dismiss him as soon as the harvest is completely got in, and then to take into his house for the winter a woman "without any child;" who would of course be more useful than the Thête for the indoor occupations of that season.[177]

In a state of society such as that which we have been describing, Grecian commerce was necessarily trifling and restricted. The Homeric poems mark either total ignorance or great vagueness of apprehension respecting all that lies beyond the coasts of Greece and Asia Minor, and the islands between or adjoining them. Libya and Egypt are supposed so distant as to be known only by name and hearsay: indeed, when the city of Kyrene was founded, a century and a half after the first Olympiad, it was difficult to find anywhere a Greek navigator who had ever visited the coast of Libya, or was fit to serve as guide to the colonists.[178] The mention of the Sikels in the Odyssey,[179] leads us to conclude that Korkyra, Italy, and Sicily were not wholly unknown to the poet: among seafaring Greeks, the knowledge of the latter implied the knowledge of the two former,—since the habitual track, even of a well-equipped Athenian trireme during the Peloponnesian war, from Peloponnêsus to Sicily, was by Korkyra and the Gulf of Tarentum. The Phokæans, long afterwards, were the first Greeks who explored either the Adriatic or Tyrrhenian sea.[180] Of the Euxine sea no knowledge is manifested in Homer, who, as a general rule, presents to us the names of distant regions only in connection with romantic or monstrous accompaniments. The Kretans, and still more the Taphians (who are supposed to have occupied the western islands off the coast of Acarnania), are mentioned as skilful mariners, and the Taphian Mentês professes to be conveying iron to Temesa to be there exchanged for copper;[181] but both Taphians and Kretans are more corsairs than traders.[182] The strong sense of the dangers of the sea, expressed by the poet Hesiod, and the imperfect structure of the early Grecian ship, attested by Thucydidês (who points out the more recent date of that improved ship-building which prevailed in his time), concur to demonstrate the then narrow range of nautical enterprise.[183]

Such was the state of the Greeks, as traders, at a time when Babylon combined a crowded and industrious population with extensive commerce, and when the Phœnician merchant-ships visited in one direction the southern coast of Arabia, perhaps even the island of Ceylon,—in another direction, the British islands.

The Phœnician, the kinsman of the ancient Jew, exhibits the type of character belonging to the latter,—with greater enterprise and ingenuity, and less of religious exclusiveness, yet still different from, and even antipathetic to, the character of the Greeks. In the Homeric poems, he appears somewhat like the Jew of the Middle Ages, a crafty trader, turning to profit the violence and rapacity of others,—bringing them ornaments, decorations, the finest and brightest products of the loom, gold, silver, electrum, ivory, tin, etc., in exchange for which he received landed produce, skins, wool, and slaves, the only commodities which even a wealthy Greek chief of those early times had to offer,—prepared at the same time for dishonest gain, in any manner which chance might throw in his way.[184] He is, however, really a trader, not undertaking expeditions with the deliberate purpose of surprise and plunder, and standing distinguished in this respect from the Tyrrhenian, Kretan, or Taphian pirate. Tin, ivory, and electrum, all of which are acknowledged in the Homeric poems, were the fruit of Phœnician trade with the West as well as with the East.[185]

Thucydidês tells us that the Phœnicians and Karians, in very early periods, occupied many of the islands of the Ægean, and we know, from the striking remnant of their mining works which Herodotus himself saw in Thasus, off the coast of Thrace, that they had once extracted gold from the mountains of that island,—at a period indeed very far back, since their occupation must have been abandoned prior to the settlement of the poet Archilochus.[186] Yet few of the islands in the Ægean were rich in such valuable products, nor was it in the usual course of Phœnician proceeding to occupy islands, except where there was an adjoining mainland with which trade could be carried on. The traffic of these active mariners required no permanent settlement, but as occasional visitors they were convenient, in enabling a Greek chief to turn his captives to account,—to get rid of slaves or friendless Thêtes who were troublesome,—and to supply himself with the metals, precious as well as useful.[187] The halls of Alkinous and Menelaus glitter with gold, copper, and electrum; while large stocks of yet unemployed metal—gold, copper, and iron —are stored up in the treasure-chamber of Odysseus and other chiefs.[188] Coined money is unknown to the Homeric age,—the trade carried on being one of barter. In reference also to the metals, it deserves to be remarked that the Homeric descriptions universally suppose copper, and not iron, to be employed for arms, both offensive and defensive. By what process the copper was tempered and hardened, so as to serve the purposes of the warrior, we do not know;[189] but the use of iron for these objects belongs to a later age, though the Works and Days of Hesiod suppose this change to have been already introduced.[190]

The mode of fighting among the Homeric heroes is not less different from the historical times, than the material of which their arms were composed. The Hoplites, or heavy-armed infantry of historical Greece, maintained a close order and well-dressed line, charging the enemy with their spears protended at even distance, and coming thus to close conflict without breaking their rank: there were special troops, bowmen, slingers, etc. armed with missiles, but the hoplite had no weapon to employ in this manner. The heroes of the Iliad and Odyssey, on the contrary, habitually employ the spear as a missile, which they launch with tremendous force: each of them is mounted in his war-chariot, drawn by two horses, and calculated to contain the warrior and his charioteer; in which latter capacity a friend or comrade will sometimes consent to serve. Advancing in his chariot at full speed, in front of his own soldiers, he hurls his spear against the enemy: sometimes, indeed, he will fight on foot, and hand to hand, but the chariot is usually near to receive him if he chooses, or to insure his retreat. The mass of the Greeks and Trojans, coming forward to the charge, without any regular step or evenly-maintained line, make their attack in the same way by hurling their spears. Each chief wears habitually a long sword and a short dagger, besides his two spears to be launched forward,—the spear being also used, if occasion serves, as a weapon for thrust. Every man is protected by shield, helmet, breastplate, and greaves: but the armor of the chiefs is greatly superior to that of the common men, while they themselves are both stronger and more expert in the use of their weapons. There are a few bowmen, as rare exceptions, but the general equipment and proceeding is as here described.

Such loose array, immortalized as it is in the Iliad, is familiar to every one; and the contrast which it presents, with those inflexible ranks, and that irresistible simultaneous charge which bore down the Persian throng at Platæa and Kunaxa,[191] is such as to illustrate forcibly the general difference between heroic and historical Greece. While in the former, a few splendid figures stand forward, in prominent relief, the remainder being a mere unorganized and ineffective mass,—in the latter, these units have been combined into a system, in which every man, officer and soldier, has his assigned place and duty, and the victory, when gained, is the joint work of all. Preëminent individual prowess is indeed materially abridged, if not wholly excluded,—no man can do more than maintain his station in the line:[192] but on the other hand, the grand purposes, aggressive or defensive, for which alone arms are taken up, become more assured and easy, and long-sighted combinations of the general are rendered for the first time practicable, when he has a disciplined body of men to obey him. In tracing the picture of civil society, we have to remark a similar transition—we pass from Hêraklês, Thêseus, Jasôn, Achilles, to Solon, Pythagoras, and Periklês—from "the shepherd of his people," (to use the phrase in which Homer depicts the good side of the heroic king,) to the legislator who introduces, and the statesman who maintains, a preconcerted system by which willing citizens consent to bind themselves. If commanding individual talent is not always to be found, the whole community is so trained as to be able to maintain its course under inferior leaders; the rights as well as the duties of each citizen being predetermined in the social order, according to principles more or less wisely laid down. The contrast is similar, and the transition equally remarkable, in the civil as in the military picture. In fact, the military organization of the Grecian republics is an element of the greatest importance in respect to the conspicuous part which they have played in human affairs,—their superiority over other contemporary nations in this respect being hardly less striking than it is in many others, as we shall have occasion to see in a subsequent stage of this history.

Even at the most advanced point of their tactics, the Greeks could effect little against a walled city, whilst the heroic weapons and array were still less available for such an undertaking as a siege. Fortifications are a feature of the age deserving considerable notice. There was a time, we are told, in which the primitive Greek towns or villages derived a precarious security, not from their walls, but merely from sites lofty and difficult of access. They were not built immediately upon the shore, or close upon any convenient landing-place, but at some distance inland, on a rock or elevation which could not be approached without notice or scaled without difficulty. It was thought sufficient at that time to guard against piratical or marauding surprise: but as the state of society became assured,—as the chance of sudden assault comparatively diminished and industry increased,—these uninviting abodes were exchanged for more convenient sites on the plain or declivity beneath; or a portion of the latter was inclosed within larger boundaries and joined on to the original foundation, which thus became the Acropolis of the new town. Thêbes, Athens, Argos, etc., belonged to the latter class of cities; but there were in many parts of Greece deserted sites on hilltops, still retaining, even in historical times, the traces of former habitation, and some of them still bearing the name of the old towns. Among the mountainous parts of Krête, in Ægina and Rhodes, in portions of Mount Ida and Parnassus, similar remnants might be perceived.[193]

Probably, in such primitive hill villages, a continuous circle of wall would hardly be required as an additional means of defence, and would often be rendered very difficult by the rugged nature of the ground. But Thucydidês represents the earliest Greeks—those whom he conceives anterior to the Trojan war—as living thus universally in unfortified villages, chiefly on account of their poverty, rudeness, and thorough carelessness for the morrow. Oppressed, and held apart from each other by perpetual fear, they had not yet contracted the sentiment of fixed abodes: they were unwilling even to plant fruit-trees because of the uncertainty of gathering the produce,—and were always ready to dislodge, because there was nothing to gain by staying, and a bare subsistence might be had any where. He compares them to the mountaineers of Ætolia and of the Ozolian Lokris in his own time, who dwelt in their unfortified hill villages with little or no intercommunication, always armed and fighting, and subsisting on the produce of their cattle and their woods,[194]—clothed in undressed hides, and eating raw meat.

The picture given by Thucydidês, of these very early and unrecorded times, can only be taken as conjectural,—the conjectures, indeed, of a statesman and a philosopher,—generalized too, in part, from the many particular instances of contention and expulsion of chiefs which he found in the old legendary poems. The Homeric poems, however, present to us a different picture. They recognize walled towns, fixed abodes, strong local attachments, hereditary individual property in land, vineyards planted and carefully cultivated, established temples of the gods, and splendid palaces of the chiefs.[195] The description of Thucydidês belongs to a lower form of society, and bears more analogy to that which the poet himself conceives as antiquated and barbarous,—to the savage Cyclopes, who dwell on the tops of mountains, in hollow caves, without the plough, without vine or fruit culture, without arts or instruments,—or to the primitive settlement of Dardanus son of Zeus, on the higher ground of Ida, while it was reserved for his descendants and successors to found the holy Ilium on the plain.[196] Ilium or Troy represents the perfection of Homeric society. It is a consecrated spot, containing temples of the gods as well as the palace of Priam, and surrounded by walls which are the fabric of the gods; while the antecedent form of ruder society, which the poet briefly glances at, is the parallel of that which the theory of Thucydidês ascribes to his own early semi-barbarous ancestors.

Walled towns serve thus as one of the evidences, that a large part of the population of Greece had, even in the Homeric times, reached a level higher than that of the Ætolians and Lokrians of the days of Thucydidês. The remains of Mykênæ and Tiryns demonstrate the massy and Cyclopian style of architecture employed in those early days: but we may remark that, while modern observers seem inclined to treat the remains of the former as very imposing, and significant of a great princely family, Thucydidês, on the contrary, speaks of it as a small place, and labors to elude the inference, which might be deduced from its insignificant size, in disproof of the grandeur of Agamemnôn.[197] Such fortifications supplied a means of defence incomparably superior to those of attack. Indeed, even in historical Greece, and after the invention of battering engines, no city could be taken except by surprise or blockade, or by ruining the country around, and thus depriving the inhabitants of their means of subsistence. And in the two great sieges of the legendary time, Troy and Thêbes, the former is captured by the stratagem of the wooden horse, while the latter is evacuated by its citizens, under the warning of the gods, after their defeat in the field.

This decided superiority of the means of defence over those of attack, in rude ages, has been one of the grand promotive causes both of the growth of civic life and of the general march of human improvement. It has enabled the progressive portions of mankind not only to maintain their acquisitions against the predatory instincts of the ruder and poorer, and to surmount the difficulties of incipient organization,—but ultimately, when their organization has been matured, both to acquire predominance, and to uphold it until their own disciplined habits have in part passed to their enemies. The important truth here stated is illustrated not less by the history of ancient Greece, than by that of modern Europe during the Middle Ages. The Homeric chief, combining superior rank with superior force, and ready to rob at every convenient opportunity, greatly resembles the feudal baron of the Middle Ages, but circumstances absorb him more easily into a city life, and convert the independent potentate into the member of a governing aristocracy.[198] Traffic by sea continued to be beset with danger from pirates, long after it had become tolerably assured by land: the "wet ways" have always been the last resort of lawlessness and violence, and the Ægean, in particular, has in all times suffered more than other waters under this calamity.

Aggressions of the sort here described were of course most numerous in those earliest times when the Ægean was not yet an Hellenic sea, and when many of the Cyclades were occupied, not by Greeks, but by Karians,—perhaps by Phœnicians: the number of Karian sepulchres discovered in the sacred island of Delus seems to attest such occupation as an historical fact. [199] According to the legendary account, espoused both by Herodotus and by Thucydidês, it was the Kretan Minôs who subdued these islands and established his sons as rulers in them; either expelling the Karians, or reducing them to servitude and tribute.[200] Thucydidês presumes that he must of course have put down piracy, in order to enable his tribute to be remitted in safety, like the Athenians during the time of their hegemony.[201] Upon the legendary thalassocraty of Minôs, I have already remarked in another place: [202] it is sufficient here to repeat, that, in the Homeric poems (long subsequent to Minôs in the current chronology), we find piracy both frequent and held in honorable estimation, as Thucydidês himself emphatically tells us, —remarking, moreover, that the vessels of those early days were only half-decked, built and equipped after the piratical fashion,[203] in a manner upon which the nautical men of his time looked back with disdain. Improved and enlarged ship-building, and the trireme, or ship with three banks of oars, common for warlike purposes during the Persian invasion, began only with the growing skill, activity, and importance of the Corinthians, three quarters of a century after the first Olympiad.[204] Corinth, even in the Homeric poems, is distinguished by the epithet of wealthy, which it acquired principally from its remarkable situation on the Isthmus, and from its two harbors of Lechæum and Kenchreæ, the one on the Corinthian, the other on the Sarônic gulf. It thus supplied a convenient connection between Epirus and Italy on the one side, and the Ægean sea on the other, without imposing upon the unskilful and timid navigator of those days the necessity of circumnavigating Peloponnêsus.

The extension of Grecian traffic and shipping is manifested by a comparison of the Homeric with the Hesiodic poems; in respect to knowledge of places and countries,—the latter being probably referable to dates between B. C. 740 and B. C. 640. In Homer, acquaintance is shown (the accuracy of such acquaintance, however, being exaggerated by Strabo and other friendly critics) with continental Greece and its neighboring islands, with Krête and the principal islands of the Ægean, and with Thrace, the Troad, the Hellespont, and Asia Minor between Paphlagonia northward and Lykia southward. The Sikels are mentioned in the Odyssey, and Sikania in the last book of that poem, but nothing is said to evince a knowledge of Italy or the realities of the western world. Libya, Egypt, and Phœnike, are known by name and by vague hearsay, but the Nile is only mentioned as "the river

Egypt:" while the Euxine sea is not mentioned at all.[205] In the Hesiodic poems, on the other hand, the Nile, the Ister, the Phasis, and the Eridanus, are all specified by name;[206] Mount Ætna, and the island of Ortygia near to Syracuse, the Tyrrhenians and Ligurians in the west, and the Scythians in the north, were also noticed.[207] Indeed, within forty years after the first Olympiad, the cities of Korkyra and Syracuse were founded from Corinth,— the first of a numerous and powerful series of colonies, destined to impart a new character both to the south of Italy and to Sicily.

In reference to the astronomy and physics of the Homeric Greek, it has already been remarked that he connected together the sensible phenomena which form the subject matter of these sciences by threads of religious and personifying fancy, to which the real analogies among them were made subordinate; and that these analogies did not begin to be studied by themselves, apart from the religious element by which they had been at first overlaid, until the age of Thales,—coinciding as that period did with the increased opportunities for visiting Egypt and the interior of Asia. The Greeks obtained access in both of these countries to an enlarged stock of astronomical observations, to the use of the gnomon, or sundial,[208] and to a more exact determination of the length of the solar year,[209] than that which served as the basis of their various lunar periods. It is pretended that Thales was the first who predicted an eclipse of the sun,—not, indeed, accurately, but with large limits of error as to the time of its occurrence,—and that he also possessed so profound an acquaintance with meteorological phenomena and probabilities, as to be able to foretell an abundant crop of olives for the coming year, and to realize a large sum of money by an olive speculation.[210]

From Thales downward we trace a succession of astronomical and physical theories, more or less successful, into which I do not intend here to enter: it is sufficient at present to contrast the father of the Ionic philosophy with the times preceding him, and to mark the first commencement of scientific prediction among the Greeks, however imperfect at the outset, as distinguished from the inspired dicta of prophets or oracles, and from those special signs of the purposes of the gods, which formed the habitual reliance of the Homeric man.[211] We shall see these two modes of anticipating the future,—one based upon the philosophical, the other upon the religious appreciation of nature,—running simultaneously on throughout Grecian history, and sharing between them in unequal portions the empire of the Greek mind; the former acquiring both greater predominance and wider application among the intellectual men, and partially restricting, but never abolishing, the spontaneous employment of the latter among the vulgar.

Neither coined money, nor the art of writing,[212] nor painting, nor sculpture, nor imaginative architecture, belong to the Homeric and Hesiodic times. Such rudiments of arts, destined ultimately to acquire so great a development in Greece, as may have existed in these early days, served only as a sort of nucleus to the fancy of the poet, to shape out for himself the fabulous creations ascribed to Hephæstus or Dædalus. No statues of the gods, not even of wood, are mentioned in the Homeric poems. All the many varieties, in Grecian music, poetry, and dancing,—the former chiefly borrowed from Lydia and Phrygia,—date from a period considerably later than the first Olympiad: Terpander, the earliest musician whose date is assigned, and the inventor of the harp with seven strings instead of that with four strings, does not come until the 26th Olympiad, or 676 B. C.: the poet Archilochus is nearly of the same date. The iambic and elegiac metres—the first deviations from the primitive epic strain and subject—do not reach up to the year 700 B. C.

It is this epic poetry which forms at once both the undoubted prerogative and the solitary jewel of the earliest era of Greece. Of the many epic poems which existed in Greece during the eight century before the Christian era, none have been preserved except the Iliad and Odyssey: the Æthiopis of Arktinus, the Ilias Minor of Lesches, the Cyprian Verses, the Capture of Œchalia, the Returns of the Heroes from Troy, the Thêbaïs and the Epigoni,— several of them passing in antiquity under the name of Homer,—have all been lost. But the two which remain are quite sufficient to demonstrate in the primitive Greeks, a mental organization unparalleled in any other people, and powers of invention and expression which prepared, as well as foreboded, the future eminence of the nation in all the various departments to which thought and language can be applied. Great as the power of thought afterwards became among the Greeks, their power of expression was still greater: in the former, other nations have built upon their foundations and surpassed them,— in the latter, they still remained unrivalled. It is not too much to say that this flexible, emphatic, and transparent character of the language as an instrument of communication,—its perfect aptitude for narrative and discussion, as well as for stirring all the veins of human emotion without ever forfeiting that character of simplicity which adapts it to all men and all times,—may be traced mainly to the existence and the wide-spread influence of the Iliad and Odyssey. To us, these compositions are interesting as beautiful poems, depicting life and manners, and unfolding certain types of character with the utmost vivacity and artlessness: to their original hearer, they possessed all these sources of attraction, together with others more powerful still, to which we are now strangers. Upon him, they bore with the full weight and solemnity of history and religion combined, while the charm of the poetry was only secondary and instrumental. The poet was then the teacher and preacher of the community, not simply the amuser of their leisure hours: they looked to him for revelations of the unknown past and for expositions of the attributes and dispensations of the gods, just as they consulted the prophet for his privileged insight into the future. The ancient epic comprised many different poets and poetical compositions, which fulfilled this purpose with more or less completeness: but it is the exclusive prerogative of the Iliad and Odyssey, that, after the minds of men had ceased to be in full harmony with their original design, they yet retained their empire by the mere force of secondary excellences: while the remaining epics—though serving as food for the curious, and as storehouses for logographers, tragedians, and artists—never seem to have acquired very wide popularity even among intellectual Greeks.

I shall, in the succeeding chapter, give some account of the epic cycle, of its relation to the Homeric poems, and of the general evidences respecting the latter, both as to antiquity and authorship.

# CHAPTER XXI.

## GRECIAN EPIC.—HOMERIC POEMS.

AT THE head of the once abundant epical compositions of Greece, most of them unfortunately lost, stand the Iliad and Odyssey, with the immortal name of Homer attached to each of them, embracing separate portions of the comprehensive legend of Troy. They form the type of what may be called the heroic epic of the Greeks, as distinguished from the genealogical, in which latter species some of the Hesiodic poems—the Catalogue of Women, the Eoiai, and the Naupaktia—stood conspicuous. Poems of the Homeric character (if so it may be called, though the expression is very indefinite,)—being confined to one of the great events, or great personages of Grecian legendary antiquity, and comprising a limited number of characters, all contemporaneous, made some approach, more or less successful, to a certain poetical unity; while the Hesiodic poems, tamer in their spirit, and unconfined both as to time and as to persons, strung together distinct events without any obvious view to concentration of interest,—without legitimate beginning or end.[213] Between these two extremes there were many gradations: biographical poems, such as the Herakleia, or Theseïs, recounting all the principal exploits performed by one single hero, present a character intermediate between the two, but bordering more closely on the Hesiodic. Even the hymns to the gods, which pass under the name of Homer, are epical fragments, narrating particular exploits or adventures of the god commemorated.

Both the didactic and the mystico-religious poetry of Greece began in Hexameter verse,—the characteristic and consecrated measure of the epic: [214] but they belong to a different species, and burst out from a different vein in the Grecian mind. It seems to have been the more common belief among the historical Greeks, that such mystic effusions were more ancient than their narrative poems, and that Orpheus, Musæus, Linus, Olên, Pamphus, and even Hesiod, etc., etc., the reputed composers of the former, were of earlier date than Homer. But there is no evidence to sustain this opinion, and the presumptions are all against it. Those compositions, which in the sixth century before the Christian era passed under the name of Orpheus and Musæus, seem to have been unquestionably post-Homeric, nor can we even admit the modified conclusion of Hermann, Ulrici, and others, that the mystic poetry as a genus (putting aside the particular compositions falsely ascribed to Orpheus and others) preceded in order of time the narrative.[215]

Besides the Iliad and Odyssey, we make out the titles of about thirty lost epic poems, sometimes with a brief hint of their contents.

Concerning the legend of Troy there were five: the Cyprian Verses, the Æthiopis, and the Capture of Troy, both ascribed to Arktinus; the lesser Iliad, ascribed to Leschês; the Returns (of the Heroes from Troy), to which the name of Hagias of Trœzên is attached; and the Telegonia, by Eugammôn, a continuation of the Odyssey. Two poems,—the Thebaïs and the Epigoni (perhaps two parts of one and the same poem) were devoted to the legend of Thebês,—the two sieges of that city by the Argeians. Another poem, called Œdipodia, had for its subject the tragical destiny of Œdipus and his family; and perhaps that which is cited as Eurôpia, or verses on Eurôpa, may have comprehended the tale of her brother Kadmus, the mythical founder of Thebês.[216]

The exploits of Hêraklês were celebrated in two compositions, each called Hêrakleia, by Kinæthôn and Pisander,—probably also in many others, of which the memory has not been preserved. The capture of Œchalia, by Hêraklês, formed the subject of a separate epic. Two other poems, the Ægimius and the Minyas, are supposed to have been founded on other achievements of this hero,—the effective aid which he lent to the Dorian king Ægimius against the Lapithæ, his descent to the under-world for the purpose of rescuing the imprisoned Thêseus, and his conquest of the city of the Minyæ, the powerful Orchomenus.[217]

Other epic poems—the Phorônis, the Danaïs, the Alkmæônis, the Atthis, the Amazonia—we know only by name, and can just guess obscurely at their contents so far as the name indicates.[218] The Titanomachia, the Gigantomachia, and the Corinthiaca, three compositions all ascribed to Eumêlus, afford by means of their titles an idea somewhat clearer of the matter which they comprised. The Theogony ascribed to Hesiod still exists, though partially corrupt and mutilated: but there seem to have been other poems, now lost, of the like import and title.

Of the poems composed in the Hesiodic style, diffusive and full of genealogical detail, the principal were, the Catalogue of Women and the Great Eoiai; the latter of which, indeed, seems to have been a continuation of the former. A large number of the celebrated women of heroic Greece were commemorated in these poems, one after the other, without any other than an arbitrary bond of connection. The Marriage of Kêyx,—the Melampodia,—and a string of fables called Astronomia, are farther ascribed to Hesiod: and the poem above mentioned, called Ægimius, is also sometimes connected with his name, sometimes with that of Kerkops. The Naupaktian Verses (so called, probably, from the birthplace of their author), and the genealogies of

Kinæthôn and Asius, were compositions of the same rambling character, as far as we can judge from the scanty fragments remaining.[219] The Orchomenian epic poet Chersias, of whom two lines only are preserved to us by Pausanias, may reasonably be referred to the same category.[220]

The oldest of the epic poets, to whom any date, carrying with it the semblance of authority, is assigned, is Arktinus of Milêtus, who is placed by Eusebius in the first Olympiad, and by Suidas in the ninth. Eugammôn, the author of the Telegonia, and the latest of the catalogue, is placed in the fifty-third Olympiad, B. C. 566. Between these two we find Asius and Leschês, about the thirtieth Olympiad,—a time when the vein of the ancient epic was drying up, and when other forms of poetry—elegiac, iambic, lyric, and choric —had either already arisen, or were on the point of arising, to compete with it.[221]

It has already been stated in a former chapter, that in the early commencements of prose-writing, Hekatæus, Pherekydês, and other logographers, made it their business to extract from the ancient fables something like a continuous narrative, chronologically arranged. It was upon a principle somewhat analogous that the Alexandrine literati, about the second century before the Christian era,[222] arranged the multitude of old epic poets into a series founded on the supposed order of time in the events narrated,— beginning with the intermarriage of Uranus and Gæa, and the Theogony,— and concluding with the death of Odysseus by the hands of his son Telegonus. This collection passed by the name of the Epic Cycle, and the poets, whose compositions were embodied in it, were termed Cyclic poets. Doubtless, the epical treasures of the Alexandrine library were larger than had ever before been brought together and submitted to men both of learning and leisure: so that multiplication of such compositions in the same museum rendered it advisable to establish some fixed order of perusal, and to copy them in one corrected and uniform edition.[223] It pleased the critics to determine precedence, neither by antiquity nor by excellence of the compositions themselves, but by the supposed sequence of narrative, so that the whole taken together constituted a readable aggregate of epical antiquity.

Much obscurity[224] exists, and many different opinions have been expressed, respecting this Epic Cycle: I view it, not as an exclusive canon, but simply as an all-comprehensive classification, with a new edition founded thereupon. It would include all the epic poems in the library older than the Telegonia, and apt for continuous narrative; it would exclude only two classes,—first, the recent epic poets, such as Panyasis and Antimachus; next, the genealogical and desultory poems, such as the Catalogue of Women, the Eoiai, and others, which could not be made to fit in to any chronological sequence of events.[225] Both the Iliad and the Odyssey were comprised in the Cycle, so that the denomination of cyclic poet did not originally or designedly carry with it any association of contempt. But as the great and capital poems were chiefly spoken of by themselves, or by the title of their own separate authors, so the general name of *poets of the Cycle* came gradually to be applied only to the worst, and thus to imply vulgarity or common-place; the more so, as many of the inferior compositions included in the collection seem to have been anonymous, and their authors in consequence describable only under some such common designation as that of the cyclic poets. It is in this manner that we are to explain the disparaging sentiment connected by Horace and others with the idea of a cyclic writer, though no such sentiment was implied in the original meaning of the Epic Cycle.

The poems of the Cycle were thus mentioned in contrast and antithesis with Homer,[226] though originally the Iliad and Odyssey had both been included among them: and this alteration of the meaning of the word has given birth to a mistake as to the primary purpose of the classification, as if it had been designed especially to part off the inferior epic productions from Homer. But while some critics are disposed to distinguish the cyclic poets too pointedly from Homer, I conceive that Welcker goes too much into the other extreme, and identifies the Cycle too closely with that poet. He construes it as a classification deliberately framed to comprise all the various productions of the Homeric epic, with its unity of action and comparative paucity, both of persons and adventures,—as opposed to the Hesiodic epic, crowded with separate persons and pedigrees, and destitute of central action as well as of closing catastrophe. This opinion does, indeed, coincide to a great degree with the fact, inasmuch as few of the Hesiodic epics appear to have been included in the Cycle: to say that *none* were included, would be too much, for we cannot venture to set aside either the Theogony or the Ægimius; but we may account for their absence perfectly well without supposing any design to exclude them, for it is obvious that their rambling character (like that of the Metamorphoses of Ovid) forbade the possibility of interweaving them in any continuous series. Continuity in the series of narrated events, coupled with a certain degree of antiquity in the poems, being the principle on which the arrangement called the Epic Cycle was based, the Hesiodic poems generally were excluded, not from any preconceived intention, but because they could not be brought into harmony with such orderly reading.

What were the particular poems which it comprised, we cannot now determine with exactness. Welcker arranges them as follows: Titanomachia, Danaïs, Amazonia (or Atthis), Œdipodia, Thebaïs (or Expedition of Amphiaräus), Epigoni (or Alkmæônis), Minyas (or Phokaïs), Capture of Œchalia, Cyprian Verses, Iliad, Æthiopis, Lesser Iliad, Iliupersis or the Taking of Troy, Returns of the Heroes, Odyssey, and Telegonia. Wuellner, Lange, and Mr. Fynes Clinton enlarge the list of cyclic poems still farther.[227] But all such reconstructions of the Cycle are conjectural and destitute of authority: the only poems which we can affirm on positive grounds to have been comprehended in it, are, first, the series respecting the heroes of Troy, from the Cypria to the Telegonia, of which Proclus has preserved the arguments, and which includes the Iliad and Odyssey,—next, the old Thebaïs, which is expressly termed cyclic,[228] in order to distinguish it from the poem of the same name composed by Antimachus. In regard to other particular compositions, we have no evidence to guide us, either for admission or exclusion, except our general views as to the scheme upon which the Cycle was framed. If my idea of that scheme be correct, the Alexandrine critics arranged therein *all* their old epical treasures, down to the Telegonia,—the good as well as the bad; gold, silver, and iron,—provided only they could be pieced in with the narrative series. But I cannot venture to include, as Mr. Clinton does, the Eurôpia, the Phorônis, and other poems of which we know only the names, because it is uncertain whether their contents were such as to fulfil their primary condition: nor can I concur with him in thinking that, where there were two or more poems of the same title and subject, one of them must necessarily have been adopted into the Cycle to the exclusion of the others. There may have been two Theogonies, or two Herakleias, both comprehended in the Cycle; the purpose being (as I before remarked), not to sift the better from the worse, but to determine some fixed order, convenient for reading and reference, amidst a multiplicity of scattered compositions, as the basis of a new, entire, and corrected edition.

Whatever may have been the principle on which the cyclic poems were originally strung together, they are all now lost, except those two unrivalled diamonds, whose brightness, dimming all the rest, has alone sufficed to confer imperishable glory even upon the earliest phase of Grecian life. It has been the natural privilege of the Iliad and Odyssey, from the rise of Grecian philology down to the present day, to provoke an intense curiosity, which, even in the historical and literary days of Greece, there were no assured facts to satisfy. These compositions are the monuments of an age essentially religious and poetical, but essentially also unphilosophical, unreflecting, and unrecording: the nature of the case forbids our having any authentic transmitted knowledge respecting such a period; and the lesson must be learned, hard and painful though it be, that no imaginable reach of critical acumen will of itself enable us to discriminate fancy from reality, in the absence of a tolerable stock of evidence. After the numberless comments and acrimonious controversies[229] to which the Homeric poems have given rise, it can hardly be said that any of the points originally doubtful have obtained a solution such as to command universal acquiescence. To glance at all these controversies, however briefly, would far transcend the limits of the present work; but the most abridged Grecian history would be incomplete without some inquiry respecting *the Poet* (so the Greek critics in their veneration denominated Homer), and the productions which pass now, or have heretofore passed, under his name.

Who or what was Homer? What date is to be assigned to him? What were his compositions?

A person, putting these questions to Greeks of different towns and ages, would have obtained answers widely discrepant and contradictory. Since the invaluable labors of Aristarchus and the other Alexandrine critics on the text of the Iliad and Odyssey, it has, indeed, been customary to regard those two (putting aside the Hymns, and a few other minor poems) as being the only genuine Homeric compositions: and the literary men called Chorizontes, or the Separators, at the head of whom were Xenôn and Hellanikus, endeavored still farther to reduce the number by disconnecting the Iliad and Odyssey, and pointing out that both could not be the work of the same author. Throughout the whole course of Grecian antiquity, the Iliad and the Odyssey, and the Hymns, have been received as Homeric: but if we go back to the time of Herodotus, or still earlier, we find that several other epics also were ascribed to Homer,—and there were not wanting[230] critics, earlier than the Alexandrine age, who regarded the whole Epic Cycle, together with the satirical poem called Margitês, the Batrachomyomachia, and other smaller pieces, as Homeric works. The cyclic Thebaïs and the Epigoni (whether they be two separate poems, or the latter a second part of the former) were in early days currently ascribed to Homer: the same was the case with the Cyprian Verses: some even attributed to him several other poems,[231] the Capture of Œchalia, the Lesser Iliad, the Phokaïs, and the Amazonia. The title of the poem called Thebaïs to be styled Homeric, depends upon evidence more ancient than any which can be produced to authenticate the Iliad and Odyssey: for Kallinus, the ancient elegiac poet (B. C. 640), mentioned Homer as the author of it,—and his opinion was shared by many other competent judges.[232] From the remarkable description given by Herodotus, of the expulsion of the rhapsodes from Sikyôn, by the despot Kleisthenês, in the time of Solôn (about B. C. 580), we may form a probable judgment that the Thebaïs and the Epigoni were then rhapsodized at Sikyôn as Homeric productions.[233] And it is clear from the language of Herodotus, that in his time the general opinion ascribed to Homer both the Cyprian Verses and the Epigoni, though he himself dissents.[234] In spite of such dissent, however, that historian must have conceived the names of Homer and Hesiod to be nearly coextensive with the whole of the ancient epic; otherwise, he would hardly have delivered his memorable judgment, that they two were the framers of Grecian theogony.

The many different cities which laid claim to the birth of Homer (seven is rather below the truth, and Smyrna and Chios are the most prominent among them,) is well known, and most of them had legends to tell respecting his romantic parentage, his alleged blindness, and his life of an itinerant bard, acquainted with poverty and sorrow.[235] The discrepancies of statement respecting the date of his reputed existence are no less worthy of remark; for out of the eight different epochs assigned to him, the oldest differs from the most recent by a period of four hundred and sixty years.

Thus conflicting would have been the answers returned in different portions of the Grecian world to any questions respecting the person of Homer. But there were a poetical gens (fraternity or guild) in the Ionic island of Chios, who, if the question had been put to them, would have answered in another manner. To them, Homer was not a mere antecedent man, of kindred nature with themselves, but a divine or semi-divine eponymus and progenitor, whom they worshipped in their gentile sacrifices, and in whose ascendent name and glory the individuality of every member of the gens was merged. The compositions of each separate Homêrid, or the combined efforts of many of them in conjunction, were the works of Homer: the name of the individual bard perishes and his authorship is forgotten, but the common gentile father lives and grows in renown, from generation to generation, by the genius of his self-renewing sons.

Such was the conception entertained of Homer by the poetical gens called Homêridæ, or Homêrids; and in the general obscurity of the whole case, I lean towards it as the most plausible conception. Homer is not only the reputed author of the various compositions emanating from the gentile members, but also the recipient of the many different legends and of the divine genealogy, which it pleases their imagination to confer upon him. Such manufacture of fictitious personality, and such perfect incorporation of the entities of religion and fancy with the real world, is a process familiar, and even habitual, in the retrospective vision of the Greeks.[236]

It is to be remarked, that the poetical gens here brought to view, the Homêrids, are of indisputable authenticity. Their existence and their considerations were maintained down to the historical times in the island of Chios.[237] If the Homêrids were still conspicuous, even in the days of Akusilaus, Pindar, Hellanikus, and Plato, when their productive invention had ceased, and when they had become only guardians and distributors, in common with others, of the treasures bequeathed by their predecessors,—far more exalted must their position have been three centuries before, while they were still the inspired creators of epic novelty, and when the absence of writing assured to them the undisputed monopoly of their own compositions.[238]

Homer, then, is no individual man, but the divine or heroic father (the ideas of worship and ancestry coalescing, as they constantly did in the Grecian mind) of the gentile Homêrids, and he is the author of the Thebaïs, the Epigoni, the Cyprian Verses, the Procems, or Hymns, and other poems, in the same sense in which he is the author of the Iliad and Odyssey,—assuming that these various compositions emanate, as perhaps they may, from different individuals numbered among the Homêrids. But this disallowance of the historical personality of Homer is quite distinct from the question, with which it has been often confounded, whether the Iliad and Odyssey are originally entire poems, and whether by one author or otherwise. To us, the name of Homer means these two poems, and little else: we desire to know as much as can be learned respecting their date, their original composition, their preservation, and their mode of communication to the public. All these questions are more or less complicated one with the other.

Concerning the date of the poems, we have no other information except the various affirmations respecting the age of Homer, which differ among themselves (as I have before observed) by an interval of four hundred and sixty years, and which for the most part determine the date of Homer by reference to some other event, itself fabulous and unauthenticated,—such as the Trojan war, the Return of the Hêrakleids, or the Ionic migration. Kratês placed Homer earlier than the Return of the Hêrakleids, and less than eighty years after the Trojan war: Eratosthenês put him one hundred years after the Trojan war: Aristotle, Aristarchus, and Castor made his birth contemporary with the Ionic migration, while Apollodôrus brings him down to one hundred years after that event, or two hundred and forty years after the taking of Troy. Thucydidês assigns to him a date much subsequent to the Trojan war.[239] On the other hand, Theopompus and Euphoriôn refer his age to the far more recent period of the Lydian king, Gyges, (Ol. 18-23, B. C. 708-688,) and put him five hundred years after the Trojan epoch.[240] What were the grounds of these various conjectures, we do not know; though in the statements of Kratês and Eratosthenês, we may pretty well divine. But the oldest dictum preserved to us respecting the date of Homer,—meaning thereby the date of the Iliad and Odyssey,—appears to me at the same time the most credible, and the most consistent with the general history of the ancient epic. Herodotus places Homer four hundred years before himself; taking his departure, not from any fabulous event, but from a point of real and authentic time.[241] Four centuries anterior to Herodotus would be a period commencing with 880 B. C. so that the composition of the Homeric poems would thus fall in a space between 850 and 800 B. C. We may gather from the language of Herodotus that this was his own judgment, opposed to a current opinion, which assigned the poet to an earlier epoch.

To place the Iliad and Odyssey at some periods between 850 B. C. and 776 B. C., appears to me more probable than any other date, anterior or posterior,— more probable than the latter, because we are justified in believing these two poems to be older than Arktinus, who comes shortly after the first Olympiad; —more probable than the former, because, the farther we push the poems back, the more do we enhance the wonder of their preservation, already sufficiently great, down from such an age and society to the historical times.

The mode in which these poems, and indeed all poems, epic as well as lyric, down to the age (probably) of Peisistratus, were circulated and brought to bear upon the public, deserves particular attention. They were not read by individuals alone and apart, but sung or recited at festivals or to assembled companies. This seems to be one of the few undisputed facts with regard to the great poet: for even those who maintain that the Iliad and Odyssey were preserved by means of writing, seldom contend that they were read.

In appreciating the effect of the poems, we must always take account of this great difference between early Greece and our own times,—between the congregation mustered at a solemn festival, stimulated by community of sympathy, listening to a measured and musical recital from the lips of trained bards or rhapsodes, whose matter was supposed to have been inspired by the Muse,—and the solitary reader, with a manuscript before him; such manuscript being, down to a very late period in Greek literature, indifferently written, without division into parts, and without marks of punctuation. As in the case of dramatic performances, in all ages, so in that of the early Grecian epic,—a very large proportion of its impressive effect was derived from the talent of the reciter and the force of the general accompaniments, and would have disappeared altogether in solitary reading. Originally, the bard sung his own epical narrative, commencing with a prœmium or hymn to one of the gods:[242] his profession was separate and special, like that of the carpenter, the leech, or the prophet: his manner and enunciation must have required particular training no less than his imaginative faculty. His character presents itself in the Odyssey as one highly esteemed; and in the Iliad, even Achilles does not disdain to touch the lyre with his own hands, and to sing heroic deeds.[243] Not only did the Iliad and Odyssey, and the poems embodied in the Epic Cycle, produce all their impression and gain all their renown by this process of oral delivery, but even the lyric and choric poets who succeeded them were known and felt in the same way by the general public, even after the full establishment of habits of reading among lettered men. While in the case of the epic, the recitation or singing had been extremely simple, and the measure comparatively little diversified, with no other accompaniment than that of the four-stringed harp,—all the variations superinduced upon the original hexameter, beginning with the pentameter and iambus, and proceeding step by step to the complicated strophês of Pindar and the tragic writers, still left the general effect of the poetry greatly dependent upon voice and accompaniments, and pointedly distinguished from mere solitary reading of the words. And in the dramatic poetry, the last in order of time, the declamation and gesture of the speaking actor alternated with the song and dance of the chorus, and with the instruments of musicians, the whole being set off by imposing visible decorations. Now both dramatic effect and song are familiar in modern times, so that every man knows the difference between reading the words and hearing them under the appropriate circumstances: but poetry, as such, is, and has now long been, so exclusively enjoyed by reading, that it requires an especial memento to bring us back to the time when the Iliad and Odyssey were addressed only to the ear and feelings of a promiscuous and sympathizing multitude. Readers there were none, at least until the century preceding Solôn and Peisistratus: from that time forward, they gradually increased both in number and influence; though doubtless small, even in the most literary period of Greece, as compared with modern European society. So far as the production of beautiful epic poetry was concerned, however, the select body of instructed readers, furnished a less potent stimulus than the unlettered and listening crowd of the earlier periods. The poems of Chœrilus and Antimachus, towards the close of the Peloponnesian war, though admired by erudite men, never acquired popularity; and the emperor Hadrian failed in his attempt to bring the latter poet into fashion at the expense of Homer.[244]

It will be seen by what has been here stated, that that class of men, who formed the medium of communication between the verse and the ear, were of the highest importance in the ancient world, and especially in the earlier periods of its career,—the bards and rhapsodes for the epic, the singers for the lyric, the actors and singers jointly with the dancers for the chorus and drama. The lyric and dramatic poets taught with their own lips the delivery of their compositions, and so prominently did this business of teaching present itself to the view of the public, that the name Didaskalia, by which the dramatic exhibition was commonly designated, derived from thence its origin.

Among the number of rhapsodes who frequented the festivals at a time when Grecian cities were multiplied and easy of access, for the recitation of the ancient epic, there must have been of course great differences of excellence; but that the more considerable individuals of the class were elaborately trained and highly accomplished in the exercise of their profession, we may assume as certain. But it happens that Socrates, with his two pupils Plato and Xenophon, speak contemptuously of their merits; and many persons have been disposed, somewhat too readily, to admit this sentence of condemnation as conclusive, without taking account of the point of view from which it was delivered.[245] These philosophers considered Homer and other poets with a view to instruction, ethical doctrine, and virtuous practice: they analyzed the characters whom the poet described, sifted the value of the lessons conveyed, and often struggled to discover a hidden meaning, where they disapproved that which was apparent. When they found a man like the rhapsode, who professed to impress the Homeric narrative upon an audience, and yet either never meddled at all, or meddled unsuccessfully, with the business of exposition, they treated him with contempt; indeed, Socrates depreciates the poets themselves, much upon the same principle, as dealing with matters of which they could render no rational account.[246] It was also the habit of Plato and Xenophôn to disparage generally professional exertion of talent for the purpose of gaining a livelihood, contrasting it often in an indelicate manner with the gratuitous teaching and ostentatious poverty of their master. But we are not warranted in judging the rhapsodes by such a standard. Though they were not philosophers or moralists, it was their province—and it had been so, long before the philosophical point of view was opened—to bring their poet home to the bosoms and emotions of an assembled crowd, and to penetrate themselves with his meaning so far as was suitable for that purpose, adapting to it the appropriate graces of action and intonation. In this their genuine task they were valuable members of the Grecian community, and seem to have possessed all the qualities necessary for success.

These rhapsodes, the successors of the primitive aœdi, or bards, seem to have been distinguished from them by the discontinuance of all musical accompaniment. Originally, the bard sung, enlivening the song with occasional touches of the simple four-stringed harp: his successor, the rhapsode, recited, holding in his hand nothing but a branch of laurel and depending for effect upon voice and manner,—a species of musical and rhythmical declamation,[247] which gradually increased in vehement emphasis and gesticulation until it approached to that of the dramatic actor. At what time this change took place, or whether the two different modes of enunciating the ancient epic may for a certain period have gone on simultaneously, we have no means of determining. Hesiod receives from the Muse a branch of laurel, as a token of his ordination into their service, which marks him for a rhapsode; while the ancient bard with his harp is still recognized in the Homeric Hymn to the Delian Apollo, as efficient and popular at the Panionic festivals in the island of Delos.[248] Perhaps the improvements made in the harp, to which three strings, in addition to the original four, were attached by Terpander (B. C. 660), and the growing complication of instrumental music generally, may have contributed to discredit the primitive accompaniment, and thus to promote the practice of recital: the story, that Terpander himself composed music, not only for hexameter poems of his own, but also for those of Homer, seems to indicate that the music which preceded him was ceasing to find favor.[249] By whatever steps the change from the bard to the rhapsode took place, certain it is that before the time of Solôn, the latter was the recognized and exclusive organ of the old Epic; sometimes in short fragments before private companies, by single rhapsodes,—sometimes several rhapsodes in continuous succession at a public festival.

Respecting the mode in which the Homeric poems were preserved, during the two centuries (or as some think, longer interval) between their original composition and the period shortly preceding Solôn,—and respecting their original composition and subsequent changes,—there are wide differences of opinion among able critics. Were they preserved with or without being written? Was the Iliad originally composed as one poem, and the Odyssey in like manner, or is each of them an aggregation of parts originally self-existent and unconnected? Was the authorship of each poem single-headed or many-headed?

Either tacitly or explicitly, these questions have been generally coupled together and discussed with reference to each other, by inquiries into the Homeric poems; though Mr. Payne Knight's Prolegomena have the merit of keeping them distinct. Half a century ago, the acute and valuable Prolegomena of F. A. Wolf, turning to account the Venetian Scholia which had then been recently published, first opened philosophical discussion as to the history of the Homeric text. A considerable part of that dissertation (though by no means the whole) is employed in vindicating the position, previously announced by Bentley, among others, that the separate constituent portions of the Iliad and Odyssey had not been cemented together into any compact body and unchangeable order until the days of Peisistratus, in the sixth century before Christ. As a step towards that conclusion, Wolf maintained that no written copies of either poem could be shown to have existed during the earlier times to which their composition is referred,—and that without writing, neither the perfect symmetry of so complicated a work could have been originally conceived by any poet, nor, if realized by him, transmitted with assurance to posterity. The absence of easy and convenient writing, such as must be indispensably supposed for long manuscripts, among the early Greeks, was thus one of the points in Wolf's case against the primitive integrity of the Iliad and Odyssey. By Nitzsch and other leading opponents of Wolf, the connection of the one with the other seems to have been accepted as he originally put it; and it has been considered incumbent on those, who defended the ancient aggregate character of the Iliad and Odyssey, to maintain that they were written poems from the beginning.

To me it appears that the architectonic functions ascribed by Wolf to Peisistratus and his associates, in reference to the Homeric poems, are nowise admissible. But much would undoubtedly be gained towards that view of the question, if it could be shown that, in order to controvert it, we were driven to the necessity of admitting long written poems in the ninth century before the Christian era. Few things, in my opinion, can be more improbable: and Mr. Payne Knight, opposed as he is to the Wolfian hypothesis, admits this no less than Wolf himself.[250] The traces of writing in Greece, even in the seventh century before the Christian era, are exceedingly trifling. We have no remaining inscription earlier than the 40th Olympiad, and the early inscriptions are rude and unskilfully executed: nor can we even assure ourselves whether Archilochus, Simonidês of Amorgus, Kallinus, Tyrtæus, Xanthus, and the other early elegiac and lyric poets, committed their compositions to writing, or at what time the practice of doing so became familiar. The first positive ground, which authorizes us to presume the existence of a manuscript of Homer, is in the famous ordinance of Solôn with regard to the rhapsodes at the Panathenæa; but for what length of time, previously, manuscripts had existed, we are unable to say.

Those who maintain the Homeric poems to have been written from the beginning, rest their case, not upon positive proofs,—nor yet upon the existing habits of society with regard to poetry, for they admit generally that the Iliad and Odyssey were not read, but recited and heard,—but upon the supposed necessity that there must have been manuscripts,[251] to insure the preservation of the poems,—the unassisted memory of reciters being neither sufficient nor trustworthy. But here we only escape a smaller difficulty by running into a greater; for the existence of trained bards, gifted with extraordinary memory, is far less astonishing than that of long manuscripts in an age essentially non-reading and non-writing, and when even suitable instruments and materials for the process are not obvious. Moreover, there is a strong positive reason for believing that the bard was under no necessity for refreshing his memory by consulting a manuscript. For if such had been the fact, blindness would have been a disqualification for the profession, which we know that it was not; as well from the example of Demodokus in the Odyssey, as from that of the blind bard of Chios, in the hymn to the Delian Apollo, whom Thucydidês, as well as the general tenor of Grecian legend, identifies with Homer himself.[252] The author of that Hymn, be he who he may, could never have described a blind man as attaining the utmost perfection in his art, if he had been conscious that the memory of the bard was only maintained by constant reference to the manuscript in his chest.

Nor will it be found, after all, that the effort of memory required, either from bards or rhapsodes, even for the longest of these old Epic poems,— though doubtless great, was at all superhuman. Taking the case with reference to the entire Iliad and Odyssey, we know that there were educated gentlemen at Athens who could repeat both poems by heart:[253] but in the professional recitations, we are not to imagine that the same person did go through the whole: the recitation was essentially a joint undertaking, and the rhapsodes who visited a festival would naturally understand among themselves which part of the poem should devolve upon each particular individual. Under such circumstances, and with such means of preparation beforehand, the quantity of verse which a rhapsode could deliver would be measured, not so much by the exhaustion of his memory, as by the physical sufficiency of his voice, having reference to the sonorous, emphatic, and rhythmical pronunciation required from him.[254]

But what guarantee have we for the exact transmission of the text for a space of two centuries by simply oral means? It may be replied, that oral transmission would hand down the text as exactly as in point of fact it was handed down. The great lines of each poem,—the order of parts,—the vein of Homeric feeling, and the general style of locution, and, for the most part, the true words,—would be maintained: for the professional training of the rhapsode, over and above the precision of his actual memory, would tend to Homerize his mind (if the expression may be permitted), and to restrain him within this magic circle. On the other hand, in respect to the details of the text, we should expect that there would be wide differences and numerous inaccuracies: and so there really were, as the records contained in the Scholia, together with the passages cited in ancient authors, but not found in our Homeric text, abundantly testify.[255]

Moreover, the state of the Iliad and Odyssey, in respect to the letter called the Digamma, affords a proof that they were recited for a considerable period before they were committed to writing, insomuch that the oral pronunciation underwent during the interval a sensible change.[256] At the time when these poems were composed, the Digamma was an effective consonant, and figured as such in the structure of the verse: at the time when they were committed to writing, it had ceased to be pronounced, and therefore never found a place in any of the manuscripts,—insomuch that the Alexandrine critics, though they knew of its existence in the much later poems of Alkæus and Sapphô, never recognized it in Homer. The hiatus, and the various perplexities of metre, occasioned by the loss of the Digamma, were corrected by different grammatical stratagems. But the whole history of this lost letter is very curious, and is rendered intelligible only by the supposition that the Iliad and Odyssey belonged for a wide space of time to the memory, the voice, and the ear, exclusively.

At what period these poems, or, indeed, any other Greek poems, first began to be written, must be matter of conjecture, though there is ground for assurance that it was before the time of Solôn. If, in the absence of evidence, we may venture upon naming any more determinate period, the question at once suggests itself, what were the purposes which, in that stage of society, a manuscript at its first commencement must have been intended to answer? For whom was a written Iliad necessary? Not for the rhapsodes; for with them it was not only planted in the memory, but also interwoven with the feelings, and conceived in conjunction with all those flexions and intonations of voice, pauses, and other oral artifices, which were required for emphatic delivery, and which the naked manuscript could never reproduce. Not for the general public,—*they* were accustomed to receive it with its rhapsodic delivery, and with its accompaniments of a solemn and crowded festival. The only persons for whom the written Iliad would be suitable, would be a select few; studious and curious men,—a class of readers, capable of analyzing the complicated emotions which they had experienced as hearers in the crowd, and who would, on perusing the written words, realize in their imaginations a sensible portion of the impression communicated by the reciter.[257]

Incredible as the statement may seem in an age like the present, there is in all early societies, and there was in early Greece, a time when no such reading class existed. If we could discover at what time such a class first began to be formed, we should be able to make a guess at the time when the old Epic poems were first committed to writing. Now the period which may with the greatest probability be fixed upon as having first witnessed the formation even of the narrowest reading class in Greece, is the middle of the seventh century before the Christian era (B. C. 660 to B. C. 630),—the age of Terpander, Kallinus, Archilochus, Simonidês of Amorgus, etc. I ground this supposition on the change then operated in the character and tendencies of Grecian poetry and music,—the elegiac and iambic measures having been introduced as rivals to the primitive hexameter, and poetical compositions having been transferred from the epical past to the affairs of present and real life. Such a change was important at a time when poetry was the only known mode of publication (to use a modern phrase not altogether suitable, yet the nearest approaching to the sense). It argued a new way of looking at the old epical treasures of the people, as well as a thirst for new poetical effect; and the men who stood forward in it may well be considered as desirous to study, and competent to criticize, from their own individual point of view, the written words of the Homeric rhapsodes, just as we are told that Kallinus both noticed and eulogized the Thebaïs as the production of Homer. There seems, therefore, ground for conjecturing, that (for the use of this newly-formed and important, but very narrow class) manuscripts of the Homeric poems and other old epics—the Thebaïs and the Cypria as well as the Iliad and the Odyssey—began to be compiled towards the middle of the seventh century B. C.:[258] and the opening of Egypt to Grecian commerce, which took place about the same period, would furnish increased facilities for obtaining the requisite papyrus to write upon. A reading class, when once formed, would doubtless slowly increase, and the number of manuscripts along with it; so that before the time of Solôn, fifty years afterwards, both readers and manuscripts, though still comparatively few, might have attained a certain recognized authority, and formed a tribunal of reference, against the carelessness of individual rhapsodes.

We may, I think, consider the Iliad and Odyssey to have been preserved without the aid of writing, for a period near upon two centuries.[259] But is it true, as Wolf imagined, and as other able critics have imagined, also, that the separate portions of which these two poems are composed were originally distinct epical ballads, each constituting a separate whole and intended for separate recitation? Is it true, that they had not only no common author, but originally, neither common purpose nor fixed order, and that their first permanent arrangement and integration was delayed for three centuries, and accomplished at last only by the taste of Peisistratus conjoined with various lettered friends?[260]

This hypothesis—to which the genius of Wolf first gave celebrity, but which has been since enforced more in detail by others, especially by William Müller and Lachmann—appears to me not only unsupported by any sufficient testimony, but also opposed to other testimony as well as to a strong force of internal probability. The authorities quoted by Wolf are Josephus, Cicero, and Pausanias:[261] Josephus mentions nothing about Peisistratus, but merely states (what we may accept as the probable fact) that the Homeric poems were originally unwritten, and preserved only in songs or recitations, from which they were at a subsequent period put into writing: hence many of the discrepancies in the text. On the other hand, Cicero and Pausanias go farther, and affirm that Peisistratus both collected, and arranged in the existing order, the rhapsodies of the Iliad and Odyssey, (implied as poems originally entire, and subsequently broken into pieces,) which he found partly confused and partly isolated from each other,—each part being then remembered only in its own portion of the Grecian world. Respecting Hipparchus the son of Peisistratus, too, we are told in the Pseudo-Platonic dialogue which bears his name, that he was the first to introduce into Attica, the poetry of Homer, and that he prescribed to the rhapsodes to recite the parts of the Panathenaic festival in regular sequence.[262]

Wolf and William Müller occasionally speak as if they admitted something like an Iliad and Odyssey as established aggregates prior to Peisistratus; but for the most part they represent him or his associates as having been the first to put together Homeric poems which were before distinct and self-existent compositions. And Lachmann, the recent expositor of the same theory, ascribes to Peisistratus still more unequivocally this original integration of parts in reference to the Iliad,—distributing the first twenty-two books of the poem into sixteen separate songs, and treating it as ridiculous to imagine that the fusion of these songs, into an order such as we now read, belongs to any date earlier than Peisistratus.[263]

Upon this theory we may remark, first, that it stands opposed to the testimony existing respecting the regulations of Solôn; who, before the time of Peisistratus, had enforced a fixed order of recitation on the rhapsodes of the Iliad at the Panathenaic festival; not only directing that they should go through the rhapsodies *seriatim*, and without omission or corruption, but also establishing a prompter or censorial authority to insure obedience,[264]— which implies the existence (at the same time that it proclaims the occasional infringement) of an orderly aggregate, as well as of manuscripts professedly complete. Next, the theory ascribes to Peisistratus a character not only materially different from what is indicated by Cicero and Pausanias,—who represent him, not as having put together atoms originally distinct, but as the renovator of an ancient order subsequently lost,—but also in itself unintelligible, and inconsistent with Grecian habit and feeling. That Peisistratus should take pains to repress the license, or make up for the unfaithful memory, of individual rhapsodes, and to ennoble the Panathenaic festival by the most correct recital of a great and venerable poem, according to the standard received among the best judges in Greece,—this is a task both suitable to his position, and requiring nothing more than an improved recension, together with exact adherence to it on the part of the rhapsodes. But what motive had he to string together several poems, previously known only as separate, into one new whole? What feeling could he gratify by introducing the extensive changes and transpositions surmised by Lachmann, for the purpose of binding together sixteen songs, which the rhapsodes are assumed to have been accustomed to recite, and the people to hear, each by itself apart? Peisistratus was not a poet, seeking to interest the public mind by new creations and combinations, but a ruler, desirous to impart solemnity to a great religious festival in his native city. Now such a purpose would be answered by selecting, amidst the divergences of rhapsodes in different parts of Greece, that order of text which intelligent men could approve as a return to the pure and pristine Iliad; but it would be defeated if he attempted large innovations of his own, and brought out for the first time a new Iliad by blending together, altering, and transposing, many old and well-known songs. A novelty so bold would have been more likely to offend than to please both the critics and the multitude. And if it were even enforced, by authority, at Athens, no probable reason can be given why all the other towns, and all the rhapsodes throughout Greece, should abnegate their previous habits in favor of it, since Athens at that time enjoyed no political ascendency such as she acquired during the following century. On the whole, it will appear that the character and position of Peisistratus himself go far to negative the function which Wolf and Lachmann put upon him. His interference presupposes a certain foreknown and ancient aggregate, the main lineaments of which were familiar to the Grecian public, although many of the rhapsodes in their practice may have deviated from it both by omission and interpolation. In correcting the Athenian recitations conformably with such understood general type, he might hope both to procure respect for Athens, and to constitute a fashion for the rest of Greece. But this step of "collecting the torn body of sacred Homer," is something generically different from the composition of a new Iliad out of preëxisting songs the former is as easy, suitable, and promising, as the latter is violent and gratuitous.[265]

To sustain the inference, that Peisistratus was the first architect of the Iliad and Odyssey, it ought at least to be shown that no other long and continuous poems existed during the earlier centuries. But the contrary of this is known to be the fact. The Æthiopis of Arktinus, which contained nine thousand one hundred verses, dates from a period more than two centuries earlier than Peisistratus: several other of the lost cyclic epics, some among them of considerable length, appear during the century succeeding Arktinus; and it is important to notice that three or four at least of these poems passed currently under the name of Homer.[266] There is no greater intrinsic difficulty in supposing long epics to have begun with the Iliad and Odyssey than with the Æthiopis: the ascendency of the name of Homer and the subordinate position of Arktinus, in the history of early Grecian poetry, tend to prove the former in preference to the latter.

Moreover, we find particular portions of the Iliad, which expressly pronounce themselves, by their own internal evidence, as belonging to a large whole, and not as separate integers. We can hardly conceive the Catalogue in the second book, except as a fractional composition, and with reference to a series of approaching exploits; for, taken apart by itself, such a barren enumeration of names could have stimulated neither the fancy of the poet, nor the attention of the listeners. But the Homeric Catalogue had acquired a sort of canonical authority even in the time of Solôn, insomuch that he interpolated a line into it, or was accused of doing so, for the purpose of gaining a disputed point against the Megarians, who, on their side, set forth another version.[267] No such established reverence could have been felt for this document, unless there had existed for a long time prior to Peisistratus, the habit of regarding and listening to the Iliad as a continuous poem. And when the philosopher Xenophanês, contemporary with Peisistratus, noticed Homer as the universal teacher, and denounced him as an unworthy describer of the gods, he must have connected this great mental sway, not with a number of unconnected rhapsodies, but with an aggregate Iliad and Odyssey; probably with other poems, also, ascribed to the same author, such as the Cypria, Epigoni, and Thebaïs.

We find, it is true, references in various authors to portions of the Iliad, each by its own separate name, such as the Teichomachy, the Aristeia (preëminent exploits) of Diomedês, or Agamemnôn, the Doloneia, or Night-expedition (of Dolon as well as of Odysseus and Diomedês), etc., and hence, it has been concluded, that these portions originally existed as separate poems, before they were cemented together into an Iliad. But such references prove nothing to the point; for until the Iliad was divided by Aristarchus and his colleagues into a given number of books, or rhapsodies, designated by the series of letters in the alphabet, there was no method of calling attention to any particular portion of the poem except by special indication of its subject-matter.[268] Authors subsequent to Peisistratus, such as Herodotus and Plato, who unquestionably conceived the Iliad as a whole, cite the separate fractions of it by designations of this sort.

The foregoing remarks on the Wolfian hypothesis respecting the text of the Iliad, tend to separate two points which are by no means necessarily connected, though that hypothesis, as set forth by Wolf himself, by W. Müller, and by Lachmann, presents the two in conjunction. First, was the Iliad originally projected and composed by one author, and as one poem, or were the different parts composed separately and by unconnected authors, and subsequently strung together into an aggregate? Secondly, assuming that the internal evidences of the poem negative the former supposition, and drive us upon the latter, was the construction of the whole poem deferred, and did the parts exist only in their separate state, until a period so late as the reign of Peisistratus? It is obvious that these two questions are essentially separate, and that a man may believe the Iliad to have been put together out of preëxisting songs, without recognizing the age of Peisistratus as the period of its first compilation. Now, whatever may be the steps through which the poem passed to its ultimate integrity, there is sufficient reason for believing that they had been accomplished long before that period: the friends of Peisistratus found an Iliad already existing and already ancient in their time, even granting that the poem had not been originally born in a state of unity. Moreover, the Alexandrine critics, whose remarks are preserved in the Scholia, do not even notice the Peisistratic recension among the many manuscripts which they had before them: and Mr. Payne Knight justly infers from their silence that either they did not possess it, or it was in their eyes of no great authority;[269] which could never have been the case if it had been the prime originator of Homeric unity.

The line of argument, by which the advocates of Wolf's hypothesis negative the primitive unity of the poem, consists in exposing gaps, incongruities, contradictions, etc., between the separate parts. Now, if in spite of all these incoherences, standing mementos of an antecedent state of separation, the component poems were made to coalesce so intimately as to appear as if they had been one from the beginning, we can better understand the complete success of the proceeding and the universal prevalence of the illusion, by supposing such coalescence to have taken place at a very early period, during the productive days of epical genius, and before the growth of reading and criticism. The longer the aggregation of the separate poems was deferred, the harder it would be to obliterate in men's minds the previous state of separation, and to make them accept the new aggregate as an original unity. The bards or rhapsodes might have found comparatively little difficulty in thus piecing together distinct songs, during the ninth or eighth century before Christ; but it we suppose the process to be deferred until the latter half of the sixth century,—if we imagine that Solôn, with all his contemporaries and predecessors, knew nothing about any aggregate Iliad, but was accustomed to read and hear only those sixteen distinct epical pieces into which Lachmann would dissect the Iliad, each of the sixteen bearing a separate name of its own,—no compilation then for the first time made by the friends of Peisistratus could have effaced the established habit, and planted itself in the general convictions of Greece as the primitive Homeric production. Had the sixteen pieces remained disunited and individualized down to the time of Peisistratus, they would in all probability have continued so ever afterwards; nor could the extensive changes and transpositions which (according to Lachmann's theory) were required to melt them down into our present Iliad, have obtained at that late period universal acceptance. Assuming it to be true that such changes and transpositions did really take place, they must at least be referred to a period greatly earlier than Peisistratus or Solôn.

The whole tenor of the poems themselves confirms what is here remarked. There is nothing either in the Iliad or Odyssey which savors of *modernism*, applying that term to the age of Peisistratus; nothing which brings to our view the alterations, brought about by two centuries, in the Greek language, the coined money, the habits of writing and reading, the despotisms and republican governments, the close military array, the improved construction of ships, the Amphiktyonic convocations, the mutual frequentation of religious festivals, the Oriental and Egyptian veins of religion, etc., familiar to the latter epoch. These alterations Onomakritus and the other literary friends of Peisistratus, could hardly have failed to notice even without design, had they then for the first time undertaken the task of piecing together many self-existent epics into one large aggregate.[270] Everything in the two great Homeric poems, both in substance and in language, belongs to an age two or three centuries earlier than Peisistratus. Indeed, even the interpolations (or those passages which on the best grounds are pronounced to be such) betray no trace of the sixth century before Christ, and may well have been heard by Archilochus and Kallinus,—in some cases even by Arktinus and Hesiod,—as genuine Homeric matter. As far as the evidences on the case, as well internal as external, enable us to judge, we seem warranted in believing that the Iliad and Odyssey were recited substantially as they now stand, (always allowing for partial divergences of text, and interpolations,) in 776 B. C., our first trustworthy mark of Grecian time. And this ancient date,—let it be added,— as it is the best-authenticated fact, so it is also the most important attribute of the Homeric poems, considered in reference to Grecian history. For they thus afford us an insight into the ante-historical character of the Greeks,—enabling us to trace the subsequent forward march of the nation, and to seize instructive contrasts between their former and their later condition.

Rejecting, therefore, the idea of compilation by Peisistratus, and referring the present state of the Iliad and Odyssey to a period more than two centuries earlier, the question still remains, by what process, or through whose agency, they reached that state? Is each poem the work of one author, or of several? If the latter, do all the parts belong to the same age? What ground is there for believing, that any or all of these parts existed before, as separate poems, and have been accommodated to the place in which they now appear, by more or less systematic alteration?

The acute and valuable Prolegomena of Wolf, half a century ago, powerfully turned the attention of scholars to the necessity of considering the Iliad and Odyssey with reference to the age and society in which they arose, and to the material differences in this respect between Homer and more recent epic poets.[271] Since that time, an elaborate study has been bestowed upon the early manifestations of poetry (Sagen-poesie) among other nations; and the German critics especially, among whom this description of literatures has been most cultivated, have selected it as the only appropriate analogy for the Homeric poems. Such poetry, consisting for the most part of short, artless effusions, with little of deliberate or far-sighted combination, has been assumed by many critics as a fit standard to apply for measuring the capacities of the Homeric age; an age exclusively of speakers, singers, and hearers, not of readers or writers. In place of the unbounded admiration which was felt for Homer, not merely as a poet of detail, but as constructor of a long epic, at the time when Wolf wrote his Prolegomena, the tone of criticism passed to the opposite extreme, and attention was fixed entirely upon the defects in the arrangement of the Iliad and Odyssey. Whatever was to be found in them of symmetry or pervading system, was pronounced to be decidedly post-Homeric. Under such preconceived anticipations, Homer seems to have been generally studied in Germany, during the generation succeeding Wolf, the negative portion of whose theory was usually admitted, though as to the positive substitute,—what explanation was to be given of the history and present constitution of the Homeric poems,—there was by no means the like agreement. During the last ten years, however, a contrary tendency has manifested itself; the Wolfian theory has been reëxamined and shaken by Nitzsch, who, as well as O. Müller, Welcker, and other scholars, have revived the idea of original Homeric unity, under certain modifications. The change in Goethe's opinion, coincident with this new direction, is recorded in one of his latest works.[272] On the other hand, the original opinion of Wolf has also been reproduced within the last five years, and fortified with several new observations on the text of the Iliad, by Lachmann.

The point is thus still under controversy among able scholars, and is probably destined to remain so. For, in truth, our means of knowledge are so limited, that no man can produce arguments sufficiently cogent to contend against opposing preconceptions; and it creates a painful sentiment of diffidence when we read the expressions of equal and absolute persuasion with which the two opposite conclusions have both been advanced.[273] We have nothing to teach us the history of these poems except the poems themselves. Not only do we possess no collateral information respecting them or their authors, but we have no one to describe to us the people or the age in which they originated; our knowledge respecting contemporary Homeric society, is collected exclusively from the Homeric compositions themselves. We are ignorant whether any other, or what other, poems preceded them, or divided with them the public favor; nor have we anything better than conjecture to determine either the circumstances under which they were brought before the hearers, or the conditions which a bard of that day was required to satisfy. On all these points, moreover, the age of Thucydidês[274] and Plato seems to have been no better informed than we are, except in so far as they could profit by the analogies of the cyclic and other epic poems, which would doubtless in many cases have afforded valuable aid.

Nevertheless, no classical scholar can be easy without *some* opinion respecting the authorship of these immortal poems. And the more defective the evidence we possess, the more essential is it that all that evidence should be marshalled in the clearest order, and its bearing upon the points in controversy distinctly understood beforehand. Both these conditions seem to have been often neglected, throughout the long-continued Homeric discussion.

To illustrate the first point: Since two poems are comprehended in the problem to be solved, the natural process would be, first, to study the easier of the two, and then to apply the conclusions thence deduced as a means of explaining the other. Now, the Odyssey, looking at its aggregate character, is incomparably more easy to comprehend than the Iliad. Yet most Homeric critics apply the microscope at once, and in the first instance, to the Iliad.

To illustrate the second point: What evidence is sufficient to negative the supposition that the Iliad or the Odyssey is a poem originally and intentionally one? Not simply particular gaps and contradictions, though they be even gross and numerous; but the preponderance of these proofs of mere unprepared coalescence over the other proofs of designed adaptation scattered throughout the whole poem. For the poet (or the coöperating poets, if more than one) may have intended to compose an harmonious whole, but may have realized their intention incompletely, and left partial faults; or, perhaps, the contradictory lines may have crept in through a corrupt text. A survey of the whole poem is necessary to determine the question; and this necessity, too, has not always been attended to.

If it had happened that the Odyssey had been preserved to us alone, without the Iliad, I think the dispute respecting Homeric unity would never have been raised. For the former is, in my judgment, pervaded almost from beginning to end by marks of designed adaptation; and the special faults which Wolf, W. Müller, and B. Thiersch,[275] have singled out for the purpose of disproving such unity of intention, are so few, and of so little importance, that they would have been universally regarded as mere instances of haste or unskilfulness on the part of the poet, had they not been seconded by the far more powerful battery opened against the Iliad. These critics, having laid down their general presumptions against the antiquity of the long epopee, illustrate their principles by exposing the many flaws and fissures in the Iliad, and then think it sufficient if they can show a few similar defects in the Odyssey,—as if the breaking up of Homeric unity in the former naturally entailed a similar necessity with regard to the latter; and their method of proceeding, contrary to the rule above laid down, puts the more difficult problem in the foreground, as a means of solution for the easier. We can hardly wonder, however, that they have applied their observations in the first instance to the Iliad, because it is in every man's esteem the more marked, striking, and impressive poem of the two,—and the character of Homer is more intimately identified with it than with the Odyssey. This may serve as an explanation of the course pursued; but be the case as it may in respect to comparative poetical merit, it is not the less true, that, as an aggregate, the Odyssey is more simple and easily understood, and, therefore, ought to come first in the order of analysis.

Now, looking at the Odyssey by itself, the proofs of an unity of design seem unequivocal and everywhere to be found. A premeditated structure, and a concentration of interest upon one prime hero, under well-defined circumstances, may be traced from the first book to the twenty-third. Odysseus is always either directly or indirectly kept before the reader, as a warrior returning from the fulness of glory at Troy, exposed to manifold and protracted calamities during his return home, on which his whole soul is so bent that he refuses even the immortality offered by Calypsô;—a victim, moreover, even after his return, to mingled injury and insult from the suitors, who have long been plundering his property, and dishonoring his house; but at length obtaining, by valor and cunning united, a signal revenge, which restores him to all that he had lost. All the persons and all the events in the poem are subsidiary to this main plot: and the divine agency, necessary to satisfy the feeling of the Homeric man, is put forth by Poseidôn and Athênê, in both cases from dispositions directly bearing upon Odysseus. To appreciate the unity of the Odyssey, we have only to read the objections taken against that of the Iliad,—especially in regard to the long withdrawal of Achilles, not only from the scene, but from the memory,—together with the independent prominence of Ajax, Diomêdês, and other heroes. How far we are entitled from hence to infer the want of premeditated unity in the Iliad, will be presently considered; but it is certain that the constitution of the Odyssey, in this respect, everywhere demonstrates the presence of such unity. Whatever may be the interest attached to Penelopê, Telemachus, or Eumæus, we never disconnect them from their association with Odysseus. The present is not the place for collecting the many marks of artistical structure dispersed throughout this poem; but it may be worth while to remark, that the final catastrophe realized in the twenty-second book,—the slaughter of the suitors in the very house which they were profaning,—is distinctly and prominently marked out in the first and second books, promised by Teiresias in the eleventh, by Athênê in the thirteenth, and by Helen in the fifteenth, and gradually matured by a series of suitable preliminaries, throughout the eight books preceding its occurrence.[276] Indeed, what is principally evident, and what has been often noticed, in the Odyssey, is, the equable flow both of the narrative and the events; the absence of that rise and fall of interest which is sufficiently conspicuous in the Iliad.

To set against these evidences of unity, there ought, at least, to be some strong cases produced of occasional incoherence or contradiction. But it is remarkable how little of such counter-evidence is to be found, although the arguments of Wolf, W. Müller, and B. Thiersch stand so much in need of it. They have discovered only one instance of undeniable inconsistency in the parts,—the number of days occupied by the absence of Telemachus at Pylus and Sparta. That young prince, though represented as in great haste to depart, and refusing pressing invitations to prolong his stay, must, nevertheless, be supposed to have continued for thirty days the guest of Menelaus, in order to bring his proceedings into chronological harmony with those of Odysseus, and to explain the first meeting of father and son in the swine-fold of Eumæus. Here is undoubtedly an inaccuracy, (so Nitzsch[277] treats it, and I think justly) on the part of the poet, who did not anticipate, and did not experience in ancient times, so strict a scrutiny; an inaccuracy certainly not at all wonderful; the matter of real wonder is, that it stands almost alone, and that there are no others in the poem.

Now, this is one of the main points on which W. Müller and B. Thiersch rest their theory,—explaining the chronological confusion by supposing that the journey of Telemachus to Pylus and Sparta, constituted the subject of an epic originally separate (comprising the first four books and a portion of the

95

fifteenth), and incorporated at second-hand with the remaining poem. And they conceive this view to be farther confirmed by the double assembly of the gods, (at the beginning of the first book as well as of the fifth,) which they treat as an awkward repetition, such as could not have formed part of the primary scheme of any epic poet. But here they only escape a small difficulty by running into another and a greater. For it is impossible to comprehend how the first four books and part of the fifteenth can ever have constituted a distinct epic; since the adventures of Telemachus have no satisfactory termination, except at the point of confluence with those of his father, when the unexpected meeting and recognition takes place under the roof of Eumæus,—nor can any epic poem ever have described that meeting and recognition without giving some account how Odysseus came thither. Moreover, the first two books of the Odyssey distinctly lay the ground, and carry expectation forward, to the final catastrophe of the poem,—treating Telemachus as a subordinate person, and his expedition as merely provisional towards an ulterior result. Nor can I agree with W. Müller, that the real Odyssey might well be supposed to begin with the fifth book. On the contrary, the exhibition of the suitors and the Ithakesian agora, presented to us in the second book, is absolutely essential to the full comprehension of the books subsequent to the thirteenth. The suitors are far too important personages in the poem to allow of their being first introduced in so informal a manner as we read in the sixteenth book: indeed, the passing allusions of Athênê (xiii. 310, 375) and Eumæus (xiv. 41, 81) to the suitors, presuppose cognizance of them on the part of the hearer.

Lastly, the twofold discussion of the gods, at the beginning of the first and fifth books, and the double interference of Athênê, far from being a needless repetition, may be shown to suit perfectly both the genuine epical conditions and the unity of the poem.[278] For although the final consummation, and the organization of measures against the suitors, was to be accomplished by Odysseus and Telemachus jointly, yet the march and adventures of the two, until the moment of their meeting in the dwelling of Eumæus, were essentially distinct. But, according to the religious ideas of the old epic, the presiding direction of Athênê was necessary for the safety and success of both of them. Her first interference arouses and inspires the son, her second produces the liberation of the father,—constituting a point of union and common origination for two lines of adventures, in both of which she takes earnest interest, but which are necessarily for a time kept apart in order to coincide at the proper moment.

It will thus appear that the twice-repeated agora of the gods in the Odyssey, bringing home, as it does to one and the same divine agent, that double start which is essential to the scheme of the poem, consists better with the supposition of premeditated unity than with that of distinct self-existent parts. And, assuredly, the manner in which Telemachus and Odysseus, both by different roads, are brought into meeting and conjunction at the dwelling of Eumæus, is something not only contrived, but very skilfully contrived. It is needless to advert to the highly interesting character of Eumæus, rendered available as a rallying-point, though in different ways, both to the father and the son, over and above the sympathy which he himself inspires.

If the Odyssey be not an original unity, of what self-existent parts can we imagine it to have consisted? To this question it is difficult to imagine a satisfactory reply: for the supposition that Telemachus and his adventures may once have formed the subject of a separate epos, apart from Odysseus, appears inconsistent with the whole character of that youth as it stands in the poem, and with the events in which he is made to take part. We could better imagine the distribution of the adventures of Odysseus himself into two parts, —one containing his wanderings and return, the other handling his ill-treatment by the suitors, and his final triumph. But though either of these two subjects might have been adequate to furnish out a separate poem, it is nevertheless certain that, as they are presented in the Odyssey, the former cannot be divorced from the latter. The simple return of Odysseus, as it now stands in the poem, could satisfy no one as a final close, so long as the suitors remain in possession of his house, and forbid his reunion with his wife. Any poem which treated his wanderings and return separately, must have represented his reunion with Penelopê and restoration to his house, as following naturally upon his arrival in Ithaka,—thus taking little or no notice of the suitors. But this would be a capital mutilation of the actual epical narrative, which considers the suitors at home as an essential portion of the destiny of the much-suffering hero, not less than his shipwrecks and trials at sea. His return (separately taken) is foredoomed, according to the curse of Polyphemus, executed by Poseidôn, to be long deferred, miserable, solitary, and ending with destruction in his house to greet him;[279] and the ground is thus laid, in the very recital of his wanderings, for a new series of events which are to happen to him after his arrival in Ithaka. There is no tenable halting-place between the departure of Odysseus from Troy, and the final restoration to his house and his wife. The distance between these two events may, indeed, be widened, by accumulating new distresses and impediments, but any separate portion of it cannot be otherwise treated than as a fraction of the whole. The beginning and the end are here the data in respect to epical genesis, though the intermediate events admit of being conceived as variables, more or less numerous: so that the conception of the whole may be said without impropriety both to precede and to govern that of the constituent parts.

The general result of a study of the Odyssey may be set down as follows: 1. The poem, as it now stands, exhibits unequivocally adaptation of parts and continuity of structure, whether by one or by several consentient hands: it may, perhaps, be a secondary formation, out of a preëxisting Odyssey of smaller dimensions; but, if so, the parts of the smaller whole must have been so far recast as to make them suitable members of the larger, and are noway recognizable by us. 2. The subject-matter of the poem not only does not favor, but goes far to exclude, the possibility of the Wolfian hypothesis. Its events cannot be so arranged as to have composed several antecedent substantive epics, afterwards put together into the present aggregate. Its authors cannot have been mere compilers of preëxisting materials, such as Peisistratus and his friends: they must have been poets, competent to work such matter as they found, into a new and enlarged design of their own. Nor can the age in which this long poem, of so many thousand lines, was turned out as a continuous aggregate, be separated from the ancient, productive, inspired age of Grecian epic.

Arriving at such conclusions from the internal evidence of the Odyssey, [280] we can apply them by analogy to the Iliad. We learn something respecting the character and capacities of that early age which has left no other mementos except these two poems. Long continuous epics (it is observed by those who support the views of Wolf), with an artistical structure, are inconsistent with the capacities of a rude and non-writing age. Such epics (we may reply) are *not inconsistent* with the early age of the Greeks, and the Odyssey is a proof of it; for in that poem the integration of the whole, and the composition of the parts, must have been simultaneous. The analogy of the Odyssey enables us to rebut that preconception under which many ingenious critics sit down to the study of the Iliad, and which induces them to explain all the incoherences of the latter by breaking it up into smaller unities, as if short epics were the only manifestation of poetical power which the age admitted. There ought to be no reluctance in admitting a presiding scheme and premeditated unity of parts, in so far as the parts themselves point to such a conclusion.

That the Iliad is not so essentially one piece as the Odyssey, every man agrees. It includes a much greater multiplicity of events, and what is yet more important, a greater multiplicity of prominent personages: the very indefinite title which it bears, as contrasted with the speciality of the name, *Odyssey*, marks the difference at once. The parts stand out more conspicuously from the whole, and admit more readily of being felt and appreciated in detached recitation. We may also add, that it is of more unequal execution than the Odyssey,—often rising to a far higher pitch of grandeur, but also, occasionally, tamer: the story does not move on continuously; incidents occur without plausible motive, nor can we shut our eyes to evidences of incoherence and contradiction.

To a certain extent, the Iliad is open to all these remarks, though Wolf and William Müller, and above all Lachmann, exaggerate the case in degree. And from hence has been deduced the hypothesis which treats the parts in their original state as separate integers, independent of, and unconnected with, each other, and forced into unity only by the afterthought of a subsequent age; or sometimes, not even themselves as integers, but as aggregates grouped together out of fragments still smaller,—short epics formed by the coalescence of still shorter songs. Now there is some plausibility in these reasonings, so long as the discrepancies are looked upon as the whole of the case. But in point of fact they are not the whole of the case: for it is not less true, that there are large portions of the Iliad which present positive and undeniable evidences of coherence as antecedent and consequent, though we are occasionally perplexed by inconsistencies of detail. To deal with these latter, is a portion of the duties of the critic. But he is not to treat the Iliad as if inconsistency prevailed everywhere throughout its parts; for coherence of parts—symmetrical antecedence and consequence—is discernible throughout the larger half of the poem.

Now the Wolfian theory explains the gaps and contradictions throughout the narrative, but it explains nothing else. If (as Lachmann thinks) the Iliad originally consisted of sixteen songs, or little substantive epics, (Lachmann's sixteen songs cover the space only as far as the 22d book, or the death of Hector, and two more songs would have to be admitted for the 23d and 24th books),—not only composed by different authors, but by each[281] without any view to conjunction with the rest,—we have then no right to expect any intrinsic continuity between them; and all that continuity which we now find must be of extraneous origin. Where are we to look for the origin? Lachmann follows Wolf, in ascribing the whole constructive process to Peisistratus and his associates, at a period when the creative epical faculty is admitted to have died out. But upon this supposition, Peisistratus (or his associates) must have done much more than omit, transpose, and interpolate, here and there; he must have gone far to rewrite the whole poem. A great poet might have recast preëxisting separate songs into one comprehensive whole, but no mere arrangers or compilers would be competent to do so: and we are thus left without any means of accounting for that degree of continuity and consistence which runs through so large a portion of the Iliad, though not through the whole. The idea that the poem, as we read it, grew out of atoms not originally designed for the places which they now occupy, involves us in new and inextricable difficulties, when we seek to elucidate either the mode of coalescence or the degree of existing unity.[282]

Admitting then premeditated adaptation of parts to a certain extent as essential to the Iliad, we may yet inquire, whether it was produced all at once, or gradually enlarged,—whether by one author, or by several; and, if the parts be of different age, which is the primitive kernel, and which are the additions.

Welcker, Lange, and Nitzsch[283] treat the Homeric poems as representing a second step in advance, in the progress of popular poetry. First, comes the age of short narrative songs; next, when these have become numerous, there arise constructive minds, who recast and blend together many of them into a larger aggregate, conceived upon some scheme of their own. The age of the epos is followed by that of the epopee,—short, spontaneous effusions preparing the way, and furnishing materials, for the architectonic genius of the poet. It is farther presumed by the above-mentioned authors, that the pre-Homeric epic included a great abundance of such smaller songs,—a fact which admits of no proof, but which seems countenanced by some passages in Homer, and is in itself no way improbable. But the transition from such songs, assuming them to be ever so numerous, to a combined and continuous poem, forms an epoch in the intellectual history of the nation, implying mental qualities of a higher order than those upon which the songs themselves depend. Nor is it to be imagined that the materials pass unaltered from their first state of isolation into their second state of combination. They must of necessity be recast, and undergo an adapting process, in which the genius of the organizing poet consists; nor can we hope, by simply knowing them as they exist in the second stage, ever to divine how they stood in the first. Such, in my judgment, is the right conception of the Homeric epoch,—an organizing poetical mind, still preserving that freshness of observation and vivacity of details which constitutes the charm of the ballad.

Nothing is gained by studying the Iliad as a congeries of fragments once independent of each other: no portion of the poem can be shown to have ever been so, and the supposition introduces difficulties greater than those which it removes. But it is not necessary to affirm that the whole poem as we now read it, belonged to the original and preconceived plan.[284] In this respect, the Iliad produces, upon my mind, an impression totally different from the Odyssey. In the latter poem, the characters and incidents are fewer, and the whole plot appears of one projection, from the beginning down to the death of the suitors: none of the parts look as if they had been composed separately, and inserted by way of addition into a preëxisting smaller poem. But the Iliad, on the contrary, presents the appearance of a house built upon a plan comparatively narrow, and subsequently enlarged by successive additions. The first book, together with the eighth, and the books from the eleventh to the twenty-second, inclusive, seem to form the primary organization of the poem, then properly an Achillêis: the twenty-third and twenty-fourth books are, perhaps, additions at the tail of this primitive poem, which still leave it nothing more than an enlarged Achillêis. But the books from the second to the seventh, inclusive, together with the tenth, are of a wider and more comprehensive character, and convert the poem from an Achillêis into an Iliad.[285] The primitive frontispiece, inscribed with the anger of Achilles, and its direct consequences, yet remains, after it has ceased to be coextensive with the poem. The parts added, however, are not necessarily inferior in merit to the original poem: so far is this from being the case, that amongst them are comprehended some of the noblest efforts of the Grecian epic. Nor are they more recent in date than the original; strictly speaking, they must be a little more recent, but they belong to the same generation and state of society as the primitive Achillêis. These qualifications are necessary to keep apart different questions, which, in discussions of Homeric criticism, are but too often confounded.

If we take those portions of the poem which I imagine to have constituted the original Achillêis, it will be found that the sequence of events contained in them is more rapid, more unbroken, and more intimately knit together in the way of cause and effect, than in the other books. Heyne and Lachmann, indeed, with other objecting critics, complains of the action in them as being too much crowded and hurried, since one day lasts from the beginning of the eleventh book to the middle of the eighteenth, without any sensible halt in the march throughout so large a portion of the journey. Lachmann, likewise, admits that those separate songs, into which he imagines that the whole Iliad may be dissected, cannot be severed with the same sharpness, in the books subsequent to the eleventh, as in those before it.[286] There is only one real halting-place from the eleventh book to the twenty-second,—the death of Patroclus; and this can never be conceived as the end of a separate poem,[287] though it is a capital step in the development of the Achillêis, and brings about that entire revolution in the temper of Achilles which was essential for the purpose of the poet. It would be a mistake to imagine that there ever could have existed a separate poem called Patrocleia, though a part of the Iliad was designated by that name. For Patroclus has no substantive position: he is the attached friend and second of Achilles, but nothing else,—standing to the latter in a relation of dependence resembling that of Telemachus to Odysseus. And the way in which Patroclus is dealt with in the Iliad, is, (in my judgment,) the most dexterous and artistical contrivance in the poem,—that which approaches nearest to the neat tissue of the Odyssey.[288]

The great and capital misfortune which prostrates the strength of the Greeks, and renders them incapable of defending themselves without Achilles, is the disablement, by wounds, of Agamemnôn, Diomêdês, and Odysseus; so that the defence of the wall and of the ships is left only to heroes of the second magnitude (Ajax alone excepted), such as Idomeneus, Leonteus, Polypœtês, Merionês, Menelaus, etc. Now, it is remarkable that all these three first-rate chiefs are in full force at the beginning of the eleventh book: all three are wounded in the battle which that book describes, and at the commencement of which Agamemnôn is full of spirits and courage.

Nothing can be more striking than the manner in which Homer concentrates our attention in the first book upon Achilles as the hero, his quarrel with Agamemnôn, and the calamities to the Greeks which are held out as about to ensue from it, through the intercession of Thetis with Zeus. But the incidents dwelt upon from the beginning of the second book down to the combat between Hector and Ajax in the seventh, animated and interesting as they are, do nothing to realize this promise. They are a splendid picture of the Trojan war generally, and eminently suitable to that larger title under which the poem has been immortalized,—but the consequences of the anger of Achilles do not appear until the eighth book. The tenth book, or Doloneia, is also a portion of the Iliad, but not of the Achillêis: while the ninth book appears to me a subsequent addition, nowise harmonizing with that main stream of the Achillêis which flows from the eleventh book to the twenty-second. The eighth book ought to be read in immediate connection with the eleventh, in order to see the structure of what seems the primitive Achillêis; for there are several passages in the eleventh and the following books, which prove that the poet who composed them could not have had present to his mind the main event of the ninth book,—the outpouring of profound humiliation by the Greeks, and from Agamemnôn, especially, before Achilles, coupled with formal offers to restore Brisêis, and pay the amplest compensation for past wrong.[289] The words of Achilles (not less than those of Patroclus and Nestor) in the eleventh and in the following books, plainly imply that the humiliation of the Greeks before him, for which he thirsts, is as yet future and contingent; that no plenary apology has yet been tendered, nor any offer made of restoring Brisêis; while both Nestor and Patroclus, with all their wish to induce him to take arms, never take notice of the offered atonement and restitution, but view him as one whose ground for quarrel stands still the same as it did at the beginning. Moreover, if we look at the first book,—the opening of the Achillêis,—we shall see that this prostration of Agamemnôn and the chief Grecian heroes before Achilles, would really be the termination of the whole poem; for Achilles asks nothing more from Thetis, nor Thetis anything more from Zeus, than that Agamemnôn and the Greeks may be brought to know the wrong they have done to their capital warrior, and humbled in the dust in expiation of it. We may add, that the abject terror in which Agamemnôn appears in the ninth book, when he sends the supplicatory message to Achilles, as it is not adequately accounted for by the degree of calamity which the Greeks have experienced in the preceding (eighth) book, so it is inconsistent with the gallantry and high spirit with which he shines at the beginning of the eleventh.[290] The situation of the Greeks only becomes desperate when the three great chiefs, Agamemnôn, Odysseus, and Diomêdês, are disabled by wounds;[291] this is the irreparable calamity which works upon Patroclus, and through him upon Achilles. The ninth book, as it now stands, seems to me an addition, by a different hand, to the original Achillêis, framed so as both to forestall and to spoil the nineteenth book, which is the real reconciliation of the two inimical heroes: I will venture to add, that it carries the pride and egotism of Achilles beyond even the largest exigences of insulted honor, and is shocking to that sentiment of Nemesis which was so deeply seated in the Grecian mind. We forgive any excess of fury against the Trojans and Hector, after the death of Patroclus; but that he should remain unmoved by restitution, by abject supplications, and by the richest atoning presents, tendered from the Greeks, indicates an implacability such as neither the first book, nor the books between the eleventh and seventeenth, convey.

It is with the Grecian agora, in the beginning of the second book, that the Iliad (as distinguished from the Achillêis) commences,—continued through the Catalogue, the muster of the two armies, the single combat between Menelaus and Paris, the renewed promiscuous battle caused by the arrow of Pandarus, the (Epipôlêsis, or) personal circuit of Agamemnôn round the army, the Aristeia, or brilliant exploits of Diomêdês, the visit of Hector to Troy for the purposes of sacrifice, his interview with Andromachê, and his combat with Ajax,—down to the seventh book. All these are beautiful poetry, presenting to us the general Trojan war, and its conspicuous individuals under different points of view, but leaving no room in the reader's mind for the thought of Achilles. Now, the difficulty for an enlarging poet, was, to pass from the Achillêis in the first book, to the Iliad in the second, and it will accordingly be found that here is an awkwardness in the structure of the poem, which counsel on the poet's behalf (ancient or modern) do not satisfactorily explain.

In the first book, Zeus has promised Thetis, that he will punish the Greeks for the wrong done to Achilles: in the beginning of the second book, he deliberates how he shall fulfil the promise, and sends down for that purpose "mischievous Oneirus" (the Dream-god) to visit Agamemnôn in his sleep, to assure him that the gods have now with one accord consented to put Troy into his hands, and to exhort him forthwith to the assembling of his army for the attack. The ancient commentators were here perplexed by the circumstance that Zeus puts a falsehood into the mouth of Oneirus. But there seems no more difficulty in explaining this, than in the narrative of the book of 1 Kings (chap. xxii. 20), where Jehovah is mentioned to have put a lying spirit into the mouth of Ahab's prophets,—the real awkwardness is, that Oneirus and his falsehood produce no effect. For in the first place, Agamemnôn takes a step very different from that which his dream recommends,—and in the next place, when the Grecian army is at length armed and goes forth to battle, it does not experience defeat, (which would be the case if the exhortation of Oneirus really proved mischievous,) but carries on a successful day's battle, chiefly through the heroism of Diomêdês. Instead of arming the Greeks forthwith, Agamemnôn convokes first a council of chiefs, and next an agora of the host. And though himself in a temper of mind highly elate with the deceitful assurances of Oneirus, he deliberately assumes the language of despair in addressing the troops, having previously prepared Nestor and Odysseus for his doing so,—merely in order to try the courage of the men, and with formal instructions, given to these two other chiefs, that they are to speak in opposition to him. Now this intervention of Zeus and Oneirus, eminently unsatisfactory when coupled with the incidents which now follow it, and making Zeus appear, but only appear, to realize his promise of honoring Achilles as well as of hurting the Greeks,—forms exactly the point of junction between the Achillêis and the Iliad.[292]

The freak which Agamemnôn plays off upon the temper of his army, though in itself childish, serves a sufficient purpose, not only because it provides a special matter of interest to be submitted to the Greeks, but also because it calls forth the splendid description, so teeming with vivacious detail, of the sudden breaking up of the assembly after Agamemnôn's harangue, and of the decisive interference of Odysseus to bring the men back, as well as to put down Thersitês. This picture of the Greeks in agora, bringing out the two chief speaking and counselling heroes, was so important a part of the general Trojan war, that the poet has permitted himself to introduce it by assuming an inexplicable folly on the part of Agamemnôn; just as he has ushered in another fine scene in the third book,—the Teichoskopy, or conversation, between Priam and Helen on the walls of Troy,—by admitting the supposition that the old king, in the tenth year of the war, did not know the persons of Agamemnôn and the other Grecian chiefs. This may serve as an explanation of the delusion practised by Agamemnôn towards his assembled host; but it does not at all explain the tame and empty intervention of Oneirus. [293]

If the initial incident of the second book, whereby we pass out of the Achillêis into the Iliad, is awkward, so also the final incident of the seventh book, immediately before we come back into the Achillêis, is not less unsatisfactory,—I mean, the construction of the wall and ditch round the Greek camp. As the poem now stands, no plausible reason is assigned why this should be done. Nestor proposes it without any constraining necessity: for the Greeks are in a career of victory, and the Trojans are making offers of compromise which imply conscious weakness,—while Diomêdês is so confident of the approaching ruin of Troy, that he dissuades his comrades from receiving even Helen herself, if the surrender should be tendered. "Many Greeks have been slain," it is true,[294] as Nestor observes; but an equal or greater number of Trojans have been slain, and all the Grecian heroes are yet in full force: the absence of Achilles is not even adverted to.

Now this account of the building of the fortification seems to be an after-thought, arising out of the enlargement of the poem beyond its original scheme. The original Achillêis, passing at once from the first to the eighth, [295] and from thence to the eleventh book, might well assume the fortification,—and talk of it as a thing existing, without adducing any special reason why it was erected. The hearer would naturally comprehend and follow the existence of a ditch and wall round the ships, as a matter of course, provided there was nothing in the previous narrative to make him believe that the Greeks had originally been without these bulwarks. And since the Achillêis, immediately after the promise of Zeus to Thetis, at the close of the first book, went on to describe the fulfilment of that promise and the ensuing disasters of the Greeks, there was nothing to surprise any one in hearing that their camp was fortified. But the case was altered when the first and the eighth books were parted asunder, in order to make room for descriptions of temporary success and glory on the part of the besieging army. The brilliant scenes sketched in the books, from the second to the seventh, mention no fortification, and even imply its nonexistence; yet, since notice of it occurs amidst the first description of Grecian disasters in the eighth book, the hearer, who had the earlier books present to his memory, might be surprised to find a fortification mentioned immediately afterwards, unless the construction of it were specially announced to have intervened. But it will at once appear, that there was some difficulty in finding a good reason why the Greeks should begin to fortify at this juncture, and that the poet who discovered the gap might not be enabled to fill it up with success. As the Greeks have got on, up to this moment, without the wall, and as we have heard nothing but tales of their success, why should they now think farther laborious precautions for security necessary? We will not ask, why the Trojans should stand quietly by and permit a wall to be built, since the truce was concluded expressly for burying the dead.[296]

The tenth book, or Doloneia, was considered by some of the ancient scholiasts,[297] and has been confidently set forth by the modern Wolfian critics, as originally a separate poem, inserted by Peisistratus into the Iliad. How it can ever have been a separate poem, I do not understand. It is framed with great specialty for the antecedent circumstances under which it occurs, and would suit for no other place; though capable of being separately recited, inasmuch as it has a definite beginning and end, like the story of Nisus and Euryalus in the Æneid. But while distinctly presupposing and resting upon the incidents in the eighth book, and in line 88 of the ninth, (probably, the appointment of sentinels on the part of the Greeks, as well of the Trojans, formed the close of the battle described in the eighth book,) it has not the slightest bearing upon the events of the eleventh or the following books: it goes to make up the general picture of the Trojan war, but lies quite apart from the Achillêis. And this is one mark of a portion subsequently inserted,— that, though fitted on to the parts which precede, it has no influence on those which follow.

If the proceedings of the combatants on the plain of Troy, between the first and the eighth book, have no reference either to Achilles, or to an Achillêis, we find Zeus in Olympus still more completely putting that hero out of the question, at the beginning of the fourth book. He is in this last-mentioned passage the Zeus of the Iliad, not of the Achillêis. Forgetful of his promise to Thetis, in the first book, he discusses nothing but the question of continuance or termination of the war, and manifests anxiety only for the salvation of Troy, in opposition to the miso-Trojan goddesses, who prevent him from giving effect to the victory of Menelaus over Paris, and the stipulated restitution of Helen,—in which case, of course, the wrong offered to Achilles would remain unexpiated. An attentive comparison will render it evident that the poet who composed the discussion among the gods, at the beginning of the fourth book, has not been careful to put himself in harmony either with the Zeus of the first book, or with the Zeus of the eighth.

So soon as we enter upon the eleventh book, the march of the poem becomes quite different. We are then in a series of events, each paving the way for that which follows, and all conducing to the result promised in the first book,—the reappearance of Achilles, as the only means of saving the Greeks from ruin,—preceded by ample atonement,[298] and followed by the maximum both of glory and revenge. The intermediate career of Patroclus introduces new elements, which, however, are admirably woven into the scheme of the poem, as disclosed in the first book. I shall not deny that there are perplexities in the detail of events, as described in the battles at the Grecian wall, and before the ships, from the eleventh to the sixteenth books, but they appear only cases of partial confusion, such as may be reasonably ascribed to imperfections of text: the main sequence remains coherent and intelligible. We find no considerable events which could be left out without breaking the thread, nor any incongruity between one considerable event and another. There is nothing between the eleventh and twenty-second books, which is at all comparable to the incongruity between the Zeus of the fourth book and the Zeus of the first and eighth. It may, perhaps, be true, that the shield of Achilles is a superadded amplification of that which was originally announced in general terms,—because the poet, from the eleventh to the twenty-second books, has observed such good economy of his materials, that he is hardly likely to have introduced one particular description of such disproportionate length, and having so little connection with the series of events. But I see no reason for believing that it is an addition materially later than the rest of the poem.

It must be confessed, that the supposition here advanced, in reference to the structure of the Iliad, is not altogether free from difficulties, because the parts constituting the original Achillêis[299] have been more or less altered or interpolated, to suit the additions made to it, particularly in the eighth book. But it presents fewer difficulties than any other supposition, and it is the only means, so far as I know, of explaining the difference between one part of the Iliad and another; both the continuity of structure, and the conformity to the opening promise, which are manifest when we read the books in the order i. viii. xi. to xxii, as contrasted with the absence of these two qualities in books ii. to vii. ix. and x. An entire organization, preconceived from the beginning, would not be likely to produce any such disparity, nor is any such visible in the Odyssey;[300] still less would the result be explained by supposing integers originally separate, and brought together without any designed organization. And it is between these three suppositions that our choice has to be made. A scheme, and a large scheme too, must unquestionably be admitted as the basis of any sufficient hypothesis. But the Achillêis would have been a long poem, half the length of the present Iliad, and probably not less compact in its structure than the Odyssey. Moreover, being parted off only by an imaginary line from the boundless range of the Trojan war, it would admit of enlargement more easily, and with greater relish to hearers, than the adventures of one single hero; while the expansion would naturally take place by adding new Grecian victory,—since the original poem arrived at the exaltation of Achilles only through a painful series of Grecian disasters. That the poem under these circumstances should have received additions, is no very violent hypothesis: in fact, when we recollect that the integrity both of the Achillêis and of the Odyssey was neither guarded by printing nor writing, we shall perhaps think it less wonderful that the former was enlarged,[301] than that the latter was not. Any relaxation of the laws of epical unity is a small price to pay for that splendid poetry, of which we find so much between the first and the eighth books of our Iliad.

The question respecting unity of authorship is different, and more difficult to determine, than that respecting consistency of parts, and sequence in the narrative. A poem conceived on a comparatively narrow scale may be enlarged afterwards by its original author, with greater or less coherence and success: the Faust of Goethe affords an example even in our own generation. On the other hand, a systematic poem may well have been conceived and executed by prearranged concert between several poets; among whom probably one will be the governing mind, though the rest may be effective, and perhaps equally effective, in respect to execution of the parts. And the age of the early Grecian epic was favorable to such fraternization of poets, of which the Gens called Homerids probably exhibited many specimens. In the recital or singing of a long unwritten poem, many bards must have conspired together, and in the earliest times the composer and the singer were one and the same person.[302] Now the individuals comprised in the Homerid Gens, though doubtless very different among themselves in respect of mental capacity, were yet homogeneous in respect of training, means of observation and instruction, social experience, religious feelings and theories, etc., to a degree much greater than individuals in modern times. Fallible as our inferences are on this point, where we have only internal evidence to guide us, without any contemporary points of comparison, or any species of collateral information respecting the age, the society, the poets, the hearers, or the language,—we must nevertheless, in the present case, take coherence of structure, together with consistency in the tone of thought, feeling, language, customs, etc., as presumptions of one author; and the contrary as presumptions of severalty; allowing, as well as we can, for that inequality of excellence which the same author may at different times present.

Now, the case made out against single-headed authorship of the Odyssey, appears to me very weak; and those who dispute it, are guided more by their *à priori* rejection of ancient epical unity, than by any positive evidence which the poem itself affords. It is otherwise with regard to the Iliad. Whatever presumptions a disjointed structure, several apparent inconsistencies of parts, and large excrescence of actual matter beyond the opening promise, can sanction,—may reasonably be indulged against the supposition that this poem all proceeds from a single author. There is a difference of opinion on the subject among the best critics, which is, probably, not destined to be adjusted, since so much depends partly upon critical feeling, partly upon the general reasonings, in respect to ancient epical unity, with which a man sits down to the study. For the champions of unity, such as Mr. Payne Knight, are very ready to strike out numerous and often considerable passages as interpolations, thus meeting the objections raised against unity of authorship, on the ground of special inconsistencies. Hermann and Boeckh, though not going the length of Lachmann in maintaining the original theory of Wolf, agree with the latter in recognizing diversity of authors in the poem, to an extent overpassing the limit of what can fairly be called interpolation. Payne Knight and Nitzsch are equally persuaded of the contrary. Here, then, is a decided contradiction among critics, all of whom have minutely studied the poems since the Wolfian question was raised. And it is such critics alone who can be said to constitute authority; for the cursory reader, who dwells upon the parts simply long enough to relish their poetical beauty, is struck only by that general sameness of coloring which Wolf himself admits to pervade the poem.[303]

Having already intimated that, in my judgment, no theory of the structure of the poem is admissible which does not admit an original and preconcerted Achillêis,—a stream which begins at the first book and ends with the death of Hector, in the twenty-second, although the higher parts of it now remain only in the condition of two detached lakes, the first book and the eighth,—I reason upon the same basis with respect to the authorship. Assuming continuity of structure as a presumptive proof, the whole of this Achillêis must be treated as composed by one author. Wolf, indeed, affirmed, that he never read the poem continuously through without being painfully impressed with the inferiority[304] and altered style of the last six books,—and Lachmann carries this feeling farther back, so as to commence with the seventeenth book. If I could enter fully into this sentiment, I should then be compelled, not to deny the existence of a preconceived scheme, but to imagine that the books from the eighteenth to the twenty-second, though forming part of that scheme, or Achillêis, had yet been executed by another and an inferior poet. But it is to be remarked, first, that inferiority of poetical merit, to a certain extent, is quite reconcilable with unity of authorship; and, secondly, that the very circumstances upon which Wolf's unfavorable judgment is built, seem to arise out of increased difficulty in the poet's task, when he came to the crowning cantos of his designed Achillêis. For that which chiefly distinguishes these books, is, the direct, incessant, and manual intervention of the gods and goddesses, formerly permitted by Zeus,—and the repetition of vast and fantastic conceptions to which such superhuman agency gives occasion; not omitting the battle of Achilles against Skamander and Simois, and the burning up of these rivers by Hêphæstus. Now, looking at this vein of ideas with the eyes of a modern reader, or even with those of a Grecian critic of the literary ages, it is certain that the effect is unpleasing: the gods, sublime elements of poetry when kept in due proportion, are here somewhat vulgarized. But though the poet here has not succeeded, and probably success was impossible, in the task which he has prescribed to himself,—yet the mere fact of his undertaking it, and the manifest distinction between his employment of divine agency in these latter cantos as compared with the preceding, seems explicable only on the supposition that they *are* the latter cantos, and come in designed sequence, as the continuance of a previous plan. The poet wishes to surround the coming forth of Achilles with the maximum of glorious and terrific circumstance; no Trojan enemy can for a moment hold out against him:[305] the gods must descend to the plain of Troy and fight in person, while Zeus, who at the beginning of the eighth book, had forbidden them to take part, expressly encourages them to do so at the beginning of the twentieth. If, then, the nineteenth book (which contains the reconciliation between Achilles and Agamemnôn, a subject naturally somewhat tame) and the three following books (where we have before us only the gods, Achilles, and the Trojans, without hope or courage) are inferior in execution and interest to the seven preceding books (which describe the long-disputed and often doubtful death-struggle between the Greeks and Trojans without Achilles), as Wolf and other critics affirm,—we may explain the difference without supposing a new poet as composer; for the conditions of the poem had become essentially more difficult, and the subject more unpromising. The necessity of keeping Achilles above the level, even of heroic prowess, restricted the poet's means of acting upon the sympathy of his hearers.[306]

The last two books of the Iliad may have formed part of the original Achillêis. But the probability rather is, that they are additions; for the death of Hector satisfies the exigencies of a coherent scheme, and we are not entitled to extend the oldest poem beyond the limit which such necessity prescribes. It has been argued on one side by Nitzsch and O. Müller, that the mind could not leave off with satisfaction at the moment in which Achilles sates his revenge, and while the bodies of Patroclus and Hector are lying unburied,— also, that the more merciful temper which he exhibits in the twenty-fourth book, must always have been an indispensable sequel, in order to create proper sympathy with his triumph. Other critics, on the contrary, have taken special grounds of exception against the last book, and have endeavored to set it aside as different from the other books, both in tone and language. To a certain extent, the peculiarities of the last book appear to me undeniable, though it is plainly a designed continuance, and not a substantive poem. Some weight also is due to the remark about the twenty-third book, that Odysseus and Diomêdês, who have been wounded and disabled during the fight, now reappear in perfect force, and contend in the games: here is no case of miraculous healing, and the inconsistency is more likely to have been admitted by a separate enlarging poet, than by the schemer of the Achillêis.

The splendid books from the second to v. 322 of the seventh,[307] are equal, in most parts, to any portion of the Achillêis, and are pointedly distinguished from the latter by the broad view which they exhibit of the general Trojan war, with all its principal personages, localities, and causes,—

yet without advancing the result promised in the first book, or, indeed, any final purpose whatever. Even the desperate wound inflicted by Tlepolemus on Sarpêdon, is forgotten, when the latter hero is called forth in the subsequent Achillêis.[308] The arguments of Lachmann, who dissects these six books into three or four separate songs,[309] carry no conviction to my mind; and I see no reason why we should not consider all of them to be by the same author, bound together by the common purpose of giving a great collective picture which may properly be termed an Iliad. The tenth book, or Doloneia, though adapted specially to the place in which it stands, agrees with the books between the first and eighth in belonging only to the general picture of the war, without helping forward the march of the Achillêis; yet it seems conceived in a lower vein, in so far as we can trust our modern ethical sentiment. One is unwilling to believe that the author of the fifth book, or Aristeia of Diomêdês, would condescend to employ the hero whom he there so brightly glorifies,—the victor even over Arês himself,—in slaughtering newly-arrived Thracian sleepers, without any large purpose or necessity.[310] The ninth book, of which I have already spoken at length, belongs to a different vein of conception, and seems to me more likely to have emanated from a separate composer.

While intimating these views respecting the authorship of the Iliad, as being in my judgment the most probable, I must repeat that, though the study of the poem carries to my mind a sufficient conviction respecting its structure, the question between unity and plurality of authors is essentially less determinable. The poem consists of a part original, and other parts superadded; yet it is certainly not impossible that the author of the former may himself have composed the latter; and such would be my belief if I regarded plurality of composers as an inadmissible idea. On this supposition, we must conclude that the poet, while anxious for the addition of new, and for the most part, highly interesting matter, has not thought fit to recast the parts and events in such manner as to impart to the whole a pervading thread of *consensus* and organization, such as we see in the Odyssey.

That the Odyssey is of later date than the Iliad, and by a different author, seems to be now the opinion of most critics, especially of Payne Knight[311] and Nitzsch; though O. Müller leans to a contrary conclusion, at the same time adding that he thinks the arguments either way not very decisive. There are considerable differences of statement in the two poems in regard to some of the gods: Iris is messenger of the gods in the Iliad, and Hermês in the Odyssey: Æolus, the dispenser of the winds in the Odyssey, is not noticed in the twenty-third book of the Iliad, but, on the contrary, Iris invites the winds, as independent gods, to come and kindle the funeral pile of Patroclus; and, unless we are to expunge the song of Demodokus in the eighth book of the

Odyssey as spurious, Aphroditê there appears as the wife of Hêphæstus,—a relationship not known to the Iliad. There are also some other points of difference enumerated by Mr. Knight and others, which tend to justify the presumption that the author of the Odyssey is not identical either with the author of the Achillêis or his enlargers, which G. Hermann considers to be a point unquestionable.[312] Indeed, the difficulty of supposing a long coherent poem to have been conceived, composed, and retained, without any aid of writing, appears to many critics even now, insurmountable, though the evidences on the other side, are, in my view, sufficient to outweigh any negative presumption thus suggested. But it is improbable that the same person should have powers of memorial combination sufficient for composing two such poems, nor is there any proof to force upon us such a supposition.

Presuming a difference of authorship between the two poems, I feel less convinced about the supposed juniority of the Odyssey. The discrepancies in manners and language in the one and the other, are so little important, that two different persons, in the same age and society, might well be imagined to exhibit as great or even greater. It is to be recollected that the subjects of the two are heterogeneous, so as to conduct the poet, even were he the same man, into totally different veins of imagination and illustration. The pictures of the Odyssey seem to delineate the same heroic life as the Iliad, though looked at from a distinct point of view: and the circumstances surrounding the residence of Odysseus, in Ithaka, are just such as we may suppose him to have left in order to attack Troy. If the scenes presented to us are for the most part pacific, as contrasted with the incessant fighting of the Iliad, this is not to be ascribed to any greater sociality or civilization in the real hearers of the Odyssey, but to the circumstances of the hero whom the poet undertakes to adorn: nor can we doubt that the poems of Arktinus and Leschês, of a later date than the Odyssey, would have given us as much combat and bloodshed as the Iliad. I am not struck by those proofs of improved civilization which some critics affirm the Odyssey to present: Mr. Knight, who is of this opinion, nevertheless admits that the mutilation of Melanthius, and the hanging up of the female slaves by Odysseus, in that poem, indicate greater barbarity than any incidents in the fights before Troy.[313] The more skilful and compact structure of the Odyssey, has been often considered as a proof of its juniority in age: and in the case of two poems by the same author, we might plausibly contend that practice would bring with it improvement in the combining faculty. But in reference to the poems before us, we must recollect, first, that in all probability the Iliad (with which the comparison is taken) is not a primitive but an enlarged poem, and that the primitive Achillêis might well have been quite as coherent as the Odyssey; secondly, that between different authors, superiority in structure is not a proof of subsequent composition, inasmuch as, on that hypothesis, we should be compelled to admit that the later poem of Arktinus would be an improvement upon the Odyssey; thirdly, that, even if it were so, we could only infer that the author of the Odyssey had *heard* the Achillêis or the Iliad; we could not infer that he lived one or two generations afterwards.[314]

On the whole, the balance of probabilities seems in favor of distinct authorship for the two poems, but the same age,—and that age a very early one, anterior to the first Olympiad. And they may thus be used as evidences, and contemporary evidences, for the phenomena of primitive Greek civilization; while they also show that the power of constructing long premeditated epics, without the aid of writing, is to be taken as a characteristic of the earliest known Greek mind. This was the point controverted by Wolf, which a full review of the case (in my judgment) decides against him: it is, moreover, a valuable result for the historian of the Greeks, inasmuch as it marks out to him the ground from which he is to start in appreciating their ulterior progress.[315]

Whatever there may be of truth in the different conjectures of critics respecting the authorship and structure of these unrivalled poems, we are not to imagine that it is the perfection of their epical symmetry which has given them their indissoluble hold upon the human mind, as well modern as ancient. There is some tendency in critics, from Aristotle downwards,[316] to invert the order of attributes in respect to the Homeric poems, so as to dwell most on recondite excellences which escape the unaided reader, and which are even to a great degree disputable. But it is given to few minds (as Goethe has remarked[317]) to appreciate fully the mechanism of a long poem; and many feel the beauty of the separate parts, who have no sentiment for the aggregate perfection of the whole.

Nor were the Homeric poems originally addressed to minds of the rarer stamp. They are intended for those feelings which the critic has in common with the unlettered mass, not for that enlarged range of vision and peculiar standard which he has acquired to himself. They are of all poems the most absolutely and unreservedly popular: had they been otherwise, they could not have lived so long in the mouth of the rhapsodes, and the ear and memory of the people: and it was *then* that their influence was first acquired, never afterwards to be shaken. Their beauties belong to the parts taken separately, which revealed themselves spontaneously to the listening crowd at the festival,—far more than to the whole poem taken together, which could hardly be appreciated unless the parts were dwelt upon and suffered to expand in the mind. The most unlettered hearer of those times could readily seize, while the most instructed reader can still recognize, the characteristic excellence of Homeric narrative,—its straightforward, unconscious, unstudied simplicity,—its concrete forms of speech[318] and happy alternation of action with dialogue,—its vivid pictures of living agents, always clearly and sharply individualized, whether in the commanding proportions of Achilles and Odysseus, in the graceful presence of Helen and Penelope, or in the more humble contrast of Eumæus and Melanthius; and always, moreover, animated by the frankness with which his heroes give utterance to all their transient emotions and even all their infirmities,—its constant reference to those coarser veins of feeling and palpable motives which belong to all men in common,—its fulness of graphic details, freshly drawn from the visible and audible world, and though often homely, never tame, nor trenching upon that limit of satiety to which the Greek mind was so keenly alive,—lastly, its perpetual junction of gods and men in the same picture, and familiar appeal to ever-present divine agency, in harmony with the interpretation of nature at that time universal.

It is undoubtedly easier to feel than to describe the impressive influence of Homeric narrative: but the time and circumstances under which that influence was first, and most powerfully felt, preclude the possibility of explaining it by comprehensive and elaborate comparisons, such as are implied in Aristotle's remarks upon the structure of the poems. The critic who seeks the explanation in the right place will not depart widely from the point of view of those rude auditors to whom the poems were originally addressed, or from the susceptibilities and capacities common to the human bosom in every stage of progressive culture. And though the refinements and delicacies of the poems, as well as their general structure, are a subject of highly interesting criticism, —yet it is not to these that Homer owes his wide-spread and imperishable popularity. Still less is it true, as the well-known observations of Horace would lead us to believe, that Homer is a teacher of ethical wisdom akin and superior to Chrysippus or Crantor.[319] No didactic purpose is to be found in the Iliad and Odyssey; a philosopher may doubtless extract, from the incidents and strongly marked characters which it contains, much illustrative matter for his exhortations,—but the ethical doctrine which he applies must emanate from his own reflection. The Homeric hero manifests virtues or infirmities, fierceness or compassion, with the same straightforward and simple-minded vivacity, unconscious of any ideal standard by which his conduct is to be tried;[320] nor can we trace in the poet any ulterior function beyond that of the inspired organ of the Muse, and the nameless, but eloquent, herald of lost adventures out of the darkness of the past.

# HISTORY OF GREECE.

PART II.

## HISTORICAL GREECE.

# CHAPTER I.

## GENERAL GEOGRAPHY AND LIMITS OF GREECE.

GREECE Proper lies between the 36th and 40th parallels of north latitude, and between the 21st and 26th degrees of east longitude. Its greatest length, from Mount Olympus to Cape Tænarus, may be stated at 250 English miles; its greatest breadth, from the western coast of Akarnania to Marathon in Attica, at 180 miles; and the distance eastward from Ambrakia across Pindus to the Magnesian mountain Homolê and the mouth of the Peneius is about 120 miles. Altogether, its area is somewhat less than that of Portugal.[321] In regard, however, to all attempts at determining the exact limits of Greece proper, we may remark, first, that these limits seem not to have been very precisely defined even among the Greeks themselves; and next, that so large a proportion of the Hellens were distributed among islands and colonies, and so much of their influence upon the world in general produced through their colonies, as to render the extent of their original domicile a matter of comparatively little moment to verify.

The chain called Olympus and the Cambunian mountains, ranging from east and west, and commencing with the Ægean sea or the gulf of Therma, near the 40th degree of north latitude, is prolonged under the name of Mount Lingon, until it touches the Adriatic at the Akrokeraunian promontory. The country south of this chain comprehended all that in ancient times was regarded as Greece, or Hellas proper, but it also comprehended something more. Hellas proper,[322] (or continuous Hellas, to use the language of Skylax and Dikæarchus) was understood to begin with the town and gulf of Ambrakia: from thence, northward to the Akrokeraunian promontory, lay the land called by the Greeks Epirus,—occupied by the Chaonians, Molossians, and Thesprotians, who were termed Epirots, and were not esteemed to belong to the Hellenic aggregate. This at least was the general understanding, though Ætolians and Akarnanians, in their more distant sections, seem to have been not less widely removed from the full type of Hellenism than the Epirots were; while Herodotus is inclined to treat even Molossians and Thesprotians as Hellens.[323]

At a point about midway between the Ægean and Ionian seas, Olympus and Lingon are traversed nearly at right angles by the still longer and vaster chain called Pindus, which stretches in a line rather west of north from the northern side of the range of Olympus: the system to which these mountains belong seems to begin with the lofty masses of greenstone comprised under the name of Mount Scardus, or Scordus, (Schardagh,)[324] which is divided only by the narrow cleft, containing the river Drin, from the limestone of the Albanian Alps. From the southern face of Olympus, Pindus strikes off nearly southward, forming the boundary between Thessaly and Epirus, and sending forth about the 39th degree of latitude the lateral chain of Othrys,—which latter takes an easterly course, forming the southern boundary of Thessaly, and reaching the sea between Thessaly and the northern coast of Eubœa. Southward of Othrys, the chain of Pindus, under the name of Tymphrêstus, still continues, until another lateral chain, called Œta, projects from it again towards the east,—forming the lofty coast immediately south of the Maliac gulf, with the narrow road of Thermopylæ between the two,—and terminating at the Eubœan strait. At the point of junction with Œta, the chain of Pindus forks into two branches; one striking to the westward of south, and reaching across Ætolia, under the names of Arakynthus, Kurius, Korax, and Taphiassus, to the promontory called Antirrhion, situated on the northern side of the narrow entrance of the Corinthian gulf, over against the corresponding promontory of Rhion in Peloponnesus; the other tending south-east, and forming Parnassus, Helicon, and Kithærôn; indeed, Ægaleus and Hymettus, even down to the southernmost cape of Attica, Sunium, may be treated as a continuance of this chain. From the eastern extremity of Œta, also, a range of hills, inferior in height to the preceding, takes its departure in a south-easterly direction, under the various names of Knêmis, Ptôon, and Teumêssus. It is joined with Kithærôn by the lateral communication, ranging from west to east, called Parnês; while the celebrated Pentelikus, abundant in marble quarries, constitutes its connecting link, to the south of Parnês with the chain from Kithærôn to Sunium.

From the promontory of Antirrhion, the line of mountains crosses into Peloponnesus, and stretches in a southerly direction down to the extremity of the peninsula called Tænarus, now Cape Matapan. Forming the boundary between Elis with Messenia on one side, and Arcadia with Laconia on the other, it bears the successive names of Olenus, Panachaikus, Pholoê, Erymanthus, Lykæus, Parrhasius, and Taygetus. Another series of mountains strikes off from Kithærôn towards the south-west, constituting, under the names of Geraneia and Oneia, the rugged and lofty Isthmus of Corinth, and then spreading itself into Peloponnesus. On entering that peninsula, one of its branches tends westward along the north of Arkadia, comprising the Akrokorinthus, or citadel of Corinth, the high peak of Kyllênê, the mountains of Aroanii and Lampeia, and ultimately joining Erymanthus and Pholoê,— while the other branch strikes southward towards the south-eastern cape of Peloponnesus, the formidable Cape Malea, or St. Angelo,—and exhibits itself under the successive names of Apesas, Artemisium, Parthenium, Parnôn, Thornax, and Zarêx.

From the eastern extremity of Olympus, in a direction rather to the eastward of south, stretches the range of mountains first called Ossa, and afterwards Pelion, down to the south-eastern corner of Thessaly. The long, lofty, and naked back-bone of the island of Eubœa, may be viewed as a continuance both of this chain and of the chain of Othrys: the line is farther prolonged by a series of islands in the Archipelago, Andros, Tênos, Mykonos, and Naxos, belonging to the group called the Cyclades, or islands encircling the sacred centre of Delos. Of these Cyclades, others are in like manner a continuance of the chain which reaches to Cape Sunium,—Keôs, Kythnos, Seriphos, and Siphnos join on to Attica, as Andros does to Eubœa. And we might even consider the great island of Krete as a prolongation of the system of mountains which breasts the winds and waves at Cape Malea, the island of Kythêra forming the intermediate link between them. Skiathus, Skopelus, and Skyrus, to the north-east of Eubœa, also mark themselves out as outlying peaks of the range comprehending Pelion and Eubœa.[325]

By this brief sketch, which the reader will naturally compare with one of the recent maps of the country, it will be seen that Greece proper is among the most mountainous territories in Europe. For although it is convenient, in giving a systematic view of the face of the country, to group the multiplicity of mountains into certain chains, or ranges, founded upon approximative uniformity of direction; yet, in point of fact, there are so many ramifications and dispersed peaks,—so vast a number of hills and crags of different magnitude and elevation,—that a comparatively small proportion of the surface is left for level ground. Not only few continuous plains, but even few continuous valleys, exist throughout all Greece proper. The largest spaces of level ground are seen in Thessaly, in Ætolia, in the western portion of Peloponnesus, and in Bœotia; but irregular mountains, valleys frequent but isolated, land-locked basins and declivities, which often occur, but seldom last long, form the character of the country.[326]

The islands of the Cyclades, Eubœa, Attica, and Laconia, consist for the most part of micaceous schist, combined with and often covered by crystalline granular limestone.[327] The centre and west of Peloponnesus, as well as the country north of the Corinthian gulf from the gulf of Ambrakia to the strait of Eubœa, present a calcareous formation, varying in different localities as to color, consistency, and hardness, but, generally, belonging or approximating to the chalk: it is often very compact, but is distinguished in a marked manner from the crystalline limestone above mentioned. The two loftiest summits in Greece[328] (both, however, lower than Olympus, estimated at nine thousand seven hundred feet) exhibit this formation,—Parnassus, which attains eight thousand feet, and the point of St. Elias in Taygetus, which is not less than seven thousand eight hundred feet. Clay-slate, and conglomerates of sand, lime, and clay, are found in many parts: a close and firm conglomerate of lime composes the Isthmus of Corinth: loose deposits of pebbles, and calcareous breccia, occupy also some portions of the territory. But the most important and essential elements of the Grecian soil, consist of the diluvial and alluvial formations, with which the troughs and basins are filled up, resulting from the decomposition of the older adjoining rocks. In these reside the productive powers of the country, and upon these the grain and vegetables for the subsistence of the people depend. The mountain regions are to a great degree barren, destitute at present of wood or any useful vegetation, though there is reason to believe that they were better wooded in antiquity: in many parts, however, and especially in Ætolia and Akarnania, they afford plenty of timber, and in all parts, pasture for the cattle during summer, at a time when the plains are thoroughly burnt up.[329] For other articles of food, dependence must be had on the valleys, which are occasionally of singular fertility. The low ground of Thessaly, the valley of the Kephisus, and the borders of the lake Kopaïs, in Bœotia, the western portion of Elis, the plains of Stratus on the confines of Akarnania and Ætolia, and those near the river Pamisus in Messenia, both are now, and were in ancient times, remarkable for their abundant produce.

Besides the scarcity of wood for fuel, there is another serious inconvenience to which the low grounds of Greece are exposed,—the want of a supply of water at once adequate and regular.[330] Abundance of rain falls during the autumnal and winter months, little or none during the summer; while the naked limestone of the numerous hills, neither absorbs nor retains moisture, so that the rain runs off as rapidly as it falls, and springs are rare. [331] Most of the rivers of Greece are torrents in early spring, and dry before the end of the summer: the copious combinations of the ancient language, designated the winter torrent by a special and separate word.[332] The most considerable rivers in the country are, the Peneius, which carries off all the waters of Thessaly, finding an exit into the Ægean through the narrow defile which parts Ossa from Olympus,—and the Achelôus, which flows from Pindus in a south-westerly direction, separating Ætolia from Akarnania, and emptying itself into the Ionian sea: the Euênus also takes its rise at a more southerly part of the same mountain chain, and falls into the same sea more to the eastward. The rivers more to the southward are unequal and inferior. Kephisus and Asôpus, in Bœotia, Alpheius, in Elis and Arcadia, Pamisus in Messenia, maintain each a languid stream throughout the summer; while the Inachus near Argos, and the Kephisus and Ilissus near Athens, present a scanty reality which falls short still more of their great poetical celebrity. Of all those rivers which have been noticed, the Achelôus is by far the most important. The quantity of mud which its turbid stream brought down and deposited, occasioned a sensible increase of the land at its embouchure, within the observation of Thucydidês.[333]

But the disposition and properties of the Grecian territory, though not maintaining permanent rivers, are favorable to the multiplication of lakes and marshes. There are numerous hollows and inclosed basins, out of which the water can find no superficial escape, and where, unless it makes for itself a subterranean passage through rifts in the mountains, it remains either as a marsh or a lake according to the time of year. In Thessaly, we find the lakes Nessônis and Bœbêis; in Ætolia, between the Achelous and Eunêus, Strabo mentions the lake of Trichônis, besides several other lakes, which it is difficult to identify individually, though the quantity of ground covered by lake and marsh is, as a whole, very considerable. In Bœotia, are situated the lakes Kopaïs, Hylikê, and Harma; the first of the three formed chiefly by the river Kephisus, flowing from Parnassus on the north-west, and shaping for itself a sinuous course through the mountains of Phokis. On the north-east and east, the lake Kopaïs is bounded by the high land of Mount Ptôon, which intercepts its communication with the strait of Eubœa. Through the limestone of this mountain, the water has either found or forced several subterraneous cavities, by which it obtains a partial egress on the other side of the rocky hill, and then flows into the strait. The Katabothra, as they were termed in antiquity, yet exist, but in an imperfect and half-obstructed condition. Even in antiquity, however, they never fully sufficed to carry off the surplus waters of the Kephisus; for the remains are still found of an artificial tunnel, pierced through the whole breadth of the rock, and with perpendicular apertures at proper intervals to let in the air from above. This tunnel—one of the most interesting remnants of antiquity, since it must date from the prosperous days of the old Orchomenus, anterior to its absorption into the Bœotian league, as well as to the preponderance of Thebes,—is now choked up and rendered useless. It may, perhaps, have been designedly obstructed by the hand of an enemy, and the scheme of Alexander the Great, who commissioned an engineer from Chalkis to reopen it, was defeated, first, by discontents in Bœotia, and ultimately by his early death.[334]

The Katabothra of the lake Kopaïs, are a specimen of the phenomenon so frequent in Greece,—lakes and rivers finding for themselves subterranean passages through the cavities in the limestone rocks, and even pursuing their unseen course for a considerable distance before they emerge to the light of day. In Arcadia, especially, several remarkable examples of subterranean water communication occur; this central region of Peloponnesus presents a cluster of such completely inclosed valleys, or basins.[335]

It will be seen from these circumstances, that Greece, considering its limited total extent, offers but little motive, and still less of convenient means, for internal communication among its various inhabitants.[336] Each village, or township, occupying its plain with the inclosing mountains,[337] supplied its own main wants whilst the transport of commodities by land was sufficiently difficult to discourage greatly any regular commerce with neighbors. In so far as the face of the interior country was concerned, it seemed as if nature had been disposed, from the beginning, to keep the population of Greece socially and politically disunited,—by providing so many hedges of separation, and so many boundaries, generally hard, sometimes impossible, to overleap. One special motive to intercourse, however, arose out of this very geographical constitution of the country, and its endless alternation of mountain and valley. The difference of climate and temperature between the high and low grounds is very great; the harvest is secured in one place before it is ripe in another, and the cattle find during the heat of summer shelter and pasture on the hills, at a time when the plains are burnt up.[338] The practice of transferring them from the mountains to the plain according to the change of season, which subsists still as it did in ancient times, is intimately connected with the structure of the country, and must from the earliest period have brought about communication among the otherwise disunited villages.[339]

Such difficulties, however, in the internal transit by land, were to a great extent counteracted by the large proportion of coast, and the accessibility of the country by sea. The prominences and indentations in the line of Grecian coast, are hardly less remarkable than the multiplicity of elevations and depressions which everywhere mark the surface.[340] The shape of Peloponnesus, with its three southern gulfs, (the Argolic, Laconian, and Messenian,) was compared by the ancient geographers to the leaf of a plane-tree: the Pagasæan gulf on the eastern side of Greece, and the Ambrakian gulf on the western, with their narrow entrances and considerable area, are equivalent to internal lakes: Xenophon boasts of the double sea which embraces so large a proportion of Attica, Ephorus of the triple sea, by which Bœotia was accessible from west, north, and south,—the Eubœan strait, opening a long line of country on both sides to coasting navigation.[341] But the most important of all Grecian gulfs are the Corinthian and the Saronic, washing the northern and north-eastern shores of Peloponnesus, and separated by the narrow barrier of the Isthmus of Corinth. The former, especially, lays open Ætolia, Phokis, and Bœotia, as well as the whole northern coast of Peloponnesus, to water approach. Corinth, in ancient times, served as an entrepôt for the trade between Italy and Asia Minor,—goods being unshipped at Lechæum, the port on the Corinthian gulf, and carried by land across to Cenchreæ, the port on the Saronic: indeed, even the merchant-vessels themselves, when not very large,[342] were conveyed across by the same route. It was accounted a prodigious advantage to escape the necessity of sailing round Cape Malea: and the violent winds and currents which modern experience attests to prevail around that formidable promontory, are quite sufficient to justify the apprehensions of the ancient Greek merchant, with his imperfect apparatus for navigation.[343]

It will thus appear that there was no part of Greece proper which could be considered as out of reach of the sea, while most parts of it were convenient and easy of access: in fact, the Arcadians were the only large section of the Hellenic name, (we may add the Doric, Tetrapolis, and the mountaineers along the chain of Pindus and Tymphrêstus,) who were altogether without a seaport.[344] But Greece proper constituted only a fraction of the entire Hellenic world, during the historical age: there were the numerous islands, and still more numerous continental colonies, all located as independent intruders on distinct points of the coast,[345] in the Euxine, the Ægean, the Mediterranean, and the Adriatic; and distant from each other by the space which separates Trebizond from Marseilles. All these various cities were comprised in the name Hellas, which implied no geographical continuity: all prided themselves on Hellenic blood, name, religion, and mythical ancestry. As the only communication between them was maritime, so the sea, important, even if we look to Greece proper exclusively, was the sole channel for transmitting ideas and improvements, as well as for maintaining sympathies—social, political, religious, and literary—throughout these outlying members of the Hellenic aggregate.

The ancient philosophers and legislators were deeply impressed with the contrast between an inland and a maritime city: in the former, simplicity and uniformity of life, tenacity of ancient habits, and dislike of what is new or foreign, great force of exclusive sympathy, and narrow range both of objects and ideas; in the latter, variety and novelty of sensations, expansive imagination, toleration, and occasional preference for extraneous customs, greater activity of the individual, and corresponding mutability of the state. This distinction stands prominent in the many comparisons instituted between the Athens of Periklês and the Athens of the earlier times down to Solôn. Both Plato and Aristotle dwell upon it emphatically,—and the former especially, whose genius conceived the comprehensive scheme of prescribing beforehand and insuring in practice the whole course of individual thought and feeling in his imaginary community, treats maritime communication, if pushed beyond the narrowest limits, as fatal to the success and permanence of any wise scheme of education. Certain it is, that a great difference of character existed between those Greeks who mingled much in maritime affairs, and those who did not. The Arcadian may stand as a type of the pure Grecian landsman, with his rustic and illiterate habits,[346]—his diet of sweet chestnuts, barley-cakes, and pork (as contrasted with the fish which formed the chief seasoning for the bread of an Athenian,)—his superior courage and endurance,—his reverence for Lacedaemonian headship as an old and customary influence,—his sterility of intellect and imagination, as well as his slackness in enterprise,—his unchangeable rudeness of relations with the gods, which led him to scourge and prick Pan, if he came back empty-handed from the chase; while the inhabitant of Phôkæa or Miletus exemplifies the Grecian mariner, eager in search of gain,—active, skilful, and daring at sea, but inferior in stedfast bravery on land,—more excitable in imagination as well as more mutable in character,—full of pomp and expense in religious manifestations towards the Ephesian Artemis or the Apollo of Branchidæ; with a mind more open to the varieties of Grecian energy and to the refining influences of Grecian civilization. The Peloponnesians generally, and the Lacedæmonians in particular, approached to the Arcadian type,—while the Athenians of the fifth century B. C. stood foremost in the other; superadding to it, however, a delicacy of taste, and a predominance of intellectual sympathy and enjoyments, which seem to have been peculiar to themselves.

The configuration of the Grecian territory, so like in many respects to that of Switzerland, produced two effects of great moment upon the character and history of the people. In the first place, it materially strengthened their powers of defence: it shut up the country against those invasions from the interior, which successively subjugated all their continental colonies; and it at the same time rendered each fraction more difficult to be attacked by the rest, so as to exercise a certain conservative influence in assuring the tenure of actual possessors: for the pass of Thermopylæ, between Thessaly and Phokis, that of Kythærôn, between Bœotia and Attica, or the mountainous range of Oneion and Geraneia along the Isthmus of Corinth, were positions which an inferior number of brave men could hold against a much greater force of assailants. But, in the next place, while it tended to protect each section of Greeks from being conquered, it also kept them politically disunited, and perpetuated their separate autonomy. It fostered that powerful principle of repulsion, which disposed even the smallest township to constitute itself a political unit apart from the rest, and to resist all idea of coalescence with others, either amicable or compulsory. To a modern leader, accustomed to large political aggregations, and securities for good government through the representative system, it requires a certain mental effort to transport himself back to a time when even the smallest town clung so tenaciously to its right of self-legislation. Nevertheless, such was the general habit and feeling of the ancient world, throughout Italy, Sicily, Spain, and Gaul. Among the Hellenes, it stands out more conspicuously, for several reasons,—first, because they seem to have pushed the multiplication of autonomous units to an extreme point, seeing that even islands not larger than Peparêthos and Amorgos had two or three separate city communities;[347] secondly, because they produced, for the first time in the history of mankind, acute systematic thinkers on matters of government, amongst all of whom the idea of the autonomous city was accepted as the indispensable basis of political speculation; thirdly, because this incurable subdivision proved finally the cause of their ruin, in spite of pronounced intellectual superiority over their conquerors: and lastly, because incapacity of political coalescence did not preclude a powerful and extensive sympathy between the inhabitants of all the separate cities, with a constant tendency to fraternize for numerous purposes, social, religious, recreative, intellectual, and æsthetical. For these reasons, the indefinite multiplication of self-governing towns, though in truth a phenomenon common to ancient Europe, as contrasted with the large monarchies of Asia, appears more marked among the ancient Greeks than elsewhere: and there cannot be any doubt that they owe it, in a considerable degree, to the multitude of insulating boundaries which the configuration of their country presented.

Nor is it rash to suppose that the same causes may have tended to promote that unborrowed intellectual development for which they stand so conspicuous. General propositions respecting the working of climate and physical agencies upon character are, indeed, treacherous; for our knowledge of the globe is now sufficient to teach us that heat and cold, mountain and plain, sea and land, moist and dry atmosphere, are all consistent with the greatest diversities of resident men: moreover, the contrast between the population of Greece itself, for the seven centuries preceding the Christian era, and the Greeks of more modern times, is alone enough to inculcate reserve in such speculations. Nevertheless, we may venture to note certain improving influences, connected with their geographical position, at a time when they had no books to study, and no more advanced predecessors to imitate. We may remark, first, that their position made them at once mountaineers and mariners, thus supplying them with great variety of objects, sensations, and adventures; next, that each petty community, nestled apart amidst its own rocks,[348] was sufficiently severed from the rest to possess an individual life and attributes of its own, yet not so far as to subtract it from the sympathies of the remainder; so that an observant Greek, commercing with a great diversity of half countrymen, whose language he understood, and whose idiosyncrasies he could appreciate, had access to a larger mass of social and political experience than any other man in so unadvanced an age could personally obtain. The Phœnician, superior to the Greek on shipboard, traversed wider distances, and saw a greater number of strangers, but had not the same means of intimate communion with a multiplicity of fellows in blood and language. His relations, confined to purchase and sale, did not comprise that mutuality of action and reaction which pervaded the crowd at a Grecian festival. The scene which here presented itself, was a mixture of uniformity and variety highly stimulating to the observant faculties of a man of genius,—who at the same time, if he sought to communicate his own impressions, or to act upon this mingled and diverse audience, was forced to shake off what was peculiar to his own town or community, and to put forth matter in harmony with the feelings of all. It is thus that we may explain, in part, that penetrating apprehension of human life and character, and that power of touching sympathies common to all ages and nations, which surprises us so much in the unlettered authors of the old epic. Such periodical intercommunion of brethren habitually isolated from each other, was the only means then open of procuring for the bard a diversified range of experience and a many-colored audience; and it was to a great degree the result of geographical causes. Perhaps among other nations such facilitating causes might have been found, yet without producing any result comparable to the Iliad and Odyssey. But Homer was, nevertheless, dependent upon the conditions of his age, and we can at least point out those peculiarities in early Grecian society, without which Homeric excellence would never have existed, —the geographical position is one, the language another.

In mineral and metallic wealth, Greece was not distinguished. Gold was obtained in considerable abundance in the island of Siphnos, which, throughout the sixth century B. C., was among the richest communities of Greece, and possessed a treasure-chamber at Delphi, distinguished for the richness of its votive offerings. At that time, gold was so rare in Greece, that the Lacedæmonians were obliged to send to the Lydian Crœsus, in order to provide enough of it for the gilding of a statue.[349] It appears to have been more abundant in Asia Minor, and the quantity of it in Greece was much multiplied by the opening of mines in Thrace, Macedonia, Epirus, and even some parts of Thessaly. In the island of Thasos, too, some mines were reopened with profitable result, which had been originally begun, and subsequently abandoned, by Phœnician settlers of an earlier century. From these same districts, also, was procured a considerable amount of silver; while, about the beginning of the fifth century B. C., the first effective commencement seems to have been made of turning to account the rich southern district of Attica, called Laureion. Copper was obtained in various parts of Greece, especially in Cyprus and Eubœa,—in which latter island was also found the earth called Cadmia, employed for the purification of the ore. Bronze was used among the Greeks for many purposes in which iron is now employed: and even the arms of the Homeric heroes (different in this respect from the later historical Greeks) are composed of copper, tempered in such a way as to impart to it an astonishing hardness. Iron was found in Eubœa, Bœôtia, and Melos,—but still more abundantly in the mountainous region of the Laconian Taygetus. There is, however no part of Greece where the remains of ancient metallurgy appear now so conspicuous, as the island of Seriphos. The excellence and varieties of marble, from Pentelikus, Hymettus, Paros, Karystus, etc., and other parts of the country,—so essential for the purposes of sculpture and architecture,—is well known.[350]

Situated under the same parallels of latitude as the coast of Asia Minor, and the southernmost regions of Italy and Spain, Greece produced wheat, barley, flax, wine, and oil, in the earliest times of which we have any knowledge;[351] though the currants, Indian corn, silk, and tobacco, which the country now exhibits, are an addition of more recent times. Theophrastus and other authors amply attest the observant and industrious agriculture prevalent among the ancient Greeks, as well as the care with which its various natural productions, comprehending a great diversity of plants, herbs, and trees, were turned to account. The cultivation of the vine and the olive,—the latter indispensable to ancient life, not merely for the purposes which it serves at present, but also from the constant habit then prevalent of anointing the body, —appears to have been particularly elaborate; and the many different accidents of soil, level, and exposure, which were to be found, not only in Hellas proper, but also among the scattered Greek settlements, afforded to observant planters materials for study and comparison. The barley-cake seems to have been more generally eaten than the wheaten loaf;[352] but one or other of them, together with vegetables and fish, (sometimes fresh, but more frequently salt,) was the common food of the population; the Arcadians fed much upon pork, and the Spartans also consumed animal food; but by the Greeks, generally, fresh meat seems to have been little eaten, except at festivals and sacrifices. The Athenians, the most commercial people in Greece proper, though their light, dry, and comparatively poor soil produced excellent barley, nevertheless, did not grow enough corn for their own consumption: they imported considerable supplies of corn from Sicily, from the coast of the Euxine, and the Tauric Chersonese, and salt-fish both from the Propontis and even from Gades:[353] the distance from whence these supplies came, when we take into consideration the extent of fine corn-land in Bœotia and Thessaly, proves how little internal trade existed between the various regions of Greece proper. The exports of Athens consisted in her figs and other fruit, olives, oil,—for all of which she was distinguished,—together with pottery, ornamental manufactures, and the silver from her mines at Laureion. Salt-fish, doubtless, found its way more or less throughout all Greece;[354] but the population of other states in Greece lived more exclusively upon their own produce than the Athenians, with less of purchase and sale,[355]—a mode of life assisted by the simple domestic economy universally prevalent, in which the women not only carded and spun all the wool, but also wove out of it the clothing and bedding employed in the family. Weaving was then considered as much a woman's business as spinning, and the same feeling and habits still prevail to the present day in modern Greece, where the loom is constantly seen in the peasants' cottages, and always worked by women.[356]

The climate of Greece appears to be generally described by modern travellers in more favorable terms than it was by the ancients, which is easily explicable from the classical interest, picturesque beauties, and transparent atmosphere, so vividly appreciate by an English or a German eye. Herodotus, [357] Hippocrates, and Aristotle, treat the climate of Asia as far more genial and favorable both to animal and vegetable life, but at the same time more enervating than that of Greece: the latter, they speak of chiefly in reference to its changeful character and diversities of local temperature, which they consider as highly stimulant to the energies of the inhabitants. There is reason to conclude that ancient Greece was much more healthy than the same territory is at present, inasmuch as it was more industriously cultivated, and the towns both more carefully administered and better supplied with water. But the differences in respect of healthiness, between one portion of Greece and another, appear always to have been considerable, and this, as well as the diversities of climate, affected the local habits and the character of the particular sections. Not merely were there great differences between the mountaineers and the inhabitants of the plains,[358]—between Lokrains, Ætolians, Phokians, Dorians, Œtæans, and Arcadians, on one hand, and the inhabitants of Attica, Bœotia, and Elis, on the other,—but each of the various tribes which went to compose these categories, had its peculiarities; and the marked contrast between Athenians and Bœotians was supposed to be represented by the light and heavy atmosphere which they respectively breathed. Nor was this all: for, even among the Bœotian aggregate, every town had its own separate attributes, physical as well as moral and political: [359] Orôpus, Tanagra, Thespiæ, Thebes, Anthêdôn, Haliartus, Korôneia, Onchêstus, and Platæa, were known to Bœotians each by its own characteristic epithet: and Dikæarchus even notices a marked distinction between the inhabitants of the city of Athens and those in the country of Attica. Sparta, Argos, Corinth, and Sikyôn, though all called Doric, had each its own dialect and peculiarities. All these differences, depending in part upon climate, site, and other physical considerations, contributed to nourish antipathies, and to perpetuate that imperfect cohesion, which has already been noticed as an indelible feature in Hellas.

The Epirotic tribes, neighbors of the Ætolians and Akarnanians, filled the space between Pindus and the Ionian sea until they joined to the northward the territory inhabited by the powerful and barbarous Illyrians. Of these Illyrians, the native Macedonian tribes appear to have been an outlying section, dwelling northward of Thessaly and Mount Olympus, eastward of the chain by which Pindus is continued, and westward of the river Axius. The Epirots were comprehended under the various denominations of Chaonians, Molossians, Thesprotians, Kassopæans, Amphilochians, Athamānes, the Æthīkes, Tymphæi, Orestæ, Paroræi, and Atintānes,[360]—most of the latter being small communities dispersed about the mountainous region of Pindus. There was, however, much confusion in the application of the comprehensive name *Epirot*, which was a title given altogether by the Greeks, and given purely upon geographical, not upon ethnical considerations. Epirus seems at first to have stood opposed to Peloponnesus, and to have signified the general region northward of the gulf of Corinth; and in this primitive sense it comprehended the Ætolians and Akarnanians, portions of whom spoke a dialect difficult to understand, and were not less widely removed than the Epirots from Hellenic habits.[361] The oracle of Dodona forms the point of ancient union between Greeks and Epirots, which was superseded by Delphi, as the civilization of Hellas developed itself. Nor is it less difficult to distinguish Epirots from Macedonians on the one hand, than from Hellenes on the other; the language, the dress, and the fashion of wearing the hair being often analogous, while the boundaries, amidst rude men and untravelled tracts, were very inaccurately understood.[362]

In describing the limits occupied by the Hellens in 776 B. C., we cannot yet take account of the important colonies of Leukas and Ambrakia, established by the Corinthians subsequently on the western coast of Epirus. The Greeks of that early time seem to comprise the islands of Kephallenia, Zakynthus, Ithaka, and Dulichium, but no settlement, either inland or insular, farther northward.

They include farther, confining ourselves to 776 B. C., the great mass of islands between the coast of Greece and that of Asia Minor, from Tenedos on the north, to Rhodes, Krete, and Kythêra southward; and the great islands of Lesbos, Chios, Samos, and Eubœa, as well as the groups called the Sporades and the Cyclades. Respecting the four considerable islands nearer to the coasts of Macedonia and Thrace,—Lemnos, Imbros, Samothrace, and Thasos, —it may be doubted whether they were at that time Hellenized. The Catalogue of the Iliad includes, under Agamemnôn, contingents from Ægina, Eubœa, Krete, Karpathus, Kasus, Kôs, and Rhodes: in the oldest epical testimony which we possess, these islands thus appear inhabited by Greeks; but the others do not occur in the Catalogue, and are never mentioned in such manner as to enable us to draw any inference. Eubœa ought, perhaps, rather to be looked upon as a portion of Grecian mainland (from which it was only separated by a strait narrow enough to be bridged over) than as an island. But the last five islands named in the Catalogue are all either wholly or partially Doric: no Ionic or Æolic island appears in it: these latter, though it was among them that the poet sung, appear to be represented by their ancestral heroes, who came from Greece proper.

The last element to be included, as going to make up the Greece of 776 B. C., is the long string of Doric, Ionic, and Æolic settlements on the coast of Asia Minor,—occupying a space bounded on the north by the Troad and the region of Ida, and extending southward as far as the peninsula of Knidus. Twelve continental cities, over and above the islands of Lesbos and Tenedos, are reckoned by Herodotus as ancient Æolic foundations,—Smyrna, Kymê, Larissa, Neon-Teichos, Têmnos, Killa, Notium, Ægirœssa, Pitana, Ægæ, Myrina, and Gryneia. Smyrna, having been at first Æolic, was afterwards acquired through a stratagem by Ionic inhabitants, and remained permanently Ionic. Phokæa, the northernmost of the Ionic settlements, bordered upon Æolis: Klazomenæ, Erythræ, Teôs, Lebedos, Kolophôn, Priênê, Myus, and Milêtus, continued the Ionic name to the southward. These, together with Samos and Chios, formed the Panionic federation.[363] To the south of Milêtus, after a considerable interval, lay the Doric establishments of Myndus, Halikarnassus, and Knidus: the two latter, together with the island of Kôs and the three townships in Rhodes, constituted the Doric Hexapolis, or communion of six cities, concerted primarily with a view to religious purposes, but producing a secondary effect analogous to political federation.

Such, then, is the extent of Hellas, as it stood at the commencement of the recorded Olympiads. To draw a picture even for this date, we possess no authentic materials, and are obliged to ante-date statements which belong to a later age: and this consideration might alone suffice to show how uncertified are all delineations of the Greece of 1183 B. C., the supposed epoch of the Trojan war, four centuries earlier.

# CHAPTER II.

## THE HELLENIC PEOPLE GENERALLY, IN THE EARLY HISTORICAL TIMES.

THE territory indicated in the last chapter—south of Mount Olympus, and south of the line which connects the city of Ambrakia with Mount Pindus,—was occupied during the historical period by the central stock of the Hellens, or Greeks, from which their numerous outlying colonies were planted out.

Both metropolitans and colonists styled themselves Hellens, and were recognized as such by each other; all glorying in the name as the prominent symbol of fraternity;—all describing non-Hellenic men, or cities, by a word which involved associations of repugnance. Our term *barbarian*, borrowed from this latter word, does not express the same idea; for the Greeks spoke thus indiscriminately of the extra-Hellenic world, with all its inhabitants;[364] whatever might be the gentleness of their character, and whatever might be their degree of civilization. The rulers and people of Egyptian Thebes, with their ancient and gigantic monuments, the wealthy Tyrians and Carthaginians, the phil-Hellene Arganthonius of Tartêssus, and the well-disciplined patricians of Rome (to the indignation of old Cato,[365]) were all comprised in it. At first, it seemed to have expressed more of repugnance than of contempt, and repugnance especially towards the sound of a foreign language.[366] Afterwards, a feeling of their own superior intelligence (in part well justified) arose among the Greeks, and their term *barbarian* was used so as to imply a low state of the temper and intelligence; in which sense it was retained by the semi-Hellenized Romans, as the proper antithesis to their state of civilization. The want of a suitable word, corresponding to *barbarian*, as the Greeks originally used it, is so inconvenient in the description of Grecian phenomena and sentiments, that I may be obliged occasionally to use the word in its primitive sense.

The Hellens were all of common blood and parentage,—were all descendants of the common patriarch Hellen. In treating of the historical Greeks, we have to accept this as a datum: it represents the sentiment under the influence of which they moved and acted. It is placed by Herodotus in the front rank, as the chief of those four ties which bound together the Hellenic aggregate: 1. Fellowship of blood; 2. Fellowship of language; 3. Fixed domiciles of gods, and sacrifices, common to all; 4. Like manners and dispositions.

*These* (say the Athenians, in their reply to the Spartan envoys, in the very crisis of the Persian invasion) "Athens will never disgrace herself by betraying." And Zeus Hellenius was recognized as the god watching over and enforcing the fraternity thus constituted.[367]

Hekatæus, Herodotus, and Thucydidês,[368] all believed that there had been an ante-Hellenic period, when different languages, mutually unintelligible, were spoken between Mount Olympus and Cape Malea. However this may be, during the historical times the Greek language was universal throughout these limits,—branching out, however, into a great variety of dialects, which were roughly classified by later literary men into Ionic, Doric, Æolic, and Attic. But the classification presents a semblance of regularity, which in point of fact does not seem to have been realized; each town, each smaller subdivision of the Hellenic name, having peculiarities of dialect belonging to itself. Now the lettered men who framed the quadruple division took notice chiefly, if not exclusively, of the written dialects,—those which had been ennobled by poets or other authors; the mere spoken idioms were for the most part neglected.[369] That there was no such thing as one Ionic dialect in the speech of the people called Ionic Greek, we know from the indisputable testimony of Herodotus,[370] who tells us that there were four capital varieties of speech among the twelve Asiatic towns especially known as Ionic. Of course, the varieties would have been much more numerous if he had given us the impressions of his ear in Eubœa, the Cyclades, Massalia, Rhegium, and Olbia,—all numbered as Greeks and as Ionians. The Ionic dialect of the grammarians was an extract from Homer, Hekatæus, Herodotus, Hippocrates, etc.; to what living speech it made the nearest approach, amidst those divergences which the historian has made known to us, we cannot tell. Sapphô and Alkæus in Lesbos, Myrtis and Korinna in Bœotia, were the great sources of reference for the Lesbian and Bœotian varieties of the Æolic dialect,—of which there was a third variety, untouched by the poets, in Thessaly.[371] The analogy between the different manifestations of Doric and Æolic, as well as that between the Doric generally and the Æolic generally, contrasted with the Attic, is only to be taken as rough and approximative.

But all these different dialects are nothing more than dialects, distinguished as modifications of one and the same language, and exhibiting evidence of certain laws and principles pervading them all. They seem capable of being traced back to a certain ideal mother-language, peculiar in itself and distinguishable from, though cognate with, the Latin; a substantive member of what has been called the Indo-European family of languages. This truth has been brought out, in recent times, by the comparative examination applied to the Sanscrit, Zend, Greek, Latin, German, and Lithuanian languages, as well as by the more accurate analysis of the Greek language itself to which such studies have given rise, in a manner much more clear than could have been imagined by the ancients themselves.[372] It is needless to dwell upon the importance of this uniformity of language in holding together the race, and in rendering the genius of its most favored members available to the civilization of all. Except in the rarest cases, the divergences of dialect were not such as to prevent every Greek from understanding, and being understood by, every other Greek,—a fact remarkable, when we consider how many of their outlying colonists, not having taken out women in their emigration, intermarried with non-Hellenic wives. And the perfection and popularity of their early epic poems, was here of inestimable value for the diffusion of a common type of language, and for thus keeping together the sympathies of the Hellenic world.[373] The Homeric dialect became the standard followed by all Greek poets for the hexameter, as may be seen particularly from the example of Hesiod,—who adheres to it in the main, though his father was a native of the Æolic Kymê, and he himself resident at Askra, in the Æolic Bœotia,—and the early iambic and elegiac compositions are framed on the same model. Intellectual Greeks in all cities, even the most distant outcasts from the central hearth, became early accustomed to one type of literary speech, and possessors of a common stock of legends, maxims, and metaphors.

That community of religious sentiments, localities, and sacrifices, which Herodotus names as the third bond of union among the Greeks, was a phenomenon, not (like the race and the language) interwoven with their primitive constitution, but of gradual growth. In the time of Herodotus, and even a century earlier, it was at its full maturity: but there had been a period when no religious meetings common to the whole Hellenic body existed. What are called the Olympic, Pythian, Nemean, and Isthmian games, (the four most conspicuous amidst many others analogous,) were, in reality, great religious festivals,—for the gods then gave their special sanction, name, and presence, to recreative meetings,—the closest association then prevailed between the feelings of common worship and the sympathy in common amusement.[374] Though this association is now no longer recognized, it is, nevertheless, essential that we should keep it fully before us, if we desire to understand the life and proceedings of the Greeks. To Herodotus and his contemporaries, these great festivals, then frequented by crowds from every part of Greece, were of overwhelming importance and interest; yet they had once been purely local, attracting no visitors except from a very narrow neighborhood. In the Homeric poems, much is said about the common gods, and about special places consecrated to and occupied by several of them: the chiefs celebrate funeral games in honor of a deceased father, which are visited by competitors from different parts of Greece, but nothing appears to manifest public or town festivals open to Grecian visitors generally.[375] And, though the rocky Pytho, with its temple, stands out in the Iliad as a place both venerated and rich,—the Pythian games, under the superintendence of the Amphiktyons, with continuous enrolment of victors, and a Pan-Hellenic reputation, do not begin until after the Sacred War, in the 48th Olympiad, or 586 B. C.[376]

The Olympic games, more conspicuous than the Pythian, as well as considerably older, are also remarkable on another ground, inasmuch as they supplied historical computers with the oldest backward record of continuous time. It was in the year 776 B. C., that the Eleians inscribed the name of their countryman, Korœbus, as victor in the competition of runners, and that they began the practice of inscribing in like manner, in each Olympic, or fifth recurring year, the name of the runner who won the prize. Even for a long time after this, however, the Olympic games seem to have remained a local festival; the prize being uniformly carried off, at the first twelve Olympiads, by some competitor either of Elis or its immediate neighborhood. The Nemean and Isthmian games did not become notorious or frequented until later even than the Pythian. Solôn,[377] in his legislation, proclaimed the large reward of five hundred drachms for every Athenian who gained an Olympic prize, and the lower sum of one hundred drachms for an Isthmiac prize. He counts the former, as Pan-Hellenic rank and renown, an ornament even to the city of which the victor was a member,—the latter, as partial, and confined to the neighborhood.

Of the beginnings of these great solemnities, we cannot presume to speak, except in mythical language: we know them only in their comparative maturity. But the habit of common sacrifice, on a small scale, and between near neighbors, is a part of the earliest habits of Greece. The sentiment of fraternity, between two tribes or villages, first manifested itself by sending a sacred legation, or Theôria,[378] to offer sacrifice at each other's festivals, and to partake in the recreations which followed; thus establishing a truce with solemn guarantee, and bringing themselves into direct connection each with the god of the other under his appropriate local surname. The pacific communion so fostered, and the increased assurance of intercourse, as Greece gradually emerged from the turbulence and pugnacity of the heroic age, operated especially in extending the range of this ancient habit: the village festivals became town festivals, largely frequented by the citizens of other towns, and sometimes with special invitations sent round to attract Theôrs from every Hellenic community,—and thus these once humble assemblages gradually swelled into the pomp and immense confluence of the Olympic and Pythian games. The city administering such holy ceremonies enjoyed inviolability of territory during the month of their occurrence, being itself under obligation at that time to refrain from all aggression, as well as to notify by heralds[379] the commencement of the truce to all other cities not in avowed hostility with it. Elis imposed heavy fines upon other towns—even on the powerful Lacedæmon—for violation of the Olympic truce, on pain of exclusion from the festival in case of non-payment.

Sometimes this tendency to religious fraternity took a form called an Amphiktyony, different from the common festival. A certain number of towns entered into an exclusive religious partnership, for the celebration of sacrifices periodically to the god of a particular temple, which was supposed to be the common property, and under the common protection of all, though one of the number was often named as permanent administrator; while all other Greeks were excluded. That there were many religious partnerships of this sort, which have never acquired a place in history, among the early Grecian villages, we may, perhaps, gather from the etymology of the word, (Amphiktyons[380] designates residents around, or neighbors, considered in the point of view of fellow-religionists,) as well as from the indications preserved to us in reference to various parts of the country. Thus there was an Amphiktyony[381] of seven cities at the holy island of Kalauria, close to the harbor of Trœzên. Hermionê, Epidaurus, Ægina, Athens, Prasiæ, Nauplia, and Orchomenus, jointly maintained the temple and sanctuary of Poseidôn in that island, (with which it would seem that the city of Trœzên, though close at hand, had no connection,) meeting there at stated periods, to offer formal sacrifices. These seven cities, indeed, were not immediate neighbors, but the speciality and exclusiveness of their interest in the temple is seen from the fact, that when the Argeians took Nauplia, they adopted and fulfilled these religious obligations on behalf of the prior inhabitants: so, also, did the Lacedæmonians, when they had captured Prasiæ. Again, in Triphylia,[382] situated between the Pisatid and Messenia, in the western part of Peloponnesus, there was a similar religious meeting and partnership of the Triphylians on Cape Samikon, at the temple of the Samian Poseidôn. Here, the inhabitants of Makiston were intrusted with the details of superintendence, as well as with the duty of notifying beforehand the exact time of meeting, (a precaution essential amidst the diversities and irregularities of the Greek calendar,) and also of proclaiming what was called the Samian truce,—a temporary abstinence from hostilities, which bound all Triphylians during the holy period. This latter custom discloses the salutary influence of such institutions in presenting to men's minds a common object of reverence, common duties, and common enjoyments; thus generating sympathies and feelings of mutual obligation amidst petty communities not less fierce than suspicious.[383] So, too, the twelve chief Ionic cities in and near Asia Minor, had their Pan-Ionic Amphiktyony peculiar to themselves: the six Doric cities, in and near the southern corner of that peninsula, combined for the like purpose at the temple of the Triopian Apollo; and the feeling of special partnership is here particularly illustrated by the fact, that Halikarnassus, one of the six, was formally extruded by the remaining five, in consequence of a violation of the rules.[384] There was also an Amphiktyonic union at Onchêstus in Bœotia, in the venerated grove and temple of Poseidôn:[385] of whom it consisted, we are not informed. These are some specimens of the sort of special religious conventions and assemblies which seem to have been frequent throughout Greece. Nor ought we to omit those religious meetings and sacrifices which were common to all the members of one Hellenic subdivision, such as the Pam-Bœotia to all the Bœotians, celebrated at the temple of the Itonian Athênê near Korôneia,[386]—the common observances, rendered to the temple of Apollo Pythaëus at Argos, by all those neighboring towns which had once been attached by this religious thread to the Argeians, —the similar periodical ceremonies, frequented by all who bore the Achæan or Ætolian name,—and the splendid and exhilarating festivals, so favorable to the diffusion of the early Grecian poetry, which brought all Ionians at stated intervals to the sacred island of Delos.[387] This latter class of festivals agreed with the Amphiktyony, in being of a special and exclusive character, not open to all Greeks.

But there was one amongst these many Amphiktyonies, which, though starting from the smallest beginnings, gradually expanded into so comprehensive a character, and acquired so marked a predominance over the rest, as to be called The Amphiktyonic Assembly, and even to have been mistaken by some authors for a sort of federal Hellenic Diet. Twelve sub-races, out of the number which made up entire Hellas, belonged to this ancient Amphiktyony, the meetings of which were held twice in every year: in spring, at the temple of Apollo at Delphi; in autumn, at Thermopylæ, in the sacred precinct of Dêmêtêr Amphiktyonis. Sacred deputies, including a chief called the Hieromnêmôn, and subordinates called the Pylagoræ, attended at these meetings from each of the twelve races: a crowd of volunteers seem to have accompanied them, for purposes of sacrifice, trade, or enjoyment. Their special, and most important function, consisted in watching over the Delphian temple, in which all the twelve sub-races had a joint interest; and it was the immense wealth and national ascendency of this temple, which enhanced to so great a pitch the dignity of its acknowledged administrators.

The twelve constituent members were as follows: Thessalians, Bœotians, Dorians, Ionians, Perrhæbians, Magnêtes, Lokrians, Œtæans, Achæans, Phokians, Dolopes, and Malians.[388] All are counted as *races*, (if we treat the Hellenes as a race, we must call these *sub-races*,) no mention being made of cities:[389] all count equally in respect to voting, two votes being given by the deputies from each of the twelve: moreover, we are told that, in determining the deputies to be sent, or the manner in which the votes of each race should be given, the powerful Athens, Sparta, and Thebes, had no more influence than the humblest Ionian, Dorian, or Bœotian city. This latter fact is distinctly stated by Æschines, himself a pylagore sent to Delphi by Athens. And so, doubtless, the theory of the case stood: the votes of the Ionic races counted for neither more nor less than two, whether given by deputies from Athens, or from the small towns of Erythræ and Priênê; and, in like manner, the Dorian votes were as good in the division, when given by deputies from Bœon and Kytinion in the little territory of Doris, as if the men delivering them had been Spartans. But there can be as little question that, in practice, the little Ionic cities, and the little Doric cities, pretended to no share in the Amphyktionic deliberations. As the Ionic vote came to be substantially the vote of Athens, so, if Sparta was ever obstructed in the management of the Doric vote, it must have been by powerful Doric cities like Argos or Corinth, not by the insignificant towns of Doris. But the theory of Amphiktyonic suffrage, as laid down by Æschines, however little realized in practice during his day, is important, inasmuch as it shows in full evidence the primitive and original constitution. The first establishment of the Amphyktionic convocation dates from a time when all twelve members were on a footing of equal independence, and when there were no overwhelming cities (such as Sparta and Athens) to cast in the shade the humbler members,—when Sparta was only one Doric city, and Athens only one Ionic city, among various others of consideration, not much inferior.

There are also other proofs which show the high antiquity of this Amphiktyonic convocation. Æschines gives us an extract from the oath which had been taken by the sacred deputies, who attended on behalf of their respective races, ever since its first establishment, and which still apparently continued to be taken in his day. The antique simplicity of this oath, and of the conditions to which the members bind themselves, betrays the early age in which it originated, as well as the humble resources of those towns to which it was applied.[390] "We will not destroy any Amphiktyonic town,—we will not cut off any Amphiktyonic town from running water,"—such are the two prominent obligations which Æschines specifies out of the old oath. The second of the two carries us back to the simplest state of society, and to towns of the smallest size, when the maidens went out with their basins to fetch water from the spring, like the daughters of Keleos at Eleusis, or those of Athens from the fountain of Kallirrhoê.[391] We may even conceive that the special mention of this detail, in the covenant between the twelve races, is borrowed literally from agreements still earlier, among the villages or little towns in which the members of each race were distributed. At any rate, it proves satisfactorily the very ancient date to which the commencement of the Amphiktyonic convocation must be referred. The belief of Æschines (perhaps, also, the belief general in his time) was, that it commenced simultaneously with the first foundation of the Delphian temple,—an event of which we have no historical knowledge; but there seems reason to suppose that its original establishment is connected with Thermopylæ and Dêmêtêr Amphiktyonis, rather than with Delphi and Apollo. The special surname by which Dêmêtêr and her temple at Thermopylæ was known,[392]—the temple of the hero Amphiktyon which stood at its side,—the word Pylæ, which obtained footing in the language to designate the half-yearly meeting of the deputies both at Thermopylæ and at Delphi,—these indications point to Thermopylæ (the real central point for all the twelve) as the primary place of meeting, and to the Delphian half-year as something secondary and superadded. On such a matter, however, we cannot go beyond a conjecture.

The hero Amphiktyon, whose temple stood at Thermopylæ, passed in mythical genealogy for the brother of Hellên. And it may be affirmed, with truth, that the habit of forming Amphiktyonic unions, and of frequenting each other's religious festivals was the great means of creating and fostering the primitive feeling of brotherhood among the children of Hellên, in those early times when rudeness, insecurity, and pugnacity did so much to isolate them. A certain number of salutary habits and sentiments, such as that which the Amphiktyonic oath embodies, in regard to abstinence from injury, as well as to mutual protection,[393] gradually found their way into men's minds: the obligations thus brought into play, acquired a substantive efficacy of their own, and the religious feeling which always remained connected with them, came afterwards to be only one out of many complex agencies by which the later historical Greek was moved. Athens and Sparta in the days of their might, and the inferior cities in relation to them, played each their own political game, in which religious considerations will be found to bear only a subordinate part.

The special function of the Amphiktyonic council, so far as we know it, consisted in watching over the safety, the interests, and the treasures of the Delphian temple. "If any one shall plunder the property of the god, or shall be cognizant thereof, or shall take treacherous counsel against the things in the temple, we will punish him with foot, and hand, and voice, and by every means in our power." So ran the old Amphiktyonic oath, with an energetic imprecation attached to it.[394] And there are some examples in which the council[395] construes its functions so largely as to receive and adjudicate upon complaints against entire cities, for offences against the religious and patriotic sentiment of the Greeks generally. But for the most part its interference relates directly to the Delphian temple. The earliest case in which it is brought to our view, is the Sacred War against Kirrha, in the 46th Olympiad, or 595 B. C., conducted by Eurylochus, the Thessalian, and Kleisthenes of Sikyôn, and proposed by Solôn of Athens:[396] we find the Amphiktyons also, about half a century afterwards, undertaking the duty of collecting subscriptions throughout the Hellenic world, and making the contract with the Alkmæonids for rebuilding the temple after a conflagration. [397] But the influence of this council is essentially of a fluctuating and intermittent character. Sometimes it appears forward to decide, and its decisions command respect; but such occasions are rare, taking the general course of known Grecian history; while there are other occasions, and those too especially affecting the Delphian temple, on which we are surprised to find nothing said about it. In the long and perturbed period which Thucydidês describes, he never once mentioned the Amphiktyons, though the temple and the safety of its treasures form the repeated subject[398] as well of dispute as of express stipulation between Athens and Sparta: moreover, among the twelve constituent members of the council, we find three—the Perrhæbians, the Magnêtes, and the Achæans of Phthia—who were not even independent, but subject to the Thessalians, so that its meetings, when they were not matters of mere form, probably expressed only the feelings of the three or four leading members. When one or more of these great powers had a party purpose to accomplish against others,—when Philip of Macedon wished to extrude one of the members in order to procure admission for himself,—it became convenient to turn this ancient form into a serious reality, and we shall see the Athenian Æschines providing a pretext for Philip to meddle in favor of the minor Bœotian cities against Thebes, by alleging that these cities were under the protection of the old Amphiktyonic oath.[399]

It is thus that we have to consider the council as an element in Grecian affairs,—an ancient institution, one amongst many instances of the primitive habit of religious fraternization, but wider and more comprehensive than the rest,—at first, purely religious, then religious and political at once; lastly, more the latter than the former,—highly valuable in the infancy, but unsuited to the maturity of Greece, and called into real working only on rare occasions, when its efficiency happened to fall in with the views of Athens, Thebes, or the king of Macedon. In such special moments it shines with a transient light which affords a partial pretence for the imposing title bestowed on it by Cicero,—"commune Græciæ concilium:"[400] but we should completely misinterpret Grecian history if we regarded it as a federal council, habitually directing or habitually obeyed. Had there existed any such "commune concilium" of tolerable wisdom and patriotism, and had the tendencies of the Hellenic mind been capable of adapting themselves to it, the whole course of later Grecian history would probably have been altered; the Macedonian kings would have remained only as respectable neighbors, borrowing civilization from Greece, and expending their military energies upon Thracians and Illyrians; while united Hellas might even have maintained her own territory against the conquering legions of Rome.

The twelve constituent Amphiktyonic races remained unchanged until the Sacred War against the Phokians (B. C. 355), after which, though the number twelve was continued, the Phokians were disfranchised, and their votes transferred to Philip of Macedon. It has been already mentioned that these twelve did not exhaust the whole of Hellas. Arcadians, Eleans, Pisans, Minyæ, Dryopes, Ætolians, all genuine Hellens, are not comprehended in it; but all of them had a right to make use of the temple of Delphi, and to contend in the Pythian and Olympic games. The Pythian games, celebrated near Delphi, were under the superintendence of the Amphiktyons,[401] or of some acting magistrate chosen by and presumed to represent them: like the Olympic games, they came round every four years (the interval between one celebration and another being four complete years, which the Greeks called a Pentaetêris): the Isthmian and Nemean games recurred every two years. In its first humble form, of a competition among bards to sing a hymn in praise of Apollo, this festival was doubtless of immemorial antiquity;[402] but the first extension of it into Pan-Hellenic notoriety (as I have already remarked), the first multiplication of the subjects of competition, and the first introduction of a continuous record of the conquerors, date only from the time when it came under the presidency of the Amphiktyons, at the close of the Sacred War against Kirrha. What is called the first Pythian contest coincides with the third year of the 48th Olympiad, or 585 B. C. From that period forward, the games become crowded and celebrated: but the date just named, nearly two centuries after the first Olympiad, is a proof that the habit of periodical frequentation of festivals, by numbers and from distant parts, grew up but slowly in the Grecian world.

The foundation of the temple of Delphi itself reaches far beyond all historical knowledge, forming one of the aboriginal institutions of Hellas. It is a sanctified and wealthy place, even in the Iliad: the legislation of Lykurgus at Sparta is introduced under its auspices, and the earliest Grecian colonies, those of Sicily and Italy in the eighth century B. C., are established in consonance with its mandate. Delphi and Dodona appear, in the most ancient circumstances of Greece, as universally venerated oracles and sanctuaries: and Delphi not only receives honors and donations, but also answers questions, from Lydians, Phrygians, Etruscans, Romans, etc.: it is not exclusively Hellenic. One of the valuable services which a Greek looked for from this and other great religious establishments was, that it should resolve his doubts in cases of perplexity,—that it should advise him whether to begin a new, or to persist in an old project,—that it should foretell what would be his fate under given circumstances, and inform him, if suffering under distress, on what conditions the gods would grant him relief. The three priestesses of Dodona with their venerable oak, and the priestess of Delphi sitting on her tripod under the influence of a certain gas or vapor exhaling from the rock, were alike competent to determine these difficult points: and we shall have constant occasion to notice in this history, with what complete faith both the question was put and the answer treasured up,—what serious influence it often exercised both upon public and private proceeding.[403] The hexameter verses, in which the Pythian priestess delivered herself, were, indeed, often so equivocal or unintelligible, that the most serious believer, with all anxiety to interpret and obey them, often found himself ruined by the result; yet the general faith in the oracle was noway shaken by such painful experience. For as the unfortunate issue always admitted of being explained upon two hypotheses,—either that the god had spoken falsely, or that his meaning had not been correctly understood,—no man of genuine piety ever hesitated to adopt the latter. There were many other oracles throughout Greece besides Delphi and Dodona: Apollo was open to the inquiries of the faithful at Ptôon in Bœotia, at Abæ in Phokis, at Branchidæ near Miletus, at Patara in Lykia, and other places: in like manner, Zeus gave answers at Olympia, Poseidôn at Tænarus, Amphiaraus at Thebes, Amphilochus at Mallas, etc. And this habit of consulting the oracle formed part of the still more general tendency of the Greek mind to undertake no enterprise without having first ascertained how the gods viewed it, and what measures they were likely to take. Sacrifices were offered, and the interior of the victim carefully examined, with the same intent: omens, prodigies, unlooked-for coincidences, casual expressions, etc., were all construed as significant of the divine will. To sacrifice with a view to this or that undertaking, or to consult the oracle with the same view, are familiar expressions[404] embodied in the language. Nor could any man set about a scheme with comfort, until he had satisfied himself in some manner or other that the gods were favorable to it.

The disposition here adverted to is one of those mental analogies pervading the whole Hellenic nation, which Herodotus indicates. And the common habit among all Greeks, of respectfully listening to the oracle of Delphi, will be found on many occasions useful in maintaining unanimity among men not accustomed to obey the same political superior. In the numerous colonies especially, founded by mixed multitudes from distant parts of Greece, the minds of the emigrants were greatly determined towards cordial coöperation by their knowledge that the expedition had been directed, the œkist indicated, and the spot either chosen or approved, by Apollo of Delphi. Such in most cases was the fact: that god, according to the conception of the Greeks, "takes delight always in the foundation of new cities, and himself in person lays the first stone."[405]

These are the elements of union—over and above the common territory, described in the last chapter—with which the historical Hellens take their start: community of blood, language, religious point of view, legends, sacrifices, festivals,[406] and also (with certain allowances) of manners and character. The analogy of manners and character between the rude inhabitants of the Arcadian Kynætha[407] and the polite Athens, was indeed accompanied with wide differences: yet if we compare the two with foreign contemporaries, we shall find certain negative characteristics, of much importance, common to both. In no city of historical Greece did there prevail either human sacrifices,[408]—or deliberate mutilation, such as cutting off the nose, ears, hands, feet, etc.,—or castration,—or selling of children into slavery,—or polygamy,—or the feeling of unlimited obedience towards one man: all customs which might be pointed out as existing among the contemporary Carthaginians, Egyptians, Persians, Thracians,[409] etc. The habit of running, wrestling, boxing, etc., in gymnastic contests, with the body perfectly naked,—was common to all Greeks, having been first adopted as a Lacedæmonian fashion in the fourteenth Olympiad: Thucydidês and Herodotus remark, that it was not only not practised, but even regarded as unseemly, among non-Hellens.[410] Of such customs, indeed, at once common to all the Greeks, and peculiar to them as distinguished from others, we cannot specify a great number; but we may see enough to convince ourselves that there did really exist, in spite of local differences, a general Hellenic sentiment and character, which counted among the cementing causes of an union apparently so little assured.

For we must recollect that, in respect to political sovereignty, complete disunion was among their most cherished principles. The only source of supreme authority to which a Greek felt respect and attachment, was to be sought within the walls of his own city. Authority seated in another city might operate upon his fears,—might procure for him increased security and advantages, as we shall have occasion hereafter to show with regard to Athens and her subject allies,—might even be mildly exercised, and inspire no special aversion: but, still, the principle of it was repugnant to the rooted sentiment of his mind, and he is always found gravitating towards the distinct sovereignty of his own boulê, or ekklêsia. This is a disposition common both to democracies and oligarchies, and operative even among the different towns belonging to the same subdivision of the Hellenic name,—Achæans, Phokians, Bœotians, etc. The twelve Achæan cities are harmonious allies, with a periodical festival which partakes of the character of a congress,—but equal and independent political communities: the Bœotian towns, under the presidency of Thebes, their reputed metropolis, recognize certain common obligations, and obey, on various particular matters, chosen officers named bœotarchs,—but we shall see, in this, as in other cases, the centrifugal tendencies constantly manifesting themselves, and resisted chiefly by the interests and power of Thebes. That great, successful, and fortunate revolution, which merged the several independent political communities of Attica into the single unity of Athens, took place before the time of authentic history: it is connected with the name of the hero Theseus, but we know not how it was effected, while its comparatively large size and extent, render it a signal exception to Hellenic tendencies generally.

Political disunion—sovereign authority within the city walls—thus formed a settled maxim in the Greek mind. The relation between one city and another was an international relation, not a relation subsisting between members of a common political aggregate. Within a few miles from his own city-walls, an Athenian found himself in the territory of another city, wherein he was nothing more than an alien,—where he could not acquire property in house or land, nor contract a legal marriage with any native woman, nor sue for legal protection against injury, except through the mediation of some friendly citizen. The right of intermarriage, and of acquiring landed property, was occasionally granted by a city to some individual non-freeman, as matter of special favor, and sometimes (though very rarely) reciprocated generally between two separate cities.[411] But the obligations between one city and another, or between the citizen of the one and the citizen of the other, are all matters of special covenant, agreed to by the sovereign authority in each. Such coexistence of entire political severance with so much fellowship in other ways, is perplexing in modern ideas, and modern language is not well furnished with expressions to describe Greek political phenomena. We may say that an Athenian citizen was an *alien* when he arrived as a visitor in Corinth, but we can hardly say that he was a *foreigner*; and though the relations between Corinth and Athens were in principle *international*, yet that word would be obviously unsuitable to the numerous petty autonomies of Hellas, besides that we require it for describing the relations of Hellenes generally with Persians or Carthaginians. We are compelled to use a word such as *interpolitical*, to describe the transactions between separate Greek cities, so numerous in the course of this history.

As, on the one hand, a Greek will not consent to look for sovereign authority beyond the limits of his own city, so, on the other hand, he must have a city to look to: scattered villages will not satisfy in his mind the exigencies of social order, security, and dignity. Though the coalescence of smaller towns into a larger is repugnant to his feelings, that of villages into a town appears to him a manifest advance in the scale of civilization. Such, at least, is the governing sentiment of Greece throughout the historical period; for there was always a certain portion of the Hellenic aggregate—the rudest and least advanced among them—who dwelt in unfortified villages, and upon whom the citizen of Athens, Corinth, or Thebes, looked down as inferiors. Such village residence was the character of the Epirots[412] universally, and prevailed throughout Hellas itself, in those very early and even ante-Homeric times upon which Thucydidês looked back as deplorably barbarous;—times of universal poverty and insecurity,—absence of pacific intercourse,—petty warfare and plunder, compelling every man to pass his life armed,—endless migration without any local attachments. Many of the considerable cities of Greece are mentioned as aggregations of preëxisting villages, some of them in times comparatively recent. Tegea and Mantineia in Arcadia, represent, in this way, the confluence of eight villages, and five villages respectively; Dymê in Achaia was brought together out of eight villages, and Elis in the same manner, at a period even later than the Persian invasion;[413] the like seems to have happened with Megara and Tanagra. A large proportion of the Arcadians continued their village life down to the time of the battle of Leuktra, and it suited the purposes of Sparta to keep them thus disunited; a policy which we shall see hereafter illustrated by the dismemberment of Mantineia (into its primitive component villages), which Agesilaus carried into effect, but which was reversed as soon as the power of Sparta was no longer paramount,—as well as by the foundation of Megalopolis out of a large number of petty Arcadian towns and villages, one of the capital measures of Epameinondas. [414] As this measure was an elevation of Arcadian importance, so the reverse proceeding—the breaking up of a city into its elementary villages—was not only a sentence of privation and suffering, but also a complete extinction of Grecian rank and dignity.

The Ozolian Lokrians, the Ætolians, and the Akarnanians maintained their separate village residence down to a still later period, preserving along with it their primitive rudeness and disorderly pugnacity.[415] Their villages were unfortified, and defended only by comparative inaccessibility; in case of need, they fled for safety with their cattle into the woods and mountains. Amidst such inauspicious circumstances, there was no room for that expansion of the social and political feelings to which protected intramural residence and increased numbers gave birth; there was no consecrated acropolis or agora,— no ornamented temples and porticos, exhibiting the continued offerings of successive generations,[416]—no theatre for music or recitation, no gymnasium for athletic exercises,—none of those fixed arrangements, for transacting public business with regularity and decorum, which the Greek citizen, with his powerful sentiment of locality, deemed essential to a dignified existence. The village was nothing more than a fraction and a subordinate, appertaining as a limb to the organized body called the city. But the city and the state are in his mind, and in his language, one and the same. While no organization less than the city can satisfy the exigencies[417] of an intelligent freeman, the city is itself a perfect and self-sufficient whole, admitting no incorporation into any higher political unity. It deserves notice that Sparta, even in the days of her greatest power, was not (properly speaking) a city, but a mere agglutination of five adjacent villages, retaining unchanged its old-fashioned trim: for the extreme defensibility of its frontier and the military prowess of its inhabitants, supplied the absence of walls, while the discipline imposed upon the Spartan, exceeded in rigor and minuteness anything known in Greece. And thus Sparta, though less than a city in respect to external appearance, was more than a city in respect to perfection of drilling and fixity of political routine. The contrast between the humble appearance and the mighty reality, is pointed out by Thucydides.[418] The inhabitants of the small territory of Pisa, wherein Olympia is situated, had once enjoyed the honorable privilege of administering the Olympic festival. Having been robbed of it, and subjected by the more powerful Eleians, they took advantage of various movements and tendencies among the larger Grecian powers to try and regain it; and on one of these occasions, we find their claim repudiated because they were villagers, and unworthy of so great a distinction.[419] There was nothing to be called a city in the Pisatid territory.

In going through historical Greece, we are compelled to accept the Hellenic aggregate with its constituent elements as a primary fact to start from, because the state of our information does not enable us to ascend any higher. By what circumstances, or out of what preëxisting elements, this aggregate was brought together and modified, we find no evidence entitled to credit. There are, indeed, various names which are affirmed to designate ante-Hellenic inhabitants of many parts of Greece,—the Pelasgi, the Leleges, the Kurêtes, the Kaukônes, the Aones, the Temmikes, the Hyantes, the Telchines, the Bœotian Thracians, the Teleboæ, the Ephyri, the Phlegyæ, etc. These are names belonging to legendary, not to historical Greece,—extracted out of a variety of conflicting legends, by the logographers and subsequent historians, who strung together out of them a supposed history of the past, at a time when the conditions of historical evidence were very little understood. That these names designated real nations, may be true, but here our knowledge ends. We have no well-informed witness to tell us their times, their limits of residence, their acts, or their character; nor do we know how far they are identical with or diverse from the historical Hellens,—whom we are warranted in calling, not, indeed, the first inhabitants of the country, but the first known to us upon any tolerable evidence. If any man is inclined to call the unknown ante-

Hellenic period of Greece by the name of Pelasgic, it is open to him to do so; but this is a name carrying with it no assured predicates, noway enlarging our insight into real history, nor enabling us to explain—what would be the real historical problem—how or from whom the Hellens acquired that stock of dispositions, aptitudes, arts, etc., with which they begin their career. Whoever has examined the many conflicting systems respecting the Pelasgi,—from the literal belief of Clavier, Larcher, and Raoul Rochette, (which appears to me, at least, the most consistent way of proceeding,) to the interpretative and half-incredulous processes applied by abler men, such as Niebuhr, or O. Müller, or Dr. Thirlwall,[420]—will not be displeased with my resolution to decline so insoluble a problem. No attested facts are now present to us—none were present to Herodotus and Thucydidês, even in their age—on which to build trustworthy affirmations respecting the ante-Hellenic Pelasgians. And where such is the case, we may without impropriety apply the remark of Herodotus, respecting one of the theories which he had heard for explaining the inundation of the Nile by a supposed connection with the circumfluous Ocean,—that "the man who carries up his story into the invisible world, passes out of the range of criticism."[421]

As far as our knowledge extends, there were no towns or villages called Pelasgian, in Greece proper, since 776 B. C. But there still existed in two different places, even in the age of Herodotus, people whom he believed to be Pelasgians. One portion of these occupied the towns of Plakia and Skylakê near Kyzikus, on the Propontis; another dwelt in a town called Krêstôn, near the Thermaic gulf.[422] There were, moreover, certain other Pelasgian townships which he does not specify,—it seems, indeed, from Thucydides, that there were some little Pelasgian townships on the peninsula of Athos.[423] Now, Herodotus acquaints us with the remarkable fact, that the people of Krêstôn, those of Plakia and Skylakê, and those of the other unnamed Pelasgian townships, all spoke the same language, and each of them respectively a different language from their neighbors around them. He informs us, moreover, that their language was a barbarous (*i. e.* a non-Hellenic) language; and this fact he quotes as an evidence to prove that the ancient Pelasgian language was a barbarous language, or distinct from the Hellenic. He at the same time states expressly that he has no positive knowledge what language the ancient Pelasgians spoke,—one proof, among others, that no memorials nor means of distinct information concerning that people, could have been open to him.

This is the one single fact, amidst so many conjectures concerning the Pelasgians, which we can be said to know upon the testimony of a competent and contemporary witness: the few townships—scattered and inconsiderable, but all that Herodotus in his day knew as Pelasgian—spoke a barbarous language. And upon such a point, he must be regarded as an excellent judge. If, then, (infers the historian,) all the early Pelasgians spoke the same language as those of Krêstôn and Plakia, they must have changed their language at the time when they passed into the Hellenic aggregate, or became Hellens. Now, Herodotus conceives that aggregate to have been gradually enlarged to its great actual size by incorporating with itself not only the Pelasgians, but several other nations once barbarians;[424] the Hellens having been originally an inconsiderable people. Among those other nations once barbarian, whom Herodotus supposes to have become Hellenized, we may probably number the Leleges; and with respect to them, as well as to the Pelasgians, we have contemporary testimony proving the existence of barbarian Leleges in later times. Philippus, the Karian historian, attested the present existence, and believed in the past existence, of Leleges in his country, as serfs or dependent cultivators under the Karians, analogous to the Helots in Laconia, or the Penestæ in Thessaly.[425] We may be very sure that there were no Hellens—no men speaking the Hellenic tongue—standing in such a relation to the Karians. Among those many barbaric-speaking nations whom Herodotus believed to have changed their language and passed into Hellens, we may, therefore, fairly consider the Leleges to have been included. For next to the Pelasgians and Pelasgus, the Leleges and Lelex figure most conspicuously in the legendary genealogies; and both together cover the larger portion of the Hellenic soil.

Confining myself to historical evidence, and believing that no assured results can be derived from the attempt to transform legend into history, I accept the statement of Herodotus with confidence, as to the barbaric language spoken by the Pelasgians of his day; and I believe the same with regard to the historical Leleges,—but without presuming to determine anything in regard to the legendary Pelasgians and Leleges, the supposed ante-Hellenic inhabitants of Greece. And I think this course more consonant to the laws of historical inquiry than that which comes recommended by the high authority of Dr. Thirlwall, who softens and explains away the statement of Herodotus, until it is made to mean only that the Pelasgians of Plakia and Krêstôn spoke a very bad Greek. The affirmation of Herodotus is distinct, and twice repeated, that the Pelasgians of these towns, and of his own time, spoke a barbaric language; and that word appears to me to admit of but one interpretation.[426] To suppose that a man, who, like Herodotus, had heard almost every variety of Greek, in the course of his long travels, as well as Egyptian, Phœnician, Assyrian, Lydian, and other languages, did not know how to distinguish bad Hellenic from non-Hellenic, is, in my judgment, inadmissible; at any rate, the supposition is not to be adopted without more cogent evidence than any which is here found.

As I do not presume to determine what were the antecedent internal elements out of which the Hellenic aggregate was formed, so I confess myself equally uninformed with regard to its external constituents. Kadmus, Danaus, Kekrops,—the eponyms of the Kadmeians, of the Danaans, and of the Attic Kekropia,—present themselves to my vision as creatures of legend, and in that character I have already adverted to them. That there may have been very early settlements in continental Greece, from Phœnicia and Egypt, is nowise impossible; but I see neither positive proof, nor ground for probable inference, that there were any such, though traces of Phœnician settlements in some of the islands may doubtless be pointed out. And if we examine the character and aptitudes of Greeks, as compared either with Egyptians or Phœnicians, it will appear that there is not only no analogy, but an obvious and fundamental contrast: the Greek may occasionally be found as a borrower from these ultramarine contemporaries, but he cannot be looked upon as their offspring or derivative. Nor can I bring myself to accept an hypothesis which implies (unless we are to regard the supposed foreign emigrants as very few in number, in which case the question loses most of its importance) that the Hellenic language—the noblest among the many varieties of human speech, and possessing within itself a pervading symmetry and organization—is a mere confluence of two foreign barbaric languages (Phœnician and Egyptian) with two or more internal barbaric languages,—Pelasgian, Lelegian, etc. In the mode of investigation pursued by different historians into this question of early foreign colonies, there is great difference (as in the case of the Pelasgi) between the different authors,—from the acquiescent Euemerism of Raoul Rochette to the refined distillation of Dr. Thirlwall, in the third chapter of his History. It will be found that the amount of positive knowledge which Dr. Thirlwall guarantees to his readers in that chapter is extremely inconsiderable; for though he proceeds upon the general theory (different from that which I hold) that historical matter may be distinguished and elicited from the legends, yet when the question arises respecting any definite historical result, his canon of credibility is too just to permit him to overlook the absence of positive evidence, even when all intrinsic incredibility is removed. That which I note as Terra Incognita, is in his view a land which may be known up to a certain point; but the map which he draws of it contains so few ascertained places as to differ very little from absolute vacuity.

The most ancient district called Hellas is affirmed by Aristotle to have been near Dôdôna and the river Achelôus,—a description which would have been unintelligible (since the river does not flow near Dôdôna), if it had not been qualified by the remark, that the river had often in former times changed its course. He states, moreover, that the deluge of Deukaliôn took place chiefly in this district, which was in those early days inhabited by the Selli, and by the people then called Græci, but now Hellenes.[427] The Selli (called by Pindar, Helli) are mentioned in the Iliad as the ministers of the Dodonæan Zeus,—"men who slept on the ground, and never washed their feet;" and Hesiod, in one of the lost poems (the Eoiai), speaks of the fat land and rich pastures of the land called Hellopia, wherein Dôdôna was situated.[428] On what authority Aristotle made his statement, we do not know; but the general feeling of the Greeks was different,—connecting Deukaliôn, Hellen, and the Hellenes, primarily and specially with the territory called Achaia Phthiôtis, between Mount Othrys and Œta. Nor can we either affirm or deny his assertion that the people in the neighborhood of Dôdôna were called Græci before they were called Hellenes. There is no ascertained instance of the mention of a people called Græci, in any author earlier than this Aristotelian treatise; for the allusions to Alkman and Sophoklês prove nothing to the point. [429] Nor can we explain how it came to pass that the Hellenes were known to the Romans only under the name of Græci, or Graii. But the name by which a people is known to foreigners is often completely different from its own domestic name, and we are not less at a loss to assign the reason, how the Rasena of Etruria came to be known to the Romans by the name of Tuscans, or Etruscans.

# CHAPTER III.

## MEMBERS OF THE HELLENIC AGGREGATE, SEPARATELY TAKEN.—GREEKS NORTH OF PELOPONNESUS.

HAVING in the preceding chapter touched upon the Greeks in their aggregate capacity, I now come to describe separately the portions of which this aggregate consisted, as they present themselves at the first discernible period of history.

It has already been mentioned that the twelve races or subdivisions, members of what is called the Amphiktyonic convocation, were as follows:—

North of the pass of Thermopylæ,—Thessalians, Perrhæbians, Magnêtes, Achæans, Melians, Ænianes, Dolopes.

South of the pass of Thermopylæ,—Dorians, Ionians, Bœotians, Lokrians, Phokians.

Other Hellenic races, not comprised among the Amphiktyons, were—

The Ætolians and Akarnanians, north of the gulf of Corinth.

The Arcadians, Eleians, Pisatans, and Triphylians, in the central and western portion of Peloponnêsus: I do not here name the Achæans, who occupied the southern or Peloponnesian coast of the Corinthian gulf, because they may be presumed to have been originally of the same race as the Phthiot Achæans, and therefore participant in the Amphiktyonic constituency, though their actual connection with it may have been disused.

The Dryopes, an inconsiderable, but seemingly peculiar subdivision, who occupied some scattered points on the sea-coast,—Hermionê on the Argolic peninsula; Styrus and Karystus in Eubœa; the island of Kythnus, etc.

Though it may be said, in a general way, that our historical discernment of the Hellenic aggregate, apart from the illusions of legend, commences with 776 B. C., yet, with regard to the larger number of its subdivisions just enumerated, we can hardly be said to possess any specific facts anterior to the invasion of Xerxes in 480 B. C. Until the year 560 B. C., (the epoch of Crœsus in Asia Minor, and of Peisistratus at Athens,) the history of the Greeks presents hardly anything of a collective character: the movements of each portion of the Hellenic world begin and end apart from the rest. The destruction of Kirrha by the Amphiktyons is the first historical incident which brings into play, in defence of the Delphian temple, a common Hellenic feeling of active obligation.

But about 560 B. C., two important changes are seen to come into operation, which alter the character of Grecian history,—extricating it out of its former chaos of detail, and centralizing its isolated phenomena: 1. The subjugation of the Asiatic Greeks by Lydia and by Persia, followed by their struggles for emancipation,—wherein the European Greeks became implicated, first as accessories, and afterwards as principals. 2. The combined action of the large mass of Greeks under Sparta, as their most powerful state and acknowledged chief, succeeded by the rapid and extraordinary growth of Athens, the complete development of Grecian maritime power, and the struggle between Athens and Sparta for the headship. These two causes, though distinct in themselves, must, nevertheless, be regarded as working together to a certain degree,—or rather, the second grew out of the first. For it was the Persian invasions of Greece which first gave birth to a wide-spread alarm and antipathy among the leading Greeks (we must not call it Pan-Hellenic, since more than half of the Amphiktyonic constituency gave earth and water to Xerxes) against the barbarians of the East, and impressed them with the necessity of joint active operations under a leader. The idea of a leadership or hegemony of collective Hellas, as a privilege necessarily vested in some one state for common security against the barbarians, thus became current,—an idea foreign to the mind of Solôn, or any one of the same age. Next, came the miraculous development of Athens, and the violent contest between her and Sparta, which should be the leader; the larger portion of Hellas taking side with one or the other, and the common quarrel against the Persian being for the time put out of sight. Athens is put down, Sparta acquires the undisputed hegemony, and again the anti-barbaric feeling manifests itself, though faintly, in the Asiatic expeditions of Agesilaus. But the Spartans, too incompetent either to deserve or maintain this exalted position, are overthrown by the Thebans,—themselves not less incompetent, with the single exception of Epameinondas. The death of that single man extinguishes the pretensions of Thebes to the hegemony, and Hellas is left, like the deserted Penelopê in the Odyssey, worried by the competition of several suitors, none of whom is strong enough to stretch the bow on which the prize depends.[430] Such a manifestation of force, as well as the trampling down of the competing suitors, is reserved, not for any legitimate Hellenic arm, but for a semi-Hellenized[431] Macedonian, "brought up at Pella," and making good his encroachments gradually from the north of Olympus. The hegemony of Greece thus passes forever out of Grecian hands; but the conqueror finds his interest in rekindling the old sentiment under the influence of which it had first sprung up. He binds to him the discordant Greeks, by the force of their ancient and common antipathy against the Great

King, until the desolation and sacrilege once committed by Xerxes at Athens is avenged by annihilation of the Persian empire. And this victorious consummation of Pan-Hellenic antipathy,—the dream of Xenophon[432] and the Ten Thousand Greeks after the battle of Kunaxa,—the hope of Jason of Pheræ,—the exhortation of Isokratês,[433]—the project of Philip, and the achievement of Alexander,—while it manifests the irresistible might of Hellenic ideas and organization in the then existing state of the world, is at the same time the closing scene of substantive Grecian life. The citizen-feelings of Greece become afterwards merely secondary forces, subordinate to the preponderance of Greek mercenaries under Macedonian order, and to the rudest of all native Hellens,—the Ætolian mountaineers. Some few individuals are indeed found, even in the third century B. C., worthy of the best times of Hellas, and the Achæan confederation of that century is an honorable attempt to contend against irresistible difficulties: but on the whole, that free, social, and political march, which gives so much interest to the earlier centuries, is irrevocably banished from Greece after the generation of Alexander the Great.

The foregoing brief sketch will show that, taking the period from Crœsus and Peisistratus down to the generation of Alexander (560-300 B. C.), the phenomena of Hellas generally, and her relations both foreign and interpolitical, admit of being grouped together in masses, with continued dependence on one or a few predominant circumstances. They may be said to constitute a sort of historical epopee, analogous to that which Herodotus has constructed out of the wars between Greeks and barbarians, from the legends of Iô and Eurôpa down to the repulse of Xerxes. But when we are called back to the period between 776 and 560 B. C., the phenomena brought to our knowledge are scanty in number,—exhibiting few common feelings or interests, and no tendency towards any one assignable purpose. To impart attraction to this first period, so obscure and unpromising, we shall be compelled to consider it in its relation with the second; partly as a preparation, partly as a contrast.

Of the extra-Peloponnesian Greeks north of Attica, during these two centuries, we know absolutely nothing; but it will be possible to furnish some information respecting the early condition and struggles of the great Dorian states in Peloponnesus, and respecting the rise of Sparta from the second to the first place in the comparative scale of Grecian powers. Athens becomes first known to us at the legislation of Drako and the attempt of Kylôn (620 B. C.) to make himself despot; and we gather some facts concerning the Ionic cities in Eubœa and Asia Minor, during the century of their chief prosperity, prior to the reign and conquests of Crœsus. In this way, we shall form to ourselves some idea of the growth of Sparta and Athens,—of the short-lived and energetic development of the Ionic Greeks,—and of the slow working of those causes which tended to bring about increased Hellenic intercommunication,—as contrasted with the enlarged range of ambition, the grand Pan-Hellenic ideas, the systematized party-antipathies, and the intensified action, both abroad and at home, which grew out of the contest with Persia.

There are also two or three remarkable manifestations which will require special notice during this first period of Grecian history: 1. The great multiplicity of colonies sent forth by individual cities, and the rise and progress of these several colonies; 2. The number of despots who arose in the various Grecian cities; 3. The lyric poetry; 4. The rudiments of that which afterwards ripened into moral philosophy, as manifested in gnomes, or aphorisms,—or the age of the Seven Wise Men.

But before I proceed to relate those earliest proceedings (unfortunately too few) of the Dorians and Ionians during the historical period, together with the other matters just alluded to, it will be convenient to go over the names and positions of those other Grecian states respecting which we have no information during these first two centuries. Some idea will thus be formed of the less important members of the Hellenic aggregate, previous to the time when they will be called into action. We begin by the territory north of the pass of Thermopylæ.

Of the different races who dwelt between this celebrated pass and the mouth of the river Peneius, by far the most powerful and important were the Thessalians. Sometimes, indeed, the whole of this area passes under the name of Thessaly,—since nominally, though not always really, the power of the Thessalians extended over the whole. We know that the Trachinian Herakleia, founded by the Lacedæmonians in the early years of the Peloponnesian war, close at the pass of Thermopylæ, was planted upon the territory of the Thessalians.[434] But there were also within these limits other races, inferior and dependent on the Thessalians, yet said to be of more ancient date, and certainly not less genuine subdivisions of the Hellenic name. The Perrhæbi[435] occupied the northern portion of the territory between the lower course of the river Peneius and Mount Olympus. The Magnêtes[436] dwelt along the eastern coast, between Mount Ossa and Pelion on one side and the Ægean on the other, comprising the south-eastern cape and the eastern coast of the gulf of Pagasæ as far as Iôlkos. The Achæans occupied the territory called Phthiôtis, extending from near Mount Pindus on the west to the gulf of Pagasæ on the east,[437]—along the mountain chain of Othrys with its lateral projections northerly into the Thessalian plain, and southerly even to its junction with Œta. The three tribes of the Malians dwelt between Achæa

Phthiôtis and Thermopylæ, including both Trachin and Herakleia. Westward of Achæa Phthiôtis, the lofty region of Pindus or Tymphrêstus, with its declivities both westward and eastward, was occupied by the Dolopes.

All these five tribes, or subdivisions,—Perrhæbians, Magnetes, Achæans of Phthiôtis, Malians, and Dolopes, together with certain Epirotic and Macedonian tribes besides, beyond the boundaries of Pindus and Olympus,— were in a state of irregular dependence upon the Thessalians, who occupied the central plain or basin drained by the Peneius. That river receives the streams from Olympus, from Pindus, and from Othrys,—flowing through a region which was supposed by its inhabitants to have been once a lake, until Poseidôn cut open the defile of Tempê, through which the waters found an efflux. In travelling northward from Thermopylæ, the commencement of this fertile region—the amplest space of land continuously productive which Hellas presents—is strikingly marked by the steep rock and ancient fortress of Thaumaki;[438] from whence the traveller, passing over the mountains of Achæa Phthiôtis and Othrys, sees before him the plains and low declivities which reach northward across Thessaly to Olympus. A narrow strip of coast —in the interior of the gulf of Pagasæ, between the Magnêtes and the Achæans, and containing the towns of Amphanæum and Pagasæ[439]— belonged to this proper territory of Thessaly, but its great expansion was inland: within it were situated the cities of Pheræ, Pharsalus, Skotussa, Larissa, Krannôn, Atrax, Pharkadôn, Trikka, Metropolis, Pelinna, etc.

The abundance of corn and cattle from the neighboring plains sustained in these cities a numerous population, and above all a proud and disorderly noblesse, whose manners bore much resemblance to those of the heroic times. They were violent in their behavior, eager in armed feud, but unaccustomed to political discussion or compromise; faithless as to obligations, yet at the same time generous in their hospitalities, and much given to the enjoyments of the table.[440] Breeding the finest horses in Greece, they were distinguished for their excellence as cavalry; but their infantry is little noticed, nor do the Thessalian cities seem to have possessed that congregation of free and tolerably equal citizens, each master of his own arms, out of whom the ranks of hoplites were constituted,—the warlike nobles, such as the Aleuadæ at Larissa, or the Skopadæ at Krannon, despising everything but equestrian service for themselves, furnished, from their extensive herds on the plain, horses for the poorer soldiers. These Thessalian cities exhibit the extreme of turbulent oligarchy, occasionally trampled down by some one man of great vigor, but little tempered by that sense of political communion and reverence for established law, which was found among the better cities of Hellas. Both in Athens and Sparta, so different in many respects from each other, this feeling will be found, if not indeed constantly predominant, yet constantly present and operative. Both of them exhibit a contrast with Larissa or Pheræ not unlike that between Rome and Capua,—the former, with her endless civil disputes constitutionally conducted, admitting the joint action of parties against a common foe; the latter, with her abundant soil enriching a luxurious oligarchy, and impelled according to the feuds of her great proprietors, the Magii, Blossii, and Jubellii.[441]

The Thessalians are, indeed, in their character and capacity as much Epirotic or Macedonian as Hellenic, forming a sort of link between the two. For the Macedonians, though trained in aftertimes upon Grecian principles by the genius of Philip and Alexander, so as to constitute the celebrated heavy-armed phalanx, were originally (even in the Peloponnesian war) distinguished chiefly for the excellence of their cavalry, like the Thessalians;[442] while the broad-brimmed hat, or kausia, and the short spreading-mantle, or chlamys, were common to both.

We are told that the Thessalians were originally emigrants from Thesprotia in Epirus, and conquerors of the plain of the Peneius, which (according to Herodotus) was then called Æolis, and which they found occupied by the Pelasgi.[443] It may be doubted whether the great Thessalian families,—such as the Aleuadæ of Larissa, descendants from Hêraklês, and placed by Pindar on the same level as the Lacedæmonian kings[444]—would have admitted this Thesprotian origin; nor does it coincide with the tenor of those legends which make the eponym, Thessalus, son of Hêraklês. Moreover, it is to be remarked that the language of the Thessalians was Hellenic, a variety of the Æolic dialect;[445] the same (so far as we can make out) as that of the people whom they must have found settled in the country at their first conquest. If then it be true that, at some period anterior to the commencement of authentic history, a body of Thesprotian warriors crossed the passes of Pindus, and established themselves as conquerors in Thessaly, we must suppose them to have been more warlike than numerous, and to have gradually dropped their primitive language.

In other respects, the condition of the population of Thessaly, such as we find it during the historical period, favors the supposition of an original mixture of conquerors and conquered: for it seems that there was among the Thessalians and their dependents a triple gradation, somewhat analogous to that of Laconia. First, a class of rich proprietors distributed throughout the principal cities, possessing most of the soil, and constituting separate oligarchies, loosely hanging together.[446] Next, the subject Achæans, Magnêtes, Perrhæbi, differing from the Laconian Periœki in this point, that they retained their ancient tribe-name and separate Amphiktyonic franchise. Thirdly, a class of serfs, or dependent cultivators, corresponding to the

Laconian Helots, who, tilling the lands of the wealthy oligarchs, paid over a proportion of its produce, furnished the retainers by which these great families were surrounded, served as their followers in the cavalry, and were in a condition of villanage,—yet with the important reserve, that they could not be sold out of the country,[447] that they had a permanent tenure in the soil, and that they maintained among one another the relations of family and village. This last mentioned order of men, in Thessaly called the Penestæ, is assimilated by all ancient authors to the Helots of Laconia, and in both cases the danger attending such a social arrangement is noticed by Plato and Aristotle. For the Helots as well as the Penestæ had their own common language and mutual sympathies, a separate residence, arms, and courage; to a certain extent, also, they possessed the means of acquiring property, since we are told that some of the Penestæ were richer than their masters.[448] So many means of action, combined with a degraded social position, gave rise to frequent revolt and incessant apprehensions. As a general rule, indeed, the cultivation of the soil by slaves, or dependents, for the benefit of proprietors in the cities, prevailed throughout most parts of Greece. The rich men of Thebes, Argos, Athens, or Elis, must have derived their incomes in the same manner; but it seems that there was often, in other places, a larger intermixture of bought foreign slaves, and also that the number, fellow-feeling, and courage of the degraded village population was nowhere so great as in Thessaly and Laconia. Now the origin of the Penestæ, in Thessaly, is ascribed to the conquest of the territory by the Thesprotians, as that of the Helots in Laconia is traced to the Dorian conquest. The victors in both countries are said to have entered into a convention with the vanquished population, whereby the latter became serfs and tillers of the land for the benefit of the former, but were at the same time protected in their holdings, constituted subjects of the state, and secured against being sold away as slaves. Even in the Thessalian cities, though inhabited in common by Thessalian proprietors and their Penestæ, the quarters assigned to each were to a great degree separated: what was called the Free Agora could not be trodden by any Penest, except when specially summoned.[449]

Who the people were, whom the conquest of Thessaly by the Thesprotians reduced to this predial villanage, we find differently stated. According to Theopompus, they were Perrhæbians and Magnêtes; according to others, Pelasgians; while Archemachus alleged them to have been Bœotians of the territory of Arnê,[450]—some emigrating, to escape the conquerors, others remaining and accepting the condition of serfs. But the conquest, assuming it as a fact, occurred at far too early a day to allow of our making out either the manner in which it came to pass, or the state of things which preceded it. The Pelasgians whom Herodotus saw at Krêstôn are affirmed by him to have been the descendants of those who quitted Thessaly to escape[451] the invading Thesprotians; though others held that the Bœotians, driven on this occasion from their habitations on the gulf of Pagasæ near the Achæans of Phthiôtis, precipitated themselves on Orchomenus and Bœotia, and settled in it, expelling the Minyæ and the Pelasgians.

Passing over the legends on this subject, and confining ourselves to historical time, we find an established quadruple division of Thessaly, said to have been introduced in the time of Aleuas, the ancestor (real or mythical) of the powerful Aleuadæ,—Thessaliôtis, Pelasgiôtis, Histiæôtis, Phthiôtis.[452] In Phthiôtis were comprehended the Achæans, whose chief towns were Melitæa, Itônus, Thebæ, Phthiôtides, Alos, Larissa, Kremastê, and Pteleon, on or near the western coast of the gulf of Pagasæ. Histiæôtis, to the north of the Peneius, comprised the Perrhæbians, with numerous towns strong in situation, but of no great size or importance; they occupied the passes of Olympus[453] and are sometimes considered as extending westward across Pindus. Pelasgiôtis included the Magnêtes, together with that which was called the Pelasgic plain, bordering on the western side of Pelion and Ossa.[454] Thessaliôtis comprised the central plain of Thessaly and the upper course of the river Peneius. This was the political classification of the Thessalian power, framed to suit a time when the separate cities were maintained in harmonious action by favorable circumstances, or by some energetic individual ascendency; for their union was in general interrupted and disorderly, and we find certain cities standing aloof while the rest went to war. [455] Though a certain political junction, and obligations of some kind towards a common authority, were recognized in theory by all, and a chief, or Tagus, [456] was nominated to enforce obedience,—yet it frequently happened that the disputes of the cities among themselves prevented the choice of a Tagus, or drove him out of the country; and left the alliance little more than nominal. Larissa, Pharsalus,[457] and Pheræ,—each with its cluster of dependent towns as adjuncts,—seem to have been nearly on a par in strength, and each torn by intestine faction, so that not only was the supremacy over common dependents relaxed, but even the means of repelling invaders greatly enfeebled. The dependence of the Perrhæbians, Magnetes, Achæans, and Malians, might, under these circumstances, be often loose and easy. But the condition of the Penestæ—who occupied the villages belonging to these great cities, in the central plain of Pelasgiôtis and Thessaliôtis, and from whom the Aleuadæ and Skopadæ derived their exuberance of landed produce—was noway mitigated, if it was not even aggravated, by such constant factions. Nor were there wanting cases in which the discontent of this subject-class was employed by members of the native oligarchy,[458] or even by foreign states, for the purpose of bringing about political revolutions.

"When Thessaly is under her Tagus, all the neighboring people pay tribute to her; she can send into the field six thousand cavalry and ten thousand hoplites, or heavy-armed infantry,"[459] observed Jason, despot of Pheræ, to Polydamas of Pharsalus, in endeavoring to prevail on the latter to second his pretensions to that dignity. The impost due from the tributaries, seemingly considerable, was then realized with arrears, and the duties upon imports at the harbors of the Pagasæan gulf, imposed for the benefit of the confederacy, were then enforced with strictness; but the observation shows that, while unanimous Thessaly was very powerful, her periods of unanimity were only occasional.[460] Among the nations which thus paid tribute to the fulness of Thessalian power, we may number not merely the Perrhæbi, Magnêtes, and Achæans of Phthiôtis, but also the Malians and Dolopes, and various tribes of Epirots extending to the westward of Pindus.[461] We may remark that they were all (except the Malians) javelin-men, or light-armed troops, not serving in rank with the full panoply; a fact which, in Greece, counts as presumptive evidence of a lower civilization: the Magnêtes, too, had a peculiar close-fitting mode of dress, probably suited to movements in a mountainous country.[462] There was even a time when the Thessalian power threatened to extend southward of Thermopylæ, subjugating the Phokians, Dorians, and Lokrians. So much were the Phokians alarmed at this danger, that they had built a wall across the pass of Thermopylæ, for the purpose of more easily defending it against Thessalian invaders, who are reported to have penetrated more than once into the Phokian valleys, and to have sustained some severe defeats.[463] At what precise time these events happened, we find no information; but it must have been considerably earlier than the invasion of Xerxes, since the defensive wall which had been built at Thermopylæ, by the Phokians, was found by Leonidas in a state of ruin. But the Phokians, though they no longer felt the necessity of keeping up this wall, had not ceased to fear and hate the Thessalians,—an antipathy which will be found to manifest itself palpably in connection with the Persian invasion. On the whole, the resistance of the Phokians was successful, for the power of the Thessalians never reached southward of the pass.[464]

It will be recollected that these different ancient races, Perrhæbi, Magnêtes, Achæans, Malians, Dolopes,—though tributaries of the Thessalians, still retained their Amphiktyonic franchise, and were considered as legitimate Hellenes: all except the Malians are, indeed, mentioned in the Iliad. We shall rarely have occasion to speak much of them in the course of this history: they are found siding with Xerxes (chiefly by constraint) in his attack of Greece, and almost indifferent in the struggle between Sparta and Athens. That the Achæans of Phthiôtis are a portion of the same race as the Achæans of Peloponnesus it seems reasonable to believe, though we trace no

157

historical evidence to authenticate it. Achæa Phthiôtis is the seat of Hellên, the patriarch of the entire race,—of the primitive Hellas, by some treated as a town, by others as a district of some breadth,—and of the great national hero, Achilles. Its connection with the Peloponnesian Achæans is not unlike that of Doris with the Peloponnesian Dorians.[465] We have, also, to notice another ethnical kindred, the date and circumstances of which are given to us only in a mythical form, but which seems, nevertheless, to be in itself a reality,—that of the Magnêtes on Pelion and Ossa, with the two divisions of Asiatic Magnêtes, or Magnesia, on Mount Sipylus and Magnesia on the river Mæander. It is said that these two Asiatic homonymous towns were founded by migrations of the Thessalian Magnêtes, a body of whom became consecrated to the Delphian god, and chose a new abode under his directions. According to one story, these emigrants were warriors, returning from the Siege of Troy; according to another, they sought fresh seats, to escape from the Thesprotian conquerors of Thessaly. There was a third story, according to which the Thessalian Magnêtes themselves were represented as colonists[466] from Delphi. Though we can elicit no distinct matter of fact from these legends, we may, nevertheless, admit the connection of race between the Thessalian and the Asiatic Magnêtes, as well as the reverential dependence of both, manifested in this supposed filiation, on the temple of Delphi. Of the Magnêtes in Krete, noticed by Plato as long extinct in his time, we cannot absolutely verify even the existence.

Of the Malians, Thucydidês notices three tribes (γένη) as existing in his time,—the Paralii, the Hierês (priests), and the Trachinii, or men of Trachin: [467] it is possible that the second of the two may have been possessors of the sacred spot on which the Amphiktyonic meetings were held. The prevalence of the hoplites or heavy-armed infantry among the Malians, indicates that we are stepping from Thessalian to more southerly Hellenic habits: the Malians recognized every man as a qualified citizen, who either had served, or was serving, in the ranks with his full panoply.[468] Yet the panoply was probably not perfectly suitable to the mountainous regions by which they were surrounded; for, at the beginning of the Peloponnesian war, the aggressive mountaineers of the neighboring region of Œta, had so harassed and overwhelmed them in war, that they were forced to throw themselves on the protection of Sparta; and the establishment of the Spartan colony of Herakleia, near Trachin, was the result of their urgent application. Of these mountaineers, described under the general name of Œtæans, the principal were the Ænianes, (or Eniênes, as they are termed in the Homeric Catalogue, as well as by Herodotus),—an ancient Hellenic[469] Amphiktyonic race, who are said to have passed through several successive migrations in Thessaly and Epirus, but who, in the historical times, had their settlement and their chief

158

town, Hypata, in the upper valley of the Spercheius, on the northern declivity of Mount Œta. But other tribes were probably also included in the name, such as those Ætolian tribes, the Bomians and Kallians, whose high and cold abodes approached near to the Maliac gulf. It is in this sense that we are to understand the name, as comprehending all the predatory tribes along this extensive mountain range, when we are told of the damage done by the Œtæans, both to the Malians on the east, and to the Dorians on the south: but there are some cases in which the name Œtæans seems to designate expressly the Ænianes, especially when they are mentioned as exercising the Amphiktyonic franchise.[470]

The fine soil, abundant moisture, and genial exposure of the southern declivities of Othrys,[471]—especially the valley of the Spercheius, through which river all these waters pass away, and which annually gives forth a fertilizing inundation,—present a marked contrast with the barren, craggy, and naked masses of Mount Œta, which forms one side of the pass of Thermopylæ. Southward of the pass, the Lokrians, Phokians, and Dorians, occupied the mountains and passes between Thessaly and Bœotia. The coast opposite to the western side of Eubœa, from the neighborhood of Thermopylæ, as far as the Bœotian frontier at Anthêdôn, was possessed by the Lokrians, whose northern frontier town, Alpêni, was conterminous with the Malians. There was, however, one narrow strip of Phokis—the town of Daphnus, where the Phokians also touched the Eubœan sea—which broke this continuity, and divided the Lokrians into two sections,—Lokrians of Mount Knêmis, or Epiknemidian Lokrians, and Lokrians of Opus, or Opuntian Lokrians. The mountain called Knêmis, running southward parallel to the coast from the end of Œta, divided the former section from the inland Phokians and the upper valley of the Kephisus: farther southward, joining continuously with Mount Ptôon by means of an intervening mountain which is now called Chlomo, it separated the Lokrians of Opus from the territories of Orchomenus, Thebes, and Anthêdôn, the north-eastern portions of Bœotia. Besides these two sections of the Lokrian name, there was also a third, completely separate, and said to have been colonized out from Opus,—the Lokrians surnamed Ozolæ,—who dwelt apart on the western side of Phokis, along the northern coast of the Corinthian gulf. They reached from Amphissa —which overhung the plain of Krissa, and stood within seven miles of Delphi —to Naupaktus. near the narrow entrance of the gulf; which latter town was taken from these Lokrians by the Athenians, a little before the Peloponnesian war. Opus prided itself on being the mother-city of the Lokrian name, and the legends of Deukaliôn and Pyrrha found a home there as well as in Phthiôtis. Alpeni, Nikæa, Thronium, and Skarpheia, were towns, ancient but unimportant, of the Epiknemidian Lokrians; but the whole length of this

Lokrian coast is celebrated for its beauty and fertility, both by Ancient and modern observers.[472]

The Phokians were bounded on the north by the little territories called Doris and Dryopis, which separated them from the Malians,—on the north-east, east, and south-west, by the different branches of Lokrians,—and on the south-east, by the Bœotians. They touched the Eubœan sea, (as has been mentioned) at Daphnus, the point where it approaches nearest to their chief town, Elateia; their territory also comprised most part of the lofty and bleak range of Parnassus, as far as its southerly termination, where a lower portion of it, called Kirphis, projects into the Corinthian gulf, between the two bays of Antikyra and Krissa; the latter, with its once fertile plain, lay immediately under the sacred rock of the Delphian Apollo. Both Delphi and Krissa originally belonged to the Phokian race, but the sanctity of the temple, together with Lacedæmonian aid, enabled the Delphians to set up for themselves, disavowing their connection with the Phokian brotherhood. Territorially speaking, the most valuable part of Phokis[473] consisted in the valley of the river Kephisus, which takes its rise from Parnassus, not far from the Phokian town of Lilæa, passes between Œta and Knêmis on one side, and Parnassus on the other, and enters Bœotia near Chæroneia, discharging itself into the lake Kôpaïs. It was on the projecting mountain ledges and rocks on each side of this river, that the numerous little Phokian towns were situated. Twenty-two of them were destroyed and broken up into villages by the Amphiktyonic order, after the second Sacred War; Abæ (one of the few, if not the only one, that was spared) being protected by the sanctity of its temple and oracle. Of these cities, the most important was Elateia, situated on the left bank of the Kephisus, and on the road from Lokris into Phokis, in the natural march of an army from Thermopylæ into Bœotia. The Phokian towns[474] were embodied in an ancient confederacy, which held its periodical meetings at a temple between Daulis and Delphi.

The little territory called Doris and Dryopis, occupied the southern declivity of Mount Œta, dividing Phokis on the north and north-west, from the Ætolians, Ænianes, and Malians. That which was called Doris in the historical times, and which reached, in the time of Herodotus, nearly as far eastward as the Maliac gulf, is said to have formed a part of what had been once called Dryopis; a territory which had comprised the summit of Œta as far as the Spercheius, northward, and which had been inhabited by an old Hellenic tribe called Dryopes. The Dorians acquired their settlement in Dryopis by gift from Hêraklês, who, along with the Malians (so ran the legend), had expelled the Dryopes, and compelled them to find for themselves new seats at Hermionê, and Asinê, in the Argolic peninsula of Peloponnesus, —at Styra and Karystus in Eubœa,—and in the island of Kythnus;[475] it is only in these five last-mentioned places, that history recognizes them. The territory of Doris was distributed into four little townships,—Pindus, or Akyphas, Bœon, Kytinion, and Erineon,—each of which seems to have occupied a separate valley belonging to one of the feeders of the river Kephisus,—the only narrow spaces of cultivated ground which this "small and sad" region presented.[476] In itself, this tetrapolis is so insignificant, that we shall rarely find occasion to mention it; but it acquired a factitious consequence by being regarded as the metropolis of the great Dorian cities in Peloponnesus, and receiving on that ground special protection from Sparta. I do not here touch upon that string of ante-historical migrations—stated by Herodotus, and illustrated by the ingenuity as well as decorated by the fancy of O. Müller—through which the Dorians are affiliated with the patriarch of the Hellenic race,—moving originally out of Phthiôtis to Histiæôtis, then to Pindus, and lastly to Doris. The residence of Dorians in Doris, is a fact which meets us at the commencement of history, like that of the Phokians and Lokrians in their respective territories.

We next pass to the Ætolians, whose extreme tribes covered the bleak heights of Œta and Korax, reaching almost within sight of the Maliac gulf, where they bordered on the Dorians and Malians,—while their central and western tribes stretched along the frontier of the Ozolian Lokrians to the flat plain, abundant in marsh and lake, near the mouth of the Euênus. In the time of Herodotus and Thucydidês, they do not seem to have extended so far westward as the Achelôus; but in later times, this latter river, throughout the greater part of its lower course, divided them from the Akarnanians:[477] on the north, they touched upon the Dolopians, and upon a parallel of latitude nearly as far north as Ambrakia. There were three great divisions of the Ætolian name,—the Apodôti, Ophioneis, and Eurytanes,—each of which was subdivided into several different village tribes. The northern and eastern portion of the territory[478] consisted of very high mountain ranges, and even in the southern portion, the mountains Arakynthus, Kurion, Chalkis, Taphiassus, are found at no great distance from the sea; while the chief towns in Ætolia, Kalydôn, Pleurôn, Chalkis,—seem to have been situated eastward of the Euênus, between the last-mentioned mountains and the sea.[479] The first two towns have been greatly ennobled in legend, but are little named in history; while, on the contrary, Thermus, the chief town of the historical Ætolians, and the place where the aggregate meeting and festival of the Ætolian name, for the choice of a Pan-Ætolic general, was convoked, is not noticed by any one earlier than Ephorus.[480] It was partly legendary renown, partly ethnical kindred (publicly acknowledged on both sides) with the Eleians in Peloponnesus, which authenticated the title of the Ætolians to rank as Hellens. But the great mass of the Apodôti, Eurytanes, and Ophioneis in the inland mountains, were so rude in their manners, and so unintelligible[481] in their speech, (which, however, was not barbaric, but very bad Hellenic,) that this title might well seem disputable,—in point of fact it was disputed, in later times, when the Ætolian power and depredations had become obnoxious nearly to all Greece. And it is, probably, to this difference of manners between the Ætolians on the sea-coast and those in the interior, that we are to trace a geographical division mentioned by Strabo, into ancient Ætolia, and Ætolia Epiktêtus, or acquired. When or by whom this division was introduced, we do not know. It cannot be founded upon any conquest, for the inland Ætolians were the most unconquerable of mankind: and the affirmation which Ephorus applied to the whole Ætolian race,—that it had never been reduced to subjection by any one,—is, most of all, beyond dispute concerning the inland portion of it.[482]

Adjoining the Ætolians were the Akarnanians, the westernmost of extra-Peloponnesian Greeks. They extended to the Ionian sea, and seem, in the time of Thucydidês, to have occupied both banks of the river Achelôus, in the lower part of its course,—though the left bank appears afterwards as belonging to the Ætolians, so that the river came to constitute the boundary, often disputed and decided by arms, between them. The principal Akarnanian towns, Stratus and Œniadæ, were both on the right bank; the latter on the marshy and overflowed land near its mouth. Near the Akarnanians, towards the gulf of Ambrakia, were found barbarian, or non-Hellenic nations,—the Agræans and the Amphilochians: in the midst of the latter, on the shores of the Ambrakian gulf, the Greek colony, called Argos Amphilochicum, was established.

Of the five Hellenic subdivisions now enumerated,—Lokrians, Phokians, Dorians (of Doris), Ætolians, and Akarnanians (of whom Lokrians, Phokians, and Ætolians are comprised in the Homeric catalogue),—we have to say the same as of those north of Thermopylæ: there is no information respecting them from the commencement of the historical period down to the Persian war. Even that important event brings into action only the Lokrians of the Eubœan sea, the Phokians, and the Dorians: we have to wait until near the Peloponnesian war, before we require information respecting the Ozolian Lokrians, the Ætolians, and the Akarnanians. These last three were unquestionably the most backward members of the Hellenic aggregate. Though not absolutely without a central town, they lived dispersed in villages, retiring, when attacked, to inaccessible heights, perpetually armed and in readiness for aggression and plunder wherever they found an opportunity.[483] Very different was the condition of the Lokrians opposite Eubœa, the Phokians, and the Dorians. These were all orderly town communities, small, indeed, and poor, but not less well administered than the average of Grecian townships, and perhaps exempt from those individual violences which so frequently troubled the Bœotian Thebes or the great cities of Thessaly. Timæus affirmed (contrary, as it seems, to the supposition of Aristotle) that, in early times, there were no slaves either among the Lokrians or Phokians, and that the work required to be done for proprietors was performed by poor freemen;[484] a habit which is alleged to have been continued until the temporary prosperity of the second Sacred War, when the plunder of the Delphian temple so greatly enriched the Phokian leaders. But this statement is too briefly given, and too imperfectly authenticated, to justify any inferences.

We find in the poet Alkman (about 610 B. C.), the Erysichæan, or Kalydonian shepherd, named as a type of rude rusticity,—the antithesis of Sardis, where the poet was born.[485] And among the suitors who are represented as coming forward to claim the daughter of the Sikyonian Kleisthenes in marriage, there appears both the Thessalian Diaktoridês from Krannôn, a member of the Skopad family,—and the Ætolian Malês, brother of that Titormus who in muscular strength surpassed all his contemporary Greeks, and who had seceded from mankind into the inmost recesses of Ætolia: this Ætolian seems to be set forth as a sort of antithesis to the delicate Smindyridês of Sybaris, the most luxurious of mankind. Herodotus introduces these characters into his dramatic picture of this memorable wedding.[486]

Between Phokis and Lokris on one side, and Attica (from which it is divided by the mountains Kithærôn and Parnês) on the other, we find the important territory called Bœotia, with its ten or twelve autonomous cities, forming a sort of confederacy under the presidency of Thebes, the most powerful among them. Even of this territory, destined during the second period of this history, to play a part so conspicuous and effective, we know nothing during the first two centuries after 776 B. C. We first acquire some insight into it, on occasion of the disputes between Thebes and Platæa, about the year 520 B. C. Orchomenus, on the north-west of the lake Kôpaïs, forms throughout the historical times one of the cities of the Bœotian league, seemingly the second after Thebes. But I have already stated that the Orchomenian legends, the Catalogue, and other allusions in Homer, and the traces of past power and importance yet visible in the historical age, attest the early political existence of Orchomenus and its neighborhood apart from Bœotia.[487] The Amphiktyony in which Orchomenus participated, at the holy island of Kalauria near the Argolic peninsula, seems to show that it must once have possessed a naval force and commerce, and that its territory must have touched the sea at Halæ and the lower town of Larymna, near the southern frontier of Lokris; this sea is separated by a very narrow space from the range of mountains which join Knêmis and Ptôon, and which inclose on the east both the basin of Orchomenus, Asplêdôn, and Kôpæ, and the lake Kôpaïs.

The migration of the Bœotians out of Thessaly into Bœotia (which is represented as a consequence of the conquest of the former country by the Thesprotians) is commonly assigned as the compulsory force which Bœotized Orchomenus. By whatever cause, or at whatever time (whether before or after 776 B. C.) the transition may have been effected, we find Orchomenus completely Bœotian throughout the known historical age,—yet still retaining its local Minyeian legends, and subject to the jealous rivalry[488] of Thebes, as being the second city in the Bœotian league. The direct road from the passes of Phokis southward into Bœotia went through Chæroneia, leaving Lebadeia on the right, and Orchomenus on the left hand, and passed the south-western edge of the lake Kôpaïs near the towns of Koroneia, Alalkomenæ, and Haliartus,—all situated on the mountain Tilphôssion, an outlying ridge connected with Helicon by the intervention of Mount Leïbethrius. The Tilphossæon was an important military post, commanding that narrow pass between the mountain and the lake which lay in the great road from Phokis to Thebes.[489] The territory of this latter city occupied the greater part of central Bœotia, south of the lake Kôpaïs; it comprehended Akræphia and Mount Ptôon, and probably touched the Eubœan sea at the village of Salganeus south of Anthêdôn. South-west of Thebes, occupying the southern descent of lofty Helicon towards the inmost corner of the Corinthian gulf, and bordering on the south-eastern extremity of Phokis with the Phokian town of Bulis, stood the city of Thespiæ. Southward of the Asôpus, between that river and Mount Kithæron, were Platæa and Tanagra; in the south-eastern corner of Bœotia stood Orôpus, the frequent subject of contention between Thebes and Athens; and in the road between the Eubœan Chalkis and Thebes, the town of Mykalêssus.

From our first view of historical Bœotia downward, there appears a confederation which embraces the whole territory: and during the Peloponnesian war, the Thebans invoke "the ancient constitutional maxims of the Bœotians" as a justification of extreme rigor, as well as of treacherous breach of the peace, against the recusant Platæans.[490] Of this confederation, the greater cities were primary members, while the lesser were attached to one or other of them in a kind of dependent union. Neither the names nor the number of these primary members can be certainly known: there seem grounds for including Thebes, Orchomenus, Lebadeia, Korôneia, Haliartus, Kôpæ, Anthêdôn, Tanagra, Thespiæ, and Platæa before its secession.[491] Akræphia, with the neighboring Mount Ptôon and its oracle, Skôlus, Glisas, and other places, were dependencies of Thebes: Chæroneia, Asplêdôn, Holmônes, and Hyêttus, of Orchomenus: Siphæ, Leuktra, Kerêssus, and Thisbê, of Thespiæ.[492] Certain generals or magistrates, called Bœotarchs, were chosen annually to manage the common affairs of the confederation. At the time of the battle of Delium in the Peloponnesian war, they were eleven in number, two of them from Thebes; but whether this number was always maintained, or in what proportions the choice was made by the different cities, we find no distinct information. There were likewise, during the Peloponnesian war, four different senates, with whom the Bœotarchs consulted on matters of importance; a curious arrangement, of which we have no explanation. Lastly, there was the general concilium and religious festival, —the Pambœotia,—held periodically at Korôneia. Such were the forms, as far as we can make them out, of the Bœotian confederacy; each of the separate cities possessing its own senate and constitution, and having its political consciousness as an autonomous unit, yet with a certain habitual deference to the federal obligations. Substantially, the affairs of the confederation will be found in the hands of Thebes, managed in the interests of Theban ascendency, which appears to have been sustained by no other feeling except respect for superior force and bravery. The discontents of the minor Bœotian towns, harshly repressed and punished, form an uninviting chapter in Grecian history.

One piece of information we find, respecting Thebes singly and apart from the other Bœotian towns anterior to the year 700 B. C. Though brief, and incompletely recorded, it is yet highly valuable, as one of the first incidents of solid and positive Grecian history. Dioklês, the Corinthian, stands enrolled as Olympic victor in the 13th Olympiad, or 728 B. C., at a time when the oligarchy called Bacchiadæ possessed the government of Corinth. The beauty of his person attracted towards him the attachment of Philolaus, one of the members of this oligarchical body,—a sentiment which Grecian manners did not proscribe; but it also provoked an incestuous passion on the part of his own mother, Halcyonê, from which Dioklês shrunk with hatred and horror. He abandoned forever his native city and retired to Thebes, whither he was followed by Philolaus, and where both of them lived and died. Their tombs were yet shown in the time of Aristotle, close adjoining to each other, yet with an opposite frontage; that of Philolaus being so placed that the inmate could command a view of the lofty peak of his native city, while that of Dioklês was so disposed as to block out all prospect of the hateful spot. That which preserves to us the memory of so remarkable an incident, is, the esteem entertained for Philolaus by the Thebans,—a feeling so profound, that they invited him to make laws for them. We shall have occasion to point out one or two similar cases, in which Grecian cities invoked the aid of an intelligent stranger; and the practice became common, among the Italian republics in the Middle Ages, to nominate a person not belonging to their city either as podesta or as arbitrator in civil dissensions. It would have been highly interesting to know, at length, what laws Philolaus made for the Thebans; but

Aristotle, with his usual conciseness, merely alludes to his regulations respecting the adoption of children and respecting the multiplication of offspring in each separate family. His laws were framed with the view to maintain the original number of lots of land, without either subdivision or consolidation; but by what means the purpose was to be fulfilled we are not informed.[493] There existed a law at Thebes, which perhaps may have been part of the scheme of Philolaus, prohibiting exposure of children, and empowering a father, under the pressure of extreme poverty, to bring his new-born infant to the magistrates, who sold it for a price to any citizen-purchaser, —taking from him the obligation to bring it up, but allowing him in return, to consider the adult as his slave.[494] From these brief allusions, coming to us without accompanying illustration, we can draw no other inference, except that the great problem of population—the relation between the well-being of the citizens and their more or less rapid increase in numbers—had engaged the serious attention even of the earliest Grecian legislators. We may, however, observe that the old Corinthian legislator, Pheidôn, (whose precise date cannot be fixed) is stated by Aristotle,[495] to have contemplated much the same object as that which is ascribed to Philolaus at Thebes; an unchangeable number both of citizens and of lots of land, without any attempt to alter the unequal ratio of the lots, one to the other.

# CHAPTER IV.

## EARLIEST HISTORICAL VIEW OF PELOPONNESUS.
## DORIANS IN ARGOS AND THE NEIGHBORING CITIES.

WE NOW pass from the northern members to the heart and head of Greece, —Peloponnesus and Attica, taking the former first in order, and giving as much as can be ascertained respecting its early historical phenomena.

The traveller who entered Peloponnesus from Bœotia during the youthful days of Herodotus and Thucydidês, found an array of powerful Doric cities conterminous to each other, and beginning at the isthmus of Corinth. First came Megara, stretching across the isthmus from sea to sea, and occupying the high and rugged mountain-ridge called Geraneia; next Corinth, with its strong and conspicuous acropolis, and its territory including Mount Oneion as well as the portion of the isthmus at once most level and narrowest, which divided its two harbors called Lechæum and Kenchreæ. Westward of Corinth, along the Corinthian gulf, stood Sikyôn, with a plain of uncommon fertility, between the two towns: southward of Sikyôn and Corinth were Phlius and Kleonæ, both conterminous, as well as Corinth, with Argos and the Argolic peninsula. The inmost bend of the Argolic gulf, including a considerable space of flat and marshy ground adjoining to the sea, was possessed by Argos; the Argolic peninsula was divided by Argos with the Doric cities of Epidaurus and Trœzen, and the Dryopian city of Hermionê, the latter possessing the south-western corner. Proceeding southward along the western coast of the gulf, and passing over the little river called Tanos, the traveller found himself in the dominion of Sparta, which comprised the entire southern region of the peninsula from its eastern to its western sea, where the river Neda flows into the latter. He first passed from Argos across the difficult mountain range called Parnôn (which bounds to the west the southern portion of Argolis), until he found himself in the valley of the river Œnus, which he followed until it joined the Eurotas. In the larger valley of the Eurotas, far removed from the sea, and accessible only through the most impracticable mountain roads, lay the five unwalled, unadorned, adjoining villages, which bore collectively the formidable name of Sparta. The whole valley of the Eurotas, from Skiritis and Beleminatis at the border of Arcadia, to the Laconian gulf,—expanding in several parts into fertile plain, especially near to its mouth, where the towns of Gythium and Helos were found,—belonged to Sparta; together with the cold and high mountain range to the eastward, which projects into the promontory of Malea,—and the still loftier chain of

Taygetus to the westward, which ends in the promontory of Tænarus. On the other side of Taygetus, on the banks of the river Pamisus, which there flows into the Messenian gulf, lay the plain of Messênê, the richest land in the peninsula. This plain had once yielded its ample produce to the free Messenian Dorians, resident in the towns of Stenyklêrus and Andania. But in the time of which we speak, the name of Messenians was borne only by a body of brave but homeless exiles, whose restoration to the land of their forefathers overpassed even the exile's proverbially sanguine hope. Their land was confounded with the western portion of Laconia, which reached in a south-westerly direction down to the extreme point of Cape Akritas, and northward as far as the river Neda.

Throughout his whole journey to the point last mentioned, from the borders of Bœotia and Megaris, the traveller would only step from one Dorian state into another. But on crossing from the south to the north bank of the river Neda, at a point near to its mouth, he would find himself out of Doric land altogether: first, in the territory called Triphylia,—next, in that of Pisa, or the Pisatid,—thirdly, in the more spacious and powerful state called Elis; these three comprising the coast-land of Peloponnesus from the mouth of the Neda to that of the Larissus. The Triphylians, distributed into a number of small townships, the largest of which was Lepreon,—and the Pisatans, equally destitute of any centralizing city,—had both, at the period of which we are now speaking, been conquered by their more powerful northern neighbors of Elis, who enjoyed the advantage of a spacious territory united under one government; the middle portion, called the Hollow Elis, being for the most part fertile, though the tracts near the sea were more sandy and barren. The Eleians were a section of Ætolian emigrants into Peloponnesus, but the Pisatans and Triphylians had both been originally independent inhabitants of the peninsula,—the latter being affirmed to belong to the same race as the Minyæ who had occupied the ante-Bœotian Orchomenos: both, too, bore the ascendency of Elis with perpetual murmur and occasional resistance.

Crossing the river Larissus, and pursuing the northern coast of Peloponnesus south of the Corinthian gulf, the traveller would pass into Achaia,—a name which designated the narrow strip of level land, and the projecting spurs and declivities, between that gulf and the northernmost mountains of the peninsula,—Skollis, Erymanthus, Aroania, Krathis, and the towering eminence called Kyllênê. Achæan cities,—twelve in number at least, if not more,—divided this long strip of land amongst them, from the mouth of the Larissus and the north-western Cape Araxus on one side, to the western boundary of the Sikyonian territory on the other. According to the accounts of the ancient legends and the belief of Herodotus, this territory had once been occupied by Ionian inhabitants whom the Achæans had expelled.

In making this journey, the traveller would have finished the circuit of Peloponnesus; but he would still have left untrodden the great central region, inclosed between the territories just enumerated,—approaching nearest to the sea on the borders of Triphylia, but never touching it anywhere. This region was Arcadia, possessed by inhabitants who are uniformly represented as all of one race, and all aboriginal. It was high and bleak, full of wild mountain, rock, and forest, and abounding, to a degree unusual even in Greece, with those land-locked basins from whence the water finds only a subterraneous issue. It was distributed among a large number of distinct villages and cities. Many of the village tribes,—the Mænalii, Parrhasii, Azanes, etc., occupying the central and the western regions, were numbered among the rudest of the Greeks: but along its eastern frontier there were several Arcadian cities which ranked deservedly among the more civilized Peloponnesians. Tegea, Mantineia, Orchomenus, Stymphalus, Pheneus, possessed the whole eastern frontier of Arcadia from the borders of Laconia to those of Sikyôn and Pellênê in Achaia: Phigaleia at the south-western corner, near the borders of Triphylia, and Heræa, on the north bank of the Alpheius, near the place where that river quits Arcadia to enter the Pisatis, were also towns deserving of notice. Towards the north of this cold and thinly-peopled region, near Pheneos, was situated the small town of Nonakris, adjoining to which rose the hardly accessible crags where the rivulet of Styx[496] flowed down: a point of common feeling for all Arcadians, from the terrific sanction which this water was understood to impart to their oaths.

The distribution of Peloponnesus here sketched, suitable to the Persian invasion and the succeeding half century, may also be said (with some allowances) to be adapted to the whole interval between about B. C. 550-370; from the time of the conquest of Thyreatis by Sparta to the battle of Leuktra. But it is not the earliest distribution which history presents to us. Not presuming to criticize the Homeric map of Peloponnesus, and going back only to 776 B. C., we find this material difference,—that Sparta occupies only a very small fraction of the large territory above described as belonging to her. Westward of the summit of Mount Taygetus are found another section of Dorians, independent of Sparta: the Messenian Dorians, whose city is on the hill of Stenyklêrus, near the south-western boundary of Arcadia, and whose possessions cover the fertile plain of Messêne along the river Pamisus to its mouth in the Messenian gulf: it is to be noted that Messêne was then the name of the plain generally, and that no town so called existed until after the battle of Leuktra. Again, eastward of the valley of the Eurotas, the mountainous region and the western shores of the Argolic gulf down to Cape Malea are also independent of Sparta; belonging to Argos, or rather to Dorian towns in unison with Argos. All the great Dorian towns, from the borders of the Megarid to the eastern frontier of Arcadia, as above enumerated, appear to have existed in 776 B. C.: Achaia was in the same condition, so far as we are able to judge, as well as Arcadia, except in regard to its southern frontier, conterminous with Sparta, of which more will hereafter be said. In respect to the western portion of Peloponnesus, Elis (properly so called) appears to have embraced the same territory in 776 B. C. as in 550 B. C.: but the Pisatid had been recently conquered, and was yet imperfectly subjected by the Eleians; while Triphylia seems to have been quite independent of them. Respecting the south-western promontory of Peloponnesus down to Cape Akritas, we are altogether without information: reasons will hereafter be given for believing that it did not at that time form part of the territory of the Messenian Dorians.

Of the different races or people whom Herodotus knew in Peloponnesus, he believed three to be aboriginal,—the Arcadians, the Achæans, and the Kynurians. The Achæans, though belonging indigenously to the peninsula, had yet removed from the southern portion of it to the northern, expelling the previous Ionian tenants: this is a part of the legend respecting the Dorian conquest, or Return of the Herakleids, and we can neither verify nor contradict it. But neither the Arcadians nor the Kynurians had ever changed their abodes. Of the latter, I have not before spoken, because they were never (so far as history knows them) an independent population. They occupied the larger portion[497] of the territory of Argolis, from Orneæ, near the northern[498] or Phliasian border, to Thyrea and the Thyreatis, on the Laconian border: and though belonging originally (as Herodotus imagines rather than asserts) to the Ionic race—they had been so long subjects of Argos in his time, that almost all evidence of their ante-Dorian condition had vanished.

But the great Dorian states in Peloponnesus—the capital powers in the peninsula—were all originally emigrants, according to the belief not only of Herodotus, but of all the Grecian world: so also were the Ætolians of Elis, the Triphylians, and the Dryopes at Hermionê and Asinê. All these emigrations are so described as to give them a root in the Grecian legendary world: the Triphylians are traced back to Lemnos, as the offspring of the Argonautic heroes,[499] and we are too uninformed about them to venture upon any historical guesses. But respecting the Dorians, it may perhaps be possible, by examining the first historical situation in which they are presented to us, to offer some conjectures as to the probable circumstances under which they arrived. The legendary narrative of it has already been given in the first chapter of this volume,—that great mythical event called the Return of the Children of Hêraklês, by which the first establishment of the Dorians in the promised land of Peloponnesus was explained to the full satisfaction of Grecian faith. One single armament and expedition, acting by the special direction of the Delphian god, and conducted by three brothers, lineal descendants of the principal Achæo-Dorian heroes through Hyllus, (the eponymus of the principal tribe,)—the national heroes of the preëxisting population vanquished and expelled, and the greater part of the peninsula both acquired and partitioned at a stroke,—the circumstances of the partition adjusted to the historical relations of Laconia and Messenia,—the friendly power of Ætolian Elis, with its Olympic games as the bond of union in Peloponnesus, attached to this event as an appendage, in the person of Oxylus,—all these particulars compose a narrative well calculated to impress the retrospective imagination of a Greek. They exhibit an epical fitness and sufficiency which it would be unseasonable to impair by historical criticism.

The Alexandrine chronology sets down a period of 328 years from the Return of the Herakleids to the first Olympiad (1104 B. C.-776 B. C.,),—a period measured by the lists of the kings of Sparta, on the trustworthiness of which some remarks have already been offered. Of these 328 years, the first 250, at the least, are altogether barren of facts; and even if we admitted them to be historical, we should have nothing to recount except a succession of royal names. Being unable either to guarantee the entire list, or to discover any valid test for discriminating the historical and the non-historical items, I here enumerate the Lacedæmonian kings as they appear in Mr. Clinton's Fasti Hellenici. There were two joint kings at Sparta, throughout nearly all the historical time of independent Greece, deducing their descent from Hêraklês through Eurysthenês and Proklês, the twin sons of Aristodêmus; the latter being one of those three Herakleid brothers to whom the conquest of the peninsula is ascribed:—

| *Line of Eurysthenês.* | | | | *Line of Proklês.* | | | |
|---|---|---|---|---|---|---|---|
| Eurysthenês reigned | 42 | years. | | Proklês | reigned | 51 | years. |
| Agis | " | 31 | " | Söus | " | — | " |
| Echestratus | " | 35 | " | Eurypôn | " | — | " |
| Labôtas | " | 37 | " | Prytanis | " | 49 | " |
| Doryssus | " | 29 | " | Eunomus | " | 45 | " |
| Agesilaus | " | 44 | " | Charilaus | " | 60 | " |
| Archelaus | " | 60 | " | Nikander | " | 38 | " |
| Teleklus | " | 40 | " | Theopompus | " | 10 | " |
| Alkamenês | " | 10 | " | | | | |
| | | 328 | | | | | |

Both Theopompus and Alkamenês reigned considerably longer, but the chronologists affirm that the year 776 B. C. (or the first Olympiad) occurred in the tenth year of each of their reigns. It is necessary to add, with regard to this list, that there are some material discrepancies between different authors even as to the names of individual kings, and still more as to the duration of their

171

reigns, as may be seen both in Mr. Clinton's chronology and in Müller's Appendix to the History of the Dorians.[500] The alleged sum total cannot be made to agree with the items without great license of conjecture. O. Müller observes,[501] in reference to this Alexandrine chronology, "that our materials only enable us to restore it to its original state, not to verify its correctness." In point of fact they are insufficient even for the former purpose, as the dissensions among learned critics attest.

We have a succession of names, still more barren of facts, in the case of the Dorian sovereigns of Corinth. This city had its own line of Herakleids, descended from Hêraklês, but not through Hyllus. Hippotês, the progenitor of the Corinthian Herakleids, was reported in the legend to have originally joined the Dorian invaders of the Peloponnesus, but to have quitted them in consequence of having slain the prophet Karnus.[502] The three brothers, when they became masters of the peninsula, sent for Alêtês, the son of Hippotês, and placed him in possession of Corinth, over which the chronologists make him begin to reign thirty years after the Herakleid conquest. His successors are thus given:—

| Aletes | reigned | 38 | years, |
|---|---|---|---|
| Ixion | " | 38 | " |
| Agelas | " | 37 | " |
| Prymnis | " | 35 | " |
| Bacchis | " | 35 | " |
| Agelas | " | 30 | " |
| Eudêmus | " | 25 | " |
| Aristomêdês | " | 35 | " |
| Agêmôn | " | 16 | " |
| Alexander | " | 25 | " |
| Telestês | " | 12 | " |
| Automenês | " | 1 | " |
| | | 327 | |

Such was the celebrity of Bacchis, we are told, that those who succeeded him took the name of Bacchiads in place of Aletiads or Herakleids. One year after the accession of Automenês, the family of the Bacchiads generally, amounting to 200 persons, determined to abolish royalty, to constitute themselves a standing oligarchy, and to elect out of their own number an annual Prytanis. Thus commenced the oligarchy of the Bacchiads, which lasted for ninety years, until it was subverted by Kypselus in 657 B. C.[503] Reckoning the thirty years previous to the beginning of the reign of Alêtês, the chronologists thus provide an interval of 447 years between the Return of the Herakleids and the accession of Kypselus, and 357 years between the same period and the commencement of the Bacchiad oligarchy. The Bacchiad oligarchy is unquestionably historical; the conquest of the Herakleids belongs to the legendary world; while the interval between the two is filled up, as in so many other cases, by a mere barren genealogy.

When we jump this vacant space, and place ourselves at the first opening of history, we find that, although ultimately Sparta came to hold the first place, not only in Peloponnesus, but in all Hellas, this was not the case at the earliest moment of which we have historical cognizance. Argos, and the neighboring towns connected with her by a bond of semi-religious, semi-political union,—Sikyôn, Phlius, Epidaurus, and Trœzên,—were at first of greater power and consideration than Sparta; a fact which the legend of the Herakleids seems to recognize by making Têmenus the eldest brother of the three. And Herodotus assures us that at one time all the eastern coast of Peloponnesus down to Cape Melea, including the island of Cythêra, all which came afterwards to constitute a material part of Laconia, had belonged to Argos.[504] Down to the time of the first Messenian war, the comparative importance of the Dorian establishments in Peloponnesus appears to have been in the order in which the legend placed them,—Argos first,[505] Sparta second, Messênê third. It will be seen hereafter that the Argeians never lost the recollection of this early preëminence, from which the growth of Sparta had extruded them; and the liberties of entire Hellas were more than once in danger from their disastrous jealousy of a more fortunate competitor.

At a short distance of about three miles from Argos, and at the exact point where that city approaches nearest to the sea,[506] was situated the isolated hillock called Temenion, noticed both by Strabo and Pausanias. It was a small village, deriving both its name and its celebrity from the chapel and tomb of the hero Têmenus, who was there worshipped by the Dorians; and the statement which Pausanias heard was, that Têmenus, with his invading Dorians, had seized and fortified the spot, and employed it as an armed post to make war upon Tisamenus and the Achæans. What renders this report deserving of the greater attention, is, that the same thing is affirmed with regard to the eminence called Solygeius, near Corinth: this too was believed to be the place which the Dorian assailants had occupied and fortified against the preëxisting Corinthians in the city. Situated close upon the Sarônic gulf, it was the spot which invaders landing from that gulf would naturally seize upon, and which Nikias with his powerful Athenian fleet did actually seize and occupy against Corinth in the Peloponnesian war.[507] In early days, the only way of overpowering the inhabitants of a fortified town, generally also planted in a position itself very defensible, was,—that the invaders, entrenching themselves in the neighborhood, harassed the inhabitants and ruined their produce until they brought them to terms. Even during the Peloponnesian war, when the art of besieging had made some progress, we read of several instances in which this mode of aggressive warfare was adopted with efficient results.[508] We may readily believe that the Dorians obtained admittance both into Argos and Corinth in this manner. And it is remarkable that, except Sikyôn (which is affirmed to have been surprised by night), these were the only towns in the Argolic region which are said to have resisted them; the story being, that Phlius, Epidaurus, and Trœzên had admitted the Dorian intruders without opposition, although a certain portion of the previous inhabitants seceded. We shall hereafter see that the non-Dorian population of Sikyôn and Corinth still remained considerable.

The separate statements which we thus find, and the position of the Temenion and the Solygeius, lead to two conjectures,—first, that the acquisitions of the Dorians in Peloponnesus were also isolated and gradual, not at all conformable to the rapid strides of the old Herakleid legend; next, that the Dorian invaders of Argos and Corinth made their attack from the Argolic and the Saronic gulfs,—by sea and not by land. It is, indeed, difficult to see how they can have got to the Temenion in any other way than by sea; and a glance at the map will show that the eminence Solygeius presents itself, [509] with reference to Corinth, as the nearest and most convenient holding-ground for a maritime invader, conformably to the scheme of operations laid by Nikias. To illustrate the supposition of a Dorian attack by sea on Corinth, we may refer to a story quoted from Aristotle (which we find embodied in the explanation of an old adage), representing Hippotês the father of Alêtês as having crossed the Maliac gulf[510] (the sea immediately bordering on the ancient Maleans, Dryopians, and Dorians) in ships, for the purpose of colonizing. And if it be safe to trust the mention of Dorians in the Odyssey, as a part of the population of the island of Crete, we there have an example of Dorian settlements which must have been effected by sea, and that too at a very early period. "We must suppose (observes O. Müller,[511] in reference to these Kretan Dorians) that the Dorians, pressed by want or restless from inactivity, constructed piratical canoes, manned these frail and narrow barks with soldiers who themselves worked at the oar, and thus being changed from mountaineers into seamen,—the Normans of Greece,—set sail for the distant island of Krête." In the same manner, we may conceive the expeditions of the Dorians against Argos and Corinth to have been effected; and whatever difficulties may attach to this hypothesis, certain it is that the difficulties of a long land-march, along such a territory as Greece, are still more serious.

The supposition of Dorian emigrations by sea, from the Maliac gulf to the north-eastern promontory of Peloponnesus, is farther borne out by the analogy of the Dryopes, or Dryopians. During the historical times, this people occupied several detached settlements in various parts of Greece, all maritime, and some insular;—they were found at Hermionê, Asinê, and Eiôn, in the Argolic peninsula (very near to the important Dorian towns constituting

174

the Amphiktyony of Argos,[512])—at Styra and Karystus in the island of Eubœa,—in the island of Kythnus, and even at Cyprus. These dispersed colonies can only have been planted by expeditions over the sea. Now we are told that the original Dryopis, the native country of this people, comprehended both the territory near the river Spercheius, and north of Œta, afterwards occupied by the Malians, as well as the neighboring district south of Œta, which was afterwards called Doris. From hence the Dryopians were expelled,—according to one story, by the Dorians,—according to another, by Hêraklês and the Malians: however this may be, it was from the Maliac gulf that they started on shipboard in quest of new homes, which some of them found on the headlands of the Argolic peninsula.[513] And it was from this very country, according to Herodotus,[514] that the Dorians also set forth, in order to reach Peloponnesus. Nor does it seem unreasonable to imagine, that the same means of conveyance, which bore the Dryopians from the Maliac gulf to Hermionê and Asinê, also carried the Dorians from the same place to the Temenion, and the hill Solygeius.

The legend represents Sikyôn, Epidaurus, Trœzên, Phlius, and Kleônæ, as all occupied by Dorian colonists from Argos, under the different sons of Têmenus: the first three are on the sea, and fit places for the occupation of maritime invaders. Argos and the Dorian towns in and near the Argolic peninsula are to be regarded as a cluster of settlements by themselves, completely distinct from Sparta and the Messenian Stenyklêrus, which appear to have been formed under totally different conditions. First, both of them are very far inland,—Stenyklêrus not easy, Sparta very difficult of access from the sea; next, we know that the conquests of Sparta were gradually made down the valley of the Eurotas seaward. Both these acquisitions present the appearance of having been made from the land-side, and perhaps in the direction which the Herakleid legend describes,—by warriors entering Peloponnesus across the narrow mouth of the Corinthian gulf, through the aid or invitation of those Ætolian settlers who at the same time colonized Elis. The early and intimate connection (on which I shall touch presently) between Sparta and the Olympic games as administered by the Eleians, as well as the leading part ascribed to Lykurgus in the constitution of the solemn Olympic truce, tend to strengthen such a persuasion.

In considering the early affairs of the Dorians in Peloponnesus, we are apt to have our minds biased, first, by the Herakleid legend, which imparts to them an impressive, but deceitful, epical unity; next, by the aspect of the later and better-known history, which presents the Spartan power as unquestionably preponderant, and Argos only as second by a long interval. But the first view (as I have already remarked) which opens to us, of real Grecian history, a little before 776 B.C., exhibits Argos with its alliance or confederacy of neighboring cities colonized from itself, as the great seat of Dorian power in the peninsula, and Sparta as an outlying state of inferior consequence. The recollection of this state of things lasted after it had ceased to be a reality, and kept alive pretensions on the part of Argos to the headship of the Greeks as a matter of right, which she became quite incapable of sustaining either by adequate power or by statesmanlike sagacity. The growth of Spartan power was a succession of encroachments upon Argos.[515]

How Sparta came constantly to gain upon Argos will be matter for future explanation: at present, it is sufficient to remark, that the ascendency of Argos was derived not exclusively from her own territory, but came in part from her position as metropolis of an alliance of autonomous neighboring cities, all Dorian and all colonized from herself,—and this was an element of power essentially fluctuating. What Thêbes was to the cities of Bœotia, of which she either was, or professed to have been, the founder,[516] the same was Argos in reference to Kleônæ, Phlius, Sikyôn, Epidaurus, Trœzên, and Ægina. These towns formed, in mythical language, "the lot of Têmenus,"[517]—in real matter of fact, the confederated allies or subordinates of Argos: the first four of them were said to have been *Dorized* by the sons or immediate relatives of Têmenus; and the kings of Argos, as acknowledged descendants of the latter, claimed and exercised a sort of *suzeraineté* over them. Hermionê, Asinê, and Nauplia seem also to have been under the supremacy of Argos, though not colonies.[518] But this supremacy was not claimed directly and nakedly: agreeably to the ideas of the time, the ostensible purposes of the Argeian confederacy or Amphiktyony were religious, though its secondary and not less real effects, were political. The great patron-god of the league was Apollo Pythaëus, in whose name the obligations incumbent on the members of the league were imposed. While in each of the confederated cities there was a temple to this god, his most holy and central sanctuary was on the Larissa or acropolis of Argos. At this central Argeian sanctuary, solemn sacrifices were offered by Epidaurus as well as by other members of the confederacy, and, as it should seem, accompanied by money-payments,[519]—which the Argeians, as chief administrators on behalf of the common god, took upon them to enforce against defaulters, and actually tried to enforce during the Peloponnesian war against Epidaurus. On another occasion, during the 66th Olympiad (B. C. 514), they imposed the large fine of 500 talents upon each of the two states Sikyôn and Ægina, for having lent ships to the Spartan king Kleomenes, wherewith he invaded the Argeian territory. The Æginetans set the claim at defiance, but the Sikyonians acknowledged its justice, and only demurred to its amount, professing themselves ready to pay 100 talents.[520] There can be no doubt that, at this later period, the ascendency of Argos over the members of her primitive confederacy had become practically inoperative;

but the tenor of the cases mentioned shows that her claims were revivals of bygone privileges, which had once been effective and valuable.

How valuable the privileges of Argos were, before the great rise of the Spartan power,—how important an ascendency they conferred, in the hands of an energetic man, and how easily they admitted of being used in furtherance of ambitious views, is shown by the remarkable case of Pheidôn, the Temenid. The few facts which we learn respecting this prince exhibit to us, for the first time, something like a real position of parties in the Peloponnesus, wherein the actual conflict of living historical men and cities, comes out in tolerable distinctness.

Pheidôn was designated by Ephorus as the tenth, and by Theopompus as the sixth, in lineal descent from Têmenus. Respecting the date of his existence, opinions the most discrepant and irreconcilable have been delivered; but there seems good reason for referring him to the period a little before and a little after the 8th Olympiad,—between 770 B. C. and 730 B. C. [521] Of the preceding kings of Argos we hear little: one of them, Eratus, is said to have expelled the Dryopian inhabitants of Asinê from their town on the Argolic peninsula, in consequence of their having coöperated with the Spartan king, Nikander, when he invaded the Argeian territory, seemingly during the generation preceding Pheidôn; there is another, Damokratidas, whose date cannot be positively determined, but he appears rather as subsequent than as anterior to Pheidôn.[522] We are informed, however, that these anterior kings, even beginning with Medôn, the grandson of Têmenus, had been forced to submit to great abridgment of their power and privileges, and that a form of government substantially popular, though nominally regal, had been established.[523] Pheidôn, breaking through the limits imposed, made himself despot of Argos. He then re-established the power of Argos over all the cities of her confederacy, which had before been so nearly dissolved as to leave all the members practically independent.[524] Next, he is said to have acquired dominion over Corinth, and to have endeavored to assure it, by treacherously entrapping a thousand of her warlike citizens; but his artifice was divulged and frustrated by Abrôn, one of his confidential friends.[525] He is farther reported to have aimed at extending his sway over the greater part of Peloponnesus,—laying claim, as the descendant of Hêraklês, through the eldest son of Hyllus, to all the cities which that restless and irresistible hero had ever taken.[526] According to Grecian ideas, this legendary title was always seriously construed, and often admitted as conclusive; though of course, where there were strong opposing interests, reasons would be found to elude it. Pheidôn would have the same ground of right as that which, two hundred and fifty years afterwards, determined the Herakleid Dôrieus, brother of Kleomenês king of Sparta, to acquire for himself the territory near Mount

Eryx in Sicily, because his progenitor,[527] Hêraklês, had conquered it before him. So numerous, however, were the legends respecting the conquests of Hêraklês, that the claim of Pheidôn must have covered the greater part of Peloponnesus, except Sparta and the plain of Messêne, which were already in the hands of Herakleids.

Nor was the ambition of Pheidôn satisfied even with these large pretensions. He farther claimed the right of presiding at the celebration of those religious games, or Agônes, which had been instituted by Hêraklês,—and among these was numbered the Olympic Agôn, then, however, enjoying but a slender fraction of the lustre which afterwards came to attach to it. The presidency of any of the more celebrated festivals current throughout Greece, was a privilege immensely prized. It was at once dignified and lucrative, and the course of our history will present more than one example in which blood was shed to determine what state should enjoy it. Pheidôn marched to Olympia, at the epoch of the 8th recorded Olympiad, or 747 B. C.; on the occasion of which event we are made acquainted with the real state of parties in the peninsula.

The plain of Olympia,—now ennobled only by immortal recollections, but once crowded with all the decorations of religion and art, and forming for many centuries the brightest centre of attraction known in the ancient world, —was situated on the river Alpheius, in the territory called the Pisatid, hard by the borders of Arcadia. At what time its agonistic festival, recurring every fifth year, at the first full moon after the summer solstice, first began or first acquired its character of special sanctity, we have no means of determining. As with so many of the native waters of Greece,—we follow the stream upward to a certain point, but the fountain-head, and the earlier flow of history, is buried under mountains of unsearchable legend. The first celebration of the Olympic contests was ascribed by Grecian legendary faith to Hêraklês,—and the site of the place, in the middle of the Pisatid, with its eight small townships, is quite sufficient to prove that the inhabitants of that little territory were warranted in describing themselves as the original administrators of the ceremony.[528] But this state of things seems to have been altered by the Ætolian settlement in Elis, which is represented as having been conducted by Oxylus and identified with the Return of the Herakleids. The Ætolo-Eleians, bordering upon the Pisatid to the north, employed their superior power in subduing their weaker neighbors,[529] who thus lost their autonomy and became annexed to the territory of Elis. It was the general rule throughout Greece, that a victorious state undertook to perform[530] the current services of the conquered people towards the gods,—such services being conceived as attaching to the soil: hence, the celebration of the Olympic games became numbered among the incumbences of Elis, just in the same way as the worship of the Eleusinian Dêmêtêr, when Eleusis lost its autonomy, was included among the religious obligations of Athens. The Pisatans, however, never willingly acquiesced in this absorption of what had once been their separate privilege; they long maintained their conviction, that the celebration of the games was their right, and strove on several occasions to regain it. On those occasions, the earliest, so far as we hear, was connected with the intervention of Pheidôn. It was at their invitation that the king of Argos went to Olympia, and celebrated the games himself, in conjunction with the Pisatans, as the lineal successor of Hêraklês; while the Eleians, being thus forcibly dispossessed, refused to include the 8th Olympiad in their register of the victorious runners. But their humiliation did not last long, for the Spartans took their part, and the contest ended in the defeat of Pheidôn. In the next Olympiad, the Eleian management and the regular enrolment appear as before, and the Spartans are even said to have confirmed Elis in her possession both of Pisatis and Triphylia.[531]

Unfortunately, these scanty particulars are all which we learn respecting the armed conflict at the 8th Olympiad, in which the religious and the political grounds of quarrel are so intimately blended,—as we shall find to be often the case in Grecian history. But there is one act of Pheidôn yet more memorable, of which also nothing beyond a meagre notice has come down to us. He first coined both copper and silver money in Ægina, and first established a scale of weights and measures,[532] which, through his influence, became adopted throughout Peloponnesus, and acquired, ultimately, footing both in all the Dorian states, and in Bœotia, Thessaly, northern Hellas generally, and Macedonia,—under the name of the Æginæan Scale. There arose subsequently another rival scale in Greece, called the Euboic, differing considerably from the Æginæan. We do not know at what time it was introduced, but it was employed both at Athens and in the Ionic cities generally, as well as in Eubœa,—being modified at Athens, so far as money was concerned, by Solon's debasement of the coinage.

The copious and valuable information contained in M. Boeckh's recent publication on Metrology, has thrown new light upon these monetary and statical scales.[533] He has shown that both the Æginæan and the Euboic scales—the former standing to the latter in the proportion of 6 : 5—had contemporaneous currency in different parts of the Persian empire; the divisions and denominations of the scale being the same in both, 100 drachmæ to a mina, and 60 minæ to a talent. The Babylonian talent, mina, and drachma are identical with the Æginæan: the word mina is of Asiatic origin; and it has now been rendered highly probable, that the scale circulated by Pheidôn was borrowed immediately from the Phœnicians, and by them originally from the Babylonians. The Babylonian, Hebraic, Phœnician,

Egyptian,[534] and Grecian scales of weight (which were subsequently followed wherever coined money was introduced) are found to be so nearly conformable, as to warrant a belief that they are all deduced from one common origin; and that origin the Chaldæan priesthood of Babylon. It is to Pheidôn, and to his position as chief of the Argeian confederacy, that the Greeks owe the first introduction of the Babylonian scale of weight, and the first employment of coined and stamped money.

If we maturely weigh the few, but striking acts of Pheidôn which have been preserved to us, and which there is no reason to discredit, we shall find ourselves introduced to an early historical state of Peloponnesus very different from that to which another century will bring us. That Argos, with the federative cities attached to her, was at this early time decidedly the commanding power in that peninsula, is sufficiently shown by the establishment and reception of the Pheidonian weights, measures, and monetary system,—while the other incidents mentioned completely harmonize with the same idea. Against the oppressions of Elis, the Pisatans invoked Pheidon,—partly as exercising a primacy in Peloponnesus, just as the inhabitants of Lepreum in Triphylia,[535] three centuries afterwards, called in the aid of Sparta for the same object, at a time when Sparta possessed the headship,—and partly as the lineal representative of Hêraklês, who had founded those games from the management of which they had been unjustly extruded. On the other hand, Sparta appears as a second-rate power. The Æginæan scale of weight and measure was adopted there as elsewhere,[536]— the Messenian Dorians were still equal and independent,—and we find Sparta interfering to assist Elis by virtue of an obligation growing (so the legend represents it) out of the common Ætolo-Dorian emigration; not at all from any acknowledged primacy, such as we shall see her enjoying hereafter. The first coinage of copper and silver money is a capital event in Grecian history, and must be held to imply considerable commerce as well as those extensive views which belong only to a conspicuous and leading position. The ambition of Pheidôn to resume all the acquisitions made by his ancestor Hêraklês, suggests the same large estimate of his actual power. He is characterized as a despot, and even as the most insolent of all despots:[537] how far he deserved such a reputation, we have no means of judging. We may remark, however, that he lived before the age of despots or tyrants, properly so called, and before the Herakleid lineage had yet lost its primary, half-political, half-religious character. Moreover, the later historians have invested his actions with a color of exorbitant aggression, by applying them to a state of things which belonged to their time and not to his. Thus Ephorus represents him as having deprived the Lacedæmonians of the headship of Peloponnesus, which they never possessed until long after him,—and also as setting at naught the sworn inviolability of the territory of the Eleians, enjoyed by the latter as celebrators of the Olympic games; whereas the Agonothesia, or right of superintendence claimed by Elis, had not at that time acquired the sanction of prescription,—while the conquest of Pisa by the Eleians themselves had proved that this sacred function did not protect the territory of a weaker people.

How Pheidôn fell, and how the Argeians lost that supremacy which they once evidently possessed, we have no positive details to inform us: with respect to the latter point, however, we can discern a sufficient explanation. The Argeians stood predominant as an entire and unanimous confederacy, which required a vigorous and able hand to render its internal organization effective or its ascendency respected without. No such leader afterwards appeared at Argos, the whole history of which city is destitute of eminent individuals: her line of kings continued at least down to the Persian war,[538] but seemingly with only titular functions, for the government had long been decidedly popular. The statements, which represent the government as popular anterior to the time of Pheidôn, appear unworthy of trust. That prince is rather to be taken as wielding the old, undiminished prerogatives of the Herakleid kings, but wielding them with unusual effect,—enforcing relaxed privileges, and appealing to the old heroic sentiment in reference to Hêraklês, rather than revolutionizing the existing relations either of Argos or of Peloponnesus. It was in fact the great and steady growth of Sparta, for three centuries after the Lykurgean institutions, which operated as a cause of subversion to the previous order of command and obedience in Greece.

The assertion made by Herodotus,—that, in earlier times, the whole eastern coast of Laconia as far as Cape Malea, including the island of Kythêra and several other islands, had belonged to Argos,—is referred by O. Müller to about the 50th Olympiad, or 580 B. C. Perhaps it had ceased to be true at that period; but that it was true in the age of Pheidôn, there seem good grounds for believing. What is probably meant is, that the Dorian towns on this coast, Prasiæ, Zarêx, Epidaurus Limêra, and Bœæ, were once autonomous, and members of the Argeian confederacy,—a fact highly probable, on independent evidence, with respect to Epidaurus Limêra, inasmuch as that town was a settlement from Epidaurus in the Argolic peninsula: and Bœæ too had its own œkist and eponymus, the Herakleid Bœus,[539] noway connected with Sparta,—perhaps derived from the same source as the name of the town Bœon in Doris. The Argeian confederated towns would thus comprehend the whole coast of the Argolic and Saronic gulfs, from Kythêra as far as Ægina, besides other islands which we do not know: Ægina had received a colony of Dorians from Argos and Epidaurus, upon which latter town it continued for some time in a state of dependence.[540] It will at once be seen that this extent of coast implies a considerable degree of commerce and maritime activity. We have besides to consider the range of Doric colonies in the southern islands of the Ægean and in the south-western corner of Asia Minor,—Krête, Kôs, Rhodes (with its three distinct cities), Halikarnassus, Knidus, Myndus, Nisyrus, Symê, Karpathus, Kalydna, etc. Of the Doric establishments here named, several are connected (as has been before stated) with the great emigration of the Têmenid Althæmenês from Argos: but what we particularly observe is, that they are often referred as colonies promiscuously to Argos, Trœzên, Epidaurus[541]—more frequently however, as it seems, to Argos. All these settlements are doubtless older than Pheidôn, and we may conceive them as proceeding conjointly from the allied Dorian towns in the Argolic peninsula, at a time when they were more in the habit of united action than they afterwards became: a captain of emigrants selected from the line of Hêraklês and Têmenus was suitable to the feelings of all of them. We may thus look back to a period, at the very beginning of the Olympiads, when the maritime Dorians on the east of Peloponnesus maintained a considerable intercourse and commerce, not only among themselves, but also with their settlements on the Asiatic coast and islands. That the Argolic peninsula formed an early centre for maritime rendezvous, we may farther infer from the very ancient Amphiktyony of the seven cities (Hermionê, Epidaurus, Ægina, Athens, Prasiæ, Nauplia, and the Minyeian Orchomenus), on the holy island of Kalauria, off the harbor of Trœzên.[542]

The view here given of the early ascendency of Argos, as the head of the Peloponnesian Dorians and the metropolis of the Asiatic Dorians, enables us to understand the capital innovation of Pheidôn,—the first coinage, and the first determinate scale of weight and measure, known in Greece. Of the value of such improvements, in the history of Grecian civilization, it is superfluous to speak, especially when we recollect that the Hellenic states, having no political unity, were only held together by the aggregate of spontaneous uniformities, in language, religion, sympathies, recreations, and general habits. We see both how Pheidôn came to contract the wish, and how he acquired the power, to introduce throughout so much of the Grecian world an uniform scale; we also see that the Asiatic Dorians form the link between him and Phœnicia, from whence the scale was derived, just as the Euboic scale came, in all probability, through the Ionic cities in Asia, from Lydia. It is asserted by Ephorus, and admitted even by the ablest modern critics, that Pheidôn first coined money "in Ægina:"[543] other authors (erroneously believing that his scale was the Euboic scale) alleged that his coinage had been carried on "in a place of Argos called Eubœa."[544] Now both these statements appear highly improbable, and both are traceable to the same mistake,—of supposing that the title, by which the scale had come to be commonly known, must necessarily be derived from the place in which the coinage had been struck. There is every reason to conclude, that what Pheidôn did was done in Argos, and nowhere else: his coinage and scale were the earliest known in Greece, and seem to have been known by his own name, "the Pheidonian measures," under which designation they were described by Aristotle, in his account of the constitution of Argos.[545] They probably did not come to bear the specific epithet of *Æginæan* until there was another scale in vogue, the *Euboic*, from which to distinguish them; and both the epithets were probably derived, not from the place where the scale first originated, but from the people whose commercial activity tended to make them most generally known,—in the one case, the Æginetans; in the other case, the inhabitants of Chalkis and Eretria. I think, therefore, that we are to look upon the Pheidonian measures as emanating from Argos, and as having no greater connection, originally, with Ægina, than with any other city dependent upon Argos.

There is, moreover, another point which deserves notice. What was known by the name of the Æginæan scale, as contrasted with and standing in a definite ratio (6 : 5) with the Euboic scale, related only to weight and money, so far as our knowledge extends:[546] we have no evidence to show that the same ratio extended either to measures of length or measures of capacity. But there seems ground for believing that the Pheidonian regulations, taken in their full comprehension, embraced measures of capacity as well as weights: Pheidôn, at the same time when he determined the talent, mina, and drachm, seems also to have fixed the dry and liquid measures,—the medimnus and metrêtês, with their parts and multiples: and there existed[547] Pheidonian measures of capacity, though not of length, so far as we know. The Æginæan scale may thus have comprised only a portion of what was established by Pheidôn, namely, that which related to weight and money.

# CHAPTER V.

## ÆTOLO-DORIAN EMIGRATION INTO PELOPONNESUS.—
## ELIS, LACONIA, AND MESSENIA.

IT HAS already been stated that the territory properly called Elis, apart from the enlargement which it acquired by conquest, included the westernmost land in Peloponnesus, south of Achaia, and west of Mount Pholoê and Olenus in Arcadia,—but not extending so far southward as the river Alpheius, the course of which lay along the southern portion of Pisatis and on the borders of Triphylia. This territory, which appears in the Odyssey as "the divine Elis, where the Epeians hold sway,"[548] is in the historical times occupied by a population of Ætolian origin. The connection of race between the historical Eleians and the historical Ætolians was recognized by both parties, nor is there any ground for disputing it.[549]

That Ætolian invaders, or emigrants, into Elis, would cross from Naupaktus, or some neighboring point in the Corinthian gulf, is in the natural course of things,—and such is the course which Oxylus, the conductor of the invasion, is represented by the Herakleid legend as taking. That legend (as has been already recounted) introduces Oxylus as the guide of the three Herakleid brothers,—Têmenus, Kresphontês, and Aristodêmus,—and as stipulating with them that, in the new distribution about to take place of Peloponnesus, he shall be allowed to possess the Eleian territory, coupled with many holy privileges as to the celebration of the Olympic games.

In the preceding chapter, I have endeavored to show that the settlements of the Dorians in and near the Argolic peninsula, so far as the probabilities of the case enable us to judge, were not accomplished by any inroad in this direction. But the localities occupied by the Dorians of Sparta, and by the Dorians of Stenyklêrus, in the territory called Messênê, lead us to a different conclusion. The easiest and most natural road through which emigrants could reach either of these two spots, is through the Eleian and the Pisatid country. Colonel Leake observes,[550] that the direct road from the Eleian territory to Sparta, ascending the valley of the Alpheius, near Olympia, to the sources of its branch, the Theius, and from thence descending the Eurotas, affords the only easy march towards that very inaccessible city: and both ancients and moderns have remarked the vicinity of the source of the Alpheius to that of the Eurotas. The situation of Stenyklêrus and Andania, the original settlements of the Messenian Dorians, adjoining closely the Arcadian

Parrhasii, is only at a short distance from the course of the Alpheius; being thus reached most easily by the same route. Dismissing the idea of a great collective Dorian armament, powerful enough to grasp at once the entire peninsula,—we may conceive two moderate detachments of hardy mountaineers, from the cold regions in and near Doris, attaching themselves to the Ætolians, their neighbors, who were proceeding to the invasion of Elis. After having aided the Ætolians, both to occupy Elis and to subdue the Pisatid, these Dorians advanced up the valley of the Alpheius in quest of settlements for themselves. One of these bodies ripens into the stately, stubborn, and victorious Spartans; the other, into the short-lived, trampled, and struggling Messenians.

Amidst the darkness which overclouds these original settlements, we seem to discern something like special causes to determine both of them. With respect to the Spartan Dorians, we are told that a person named Philonomus betrayed Sparta to them, persuading the sovereign in possession to retire with his people into the habitations of the Ionians, in the north of the peninsula,—and that he received as a recompense for this acceptable service Amyklæ, with the district around it. It is farther stated,—and this important fact there seems no reason to doubt,—that Amyklæ,—though only twenty stadia or two miles and a half distant from Sparta, retained both its independence and its Achæan inhabitants, long after the Dorian emigrants had acquired possession of the latter place, and was only taken by them under the reign of Têleklus, one generation before the first Olympiad.[551] Without presuming to fill up by conjecture incurable gaps in the statements of our authorities, we may from hence reasonably presume that the Dorians were induced to invade, and enabled to acquire, Sparta, by the invitation and assistance of a party in the interior of the country. Again, with respect to the Messenian Dorians, a different, but not less effectual temptation was presented by the alliance of the Arcadians, in the south-western portion of that central region of Peloponnesus. Kresphontês, the Herakleid leader, it is said, espoused the daughter[552] of the Arcadian king, Kypselus, which procured for him the support of a powerful section of Arcadia. His settlement at Stenyklêrus was a considerable distance from the sea, at the north-east corner of Messenia,[553] close to the Arcadian frontier; and it will be seen hereafter that this Arcadian alliance is a constant and material element in the disputes of the Messenian Dorians with Sparta.

We may thus trace a reasonable sequence of events, showing how two bodies of Dorians, having first assisted the Ætolo-Eleians to conquer the Pisatid, and thus finding themselves on the banks of the Alpheius, followed the upward course of that river, the one to settle at Sparta, the other at Stenyklêrus. The historian Ephorus, from whom our scanty fragments of information respecting these early settlements are derived,—it is important to note that he lived in the age immediately succeeding the first foundation of Messênê as a city, the restitution of the long-exiled Messenians, and the amputation of the fertile western half of Laconia, for their benefit, by Epameinondas,—imparts to these proceedings an immediate decisiveness of effect which does not properly belong to them: as if the Spartans had become at once possessed of all Laconia, and the Messenians of all Messenia: Pausanias, too, speaks as if the Arcadians collectively had assisted and allied themselves with Kresphontês. This is the general spirit which pervades his account, though the particular facts in so far as we find any such, do not always harmonize with it. Now we are ignorant of the preëxisting divisions of the country, either east or west of Mount Taygetus, at the time when the Dorians invaded it. But to treat the one and the other as integral kingdoms, handed over at once to two Dorian leaders, is an illusion borrowed from the old legend, from the historicizing fancies of Ephorus, and from the fact that, in the well-known times, this whole territory came to be really united under the Spartan power.

At what date the Dorian settlements at Sparta and Stenyklêrus were effected, we have no means of determining. Yet, that there existed between them in the earliest times a degree of fraternity which did not prevail between Lacedæmon and Argos, we may fairly presume from the common temple, with joint religious sacrifices, of Artemis Limnatis, or Artemis on the Marsh, erected on the confines of Messenia and Laconia.[554] Our first view of the two, at all approaching to distinctness, seems to date from a period about half a century earlier than the first Olympiad (776 B. C.),—about the reign of king Têleklus of the Eurystheneid or Agid line, and the introduction of the Lykurgean discipline. Têleklus stands in the list as the eighth king dating from Eurysthenes. But how many of the seven kings before him are to be considered as real persons,—or how much, out of the brief warlike expeditions ascribed to them, is to be treated as authentic history,—I pretend not to define.

The earliest determinable event in the *internal* history of Sparta is the introduction of the Lykurgean discipline; the earliest *external* events are the conquest of Amyklæ, Pharis, and Geronthræ, effected by king Têleklus, and the first quarrel with the Messenians, in which that prince was slain. When we come to see how deplorably great was the confusion and ignorance which reigned with reference to a matter so preëminently important as Lykurgus and his legislation, we shall not be inclined to think that facts much less important, and belonging to an earlier epoch, can have been handed down upon any good authority. And in like manner, when we learn that Amyklæ, Pharis, and Geronthræ (all south of Sparta, and the first only two and a half

186

miles distant from that city) were independent of the Spartans until the reign of Têleklus, we shall require some decisive testimony before we can believe that a community so small, and so hemmed in as Sparta must then have been, had in earlier times undertaken expeditions against Helos on the sea-coast, against Kleitor on the extreme northern side of Arcadia, against the Kynurians, or against the Argeians. If Helos and Kynuria were conquered by these early kings, it appears that they had to be conquered a second time by kings succeeding Têleklus. It would be more natural that we should hear when and how they conquered the places nearer to them,—Sellasia, or Belemina, the valley of the Œnus, or the upper valley of the Eurotas. But these seem to be assumed as matters of course; the proceedings ascribed to the early Spartan kings are such only as might beseem the palmy days when Sparta was undisputed mistress of all Laconia.

The succession of Messenian kings, beginning with Kresphontês, the Herakleid brother, and continuing from father to son,—Æpytus, Glaukus, Isthnius, Dotadas, Subotas, Phintas, the last being contemporary with Têleklus,—is still less marked by incident than that of the early Spartan kings. It is said that the reign of Kresphontês was troubled, and himself ultimately slain by mutinies among his subjects: Æpytus, then a youth, having escaped into Arcadia, was afterwards restored to the throne by the Arcadians, Spartans, and Argeians.[555] From Æpytus, the Messenian line of kings are stated to have been denominated Æpytids in preference to Herakleids,— which affords another proof of their intimate connection with the Arcadians, since Æpytus was a very ancient name in Arcadian heroic antiquity.[556]

There is considerable resemblance between the alleged behavior of Kresphontês on first settling at Stenyklêrus, and that of Eurysthenês and Proklês at Sparta,—so far as we gather from statements alike meagre and uncertified, resting on the authority of Ephorus. Both are said to have tried to place the preëxisting inhabitants of the country on a level with their own Dorian bands; both provoked discontents and incurred obloquy, with their contemporaries as well as with posterity, by the attempt; nor did either permanently succeed. Kresphontês was forced to concentrate all his Dorians in Stenyklêrus, while after all, the discontents ended in his violent death. And Agis, the son of Eurysthenês, is said to have reversed all the liberal tentatives of his father, so as to bring the whole of Laconia into subjection and dependence on the Dorians at Sparta, with the single exception of Amyklæ. So odious to the Spartan Dorians was the conduct of Eurysthenês, that they refused to acknowledge him as their œkist, and conferred that honor upon Agis; the two lines of kings being called Agiads and Eurypontids, instead of Eurystheneids and Prokleids.[557] We see in these statements the same tone of mind as that which pervades the Panathenaic oration of Isokratês, the master of Ephorus,—the facts of an unknown period, so colored as to suit an *idéal* of haughty Dorian exclusiveness.

Again, as Eurysthenês and Proklês appear, in the picture of Ephorus, to carry their authority at once over the whole of Laconia, so too does Kresphontês over the whole of Messenia,—over the entire south-western region of Peloponnesus, westward of Mount Taygetus and Cape Tænarus, and southward of the river Neda. He sends an envoy to Pylus and Rhium, the western and southern portions of the south-western promontory of Peloponnesus, treating the entire territory as if it were one sovereignty, and inviting the inhabitants to submit under equal laws.[558] But it has already been observed, that this supposed oneness and indivisibility is not less uncertified in regard to Messenia than in regard to Laconia. How large a proportion of the former territory these kings of Stenyklêrus may have ruled, we have no means of determining, but there were certainly portions of it which they did not rule,—not merely during the reign of Têleklus at Sparta, but still later, during the first Messenian war. For not only are we informed that Têleklus established three townships, Poiêessa, Echeiæ,[559] and Tragium, near the Messenian gulf, and on the course of the river Nedon, but we read also a farther matter of evidence in the roll of Olympic victors. Every competitor for the prize at one of these great festivals was always entered as member of some autonomous Hellenic community, which constituted his title to approach the lists; if successful, he was proclaimed with the name of the community to which he belonged. Now during the first ten Olympiads, seven winners are proclaimed as Messenians; in the 11th Olympiad, we find the name of Oxythemis Korônæus,—Oxythemis, not of Korôneia in Bœotia, but of Korônê in the western bend of the Messenian gulf,[560] some miles on the right bank of the Pamisus, and a considerable distance to the north of the modern Coron. Now if Korônê had then been comprehended in Messenia, Oxythemis would have been proclaimed as a Messenian, like the seven winners who preceded him; and the fact of his being proclaimed as a Korônæan, proves that Korônê was then an independent community, not under the dominion of the Dorians of Stenyklêrus. It seems clear, therefore, that the latter did not reign over the whole territory commonly known as Messenia, though we are unable to assign the proportion of it which they actually possessed.

The Olympic festival, in its origin doubtless a privilege of the neighboring Pisatans, seems to have derived its great and gradually expanding importance from the Ætolo-Eleian settlement in Peloponnesus, combined with the Dorians of Laconia and Messenia. Lykurgus of Sparta, and Iphitus of Elis, are alleged to have joined their efforts for the purpose of establishing both the sanctity of the Olympic truce and the inviolability of the Eleian territory.

Hence, though this tale is not to be construed as matter of fact, we may see that the Lacedæmonians regarded the Olympic games as a portion of their own antiquities. Moreover, it is certain, both that the dignity of the festival increased simultaneously with their ascendency,[561] and that their peculiar fashions were very early introduced into the practice of the Olympic competitors. Probably, the three bands of coöperating invaders, Ætolians and Spartan and Messenian Dorians, may have adopted this festival as a periodical renovation of mutual union and fraternity; from which cause the games became an attractive centre for the western portion of Peloponnesus, before they were much frequented by people from the eastern, or still more from extra-Peloponnesian Hellas. For it cannot be altogether accidental, when we read the names of the first twelve proclaimed Olympic victors (occupying nearly half a century from 776 B. C. downwards), to find that seven of them are Messenians, three Eleians, one from Dymê, in Achaia, and one from Korônê; while after the 12th Olympiad, Corinthians and Megarians and Epidaurians begin to occur; later still, extra-Peloponnesian victors. We may reasonably infer from hence that the Olympic ceremonies were at this early period chiefly frequented by visitors and competitors from the western regions of Peloponnesus, and that the affluence to them, from the more distant parts of the Hellenic world, did not become considerable until the first Messenian war had closed.

Having thus set forth the conjectures, to which our very scanty knowledge points, respecting the first establishment of the Ætolian and Dorian settlements in Elis, Laconia, and Messenia, connected as they are with the steadily increasing dignity and frequentation of the Olympic festival, I proceed, in the next chapter, to that memorable circumstance which both determined the character, and brought about the political ascendency, of the Spartans separately: I mean, the laws and discipline of Lykurgus.

Of the preëxisting inhabitants of Laconia and Messenia, whom we are accustomed to call Achæans and Pylians, so little is known, that we cannot at all measure the difference between them and their Dorian invaders, either in dialect, in habits, or in intelligence. There appear no traces of any difference of dialect among the various parts of the population of Laconia: the Messenian allies of Athens, in the Peloponnesian war, speak the same dialect as the Helots, and the same also as the Ambrakiotic colonists from Corinth: all Doric.[562] Nor are we to suppose that the Doric dialect was at all peculiar to the people called Dorians. As far as can be made out by the evidence of Inscriptions, it seems to have been the dialect of the Phokians, Delphians, Lokrians, Ætolians, and Achæans of Phthiôtis: with respect to the latter, the Inscriptions of Thaumaki, in Achæa Phthiôtis, afford a proof the more curious and the more cogent of native dialect, because the Phthiôts were both immediate neighbors and subjects of the Thessalians, who spoke a variety of the Æolic. So, too, within Peloponnesus, we find evidences of Doric dialect among the Achæans in the north of Peloponnesus,—the Dryopic inhabitants of Hermionê,[563]—and the Eleuthero-Lacones, or Laconian townships (compounded of Periœki and Helots), emancipated by the Romans in the second century B. C. Concerning the speech of that population whom the invading Dorians found in Laconia, we have no means of judging: the presumption would rather be that it did not differ materially from the Doric. Thucydidês designates the Corinthians, whom the invading Dorians attacked from the hill Solygeius, as being Æolians, and Strabo speaks both of the Achæans as an Æolic nation, and of the Æolic dialect as having been originally preponderant in Peloponnesus.[564] But we do not readily see what means of information either of these authors possessed respecting the speech of a time which must have been four centuries anterior even to Thucydidês.

Of that which is called the Æolic dialect there are three marked and distinguishable varieties,—the Lesbian, the Thessalian, and the Bœotian; the Thessalian forming a mean term between the other two. Ahrens has shown that the ancient grammatical critics are accustomed to affirm peculiarities, as belonging to the Æolic dialect generally, which in truth belong only to the Lesbian variety of it, or to the poems of Alkæus and Sappho, which these critics attentively studied. Lesbian Æolic, Thessalian Æolic, and Bœotian Æolic, are all different: and if, abstracting from these differences, we confine our attention to that which is common to all three, we shall find little to distinguish this abstract Æolic from the abstract Doric, or that which is common to the many varieties of the Doric dialect.[565] These two are sisters, presenting, both of them, more or less the Latin side of the Greek language, while the relationship of either of them to the Attic and Ionic is more distant. Now it seems that, putting aside Attica, the speech of all Greece,[566] from Perrhæbia and Mount Olympus to Cape Malea and Cape Akritas, consisted of different varieties, either of the Doric or of the Æolic dialect; this being true (as far as we are able to judge) not less of the aboriginal Arcadians than of the rest. The Laconian dialect contained more specialties of its own, and approached nearer to the Æolic and to the Eleian, than any other variety of the Dorian: it stands at the extreme of what has been classified as the strict Dorian,—that is, the farthest removed from Ionic and Attic. The Kretan towns manifest also a strict Dorism; as well as the Lacedæmonian colony of Tarentum, and, seemingly, most of the Italiotic Greeks, though some of them are called Achæan colonies. Most of the other varieties of the Doric dialect (Phokian, Lokrian, Delphian, Achæan of Phthiôtis) exhibit a form departing less widely from the Ionic and Attic: Argos, and the towns in the Argolic peninsula, seem to form a stepping-stone between the two.

These positions represent the little which can be known respecting those varieties of Grecian speech which are not known to us by written works. The little presumption which can be raised upon them favors the belief that the Dorian invaders of Laconia and Messenia found there a dialect little different from that which they brought with them,—a conclusion which it is the more necessary to state distinctly, since the work of O. Müller has caused an exaggerated estimate to be formed of the distinctive peculiarities whereby Dorism was parted off from the rest of Hellas.

# CHAPTER VI.

## LAWS AND DISCIPLINE OF LYKURGUS AT SPARTA.

PLUTARCH begins his biography of Lykurgus with the following ominous words:—

"Concerning the lawgiver Lykurgus, we can assert absolutely nothing which is not controverted: there are different stories in respect to his birth, his travels, his death, and also his mode of proceeding, political as well as legislative: least of all is the time in which he lived agreed upon."

And this exordium is but too well borne out by the unsatisfactory nature of the accounts which we read, not only in Plutarch himself, but in those other authors out of whom we are obliged to make up our idea of the memorable Lykurgean system. If we examine the sources from which Plutarch's life of Lykurgus is deduced, it will appear that—excepting the poets Alkman, Tyrtæus, and Simonidês, from whom he has borrowed less than we could have wished—he has no authorities older than Xenophon and Plato: Aristotle is cited several times, and is unquestionably the best of his witnesses, but the greater number of them belong to the century subsequent to that philosopher. Neither Herodotus nor Ephorus are named, though the former furnishes some brief, but interesting particulars,—and the latter also (as far as we can judge from the fragments remaining) entered at large into the proceedings of the Spartan lawgiver.[567]

Lykurgus is described by Herodotus as uncle and guardian to king Labôtas, of the Eurystheneid or Agid line of Spartan kings; and this would place him, according to the received chronology, about 220 years before the first recorded Olympiad (about B. C. 996).[568] All the other accounts, on the contrary, seem to represent him as a younger brother, belonging to the other or Prokleid line of Spartan kings, though they do not perfectly agree respecting his parentage. While Simonidês stated him to be the son of Prytanis, Dieutychidas described him as grandson of Prytanis, son of Eunomus, brother of Polydektês, and uncle as well as guardian to Charilaus,—thus making him eleventh in descent from Hêraklês.[569] This latter account was adopted by Aristotle, coinciding, according to the received chronology, with the date of Iphitus the Eleian, and the first celebration of the Olympic games by Lykurgus and Iphitus conjointly,[570] which Aristotle accepted as a fact. Lykurgus, on the hypothesis here mentioned, would stand about B. C. 880, a century before the recorded Olympiads. Eratosthenês and Apollodorus placed him "not a few years earlier than the first Olympiad." If they meant hereby the epoch commonly assigned as the Olympiad of Iphitus, their date would coincide pretty nearly with that of Herodotus: if, on the other hand, they meant the first recorded Olympiad (B. C. 776), they would be found not much removed from the opinion of Aristotle. An unequivocal proof of the inextricable confusion in ancient times respecting the epoch of the great Spartan lawgiver is indirectly afforded by Timæus, who supposed that there had existed two persons named Lykurgus, and that the acts of both had been ascribed to one. It is plain from hence that there was no certainty attainable, even in the third century before the Christian era, respecting the date or parentage of Lykurgus.

Thucydidês, without mentioning the name of Lykurgus, informs us that it was "400 years and somewhat more" anterior to the close of the Peloponnesian war,[571] when the Spartans emerged from their previous state of desperate internal disorder, and entered upon "their present polity." We may fairly presume that this alludes to the Lykurgean discipline and constitution, which Thucydides must thus have conceived as introduced about B. C. 830-820,—coinciding with something near the commencement of the reign of king Têleklus. In so far as it is possible to form an opinion, amidst evidence at once so scanty and so discordant, I incline to adopt the opinion of Thucydidês as to the time at which the Lykurgean constitution was introduced at Sparta. The state of "eunomy" and good order which that constitution brought about,—combined with the healing of great previous internal sedition, which had tended much to enfeeble them,—is represented (and with great plausibility) as the grand cause of the victorious career beginning with king Têleklus, the conqueror of Amyklæ, Pharis, and Geronthræ. Therefore it would seem, in the absence of better evidence, that a date, connecting the fresh stimulus of the new discipline with the reign of Têleklus, is more probable than any epoch either later or earlier.[572]

O. Müller,[573] after glancing at the strange and improbable circumstances handed down to us respecting Lykurgus, observes, "that we have absolutely no account of him as an individual person." This remark is perfectly just: but another remark, made by the same distinguished author, respecting the Lykurgean system of laws, appears to me erroneous,—and requires more especially to be noticed, inasmuch as the corollaries deduced from it pervade a large portion of his valuable History of the Dorians. He affirms that the laws of Sparta were considered the true Doric institutions, and that their origin was identical with that of the people: Sparta is, in his view, the full type of Dorian principles, tendencies, and sentiments,—and is so treated throughout his entire work.[574] But such an opinion is at once gratuitous (for the passage of Pindar cited in support of it is scarcely of any value) and contrary to the whole tenor of ancient evidence. The institutions of Sparta were not Dorian, but peculiar to herself;[575] distinguishing her not less from Argos, Corinth, Megara, Epidaurus, Sikyôn, Korkyra, or Knidus, than from Athens or Thebes. Krête was the only other portion of Greece in which there prevailed institutions in many respects analogous, yet still dissimilar in those two attributes which form the real mark and pinch of Spartan legislation, namely, the military discipline and the rigorous private training. There were doubtless Dorians in Krête, but we have no proof that these peculiar institutions belonged to them more than to the other inhabitants of the island. That the Spartans had an original organization, and tendencies common to them with the other Dorians, we may readily concede; but the Lykurgean constitution impressed upon them a peculiar tendency, which took them out of the general march, and rendered them the least fit of all states to be cited as an example of the class-attributes of Dorism. One of the essential causes, which made the Spartan institutions work so impressively upon the Grecian mind, was their perfect singularity, combined with the conspicuous ascendency of the state in which they were manifested; while the Kretan communities, even admitting their partial resemblance (which was chiefly in the institution of the Syssitia, and was altogether more in form than in spirit) to Sparta, were too insignificant to attract notice except from speculative observers. It is therefore a mistake on the part of O. Müller, to treat Sparta as the type and representative of Dorians generally, and very many of the positions advanced in his History of the Dorians require to be modified when this mistake is pointed out.

The first capital fact to notice respecting the institutions ascribed to Lykurgus, is the very early period at which they had their commencement: it seems impossible to place this period later than 825 B. C. We do not find, nor have we a right to expect, trustworthy history in reference to events so early. If we have one foot on historical ground, inasmuch as the institutions themselves are real,—the other foot still floats in the unfaithful region of mythe, when we strive to comprehend the generating causes: the mist yet prevails which hinders us from distinguishing between the god and the man. The light in which Lykurgus appeared, to an intelligent Greek of the fifth century before the Christian era, is so clearly, yet briefly depicted, in the following passage of Herodotus, that I cannot do better than translate it:—

"In the very early times (Herodotus observes) the Spartans were among themselves the most lawless of all Greeks, and unapproachable by foreigners. Their transition to good legal order took place in the following manner. When Lycurgus, a Spartan of consideration, visited Delphi to consult the oracle, the instant that he entered the sanctuary, the Pythian priestess exclaimed,—

"Thou art come, Lycurgus, to my fat shrine, beloved by Zeus, and by all the Olympic gods. Is it as god or as man that I am to address thee in the spirit? I hesitate,—and yet, Lycurgus, I incline more to call thee a god."

So spake the Pythian priestess. "Moreover, in addition to these words, some affirm that the Pythia revealed to him the order of things now established among the Spartans. *But the Lacedæmonians themselves* say, that Lycurgus, when guardian of his nephew Labôtas, king of the Spartans, introduced these institutions out of Krete. No sooner had he obtained this guardianship, than he changed all the institutions into their present form, and took security against any transgression of it. Next, he constituted the military divisions, the Enômoties and the Triakads, as well as the Syssitia, or public mess: he also, farther, appointed the ephors and the senate. By this means the Spartans passed from bad to good order: to Lycurgus, after his death, they built a temple, and they still worship him reverentially. And as might naturally be expected in a productive soil, and with no inconsiderable numbers of men, they immediately took a start forward, and flourished so much that they could not be content to remain tranquil within their own limits," etc.

Such is our oldest statement (coming from Herodotus) respecting Lykurgus, ascribing to him that entire order of things which the writer witnessed at Sparta. Thucydidês also, though not mentioning Lykurgus, agrees in stating that the system among the Lacedæmonians, as he saw it, had been adopted by them four centuries previously,—had rescued them from the most intolerable disorders, and had immediately conducted them to prosperity and success.[576] Hellanikus, whose writings a little preceded those of Herodotus, not only did not (any more than Thucydidês) make mention of Lykurgus, but can hardly be thought to have attached any importance to the name; since he attributed the constitution of Sparta to the first kings, Eurysthenes and Prokles.[577]

But those later writers, from whom Plutarch chiefly compiled his biography, profess to be far better informed on the subject of Lykurgus, and enter more into detail. His father, we are told, was assassinated during the preceding state of lawlessness; his elder brother Polydektês died early, leaving a pregnant widow, who made to Lykurgus propositions that he should marry her and become king. But Lykurgus, repudiating the offer with indignation, awaited the birth of his young nephew Charilaus, held up the child publicly in the agora, as the future king of Sparta, and immediately relinquished the authority which he had provisionally exercised. However, the widow and her brother Leonidas raised slanderous accusations against him, of designs menacing to the life of the infant king,—accusations which he deemed it proper to obviate, by a temporary absence. Accordingly, he left Sparta and went to Krête, where he studied the polity and customs of the different cities; next, he visited Ionia and Egypt, and (as some authors affirmed) Libya, Iberia, and even India. While in Ionia, he is reported to have obtained from the descendants of Kreophylus a copy of the Homeric poems, which had not up to that time become known in Peloponnesus: there were not wanting authors, indeed, who said that he had conversed with Homer himself.[578]

Meanwhile, the young king Charilaus grew up and assumed the sceptre, as representing the Prokleid or Eurypontid family. But the reins of government had become more relaxed, and the disorders worse than ever, when Lykurgus returned. Finding that the two kings as well as the people were weary of so disastrous a condition, he set himself to the task of applying a corrective, and with this view consulted the Delphian oracle; from which he received strong assurances of the divine encouragement, together with one or more special injunctions (the primitive Rhetræ of the constitution), which he brought with him to Sparta.[579] He then suddenly presented himself in the agora, with thirty of the most distinguished Spartans, all in arms, as his guards and partisans. King Charilaus, though at first terrified, when informed of the designs of his uncle, stood forward willingly to second them; while the bulk of the Spartans respectfully submitted to the venerable Herakleid, who came as reformer and missionary from Delphi.[580] Such were the steps by which Lykurgus acquired his ascendency: we have now to see how he employed it.

His first proceeding, pursuant to the Rhetra or Compact brought from Delphi, was to constitute the Spartan senate, consisting of twenty-eight ancient men; making an aggregate of thirty in conjunction with the two kings, who sat and voted in it. With this were combined periodical assemblies of the Spartan people, in the open air, between the river Knakiôn and the bridge Babyka. Yet no discussion was permitted in these assemblies,—their functions were limited to the simple acceptance or rejection of that which had previously been determined in the senate.[581] Such was the Spartan political constitution as fixed by Lykurgus; but a century afterwards (so Plutarch's account runs), under the kings Polydôrus and Theopompus, two important alterations were made. A rider was then attached to the old Lykurgean Rhetra, by which it was provided that, "in case the people decided crookedly, the senate, with the kings, should reverse their decisions;"[582] while another change, perhaps intended as a sort of compensation for this bridle on the popular assembly, introduced into the constitution a new executive Directory of five men, called Ephors. This Board—annually chosen, by some capricious method, the result of which could not well be foreseen, and open to be filled by every Spartan citizen—either originally received, or gradually drew to itself, functions so extensive and commanding, in regard to internal administration and police, as to limit the authority of the kings to little more than the exclusive command of the military force. Herodotus was informed, at Sparta, that the ephors as well as the senate had been constituted by Lykurgus; but the authority of Aristotle, as well as the internal probability of the case, sanctions the belief that they were subsequently added.[583]

Taking the political constitution of Sparta ascribed to Lykurgus, it appears not to have differed materially from the rude organization exhibited in the Homeric poems, where we always find a council of chiefs or old men, and occasional meetings of a listening agora. It is hard to suppose that the Spartan kings can ever have governed without some formalities of this sort; so that the innovation (if innovation there really was) ascribed to Lykurgus, must have consisted in some new details respecting the senate and the agora,—in fixing the number[584] thirty, and the life-tenure of the former,—and the special place of meeting of the latter, as well as the extent of privilege which it was to exercise; consecrating the whole by the erection of the temples of Zeus Hellanius and Athênê Hellania. The view of the subject presented by Plutarch as well as by Plato,[585] as if the senate were an entire novelty, does not consist with the pictures of the old epic. Hence we may more naturally imagine that the Lykurgean political constitution, apart from the ephors who were afterwards tacked to it, presents only the old features of the heroic government of Greece, defined and regularized in a particular manner. The presence of two coexistent and coordinate kings, indeed, succeeding in hereditary descent, and both belonging to the gens of Herakleids, is something peculiar to Sparta,—the origin of which receives no other explanation than a reference to the twin sons of Aristodêmus, Eurysthenês and Proklês. These two primitive ancestors are a type of the two lines of Spartan kings; for they are said to have passed their lives in perpetual dissensions, which was the habitual state of the two contemporaneous kings at Sparta. While the coexistence of the pair of kings, equal in power and constantly thwarting each other, had often a baneful effect upon the course of public measures, it was, nevertheless, a security to the state against successful violence,[586] ending in the establishment of a despotism, on the part of any ambitious individual among the regal line.

During five successive centuries of Spartan history, from Polydôrus and Theopompus downward, no such violence was attempted by any of the kings, [587] until the times of Agis the Third and Kleomenês the Third,—240 B. C. to 220 B. C. The importance of Greece had at this last-mentioned period irretrievably declined, and the independent political action which she once possessed had become subordinate to the more powerful force either of the Ætolian mountaineers (the rudest among her own sons) or to Epirotic, Macedonian, and Asiatic foreigners, preparatory to the final absorption by the

Romans. But amongst all the Grecian states, Sparta had declined the most; her ascendency was totally gone, and her peculiar training and discipline (to which she had chiefly owed it) had degenerated in every way. Under these untoward circumstances, two young kings, Agis and Kleomenês,—the former a generous enthusiast, the latter more violent and ambitious,—conceived the design of restoring the Lykurgean constitution in its supposed pristine purity, with the hope of reviving both the spirit of the people and the ascendency of the state. But the Lykurgean constitution had been, even in the time of Xenophon,[588] in part, an *idéal* not fully realized in practice—much less was it a reality in the days of Kleomenês and Agis moreover, it was an *idéal* which admitted of being colored according to the fancy or feelings of those reformers who professed, and probably believed, that they were aiming at its genuine restoration. What the reforming kings found most in their way, was the uncontrolled authority, and the conservative dispositions, of the ephors,— which they naturally contrasted with the original fulness of the kingly power, when kings and senate stood alone. Among the various ways in which men's ideas of what the primitive constitution *had* been, were modified by the feelings of their own time (we shall presently see some other instances of this), is probably to be reckoned the assertion of Kleomenês respecting the first appointment of the ephors. Kleomenês affirmed that the ephors had originally been nothing more than subordinates and deputies of the kings, chosen by the latter to perform for a time their duties during the long absence of the Messenian war. Starting from this humble position, and profiting by the dissensions of the two kings,[589] they had in process of time, especially by the ambition of the ephor Asterôpus, found means first to constitute themselves an independent board, then to usurp to themselves more and more of the kingly authority, until they at last reduced the kings to a state of intolerable humiliation and impotence. As a proof of the primitive relation between the kings and the ephors, he alluded to that which was the custom at Sparta in his own time. When the ephors sent for either of the kings, the latter had a right to refuse obedience to two successive summonses, but the third summons he was bound to obey.[590]

It is obvious that the fact here adduced by Kleomenês (a curious point in Spartan manners) contributes little to prove the conclusion which he deduced from it, of the original nomination of the ephors as mere deputies by the kings. That they were first appointed at the time of the Messenian war is probable, and coincides with the tale that king Theopompus was a consenting party to the measure,—that their functions were at first comparatively circumscribed, and extended by successive encroachments, is also probable; but they seem to have been from the beginning a board of specially popular origin, in contraposition to the kings and the senate. One proof of this is to be found in the ancient oath, which was every month interchanged between the kings and the ephors; the king swearing for himself, that he would exercise his regal functions according to the established laws,—the ephors swearing on behalf of the city, that his authority should on that condition remain unshaken. [591] This mutual compact, which probably formed a part of the ceremony during the monthly sacrifices offered by the king,[592] continued down to a time when it must have become a pure form, and when the kings had long been subordinate in power to the ephors. But it evidently began first as a reality,—when the king was predominant and effective chief of the state, and when the ephors, clothed with functions chiefly defensive, served as guarantees to the people against abuse of the regal authority. Plato, Aristotle, and Cicero,[593] all interpret the original institution of the ephors as designed to protect the people and restrain the kings: the latter assimilates them to the tribunes at Rome.

Such were the relations which had once subsisted between the kings and the ephors: though in later times these relations had been so completely reversed, that Polybius considers the former as essentially subordinate to the latter,—reckoning it as a point of duty in the kings to respect the ephors "as their fathers."[594] And such is decidedly the state of things throughout all the better-known period of history which we shall hereafter traverse. The ephors are the general directors of public affairs[595] and the supreme controlling board, holding in check every other authority in the state, without any assignable limit to their powers. The extraordinary ascendency of these magistrates is particularly manifested in the fact stated by Aristotle, that they exempted themselves from the public discipline, so that their self-indulgent year of office stood in marked contrast with the toilsome exercises and sober mess common to rich and poor alike. The kings are reduced to a certain number of special functions, combined with privileges partly religious, partly honorary: their most important political attribute is, that they are *ex officio* generals of the military force on foreign expeditions. But even here, we trace the sensible decline of their power. For whereas Herodotus was informed, and it probably had been the old privilege, that the king could levy war against whomsoever he chose, and that no Spartan could impede him on pain of committing sacrilege,[596]—we shall see, throughout the best-known periods of this history, that it is usually the ephors (with or without the senate and public assembly) who determine upon war,—the king only takes the command when the army is put on the march. Aristotle seems to treat the Spartan king as a sort of hereditary general; but even in this privilege, shackles were put upon him,—for two, out of the five ephors, accompanied the army, and their power seems to have been not seldom invoked to insure obedience to his orders.[597]

The direct political powers of the kings were thus greatly curtailed; yet importance, in many ways, was still left to them. They possessed large royal domains, in many of the townships of the Periœki: they received frequent occasional presents, and when victims were offered to the gods, the skins and other portions belonged to them as perquisites:[598] they had their votes in the senate, which, if they were absent, were given on their behalf, by such of the other senators as were most nearly related to them: the adoption of children received its formal accomplishment in their presence,—and conflicting claims at law, for the hand of an unbequeathed orphan heiress, were adjudicated by them. But above all, their root was deep in the religious feelings of the people. Their preëminent lineage connected the entire state with a divine paternity. They, the chiefs of the Herakleids, were the special grantees of the soil of Sparta from the gods,—the occupation of the Dorians being only sanctified and blest by Zeus for the purpose of establishing the children of Hêraklês in the valley of the Eurotas.[599] They represented the state in its relations with the gods, being by right priests of Zeus Lacedæmon, (the ideas of the god and the country coalescing into one), and of Zeus Uranius, and offering the monthly sacrifices necessary to insure divine protection to the people. Though individual persons might sometimes be put aside, nothing short of a new divine revelation could induce the Spartans to step out of the genuine lineage of Eurysthenês and Proklês. Moreover, the remarkable mourning ceremony, which took place at the death of every king, seems to indicate that the two kingly families—which counted themselves Achæan,[600] not Dorian—were considered as the great common bond of union between the three component parts of the population of Laconia,—Spartans, Periœki, and Helots. Not merely was it required, on this occasion, that two members of every house in Sparta should appear in sackcloth and ashes,—but the death of the king was formally made known throughout every part of Laconia, and deputies from the townships of the Periœki, and the villages of the Helots, to the number of several thousand, were summoned to Sparta to take their share in the profuse and public demonstrations of sorrow,[601] which lasted for ten days, and which imparted to the funeral obsequies a superhuman solemnity. Nor ought we to forget, in enumerating the privileges of the Spartan king, that he (conjointly with two officers called Pythii, nominated by him,) carried on the communications between the state and the temple of Delphi, and had the custody of oracles and prophecies generally. In most of the Grecian states, such inspired declarations were treasured up, and consulted in cases of public emergency: but the intercourse of Sparta with the Delphian oracle was peculiarly frequent and intimate, and the responses of the Pythian priestess met with more reverential attention from the Spartans than from any other Greeks.[602] So much the more important were the king's functions, as the medium of this intercourse: the oracle always upheld his dignity, and often even seconded his underhand personal schemes.[603]

Sustained by so great a force of traditional reverence, a Spartan king, of military talent and individual energy, like Agesilaus, exercised great ascendency; but such cases were very rare, and we shall find the king throughout the historical period only a secondary force, available on special occasions. For real political orders, in the greatest cases as well as the least, the Spartan looks to the council of ephors, to whom obedience is paid with a degree of precision which nothing short of the Spartan discipline could have brought about,—by the most powerful citizens not less than by the meanest. [604] Both the internal police and the foreign affairs of the state are in the hands of the ephors, who exercise an authority approaching to despotism, and altogether without accountability. They appoint and direct the body of three hundred young and active citizens, who performed the immediate police service of Laconia: they cashier at pleasure any subordinate functionary, and inflict fine or arrest at their own discretion: they assemble the military force, on occasion of foreign war, and determine its destination, though the king has the actual command of it: they imprison on suspicion even the regent or the king himself:[605] they sit as judges, sometimes individually and sometimes as a board, upon causes and complaints of great moment, and they judge without the restraint of written laws, the use of which was peremptorily forbidden by a special Rhetra,[606] erroneously connected with Lykurgus himself, but at any rate ancient. On certain occasions of peculiar moment, they take the sense of the senate and the public assembly,[607]—such seems to have been the habit on questions of war and peace. It appears, however, that persons charged with homicide, treason, or capital offences generally, were tried before the senate. We read of several instances in which the kings were tried and severely fined, and in which their houses were condemned to be razed to the ground, probably by the senate, on the proposition of the ephors: in one instance, it seems that the ephors inflicted by their own authority a fine even upon Agesilaus.[608]

War and peace appear to have been submitted, on most, if not on all occasions, to the senate and the public assembly; no matter could reach the latter until it had passed through the former. And we find some few occasions on which the decision of the public assembly was a real expression of opinion, and operative as to the result,—as, for example, the assembly which immediately preceded and resolved upon the Peloponnesian war. Here, in addition to the serious hazard of the case, and the general caution of a Spartan temperament, there was the great personal weight and experience of king Archidamus opposed to the war, though the ephors were favorable to it.[609] The public assembly, under such peculiar circumstances, really manifested an opinion and came to a division. But, for the most part, it seems to have been little better than an inoperative formality. The general rule permitted no open discussion, nor could any private citizen speak except by special leave from the magistrates. Perhaps even the general liberty to discuss, if given, might have been of no avail, for not only was there no power of public speaking, but no habit of canvassing public measures, at Sparta; nothing was more characteristic of the government than the extreme secrecy of its proceedings. [610] The propositions brought forward by the magistrates were either accepted or rejected, without any license of amending. There could be no attraction to invite the citizen to be present at such an assembly: and we may gather from the language of Xenophon that, in his time, it consisted only of a certain number of notables specially summoned in addition to the senate, which latter body is itself called "the lesser Ekklesia.[611]" Indeed, the constant and formidable diminution in the number of qualified citizens was alone sufficient to thin the attendance of the assembly, as well as to break down any imposing force which it might once have possessed.

An assembly thus circumstanced,—though always retained as a formality, and though its consent on considerable matters and for the passing of laws (which, however, seems to have been a rare occurrence at Sparta) was indispensable,—could be very little of a practical check upon the administration of the ephors. The senate, a permanent body, with the kings included in it, was the only real check upon them, and must have been to a certain extent a concurrent body in the government,—though the large and imposing language in which its political supremacy is spoken of by Demosthenês and Isokratês exceeds greatly the reality of the case. Its most important function was that of a court of criminal justice, before whom every man put on trial for his life was arraigned.[612] But both in this and in their other duties, we find the senators as well as the kings and the ephors charged with corruption and venality.[613] As they were not appointed until sixty years of age, and then held their offices for life, we may readily believe that some of them continued to act after the period of extreme and disqualifying senility, —which, though the extraordinary respect of the Lacedæmonians for old age would doubtless tolerate it, could not fail to impair the influence of the body as a concurrent element of government.

The brief sketch here given of the Spartan government will show that, though Greek theorists found a difficulty in determining under what class they should arrange it,[614] it was in substance a close, unscrupulous, and well-obeyed oligarchy,—including within it, as subordinate, those portions which had once been dominant, the kings and the senate, and softening the odium, without abating the mischief, of the system, by its annual change of the ruling ephors. We must at the same time distinguish the government from the Lykurgean discipline and education, which doubtless tended much to equalize rich and poor, in respect to practical life, habits, and enjoyments. Herodotus (and seemingly, also, Xenophon) thought that the form just described was that which the government had originally received from the hand of Lykurgus. Now, though there is good reason for supposing otherwise, and for believing the ephors to be a subsequent addition,—yet, the mere fact that Herodotus was so informed at Sparta, points our attention to one important attribute of the Spartan polity, which it is proper to bring into view. This attribute is, its unparalleled steadiness, for four or five successive centuries, in the midst of governments like the Grecian, all of which had undergone more or less of fluctuation. No considerable revolution—not even any palpable or formal change—occurred in it, from the days of the Messenian war, down to those of Agis the Third: in spite of the irreparable blow which the power and territory of the state sustained from Epameinondas and the Thebans, the form of government, nevertheless, remained unchanged. It was the only government in Greece which could trace an unbroken, peaceable descent from a high antiquity, and from its real or supposed founder. Now this was one of the main circumstances (among others which will hereafter be mentioned) of the astonishing ascendency which the Spartans acquired over the Hellenic mind, and which they will not be found at all to deserve by any superior ability in the conduct of affairs. The steadiness of their political sympathies,—exhibited at one time, by putting down the tyrants, or despots, at another, by overthrowing the democracies,—stood in the place of ability; and even the recognized failings of their government were often covered by the sentiment of respect for its early commencement and uninterrupted continuance. If such a feeling acted on the Greeks generally,[615] much more powerful was its action upon the Spartans themselves, in inflaming that haughty exclusiveness for which they stood distinguished. And it is to be observed that the Spartan mind continued to be cast on the old-fashioned scale, and unsusceptible of modernizing influences, longer than that of most other people of Greece. The ancient legendary faith, and devoted submission to the Delphian oracle, remained among them unabated, at a time when various influences had considerably undermined it among their fellow-Hellens and neighbors. But though the unchanged title and forms of the government thus contributed to its imposing effect, both at home and abroad, the causes of internal degeneracy were not the less really at work, in undermining its efficiency. It has been already stated, that the number of qualified citizens went on continually diminishing, and even of this diminished number a larger proportion than before were needy, since the landed property tended constantly to concentrate itself in fewer hands. There grew up in this way a body of discontent, which had not originally existed, both among the poorer citizens, and among those who had lost their franchise as citizens; thus aggravating the danger arising from Periœki and Helots, who will be presently noticed.

We pass from the political constitution of Sparta to the civil ranks and distribution, economical relations, and lastly, the peculiar system of habits, education, and discipline, said to have been established among the Lacedæmonians by Lykurgus. Here, again, we shall find ourselves imperfectly informed as to the existing institutions, and surrounded by confusion when we try to explain how those institutions arose.

It seems, however, ascertained that the Dorians, in all their settlements, were divided into three tribes,—the Hylleis, the Pamphyli, and the Dymanes: in all Dorian cities, moreover, there were distinguished Herakleid families, from whom œkists were chosen when new colonies were formed. These three tribes can be traced at Argos, Sikyôn, Epidaurus, Trœzên, Megara, Korkyra, and seemingly, also, at Sparta.[616] The Hylleis recognized, as their eponym and progenitor, Hyllus, the son of Hêraklês, and were therefore, in their own belief, descended from Hêraklês himself: we may suppose the Herakleids, specially so called, comprising the two regal families, to have been the elder brethren of the tribe of Hylleis, the whole of whom are sometimes spoken of as Herakleids, or descendants of Hêraklês.[617] But there seem to have been also at Sparta, as in other Dorian towns, non-Dorian inhabitants, apart from these three tribes, and embodied in tribes of their own. One of these, the Ægeids, said to have come from Thebes as allies of the Dorian invaders, is named by Aristotle, Pindar, and Herodotus,[618]—while the Ægialeis at Sikyôn, the tribe Hyrnêthia at Argos and Epidaurus, and others, whose titles we do not know, at Corinth, represent, in like manner, the non-Dorian portions of their respective communities.[619] At Corinth, the total number of tribes is said to have been eight.[620] But at Sparta, though we seem to make out the existence of the three Dorian tribes, we do not know how many tribes there were in all: still less do we know what relation the Obæ, or Obes, another subordinate distribution of the people, bore to the tribes. In the ancient Rhetra of Lykurgus, the Tribes and Obês are directed to be maintained unaltered: but the statement of O. Müller and Boeckh[621]—that there were thirty Obês in all, ten to each tribe—rests upon no other evidence than a peculiar punctuation of this Rhetra, which various other critics reject; and seemingly, with good reason. We are thus left without any information respecting the Obê, though we know that it was an old, peculiar, and lasting division among the Spartan people, since it occurs in the oldest Rhetra of Lykurgus, as well as in late inscriptions of the date of the Roman empire. In similar inscriptions, and in the account of Pausanias, there is, however, recognized a classification of Spartans distinct from and independent of the three old Dorian tribes, and founded upon the different quarters of the city,— Limnæ, Mesoa, Pitanê, and Kynosura;[622] from one of these four was derived the usual description of a Spartan in the days of Herodotus. There is reason to suppose that the old Dorian tribes became antiquated at Sparta, (as the four old Ionian tribes did at Athens,) and that the topical classification derived from the quarters of the city superseded it,—these quarters having been originally the separate villages, of the aggregate of which Sparta was composed.[623] That the number of the old senators, thirty, was connected with the three Dorian tribes, deriving ten members from each, is probable enough, though there is no proof of it.

Of the population of Laconia, three main divisions are recognized,— Spartans, Periœki, and Helots. The first of the three were the full qualified citizens, who lived in Sparta itself, fulfilled all the exigences of the Lykurgean discipline, paid their quota to the Syssitia, or public mess, and were alone eligible to honors[624] or public offices. These men had neither time, nor taste even, for cultivation of the land, still less for trade or handicraft: such occupations were inconsistent with the prescribed training, even if they had not been positively interdicted. They were maintained from the lands round the city, and from the large proportion of Laconia which belonged to them; the land being tilled for them by Helots, who seem to have paid over to them a fixed proportion of the produce; in some cases, at least, as much as one-half. [625] Each Spartan retained his qualification, and transmitted it to his children, on two conditions,—first, that of submitting to the prescribed discipline; next, that of paying, each, his stipulated quota to the public mess, which was only maintained by these individual contributions. The multiplication of children in the poorer families, after acquisitions of new territory ceased, continually augmented both the number and the proportion of citizens who were unable to fulfil the second of these conditions, and who therefore lost their franchise: so that there arose towards the close of the Peloponnesian war, a distinction, among the Spartans themselves, unknown to the earlier times,—the reduced number of fully qualified citizens being called The Equals, or Peers,—the disfranchised poor, The Inferiors. The latter, disfranchised as they were, nevertheless, did not become Periœki: it was probably still competent to them to resume their qualification, should any favorable accident enable them to make their contributions to the public mess.

The Periœkus was also a freeman and a citizen, not of Sparta, but of some one of the hundred townships of Laconia.[626] Both he and the community to which he belonged received their orders only from Sparta, having no political sphere of their own, and no share in determining the movements of the Spartan authorities. In the island of Kythêra,[627] which formed one of the Periœkic townships, a Spartan bailiff resided as administrator. But whether the same was the case with others, we cannot affirm: nor is it safe to reason from one of these townships to all,—there may have been considerable differences in the mode of dealing with one and another. For they were spread through the whole of Laconia, some near and some distant from Sparta: the free inhabitants of Amyklæ must have been Periœki, as well as those of Kythêra, Thuria, Ætheia, or Aulôn: nor can we presume that the feeling on the part of the Spartan authorities towards all of them was the same. Between the Spartans and their neighbors, the numerous Periœki of Amyklæ, there must have subsisted a degree of intercourse and mutual relation in which the more distant Periœki did not partake,—besides, that both the religious edifices and the festivals of Amyklæ were most reverentially adopted by the Spartans and exalted into a national dignity: and we seem to perceive, on some occasions, a degree of consideration manifested for the Amyklæan hoplites,[628] such as perhaps other Periœki might not have obtained. The class-name, Periœki,[629] —circumresidents, or dwellers around the city,—usually denoted native inhabitants of inferior political condition as contrasted with the full-privileged burghers who lived in the city, but it did not mark any precise or uniform degree of inferiority. It is sometimes so used by Aristotle as to imply a condition no better than that of the Helots, so that, in a large sense, all the inhabitants of Laconia (Helots as well as the rest) might have been included in it. But when used in reference to Laconia, it bears a technical sense, whereby it is placed in contraposition with the Spartan on one side, and with the Helot on the other: it means, native freemen and proprietors, grouped in subordinate communities[630] with more or less power of local management, but (like the subject towns belonging to Bern, Zurich, and most of the old thirteen cantons of Switzerland) embodied in the Lacedæmonian aggregate, which was governed exclusively by the kings, senate, and citizens of Sparta.

When we come to describe the democracy of Athens after the revolution of Kleisthenes, we shall find the demes, or local townships and villages of Attica, incorporated as equal and constituent fractions of the integer called The Deme (or The City) of Athens, so that a demot of Acharnæ or Sphêttus is at the same time a full Athenian citizen. But the relation of the Periœkic townships to Sparta is one of inequality and obedience, though both belong to the same political aggregate, and make up together the free Lacedæmonian community. In like manner, Orneæ and other places were townships of men personally free, but politically dependent on Argos,—Akræphiæ on Thebes, —Chæroneia on Orchomenus,—and various Thessalian towns on Pharsalus and Larissa.[631] Such, moreover, was, in the main, the state into which Athens would have brought her allies, and Thebes the free Bœotian communities,[632] if the policy of either of these cities had permanently prospered. This condition carried with it a sentiment of degradation, and a painful negation of that autonomy for which every Grecian community thirsted; while being maintained through superior force, it had a natural tendency, perhaps without the deliberate wish of the reigning city, to degenerate into practical oppression. But in addition to this general tendency, the peculiar education of a Spartan, while it imparted force, fortitude, and regimental precision, was at the same time so rigorously peculiar, that it rendered him harsh, unaccommodating, and incapable of sympathizing with the ordinary march of Grecian feeling,—not to mention the rapacity and love of money, which is attested, by good evidence, as belonging to the Spartan character,[633] and which we should hardly have expected to find in the pupils of Lykurgus. As Harmosts out of their native city,[634] and in relations with inferiors, the Spartans seem to have been more unpopular than other Greeks, and we may presume that a similar haughty roughness pervaded their dealings with their own Periœki; who were bound to them certainly by no tie of affection, and who for the most part revolted after the battle of Leuktra, as soon as the invasion of Laconia by Epameinondas enabled them to do so with safety.

Isokratês, taking his point of departure from the old Herakleid legend, with its instantaneous conquest and triple partition of all Dorian Peloponnesus, among the three Herakleid brethren, deduces the first origin of the Periœkic townships from internal seditions among the conquerors of Sparta. According to him, the period immediately succeeding the conquest was one of fierce intestine warfare in newly-conquered Sparta, between the Few and the Many,—the oligarchy and the demus. The former being victorious, two important measures were the consequences of their victory. They banished the defeated Many from Sparta into Laconia, retaining the residence in Sparta exclusively for themselves; they assigned to them the smallest and least fertile half of Laconia, monopolizing the larger and better for themselves; and they disseminated them into many very small townships, or subordinate little communities, while they concentrated themselves entirely at Sparta. To these precautions for insuring dominion, they added another not less important. They established among their own Spartan citizens equality of legal privilege and democratical government, so as to take the greatest securities for internal harmony; which harmony, according to the judgment of Isokratês, had been but too effectually perpetuated, enabling the Spartans to achieve their dominion over oppressed Greece,—like the accord of pirates[635] for the spoliation of the peaceful. The Periœkic townships, he tells us, while deprived of all the privileges of freemen, were exposed to all the toils, as well as to an unfair share of the dangers, of war. The Spartan authorities put them in situations and upon enterprises which they deemed too dangerous for their own citizens; and, what was still worse, the ephors possessed the power of putting to death, without any form of preliminary trial, as many Periœki as they pleased.[636]

The statement here delivered by Isokratês, respecting the first origin of the distinction of Spartans and Periœki, is nothing better than a conjecture, nor is it even a probable conjecture, since it is based on the historical truth of the old Herakleid legend, and transports the disputes of his own time, between the oligarchy and the demus, into an early period, to which such disputes do not belong. Nor is there anything, so far as our knowledge of Grecian history extends, to bear out his assertion, that the Spartans took to themselves the least dangerous post in the field, and threw undue peril upon their Periœki. Such dastardly temper was not among the sins of Sparta; but it is undoubtedly true that, as the number of citizens continually diminished, so the Periœki came to constitute, in the later times, a larger and larger proportion of the Spartan force. Yet the power which Isokratês represents to have been vested in the ephors, of putting to death Periœki without preliminary trial, we may fully believe to be real, and to have been exercised as often as the occasion seemed to call for it. We shall notice, presently, the way in which these magistrates dealt with the Helots, and shall see ample reason from thence to draw the conclusion that, whenever the ephors believed any man to be dangerous to the public peace,—whether an inferior Spartan, a Periœkus, or a Helot,—the most summary mode of getting rid of him would be considered as the best. Towards Spartans of rank and consideration, they were doubtless careful and measured in their application of punishment, but the same necessity for circumspection did not exist with regard to the inferior classes: moreover, the feeling that the exigences of justice required a fair trial before punishment was inflicted, belongs to Athenian associations much more than to Spartan. How often any such summary executions may have taken place, we have no information.

We may remark that the account which Isokratês has here given of the origin of the Laconian Periœki is not essentially irreconcilable with that of Ephorus,[637] who recounted that Eurysthenês and Proklês, on first conquering Laconia, had granted to the preëxisting population equal rights with the Dorians,—but that Agis, son of Eurysthenês, had deprived them of this equal position, and degraded them into dependent subjects of the latter. At least, the two narratives both agree in presuming that the Periœki had once enjoyed a better position, from which they had been extruded by violence. And the policy which Isokratês ascribes to the victorious Spartan oligarchs,—of driving out the demus from concentrated residence in the city to disseminated residence in many separate and insignificant townships,—seems to be the expression of that proceeding which in his time was numbered among the most efficient precautions against refractory subjects,—the Diœkisis, or breaking up of a town-aggregate into villages. We cannot assign to the statement any historical authority.[638] Moreover, the division of Laconia into six districts, together with its distribution into townships (or the distribution of settlers into preëxisting townships), which Ephorus ascribed to the first Dorian kings, are all deductions from the primitive legendary account, which described the Dorian conquest as achieved by one stroke, and must all be dismissed, if we suppose it to have been achieved gradually. This gradual conquest is admitted by O. Müller, and by many of the ablest subsequent inquirers,—who, nevertheless, seem to have the contrary supposition involuntarily present to their minds when they criticize the early Spartan history, and always unconsciously imagine the Spartans as masters of all Laconia. We cannot even assert that Laconia was ever under one government before the consummation of the successive conquests of Sparta.

Of the assertion of O. Müller—repeated by Schömann[639]—"that the difference of races was strictly preserved, and that the Periœki were always considered as Achæans,"—I find no proof, and I believe it to be erroneous. Respecting Pharis, Geronthræ, and Amyklæ, three Periœkic towns, Pausanias gives us to understand that the preëxisting inhabitants either retired or were expelled on the Dorian conquest, and that a Dorian population replaced them. [640] Without placing great faith in this statement, for which Pausanias could hardly have any good authority, we may yet accept it as representing the probabilities of the case, and as counterbalancing the unsupported hypothesis of Müller. The Periœkic townships were probably composed either of Dorians entirely, or of Dorians incorporated in greater or less proportion with the preëxisting inhabitants. But whatever difference of race there may once have been, it was effaced before the historical times,[641] during which we find no proof of Achæans, known as such, in Laconia. The Herakleids, the Ægeids, and the Talthybiads, all of whom belong to Sparta, seem to be the only examples of separate races, partially distinguishable from Dorians, known after the beginning of authentic history. The Spartans and the Periœki constitute one political aggregate, and that too so completely melted together in the general opinion (speaking of the times before the battle of Leuktra), that the peace of Antalkidas, which guaranteed autonomy to every separate Grecian city, was never so construed as to divorce the Periœkic towns from Sparta. Both are known as Laconians, or Lacedæmonians, and Sparta is regarded by Herodotus only as the first and bravest among the many and brave Lacedæmonian cities.[642] The victors at Olympia are proclaimed, not as Spartans, but as Laconians,—a title alike borne by the Periœki. And many of the numerous winners, whose names we read in the Olympic lists as Laconians, may probably have belonged to Amyklæ or other Periœkic towns.

The Periœkic hoplites constituted always a large—in later times a preponderant—numerical proportion of the Lacedæmonian army, and must undoubtedly have been trained, more or less perfectly, in the peculiar military tactics of Sparta; since they were called upon to obey the same orders as the Spartans in the field,[643] and to perform the same evolutions. Some cases appear, though rare, in which a Periœkus has high command in a foreign expedition. In the time of Aristotle, the larger proportion of Laconia (then meaning only the country eastward of Taygetus, since the foundation of Messênê by Epameinondas had been consummated) belonged to Spartan citizens,[644] but the remaining smaller half must have been the property of the Periœki, who must besides have carried on most of the commerce of export and import,—the metallurgic enterprise, and the distribution of internal produce,—which the territory exhibited; since no Spartan ever meddled in such occupations. And thus the peculiar training of Lykurgus, by throwing all these employments into the hands of the Periœki, opened to them a new source of importance, which the dependent townships of Argos, of Thebes, or of Orchomenus, would not enjoy.

The Helots of Laconia were Coloni, or serfs, bound to the soil, who tilled it for the benefit of the Spartan proprietors certainly,—probably, of Periœkic proprietors also. They were the rustic population of the country, who dwelt, not in towns, but either in small villages[645] or in detached farms, both in the district immediately surrounding Sparta, and round the Periœkic Laconian towns also. Of course, there were also Helots who lived in Sparta and other towns, and did the work of domestic slaves,—but such was not the general character of the class. We cannot doubt that the Dorian conquest from Sparta found this class in the condition of villagers and detached rustics; but whether they were dependent upon preëxisting Achæan proprietors, or independent, like much of the Arcadian village population, is a question which we cannot answer. In either case, however, it is easy to conceive that the village lands (with the cultivators upon them) were the most easy to appropriate for the benefit of masters resident at Sparta; while the towns, with the district immediately around them, furnished both dwelling and maintenance to the outgoing detachments of Dorians. If the Spartans had succeeded in their attempt to enlarge their territory by the conquest of Arcadia,[646] they might very probably have converted Tegea and Mantineia into Periœkic towns, with a diminished territory inhabited (either wholly or in part) by Dorian settlers, —while they would have made over to proprietors in Sparta much of the village lands of the Mænalii, Azanes, and Parrhasii, helotizing the inhabitants. The distinction between a town and a village population seems the main ground of the different treatment of Helots and Periœki in Laconia. A considerable proportion of the Helots were of genuine Dorian race, being the Dorian Messenians west of Mount Taygetus, subsequently conquered and aggregated to this class of dependent cultivators, who, as a class, must have begun to exist from the very first establishment of the invading Dorians in the district round Sparta. From whence the name of Helots arose, we do not clearly make out: Ephorus deduced it from the town of Helus, on the southern coast, which the Spartans are said to have taken after a resistance so obstinate as to provoke them to deal very rigorously with the captives. There are many reasons for rejecting this story, and another etymology has been proposed, according to which Helot is synonymous with *captive*: this is more plausible, yet still not convincing.[647] The Helots lived in the rural villages, as *adscripti glebæ*, cultivating their lands and paying over their rent to the master at Sparta, but enjoying their homes, wives, families, and mutual neighborly feelings, apart from the master's view. They were never sold out of the country, and probably never sold at all; belonging, not so much to the master as to the state, which constantly called upon them for military service, and recompensed their bravery or activity with a grant of freedom. Meno, the Thessalian of Pharsalus, took out three hundred Penestæ of his own, to aid the Athenians against Amphipolis: these Thessalian Penestæ were in many points analogous to the Helots, but no individual Spartan possessed the like power over the latter. The Helots were thus a part of the state, having their domestic and social sympathies developed, a certain power of acquiring property,[648] and the consciousness of Grecian lineage and dialect,—points of marked superiority over the foreigners who formed the slave population of Athens or Chios. They seem to have been noway inferior to any village population of Greece; while the Grecian observer sympathized with them more strongly than with the bought slaves of other states,—not to mention that their homogeneous aspect, their numbers, and their employment in military service, rendered them more conspicuous to the eye.

The service in the Spartan house was all performed by members of the Helot class; for there seem to have been few, if any, other slaves in the country. The various anecdotes which are told respecting their treatment at Sparta, betoken less of cruelty than of ostentatious scorn,[649]—a sentiment which we are noway surprised to discover among the citizens at the mess-table. But the great mass of the Helots, who dwelt in the country, were objects of a very different sentiment on the part of the Spartan ephors, who knew their bravery, energy, and standing discontent, and yet were forced to employ them as an essential portion of the state army. The Helots commonly served as light-armed, in which capacity the Spartan hoplites could not dispense with their attendance. At the battle of Platæa, every Spartan hoplite had seven Helots,[650] and every Periœkic hoplite one Helot, to attend him:[651] but, even in camp, the Spartan arrangements were framed to guard against any sudden mutiny of these light-armed companions, while, at home, the citizen habitually kept his shield disjoined from its holding-ring, to prevent the possibility of its being snatched for the like purpose. Sometimes, select Helots were clothed in heavy armor, and thus served in the ranks, receiving manumission from the state as the reward of distinguished bravery.[652]

But Sparta, even at the maximum of her power, was more than once endangered by the reality, and always beset with the apprehension, of Helotic revolt. To prevent or suppress it, the ephors submitted to insert express stipulations for aid in their treaties with Athens,—to invite Athenian troops into the heart of Laconia,—and to practice combinations of cunning and atrocity which even yet stand without parallel in the long list of precautions for fortifying unjust dominion. It was in the eighth year of the Peloponnesian war, after the Helots had been called upon for signal military efforts in various ways, and when the Athenians and Messenians were in possession of Pylus, that the ephors felt especially apprehensive of an outbreak. Anxious to single out the most forward and daring Helots, as the men from whom they had most to dread, they issued proclamation that every member of that class who had rendered distinguished services should make his claims known at Sparta, promising liberty to the most deserving. A large number of Helots came forward to claim the boon: not less than two thousand of them were approved, formally manumitted, and led in solemn procession round the temples, with garlands on their heads, as an inauguration to their coming life of freedom. But the treacherous garland only marked them out as victims for the sacrifice: every man of them forthwith disappeared,—the manner of their death was an untold mystery.

For this dark and bloody deed, Thucydidês is our witness,[653] and Thucydidês describing a contemporary matter into which he had inquired. Upon any less evidence we should have hesitated to believe the statement; but standing as it thus does above all suspicion, it speaks volumes as to the inhuman character of the Lacedæmonian government, while it lays open to us at the same time the intensity of their fears from the Helots. In the assassination of this fated regiment of brave men, a large number of auxiliaries and instruments must have been concerned: yet Thucydidês, with all his inquiries, could not find out how any of them perished: he tells us, that no man knew. We see here a fact which demonstrates unequivocally the impenetrable mystery in which the proceedings of the Spartan government were wrapped,—the absence not only of public discussion, but of public curiosity,—and the perfection with which the ephors reigned over the will, the hands, and the tongues, of their Spartan subjects. The Venetian Council of Ten, with all the facilities for nocturnal drowning which their city presented, could hardly have accomplished so vast a *coup-d'état* with such invisible means. And we may judge from hence, even if we had no other evidence, how little the habits of a public assembly could have suited either the temper of mind or the march of government at Sparta.

Other proceedings, ascribed to the ephors against the Helots, are conceived in the same spirit as the incident just recounted from Thucydidês, though they do not carry with them the same certain attestation. It was a part of the institutions of Lykurgus (according to a statement which Plutarch professes to have borrowed from Aristotle) that the ephors should every year declare war against the Helots, in order that the murder of them might be rendered innocent; and that active young Spartans should be armed with daggers and sent about Laconia, in order that they might, either in solitude or at night, assassinate such of the Helots as were considered formidable.[654] This last measure passes by the name of the Krypteia, yet we find some difficulty in determining to what extent it was ever realized. That the ephors, indeed, would not be restrained by any scruples of justice or humanity, is plainly shown by the murder of the two thousand Helots above noticed; but this latter incident really answered its purpose, while a standing practice, such as that of the Krypteia, and a formal notice of war given beforehand, would provoke the reaction of despair rather than enforce tranquillity. There seems, indeed, good evidence that the Krypteia was a real practice,[655]—that the ephors kept up a system of police or espionage throughout Laconia, by the employment of active young citizens, who lived a hard and solitary life, and suffered their motions to be as little detected as possible. The ephors might naturally enough take this method of keeping watch both over the Periœkic townships and the Helot villages, and the assassination of individual Helots by these police-men, or Krypts, would probably pass unnoticed. But it is impossible to believe in any standing murderous order, or deliberate annual assassination of Helots, for the purpose of intimidation, as Aristotle is alleged to have represented,—for we may well doubt whether he really did make such a representation, when we see that he takes no notice of this measure in his Politics, where he speaks at some length both of the Spartan constitution and of the Helots. The well-known hatred and fear, entertained by the Spartans towards their Helots, has probably colored Plutarch's description of the Krypteia, so as to exaggerate those unpunished murders which occasionally happened into a constant phenomenon with express design. A similar deduction is to be made from the statement of Myrôn of Priênê,[656] who alleged that they were beaten every year without any special fault, in order to put them in mind of their slavery,—and that those Helots, whose superior beauty or stature placed them above the visible stamp of their condition, were put to death; while such masters as neglected to keep down the spirit of their vigorous Helots were punished. That secrecy, for which the ephors were so remarkable, seems enough of itself to refute the assertion that they publicly proclaimed war against the Helots; though we may well believe that this unhappy class of men may have been noticed as objects for jealous observation in the annual ephoric oath of office. Whatever may have been the treatment of the Helots in later times, it is at all events hardly to be supposed

213

that any regulation hostile to them can have emanated from Lykurgus. For the dangers arising from that source did not become serious until after the Messenian war,—nor, indeed, until after the gradual diminution of the number of Spartan citizens had made itself felt.

The manumitted Helots did not pass into the class of Periœki,—for this purpose a special grant, of the freedom of some Periœkic township, would probably be required,—but constituted a class apart, known at the time of the Peloponnesian war by the name of Neodamôdes. Being persons who had earned their liberty by signal bravery, they were of course regarded by the ephors with peculiar apprehension, and, if possible, employed on foreign service,[657] or planted on some foreign soil as settlers. In what manner these freedmen employed themselves, we find no distinct information; but we can hardly doubt that they quitted the Helot village and field, together with the rural costume (the leather cap and sheepskin) which the Helot commonly wore, and the change of which exposed him to suspicion, if not to punishment, from his jealous masters. Probably they, as well as the disfranchised Spartan citizens (called Hypomeiones, or Inferiors), became congregated at Sparta, and found employment either in various trades or in the service of the government.

It has been necessary to give this short sketch of the orders of men who inhabited Laconia, in order to enable us to understand the statements given about the legislation of Lykurgus. The arrangements ascribed to that lawgiver, in the way that Plutarch describes them, presuppose, and do not create, the three orders of Spartans, Periœki, and Helots. We are told by Plutarch that the disorders which Lykurgus found existing in the state arose in a great measure from the gross inequality of property, and from the luxurious indulgence and unprincipled rapacity of the rich,—who had drawn to themselves the greater proportion of the lands in the country, leaving a large body of poor, without any lot of land, in hopeless misery and degradation. To this inequality (according to Plutarch) the reforming legislator applied at once a stringent remedy. He redistributed the whole territory belonging to Sparta, as well as the remainder of Laconia; the former, in nine thousand equal lots, one to each Spartan citizen; the latter, in thirty thousand equal lots, one to each Periœkus: of this alleged distribution, I shall speak farther presently. Moreover, he banished the use of gold and silver money, tolerating nothing in the shape of circulating medium but pieces of iron, heavy and scarcely portable; and he forbade[658] to the Spartan citizen every species of industrious or money-seeking occupation, agriculture included. He farther constituted,—though not without strenuous opposition, during the course of which his eye is said to have been knocked out by a violent youth, named Alkander,—the Syssitia, or public mess. A certain number of joint tables were provided, and every citizen was required to belong to some one of them, and habitually to take his meals at it,[659]—no new member being admissible without an unanimous ballot in his favor by the previous occupants. Each provided from his lot of land a specified quota of barley-meal, wine, cheese, and figs, and a small contribution of money for condiments: game was obtained in addition by hunting in the public forests of the state, while every one who sacrificed to the gods,[660] sent to his mess-table a part of the victim killed. From boyhood to old age, every Spartan citizen took his sober meals at this public mess, where all shared alike; nor was distinction of any kind allowed, except on signal occasions of service rendered by an individual to the state.

These public Syssitia, under the management of the Polemarchs, were connected with the military distribution, the constant gymnastic training, and the rigorous discipline of detail, enforced by Lykurgus. From the early age of seven years, throughout his whole life, as youth and man no less than as boy, the Spartan citizen lived habitually in public, always either himself under drill, gymnastic and military, or a critic and spectator of others,—always under the fetters and observances of a rule partly military, partly monastic,—estranged from the independence of a separate home,—seeing his wife, during the first years after marriage, only by stealth, and maintaining little peculiar relation with his children. The supervision, not only of his fellow-citizens, but also of authorized censors, or captains nominated by the state, was perpetually acting upon him: his day was passed in public exercises and meals, his nights in the public barrack to which he belonged. Besides the particular military drill, whereby the complicated movements required from a body of Lacedæmonian hoplites in the field, were made familiar to him from his youth,—he also became subject to severe bodily discipline of other kinds, calculated to impart strength, activity, and endurance. To manifest a daring and pugnacious spirit,—to sustain the greatest bodily torture unmoved,—to endure hunger and thirst, heat, cold, and fatigue,—to tread the worst ground barefoot,—to wear the same garment winter and summer,—to suppress external manifestations of feeling, and to exhibit in public, when action was not called for, a bearing shy, silent, and motionless as a statue,—all these were the virtues of the accomplished Spartan youth.[661] Two squadrons were often matched against each other to contend (without arms) in the little insular circumscription called the Platanistûs, and these contests were carried on, under the eye of the authorities, with the utmost extremity of fury. Nor was the competition among them less obstinate, to bear without murmuring the cruel scourgings inflicted before the altar of Artemis Orthia, supposed to be highly acceptable to the goddess, though they sometimes terminated even in the death of the uncomplaining sufferer.[662] Besides the various descriptions of gymnastic contests, the youths were instructed in the choric dances employed in festivals of the gods, which contributed to impart to them methodized and harmonious movements. Hunting in the woods and mountains of Laconia was encouraged, as a means of inuring them to fatigue and privation. The nourishment supplied to the youthful Spartans was purposely kept insufficient, but they were allowed to make up the deficiency not only by hunting, but even by stealing whatever they could lay hands upon, provided they could do so without being detected in the fact; in which latter case they were severely chastised.[663] In reference simply to bodily results, [664] the training at Sparta was excellent, combining strength and agility with universal aptitude and endurance, and steering clear of that mistake by which Thebes and other cities impaired the effect of their gymnastics,—the attempt to create an athletic habit, suited for the games, but suited for nothing else.

Of all the attributes of this remarkable community, there is none more difficult to make out clearly than the condition and character of the Spartan women. Aristotle asserts that, in his time, they were imperious and unruly, without being really so brave and useful in moments of danger as other Grecian females;[665] that they possessed great influence over the men, and even exercised much ascendency over the course of public affairs; and that nearly half the landed property of Laconia had come to belong to them. The exemption of the women from all control, formed, in his eye, a pointed contrast with the rigorous discipline imposed upon the men,—and a contrast hardly less pointed with the condition of women in other Grecian cities, where they were habitually confined to the interior of the house, and seldom appeared in public. While the Spartan husband went through the hard details of his ascetic life, and dined on the plainest fare at the Pheidition, or mess, the wife (it appears) maintained an ample and luxurious establishment at home; and the desire to provide for such outlay was one of the causes of that love of money which prevailed among men forbidden to enjoy it in the ordinary ways. To explain this antithesis between the treatment of the two sexes at Sparta, Aristotle was informed that Lykurgus had tried to bring the women no less than the men under a system of discipline, but that they made so obstinate a resistance as to compel him to desist.[666]

The view here given by the philosopher, and deserving of course careful attention, is not easy to reconcile with that of Xenophon and Plutarch, who look upon the Spartan women from a different side, and represent them as worthy and homogeneous companions to the men. The Lykurgean system (as these authors describe it) considering the women as a part of the state, and not as a part of the house, placed them under training hardly less than the men. Its grand purpose, the maintenance of a vigorous breed of citizens, determined both the treatment of the younger women, and the regulations as to the intercourse of the sexes. "Female slaves are good enough (Lykurgus thought) to sit at home spinning and weaving,—but who can expect a splendid offspring, the appropriate mission and duty of a free Spartan woman towards her country, from mothers brought up in such occupations?"[667] Pursuant to these views, the Spartan damsels underwent a bodily training analogous to that of the Spartan youth,—being formally exercised, and contending with each other in running, wrestling, and boxing, agreeably to the forms of the Grecian agônes. They seem to have worn a light tunic, cut open at the skirts, so as to leave the limbs both free and exposed to view,—hence Plutarch speaks of them as completely uncovered, while other critics, in different quarters of Greece, heaped similar reproach upon the practice, as if it had been perfect nakedness.[668] The presence of the Spartan youths, and even of the kings and the body of citizens, at these exercises, lent animation to the scene. In like manner, the young women marched in the religious processions, sung and danced at particular festivals, and witnessed as spectators the exercises and contentions of the youths; so that the two sexes were perpetually intermingled with each other in public, in a way foreign to the habits, as well as repugnant to the feelings, of other Grecian states. We may well conceive that such an education imparted to the women both a demonstrative character and an eager interest in masculine accomplishments, so that the expression of their praise was the strongest stimulus, and that of their reproach the bitterest humiliation, to the youthful troop who heard it.

The age of marriage (which in some of the unrestricted cities of Greece was so early as to deteriorate visibly the breed of citizens)[669] was deferred by the Spartan law, both in women and men, until the period supposed to be most consistent with the perfection of the offspring. And when we read the restriction which Spartan custom imposed upon the intercourse even between married persons, we shall conclude without hesitation that the public intermixture of the sexes, in the way just described, led to no such liberties, between persons not married, as might be likely to arise from it under other circumstances.[670] Marriage was almost universal among the citizens, enforced by general opinion at least, if not by law. The young Spartan carried away his bride by a simulated abduction, but she still seems, for some time at least, to have continued to reside with her family, visiting her husband in his barrack in the disguise of male attire, and on short and stolen occasions.[671] To some married couples, according to Plutarch, it happened, that they had been married long enough to have two or three children, while they had scarcely seen each other apart by daylight. Secret intrigue on the part of married women was unknown at Sparta; but to bring together the finest couples was regarded by the citizens as desirable, and by the lawgiver as a duty. No personal feeling or jealousy on the part of the husband found sympathy from any one,—and he permitted without difficulty, sometimes actively encouraged, compliances on the part of his wife, consistent with this generally acknowledged object. So far was such toleration carried, that there were some married women who were recognized mistresses of two houses, [672] and mothers of two distinct families,—a sort of bigamy strictly forbidden to the men, and never permitted, except in the remarkable case of king Anaxandrides, when the royal Herakleidan line of Eurysthenes was in danger of becoming extinct. The wife of Anaxandrides being childless, the ephors strongly urged him, on grounds of public necessity, to repudiate her and marry another. But he refused to dismiss a wife who had given him no cause of complaint; upon which, when they found him inexorable, they desired him to retain her, but to marry another wife besides, in order that at any rate there might be issue to the Eurystheneid line. "He thus (says Herodotus) married two wives, and inhabited two family-hearths, a proceeding unknown at Sparta;"[673] yet the same privilege which, according to Xenophon, some Spartan women enjoyed without reproach from any one, and with perfect harmony between the inmates of both their houses. O. Müller[674] remarks— and the evidence, as far as we know it, bears him out—that love-marriages and genuine affection towards a wife were more familiar to Sparta than to Athens; though in the former, marital jealousy was a sentiment neither indulged nor recognized,—while in the latter, it was intense and universal. [675]

To reconcile the careful gymnastic training, which Xenophon and Plutarch mention, with that uncontrolled luxury and relaxation which Aristotle condemns in the Spartan women, we may perhaps suppose that, in the time of the latter, the women of high position and wealth had contrived to emancipate themselves from the general obligation, and that it is of such particular cases that he chiefly speaks. He dwells especially upon the increasing tendency to accumulate property in the hands of the women,[676] which seems to have been still more conspicuous a century afterwards, in the reign of Agis the Third. And we may readily imagine that one of the employments of wealth thus acquired would be to purchase exemption from laborious training,—an object more easy to accomplish in their case than in that of the men, whose services were required by the state as soldiers. By what steps so large a proportion as two-fifths of the landed property of the state came to be possessed by women, he partially explains to us. There were (he says) many sole heiresses,—the dowries given by fathers to their daughters were very large,—and the father had unlimited power of testamentary bequest, which he was disposed to use to the advantage of his daughter over his son. In conjunction with this last circumstance, we have to notice that peculiar sympathy and yielding disposition towards women in the Spartan mind, of which Aristotle also speaks,[677] and which he ascribes to the warlike temper both of the citizen and the state,—Arês bearing the yoke of Aphroditê. But, apart from such a consideration, if we suppose, on the part of a wealthy

Spartan father, the simple disposition to treat sons and daughters alike as to bequest,—nearly one half of the inherited mass of property would naturally be found in the hands of the daughters, since on an average of families the number of the two sexes born is nearly equal. In most societies, it is the men who make new acquisitions: but this seldom or never happened with Spartan men, who disdained all money-getting occupations.

Xenophon, a warm panegyrist of Spartan manners, points with some pride to the tall and vigorous breed of citizens which the Lykurgic institutions had produced. The beauty of the Lacedæmonian women was notorious throughout Greece, and Lampitô, the Lacedæmonian woman introduced in the Lysistrata of Aristophanês, is made to receive from the Athenian women the loudest compliments upon her fine shape and masculine vigor.[678] We may remark that, on this as well as on the other points, Xenophon emphatically insists on the peculiarity of Spartan institutions, contradicting thus the views of those who regard them merely as something a little Hyper-Dorian. Indeed, such peculiarity seems never to have been questioned in antiquity, either by the enemies or by the admirers of Sparta. And those who censured the public masculine exercises of the Spartan maidens, as well as the liberty tolerated in married women, allowed at the same time that the feelings of both were actively identified with the state to a degree hardly known in Greece; that the patriotism of the men greatly depended upon the sympathy of the other sex, which manifested itself publicly, in a manner not compatible with the recluse life of Grecian women generally, to the exaltation of the brave as well as to the abasement of the recreant; and that the dignified bearing of the Spartan matrons under private family loss seriously assisted the state in the task of bearing up against public reverses. "Return either with your shield or upon it," was their exhortation to their sons when departing for foreign service: and after the fatal day of Leuktra, those mothers who had to welcome home their surviving sons in dishonor and defeat, were the bitter sufferers; while those whose sons had perished, maintained a bearing comparatively cheerful.[679]

Such were the leading points of the memorable Spartan discipline, strengthened in its effect on the mind by the absence of communication with strangers. For no Spartan could go abroad without leave, nor were strangers permitted to stay at Sparta; they came thither, it seems, by a sort of sufferance, but the uncourteous process called xenêlasy[680] was always available to remove them, nor could there arise in Sparta that class of resident metics or aliens who constituted a large part of the population of Athens, and seem to have been found in most other Grecian towns. It is in this universal schooling, training, and drilling, imposed alike upon boys and men, youths and virgins, rich and poor, that the distinctive attribute of Sparta is to be sought,—not in her laws or political constitution.

Lykurgus (or the individual to whom this system is owing, whoever he was) is the founder of a warlike brotherhood rather than the lawgiver of a political community; his brethren live together like bees in a hive (to borrow a simile from Plutarch), with all their feelings implicated in the commonwealth, and divorced from house and home.[681] Far from contemplating the society as a whole, with its multifarious wants and liabilities, he interdicts beforehand, by one of the three primitive Rhetræ, all written laws, that is to say, all formal and premeditated enactments on any special subject. When disputes are to be settled or judicial interference is required, the magistrate is to decide from his own sense of equity; that the magistrate will not depart from the established customs and recognized purposes of the city, is presumed from the personal discipline which he and the select body to whom he belongs, have undergone. It is this select body, maintained by the labor of others, over whom Lykurgus exclusively watches, with the provident eye of a trainer, for the purpose of disciplining them into a state of regimental preparation,[682] single-minded obedience, and bodily efficiency and endurance, so that they may be always fit and ready for defence, for conquest and for dominion. The parallel of the Lykurgean institutions is to be found in the Republic of Plato, who approves the Spartan principle of select guardians carefully trained and administering the community at discretion; with this momentous difference, indeed, that the Spartan character[683] formed by Lykurgus is of a low type, rendered savage and fierce by exclusive and overdone bodily discipline,—destitute even of the elements of letters,— immersed in their own narrow specialities, and taught to despise all that lay beyond,—possessing all the qualities requisite to procure dominion, but none of those calculated to render dominion popular or salutary to the subject; while the habits and attributes of the guardians, as shadowed forth by Plato, are enlarged as well as philanthropic, qualifying them not simply to govern, but to govern for purposes protective, conciliatory, and exalted. Both Plato and Aristotle conceive as the perfection of society something of the Spartan type,—a select body of equally privileged citizens, disengaged from industrious pursuits, and subjected to public and uniform training. Both admit (with Lykurgus) that the citizen belongs neither to himself nor to his family, but to his city; both at the same time note with regret, that the Spartan training was turned only to one portion of human virtue,—that which is called forth in a state of war;[684] the citizens being converted into a sort of garrison, always under drill, and always ready to be called forth either against Helots at home or against enemies abroad. Such exclusive tendency will appear less astonishing if we consider the very early and insecure period at which the Lykurgean institutions arose, when none of those guarantees which afterwards maintained the peace of the Hellenic world had as yet become effective,—no constant habits of intercourse, no custom of meeting in Amphiktyony from the distant parts of Greece, no common or largely frequented festivals, no multiplication of proxenies (or standing tickets of hospitality) between the important cities, no pacific or industrious habits anywhere. When we contemplate the general insecurity of Grecian life in the ninth or eighth century before the Christian era, and especially the precarious condition of a small band of Dorian conquerors in Sparta and its district, with subdued Helots on their own lands and Achæans unsubdued all around them,—we shall not be surprised that the language which Brasidas in the Peloponnesian war addresses to his army in reference to the original Spartan settlement, was still more powerfully present to the mind of Lykurgus four centuries earlier —"We are a few in the midst of many enemies; we can only maintain ourselves by fighting and conquering."[685]

Under such circumstances, the exclusive aim which Lykurgus proposed to himself is easily understood; but what is truly surprising, is the violence of his means and the success of the result. He realized his project of creating, in the eight thousand or nine thousand Spartan citizens, unrivalled habits of obedience, hardihood, self-denial, and military aptitude,—complete subjection on the part of each individual to the local public opinion, and preference of death to the abandonment of Spartan maxims, intense ambition on the part of every one to distinguish himself within the prescribed sphere of duties, with little ambition for anything else. In what manner so rigorous a system of individual training can have been first brought to bear upon any community, mastering the course of the thoughts and actions from boyhood to old age,—a work far more difficult than any political revolution,—we are not permitted to discover. Nor does the influence of an earnest and energetic Herakleidman,—seconded by the still more powerful working of the Delphian god behind, upon the strong pious susceptibilities of the Spartan mind,— sufficiently explain a phenomenon so remarkable in the history of mankind, unless we suppose them aided by some combination of coöperating circumstances which history has not transmitted to us,[686] and preceded by disorders so exaggerated as to render the citizens glad to escape from them at any price.

Respecting the ante-Lykurgean Sparta we possess no positive information whatever. But although this unfortunate gap cannot be filled up, we may yet master the negative probabilities of the case sufficiently to see that, in what Plutarch has told us (and from Plutarch the modern views have, until lately, been derived), there is indeed a basis of reality, but there is also a large superstructure of romance,—in not a few particulars essentially misleading. For example, Plutarch treats Lykurgus as introducing his reforms at a time when Sparta was mistress of Laconia, and distributing the whole of that territory among the Periœki. Now we know that Laconia was not then in possession of Sparta, and that the partition of Lykurgus (assuming it to be real) could only have been applied to the land in the immediate vicinity of the latter. For even Amyklæ, Pharis, and Geronthræ, were not conquered until the reign of Têleklus, posterior to any period which we can reasonably assign to Lykurgus: nor can any such distribution of Laconia have really occurred. Farther, we are told that Lykurgus banished from Sparta coined gold and silver, useless professions and frivolities, eager pursuit of gain, and ostentatious display. Without dwelling upon the improbability that any one of these anti-Spartan characteristics should have existed at so early a period as the ninth century before the Christian era, we may at least be certain that coined silver was not then to be found, since it was first introduced into Greece by Pheidon of Argos in the succeeding century, as has been stated in the preceding section.

But amongst all the points stated by Plutarch, the most suspicious by far, and the most misleading, because endless calculations have been built upon it, is the alleged redivision of landed property. He tells us that Lykurgus found fearful inequality in the landed possessions of the Spartans; nearly all the land in the hands of a few, and a great multitude without any land; that he rectified this evil by a redivision of the Spartan district into nine thousand equal lots, and the rest of Laconia into thirty thousand, giving to each citizen as much as would produce a given quota of barley, etc.; and that he wished, moreover, to have divided the movable property upon similar principles of equality, but was deterred by the difficulties of carrying his design into execution.

Now we shall find on consideration that this new and equal partition of lands by Lykurgus is still more at variance with fact and probability than the two former alleged proceedings. All the historical evidences exhibit decided inequalities of property among the Spartans,—inequalities which tended constantly to increase; moreover, the earlier authors do not conceive this evil as having grown up by way of abuse out of a primeval system of perfect equality, nor do they know anything of the original equal redivision by Lykurgus. Even as early as the poet Alkæus (B. C. 600-580) we find bitter complaints of the oppressive ascendency of wealth, and the degradation of the poor man, cited as having been pronounced by Aristodêmus at Sparta: "Wealth (said he) makes the man,—no poor person is either accounted good or honored."[687] Next, the historian Hellanikus certainly knew nothing of the Lykurgean redivision,—for he ascribed the whole Spartan polity to Eurysthenês and Proklês, the original founders, and hardly noticed Lykurgus at all. Again, in the brief, but impressive description of the Spartan lawgiver by Herodotus, several other institutions are alluded to, but nothing is said about a redivision of the lands; and this latter point is in itself of such transcendent moment, and was so recognized among all Grecian thinkers, that the omission is almost a demonstration of ignorance. Thucydidês certainly could not have believed that equality of property was an original feature in the Lykurgean system; for he says that, at Lacedæmon, "the rich men assimilated themselves greatly in respect of clothing and general habits of life to the simplicity of the poor, and thus set an example which was partially followed in the rest of Greece:" a remark which both implies the existence of unequal property, and gives a just appreciation of the real working of Lykurgic institutions.[688] The like is the sentiment of Xenophon:[689] he observes that the rich at Sparta gained little by their wealth in point of superior comfort; but he never glances at any original measure carried into effect by Lykurgus for equalizing possessions. Plato too,[690] while he touches upon the great advantage possessed by the Dorians, immediately after their conquest of Peloponnesus, in being able to apportion land suitably to all,—never hints that this original distribution had degenerated into an abuse, and that an entire subsequent redivision had been resorted to by Lykurgus: moreover, he is himself deeply sensible of the hazards of that formidable proceeding. Lastly, Aristotle clearly did not believe that Lykurgus had redivided the soil. For he informs us first, that, "both in Lacedæmon and in Krete,[691] the legislator had rendered the enjoyment of property common through the establishment of the Syssitia, or public mess." Now this remark (if read in the chapter of which it forms a part, a refutation of the scheme of Communism for the select guardians in the Platonic Republic) will be seen to tell little for its point, if we assume that Lykurgus at the same time equalized all individual possessions. Had Aristotle known that fact, he could not have failed to notice it: nor could he have assimilated the legislators in Lacedæmon and Krete, seeing that in the latter no one pretends that any such equalization was ever brought about. Next, not only does Aristotle dwell upon the actual inequality of property at Sparta as a serious public evil, but he nowhere treats this as having grown out of a system of absolute equality once enacted by the lawgiver as a part of the primitive constitution: he expressly notices inequality of property so far back as the second Messenian war. Moreover, in that valuable chapter of his Politics, where the scheme of equality of possessions is discussed, Phaleas of Chalkedôn is expressly mentioned as the first author of it, thus indirectly excluding Lykurgus.[692] The mere silence of Aristotle is in this discussion a negative argument of the greatest weight. Isokratês,[693] too, speaks much about Sparta for good and for evil,—mentions Lykurgus as having established a political constitution much like that of the earliest days of Athens,—praises the gymnasia and the discipline, and compliments the Spartans upon the many centuries which they have gone through without violent sedition, extinction of debts, and redivision of the land,—those "monstrous evils," as he terms them. Had he conceived Lykurgus as being himself the author of a complete redivision of land, he could hardly have avoided some allusion to it.

It appears, then, that none of the authors down to Aristotle ascribe to Lykurgus a redivision of the lands, either of Sparta or of Laconia. The statement to this effect in Plutarch, given in great detail and with precise specification of number and produce, must have been borrowed from some author later than Aristotle; and I think we may trace the source of it, when we study Plutarch's biography of Lykurgus in conjunction with that of Agis and Kleomenês. The statement is taken from authors of the century after Aristotle, either in, or shortly before, the age when both those kings tried extreme measures to renovate the sinking state: the former by a thorough change of system and property, yet proposed and accepted according to constitutional forms; the latter by projects substantially similar, with violence to enforce them. The accumulation of landed property in few hands, the multiplication of poor, and the decline in the number of citizens, which are depicted as grave mischiefs by Aristotle, had become greatly aggravated during the century between him and Agis. The number of citizens, reckoned by Herodotus in the time of the Persian invasion at eight thousand, had dwindled down in the time of Aristotle to one thousand, and in that of Agis to seven hundred, out of which latter number one hundred alone possessed most of the landed property of the state.[694] Now, by the ancient rule of Lykurgus, the qualification for citizenship was the ability to furnish the prescribed quota, incumbent on each individual, at the public mess: so soon as a citizen became too poor to answer to this requisition, he lost his franchise and his eligibility to offices.[695] The smaller lots of land, though it was held discreditable either to buy or sell them,[696] and though some have asserted (without ground, I think) that it was forbidden to divide them,—became insufficient for numerous families, and seem to have been alienated in some indirect manner to the rich; while every industrious occupation being both interdicted to a Spartan citizen and really inconsistent with his rigorous personal discipline, no other means of furnishing his quota, except the lot of land, was open to him. The difficulty felt with regard to these smaller lots of land may be judged of from the fact stated by Polybius,[697] that three or four Spartan brothers had often one and the same wife, the paternal land being just sufficient to furnish contributions for all to the public mess, and thus to keep alive the citizen-rights of all the sons. The tendency to diminution in the number of Spartan citizens seems to have gone on uninterruptedly from the time of the Persian war, and must have been aggravated by the foundation of Messênê, with its independent territory around, after the battle of Leuktra, an event which robbed the Spartans of a large portion of their property. Apart from these special causes, moreover, it has been observed often as a statistical fact, that a close corporation of citizens, or any small number of families, intermarrying habitually among one another, and not reinforced from without, have usually a tendency to diminish.

The present is not the occasion to enter at length into that combination of causes which partly sapped, partly overthrew, both the institutions of Lykurgus and the power of Sparta. But taking the condition of that city as it stood in the time of Agis the Third (say about 250 B. C.), we know that its citizens had become few in number, the bulk of them miserably poor, and all the land in a small number of hands. The old discipline and the public mess (as far as the rich were concerned) had degenerated into mere forms,—a numerous body of strangers or non-citizens (the old xenêlasy, or prohibition of resident strangers, being long discontinued) were domiciled in the town, forming a powerful moneyed interest; and lastly, the dignity and ascendency of the state amongst its neighbors were altogether ruined. It was insupportable to a young enthusiast like king Agis, as well as to many ardent spirits among his contemporaries, to contrast this degradation with the previous glories of their country: nor did they see any other way of reconstructing the old Sparta except by again admitting the disfranchised poor citizens, redividing the lands, cancelling all debts, and restoring the public mess and military training in all their strictness. Agis endeavored to carry through these subversive measures, (such as no demagogue in the extreme democracy of Athens would ever have ventured to glance at,) with the consent of the senate and public assembly, and the acquiescence of the rich. His sincerity is attested by the fact, that his own property, and that of his female relatives, among the largest in the state, was cast as the first sacrifice into the common stock. But he became the dupe of unprincipled coadjutors, and perished in the unavailing attempt to realize his scheme by persuasion. His successor, Kleomenês, afterwards accomplished by violence a change substantially similar, though the intervention of foreign arms speedily overthrew both himself and his institutions.

Now it was under the state of public feeling which gave birth to these projects of Agis and Kleomenês at Sparta, that the historic fancy, unknown to Aristotle and his predecessors, first gained ground, of the absolute equality of property as a primitive institution of Lykurgus. How much such a belief would favor the schemes of innovation is too obvious to require notice; and without supposing any deliberate imposture, we cannot be astonished that the predispositions of enthusiastic patriots interpreted, according to their own partialities, an old unrecorded legislation from which they were separated by more than five centuries. The Lykurgean discipline tended forcibly to suggest to men's minds the *idea* of equality among the citizens,—that is, the negation of all inequality not founded on some personal attribute,—inasmuch as it assimilated the habits, enjoyments, and capacities of the rich to those of the poor; and the equality thus existing in idea and tendency, which seemed to proclaim the wish of the founder, was strained by the later reformers into a positive institution which he had at first realized, but from which his degenerate followers had receded. It was thus that the fancies, longings, and indirect suggestions of the present assumed the character of recollections out of the early, obscure, and extinct historical past. Perhaps the philosopher Sphærus of Borysthenês (friend and companion of Kleomenês,[698] disciple of Zeno the Stoic, and author of works now lost, both on Lykurgus and Socrates, and on the constitution of Sparta) may have been one of those who gave currency to such an hypothesis. And we shall readily believe that, if advanced, it would find easy and sincere credence, when we recollect how many similar delusions have obtained vogue in modern times, far more favorable to historical accuracy,—how much false coloring has been attached by the political feeling of recent days to matters of ancient history, such as the Saxon Witenagemote, the Great Charter, the rise and growth of the English House of Commons, or even the Poor Law of Elizabeth.

When we read the division of lands really proposed by king Agis, it is found to be a very close copy of the original division ascribed to Lykurgus. He parcels the lands bounded by the four limits of Pellênê, Sellasia, Malea, and Taygetus, into four thousand five hundred lots, one to every Spartan; and the lands beyond these limits into fifteen thousand lots, one to each Periœkus; and he proposes to constitute in Sparta fifteen pheiditia, or public mess-tables, some including four hundred individuals, others two hundred,—thus providing a place for each of his four thousand five hundred Spartans. With respect to the division originally ascribed to Lykurgus, different accounts were given. Some considered it to have set out nine thousand lots for the district of Sparta, and thirty thousand for the rest of Laconia;[699] others affirmed that six thousand lots had been given by Lykurgus, and three thousand added afterwards by king Polydorus; a third tale was, that Lykurgus had assigned four thousand five hundred lots, and king Polydorus as many more. This last scheme is much the same as what was really proposed by Agis.

In the preceding argument respecting the redivision of land ascribed to Lykurgus, I have taken that measure as it is described by Plutarch. But there has been a tendency, in some able modern writers, while admitting the general fact of such redivision, to reject the account given by Plutarch in some of its main circumstances. That, for instance, which is the capital feature in Plutarch's narrative, and which gives soul and meaning to his picture of the lawgiver—the equality of partition—is now rejected by many as incorrect, and it is supposed that Lykurgus made some new agrarian regulations tending towards a general equality of landed property, but not an entirely new partition; that he may have resumed from the wealthy men lands which they had unjustly taken from the conquered Achæans, and thus provided

226

allotments both for the poorer citizens and for the subject Laconians. Such is the opinion of Dr. Thirlwall, who at the same time admits that the exact proportion of the Lykurgean distribution can hardly be ascertained.[700]

I cannot but take a different view of the statement made by Plutarch. The moment that we depart from that rule of equality, which stands so prominently marked in his biography of Lykurgus, we step into a boundless field of possibility, in which there is nothing to determine us to one point more than to another. The surmise started by Dr. Thirlwall, of lands unjustly taken from the conquered Achæans by wealthy Spartan proprietors, is altogether gratuitous; and granting it to be correct, we have still to explain how it happened that this correction of a partial injustice came to be transformed into the comprehensive and systematic measure which Plutarch describes; and to explain, farther, from whence it arose that none of the authors earlier than Plutarch take any notice of Lykurgus as an agrarian equalizer. These two difficulties will still remain, even if we overlook the gratuitous nature of Dr. Thirlwall's supposition, or of any other supposition which can be proposed respecting the real Lykurgean measure which Plutarch is affirmed to have misrepresented.

It appears to me that these difficulties are best obviated by adopting a different canon of historical interpretation. We cannot accept as real the Lykurgean land division described in the life of the lawgiver; but treating this account as a fiction, two modes of proceeding are open to us. We may either consider the fiction, as it now stands, to be the exaggeration and distortion of some small fact, and then try to guess, without any assistance, what the small fact was. Or we may regard it as fiction from first to last, the expression of some large idea and sentiment so powerful in its action on men's minds at a given time, as to induce them to make a place for it among the realities of the past. Now the latter supposition, applied to the times of Agis the Third, best meets the case before us. The eighth chapter of the life of Lykurgus by Plutarch, in recounting the partition of land, describes the dream of king Agis, whose mind is full of two sentiments,—grief and shame for the actual condition of his country,—together with reverence for its past glories, as well as for the lawgiver from whose institutions those glories had emanated. Absorbed with this double feeling, the reveries of Agis go back to the old ante-Lykurgean Sparta, as it stood more than five centuries before. He sees, in the spirit, the same mischiefs and disorders as those which afflict his waking eye,—gross inequalities of property, with a few insolent and luxurious rich, a crowd of mutinous and suffering poor, and nothing but fierce antipathy reigning between the two. Into the midst of this froward, lawless, and distempered community, steps the venerable missionary from Delphi,—breathes into men's minds new impulses, and an impatience to shake off the old social and political Adam,—and persuades the rich, voluntarily abnegating their temporal advantages, to welcome with satisfaction a new system, wherein no distinction shall be recognized, except that of good or evil desert.[701] Having thus regenerated the national mind, he parcels out the territory of Laconia into equal lots, leaving no superiority to any one. Fraternal harmony becomes the reigning sentiment, while the coming harvests present the gratifying spectacle of a paternal inheritance recently distributed, with the brotherhood contented, modest, and docile. Such is the picture with which "mischievous Oneirus" cheats the fancy of the patriotic Agis, whispering the treacherous message that the gods have promised *him* success in a similar attempt, and thus seducing him into that fatal revolutionary course, which is destined to bring himself, his wife, and his aged mother, to the dungeon and the hangman's rope.[702]

That the golden dream just described was dreamed by some Spartan patriots is certain, because it stands recorded in Plutarch; that it was not dreamed by the authors of centuries preceding Agis, I have already endeavored to show; that the earnest feelings, of sickness of the present and yearning for a better future under the colors of a restored past, which filled the soul of this king and his brother-reformers,—combined with the levelling tendency between rich and poor which really was inherent in the Lykurgean discipline,—were amply sufficient to beget such a dream, and to procure for it a place among the great deeds of the old lawgiver, so much venerated and so little known,—this too I hold to be unquestionable. Had there been any evidence that Lykurgus had interfered with private property, to the limited extent which Dr. Thirlwall and other able critics imagine,—that he had resumed certain lands unjustly taken by the rich from the Achæans,—I should have been glad to record it; but, finding no such evidence, I cannot think it necessary to presume the fact, simply in order to account for the story in Plutarch.[703]

The various items in that story all hang together, and must be understood as forming parts of the same comprehensive fact, or comprehensive fancy. The fixed total of nine thousand Spartan, and thirty thousand Laconian lots, [704] the equality between them, and the rent accruing from each, represented by a given quantity of moist and dry produce,—all these particulars are alike true or alike uncertified. Upon the various numbers here given, many authors have raised calculations as to the population and produce of Laconia, which appear to me destitute of any trustworthy foundation. Those who accept the history, that Lykurgus constituted the above-mentioned numbers both of citizens and of lots of land, and that he contemplated the maintenance of both numbers in unchangeable proportion,—are perplexed to assign the means whereby this adjustment was kept undisturbed. Nor are they much assisted in the solution of this embarrassing problem by the statement of Plutarch, who tells us that the number remained fixed of itself, and that the succession ran on from father to son, without either consolidation or multiplication of parcels, down to the period when foreign wealth flowed into Sparta, as a consequence of the successful conclusion of the Peloponnesian war. Shortly after that period (he tells us) a citizen named Epitadeus became ephor,—a vindictive and malignant man, who, having had a quarrel with his son, and wishing to oust him from the succession, introduced and obtained sanction to a new Rhetra, whereby power was granted to every father of a family either to make over during life, or to bequeathe after death, his house and his estate to any one whom he chose.[705] But it is plain that this story (whatever be the truth about the family quarrel of Epitadeus) does not help us out of the difficulty. From the time of Lykurgus to that of this disinheriting ephor, more than four centuries must be reckoned: now, had there been real causes at work sufficient to maintain inviolate the identical number of lots and families during this long period, we see no reason why his new law, simply permissive and nothing more, should have overthrown it. We are not told by Plutarch what was the law of succession prior to Epitadeus. If the whole estate went by law to one son in the family, what became of the other sons, to whom industrious acquisition in any shape was repulsive as well as interdicted? If, on the other hand, the estate was divided between the sons equally (as it was by the law of succession at Athens), how can we defend the maintenance of an unchanged aggregate number of parcels?

Dr. Thirlwall, after having admitted a modified interference with private property by Lykurgus, so as to exact from the wealthy a certain sacrifice in order to create lots for the poor, and to bring about something approaching to equi-producing lots for all, observes: "The average amount of the rent, paid by the cultivating Helots from each lot, seems to have been no more than was required for the frugal maintenance of a family with six persons. The right of transfer was as strictly confined as that of enjoyment; the patrimony was indivisible, inalienable, and descended to the eldest son; in default of a male heir, to the eldest daughter. The object seems to have been, after the number of the allotments became fixed, that each should be constantly represented by one head of a household. But the nature of the means employed for this end is one of the most obscure points of the Spartan system.... In the better times of the commonwealth, this seems to have been principally effected by adoptions and marriages with heiresses, which provided for the marriages of younger sons in families too numerous to be supported on their own hereditary property. It was then probably seldom necessary for the state to interfere, in order to direct the childless owner of an estate, or the father of a rich heiress, to a proper choice. But as all adoption required the sanction of the kings, and they had also the disposal of the hand of orphan heiresses, there can be little doubt that the magistrate had the power of interposing on such occasions, even in opposition to the wishes of individuals, to relieve poverty and check the accumulation of wealth." (Hist. Gr. ch. 8, vol. i. p. 367).

I cannot concur in the view which Dr. Thirlwall here takes of the state of property, or the arrangements respecting its transmission, in ancient Sparta. Neither the equal modesty of possession which he supposes, nor the precautions for perpetuating it, can be shown to have ever existed among the pupils of Lykurgus. Our earliest information intimates the existence of rich men at Sparta: the story of king Aristo and Agêtus, in Herodotus, exhibits to us the latter as a man who cannot be supposed to have had only just "enough to maintain six persons frugally,"—while his beautiful wife, whom Aristo coveted and entrapped from him, is expressly described as the daughter of opulent parents. Sperthiês and Bulis, the Talthybiads, are designated as belonging to a distinguished race, and among the wealthiest men in Sparta. [706] Demaratus was the only king of Sparta, in the days of Herodotus, who had ever gained a chariot-victory in the Olympic games; but we know by the case of Lichas, during the Peloponnesian war, Evagoras, and others, that private Spartans were equally successful;[707] and for one Spartan who won the prize, there must of course have been many who bred their horses and started their chariots unsuccessfully. It need hardly be remarked, that chariot-competition at Olympia was one of the most significant evidences of a wealthy house: nor were there wanting Spartans who kept horses and dogs without any exclusive view to the games. We know from Xenophon that, at the time of the battle of Leuktra, "the very rich Spartans" provided the horses to be mounted for the state-cavalry.[708] These and other proofs, of the existence of rich men at Sparta, are inconsistent with the idea of a body of citizens each possessing what was about enough for the frugal maintenance of six persons, and no more.

As we do not find that such was in practice the state of property in the Spartan community, so neither can we discover that the lawgiver ever tried either to make or to keep it so. What he did was to impose a rigorous public discipline, with simple clothing and fare, incumbent alike upon the rich and the poor (this was his special present to Greece, according to Thucydidês,[709] and his great point of contact with democracy, according to Aristotle); but he took no pains either to restrain the enrichment of the former, or to prevent the impoverishment of the latter. He meddled little with the distribution of property, and such neglect is one of the capital deficiencies for which Aristotle censures him. That philosopher tells us, indeed, that the Spartan law had made it dishonorable (he does not say, peremptorily forbidden) to buy or sell landed property, but that there was the fullest liberty both of donation and bequest: and the same results, he justly observes, ensued from the practice tolerated as would have ensued from the practice discountenanced,—since it was easy to disguise a real sale under an ostensible donation. He notices pointedly the tendency of property at Sparta to concentrate itself in fewer hands, unopposed by any legal hindrances: the fathers married their daughters to whomsoever they chose, and gave dowries according to their own discretion, generally very large: the rich families, moreover, intermarried among one another habitually, and without restriction. Now all these are indicated by Aristotle as cases in which the law might have interfered, and ought to have interfered, but did not,—for the great purpose of disseminating the benefits of landed property as much as possible among the mass of the citizens. Again, he tells us that the law encouraged the multiplication of progeny, and granted exemptions to such citizens as had three or four children,—but took no thought how the numerous families of poorer citizens were to live, or to maintain their qualification at the public tables, most of the lands of the state being in the hands of the rich.[710] His notice, and condemnation, of that law, which made the franchise of the Spartan citizen dependent upon his continuing to furnish his quota to the public table,—has been already adverted to; as well as the potent love of money[711] which he notes in the Spartan character, and which must have tended continually to keep together the richer families among themselves: while amongst a community where industry was unknown, no poor citizen could ever become rich.

If we duly weigh these evidences, we shall see that equality of possessions neither existed in fact, nor ever entered into the scheme and tendencies of the lawgiver at Sparta. And the picture which Dr. Thirlwall[712] has drawn of a body of citizens each possessing a lot of land about adequate to the frugal maintenance of six persons,—of adoptions and marriages of heiresses arranged with a deliberate view of providing for the younger children of numerous families,—of interference on the part of the kings to insure this object,—of a fixed number of lots of land, each represented by one head of a household,—this picture is one, of which the reality must not be sought on the banks of the Eurotas. The "better times of the commonwealth," to which he refers, may have existed in the glowing retrospect of Agis, but are not acknowledged in the sober appreciation of Aristotle. That the citizens were far more numerous in early times, the philosopher tells us, and that the community had in his day greatly declined in power, we also know: in this sense, the times of Sparta had doubtless once been better. We may even concede that during the three centuries succeeding Lykurgus, when they were continually acquiring new territory, and when Aristotle had been told that they had occasionally admitted new citizens, so that the aggregate number of citizens had once been ten thousand,—we may concede that in these previous centuries the distribution of land had been less unequal, so that the disproportion between the great size of the territory and the small number of citizens was not so marked as it had become at the period which the philosopher personally witnessed; for the causes tending to augmented inequality were constant and uninterrupted in their working. But this admission will still leave us far removed from the sketch drawn by Dr. Thirlwall, which depicts the Lykurgean Sparta as starting from a new agrarian scheme not far removed from equality of landed property,—the citizens as spontaneously disposed to uphold this equality, by giving to unprovided men the benefit of adoptions and heiress-marriages,—and the magistrate as interfering to enforce this latter purpose, even in cases where the citizens were themselves unwilling. All our evidence exhibits to us both decided inequality of possessions and inclinations on the part of rich men, the reverse of those which Dr. Thirlwall indicates; nor will the powers of interference which he ascribes to the magistrate be found sustained by the chapter of Herodotus on which he seems to rest them.[713]

To conceive correctly, then, the Lykurgean system, as far as obscurity and want of evidence will permit, it seems to me that there are two current misconceptions which it is essential to discard. One of these is, that the system included a repartition of landed property, upon principles of exact or approximative equality (distinct from that appropriation which belonged to the Dorian conquest and settlement), and provisions for perpetuating the number of distinct and equal lots. The other is, that it was first brought to bear when the Spartans were masters of all Laconia. The illusions created by the old legend,—which depicts Laconia as all one country, and all conquered at one stroke,—yet survive after the legend itself has been set aside as bad evidence: we cannot conceive Sparta as subsisting by itself without dominion over Laconia; nor Amyklæ, Pharis, and Geronthræ, as really and truly independent of Sparta. Yet, if these towns were independent in the time of Lykurgus, much more confidently may the same independence be affirmed of the portions of Laconia which lie lower than Amyklæ down the valley of the Eurotas, as well as of the eastern coast, which Herodotus expressly states to have been originally connected with Argos.

Discarding, then, these two suppositions, we have to consider the Lykurgean system as brought to bear upon Sparta and its immediate circumjacent district, apart from the rest of Laconia, and as not meddling systematically with the partition of property, whatever that may have been, which the Dorian conquerors established at their original settlement. Lykurgus does not try to make the poor rich, nor the rich poor; but he imposes upon both the same subjugating drill,[714]—the same habits of life, gentlemanlike idleness, and unlettered strength,—the same fare, clothing, labors, privations, endurance, punishments, and subordination. It is a lesson instructive at least, however unsatisfactory, to political students,—that, with all this equality of dealing, he ends in creating a community in whom not merely the love of preëminence, but even the love of money, stands powerfully and specially developed.[715]

How far the peculiar of the primitive Sparta extended we have no means of determining; but its limits down the valley of the Eurotas were certainly narrow, inasmuch as it did not reach so far as Amyklæ. Nor can we tell what principles the Dorian conquerors may have followed in the original allotment of lands within the limits of that peculiar. Equal apportionment is not probable, because all the individuals of a conquering band are seldom regarded as possessing equal claims; but whatever the original apportionment may have been, it remained without any general or avowed disturbance until the days of Agis the Third, and Kleomenês the Third. Here, then, we have the primitive Sparta, including Dorian warriors with their Helot subjects, but no Periœki. And it is upon these Spartans separately, perhaps after the period of aggravated disorder and lawlessness noticed by Herodotus and Thucydidês, that the painful but invigorating discipline, above sketched, must have been originally brought to bear.

The gradual conquest of Laconia, with the acquisition of additional lands and new Helots, and the formation of the order of Periœki, both of which were a consequence of it,—is to be considered as posterior to the introduction of the Lykurgean system at Sparta, and as resulting partly from the increased force which that system imparted. The career of conquest went on, beginning from Têleklus, for nearly three centuries,—with some interruptions, indeed, and in the case of the Messenian war, with a desperate and even precarious struggle,—so that in the time of Thucydidês, and for some time previously, the Spartans possessed two-fifths of Peloponnesus. And this series of new acquisitions and victories disguised the really weak point of the Spartan system, by rendering it possible either to plant the poorer citizens as Periœki in a conquered township, or to supply them with lots of land, of which they could receive the produce without leaving the city,—so that their numbers and their military strength were prevented from declining. It is even affirmed by Aristotle,[716] that during these early times they augmented the numbers of their citizens by fresh admissions, which of course implies the acquisition of additional lots of land. But successful war, to use an expression substantially borrowed from the same philosopher, was necessary to their salvation: the establishment of their ascendency, and of their maximum of territory, was followed, after no very long interval, by symptoms of decline.[717] It will hereafter be seen that, at the period of the conspiracy of Kinadôn (395 B. C.), the full citizens (called Homoioi, or Peers) were considerably inferior in number to the Hypomeiŏnes, or Spartans, who could no longer furnish their qualification, and had become disfranchised. And the loss thus sustained was very imperfectly repaired by the admitted practice, sometimes resorted to by rich men, of associating with their own children the children of poorer citizens, and paying the contribution for these latter to the public tables, so as to enable them to go through the prescribed course of education and discipline,—whereby they became (under the title or sobriquet of Mothãkes[718]) citizens, with a certain taint of inferiority, yet were sometimes appointed to honorable commands.

Laconia, the state and territory of the Lacedæmonians, was affirmed, at the time of its greatest extension, to have comprehended a hundred cities,[719] —this after the conquest of Messenia; so that it would include all the southern portion of Peloponnesus, from Thyrea, on the Argolic gulf, to the southern bank of the river Nedon, in its course into the Ionian sea. But Laconia, more strictly so called, was distinguished from Messenia, and was understood to designate the portion of the above-mentioned territory which lay to the east of Mount Taygetus. The conquest of Messenia by the Spartans we shall presently touch upon; but that of Laconia proper is very imperfectly narrated to us. Down to the reign of Têleklus, as has been before remarked, Amyklæ, Pharis, and Geronthræ, were still Achæan: in the reign of that prince they were first conquered, and the Achæans either expelled or subjugated. It cannot be doubted that Amyklæ had been previously a place of consequence: in point of heroic antiquity and memorials, this city, as well as Therapnæ, seems to have surpassed Sparta. And the war of the Spartans against it is represented as a struggle of some moment,—indeed, in those times, the capture of any walled city was tedious and difficult. Timomachus, an Ægeid from Thebes,[720] at the head of a body of his countrymen, is said to have rendered essential service to the Spartans in the conquest of the Achæans of Amyklæ; and the brave resistance of the latter was commemorated by a monument erected to Zeus Tropæus, at Sparta, which was still to be seen in the time of Pausanias.[721] The Achæans of Pharis and Geronthræ, alarmed by the fate of Amyklæ, are said to have surrendered their towns with little or no resistance: after which the inhabitants of all the three cities, either wholly or in part, went into exile beyond sea, giving place to colonists from Sparta.[722] From this time forward, according to Pausanias, Amyklæ continued as a village.[723] But as the Amyklæan hoplites constituted a valuable portion of the Spartan army, it must have been numbered among the cities of the Periœki, as one of the hundred;[724] the distinction between a dependent city and a village not being very strictly drawn. The festival of the Hyacinthia, celebrated at the great temple of the Amyklæan Apollo, was among the most solemn and venerated in the Spartan calendar.

It was in the time of Alkamenês, the son of Têleklus, that the Spartans conquered Helus, a maritime town on the left bank of the Eurotas, and reduced its inhabitants to bondage,—from whose name,[725] according to various authors, the general title *Helots*, belonging to all the serfs of Laconia, was derived. But of the conquest of the other towns of Laconia,—Gytheium,

Akriæ, Therapnæ, etc.,—or of the eastern land on the coast of the Argolic gulf, including Brasiæ and Epidaurus Limêra, or the island of Kythêra, all which at one time belonged to the Argeian confederacy, we have no accounts.

Scanty as our information is, it just enables us to make out a progressive increase of force and dominion on the part of the Spartans, resulting from the organization of Lykurgus. Of this progress, a farther manifestation is found, besides the conquest of the Achæans in the south by Têleklus and Alkamenês, in their successful opposition to the great power of Pheidôn the Argeian, related in a previous chapter. We now approach the long and arduous efforts by which they accomplished the subjugation of their brethren the Messenian Dorians.

# CHAPTER VII.

## FIRST AND SECOND MESSENIAN WARS.

THAT there were two long contests between the Lacedæmonians and Messenians, and that in both the former were completely victorious, is a fact sufficiently attested. And if we could trust the statements in Pausanias,—our chief and almost only authority on the subject,—we should be in a situation to recount the history of both these wars in considerable detail. But unfortunately, the incidents narrated in that writer have been gathered from sources which are, even by his own admission, undeserving of credit,—from Rhianus, the poet of Bênê in Krete, who had composed an epic poem on Aristomenês and the second Messenian war, about B. C. 220,—and from Myrôn of Priênê, a prose author whose date is not exactly known, but belonging to the Alexandrine age, and not earlier than the third century before the Christian era. From Rhianus, we have no right to expect trustworthy information, while the accuracy of Myrôn is much depreciated by Pausanias himself,—on some points even too much, as will presently be shown. But apart from the mental habits either of the prose writer or the poet, it does not seem that any good means of knowledge were open to either of them, except the poems of Tyrtæus, which we are by no means sure that they ever consulted. The account of the two wars, extracted from these two authors by Pausanias, is a string of *tableaux*, several of them, indeed, highly poetical, but destitute of historical coherence or sufficiency: and O. Müller has justly observed, that "absolutely no reason is given in them for the subjection of Messenia."[726] They are accounts unworthy of being transcribed in detail into the pages of genuine history, nor can we pretend to do anything more than verify a few leading facts of the war.

The poet Tyrtæus was himself engaged on the side of the Spartans in the second war, and it is from him that we learn the few indisputable facts respecting both the first and the second. If the Messenians had never been reëstablished in Peloponnesus, we should probably never have heard any farther details respecting these early contests. That reëstablishment, together with the first foundation of the city called Messênê on Mount Ithomê, was among the capital wounds inflicted on Sparta by Epameinondas, in the year B. C. 369,—between three hundred and two hundred and fifty years after the conclusion of the second Messenian war. The descendants of the old Messenians, who had remained for so long a period without any fixed position in Greece, were incorporated in the new city, together with various

Helots and miscellaneous settlers who had no claim to a similar genealogy. The gods and heroes of the Messenian race were reverentially invoked at this great ceremony, especially the great hero Aristomenês;[727] and the site of Mount Ithomê, the ardor of the newly established citizens, the hatred and apprehension of Sparta, operating as a powerful stimulus to the creation and multiplication of what are called *traditions*, sufficed to expand the few facts known respecting the struggles of the old Messenians into a variety of details. In almost all these stories we discover a coloring unfavorable to Sparta, contrasting forcibly with the account given by Isokratês, in his Discourse called Archidamus, wherein we read the view which a Spartan might take of the ancient conquests of his forefathers. But a clear proof that these Messenian stories had no real basis of tradition, is shown in the contradictory statements respecting the principal Hero Aristomenês; for some place him in the first, others in the second, of the two wars. Diodôrus and Myrôn both placed him in the first; Rhianus, in the second. Though Pausanias gives it as his opinion that the account of the latter is preferable, and that Aristomenês really belongs to the second Messenian war, it appears to me that the one statement is as much worthy of belief as the other, and that there is no sufficient evidence for deciding between them,—a conclusion which is substantially the same with that of Wesseling, who thinks that there were two persons named Aristomenês, one in the first and one in the second war.[728] This inextricable confusion respecting the greatest name in Messenian antiquity, shows how little any genuine stream of tradition can here be recognized.

Pausanias states the first Messenian war as beginning in B. C. 743 and lasting till B. C. 724,—the second, as beginning in B. C. 685 and lasting till B. C. 668. Neither of these dates rest upon any assignable positive authority; but the time assigned to the first war seems probable, while that of the second is apparently too early. Tyrtæus authenticates both the duration of the first war, twenty years, and the eminent services rendered in it by the Spartan king Theopompus.[729] He says, moreover, speaking during the second war, "the fathers of our fathers conquered Messênê;" thus loosely indicating the relative dates of the two.

The Spartans (as we learn from Isokratês, whose words date from a time when the city of Messênê was only a recent foundation) professed to have seized the territory, partly in revenge for the impiety of the Messenians in killing their own king, the Herakleid Kresphontês, whose relative had appealed to Sparta for aid,—partly by sentence of the Delphian oracle. Such were the causes which had induced them first to invade the country, and they had conquered it after a struggle of twenty years.[730] The Lacedæmonian explanations, as given in Pausanias, seem for the most part to be counterstatements arranged after the time when the Messenian version, evidently the interesting and popular account, had become circulated.

It has already been stated that the Lacedæmonians and Messenians had a joint border temple and sacrifice in honor of Artemis Limnatis, dating from the earliest times of their establishment in Peloponnesus. The site of this temple, near the upper course of the river Nedon, in the mountainous territory north-east of Kalamata, but west of the highest ridge of Taygetus, has recently been exactly verified,—and it seems in these early days to have belonged to Sparta. That the quarrel began at one of these border sacrifices was the statement of both parties, Lacedæmonians and Messenians. According to the latter, the Lacedæmonian king Têleklus laid a snare for the Messenians, by dressing up some youthful Spartans as virgins, and giving them daggers; whereupon a contest ensued, in which the Spartans were worsted and Têleklus slain. That Têleklus was slain at the temple by the Messenians, was also the account of the Spartans,—but they affirmed that he was slain in attempting to defend some young Lacedæmonian maidens, who were sacrificing at the temple, against outrageous violence from the Messenian youth.[731] In spite of the death of this king, however, the war did not actually break out until some little time after, when Alkamenês and Theopompus were kings at Sparta, and Antiochus and Androklês, sons of Phintas, kings of Messenia. The immediate cause of it was a private altercation between the Messenian Polycharês (victor at the fourth Olympiad, B. C. 764) and the Spartan Euæphnus. Polycharês, having been grossly injured by Euæphnus, and his claim for redress having been rejected at Sparta, took revenge by aggressions upon other Lacedæmonians; the Messenians refused to give him up, though one of the two kings, Androklês, strongly insisted upon doing so, and maintained his opinion so earnestly against the opposite sense of the majority and of his brother Antiochus, that a tumult arose, and he was slain. The Lacedæmonians, now resolving upon war, struck the first blow without any formal declaration, by surprising the border town of Ampheia, and putting its defenders to the sword. They farther overran the Messenian territory, and attacked some other towns, but without success. Euphaês, who had now succeeded his father Antiochus as king of Messenia, summoned the forces of the country and carried on the war against them with energy and boldness. For the first four years of the war, the Lacedæmonians made no progress, and even incurred the ridicule of the old men of their nation as faint-hearted warriors: in the fifth year, however, they undertook a more vigorous invasion, under their two kings, Theopompus and Polydôrus, who were met by Euphaês with the full force of the Messenians. A desperate battle ensued, in which it does not seem that either side gained much advantage: nevertheless, the Messenians found themselves so much enfeebled by it, that they were forced to take refuge on the fortified mountain of Ithômê, abandoning the rest of the country. In their distress, they sent to solicit counsel and protection from Delphi, but their messenger brought back the appalling answer that a virgin, of the royal race of Æpytus, must be sacrificed for their salvation: in the tragic scene which ensues, Aristodêmus puts to death his own daughter, yet without satisfying the exigencies of the oracle. The war still continued, and in the thirteenth year of it another hard-fought battle took place, in which the brave Euphaês was slain, but the result was again indecisive. Aristodêmus, being elected king in his place, prosecuted the war strenuously: the fifth year of his reign is signalized by a third general battle, wherein the Corinthians assist the Spartans, and the Arcadians and Sikyonians are on the side of Messenia; the victory is here decisive on the side of Aristodêmus, and the Lacedæmonians are driven, back into their own territory.[732] It was now their turn to send envoys and ask advice from the Delphian oracle; while the remaining events of the war exhibit a series, partly of stratagems to fulfil the injunctions of the priestess,—partly of prodigies in which the divine wrath is manifested against the Messenians. The king Aristodêmus, agonized with the thought that he has slain his own daughter without saving his country, puts an end to his own life.[733] In the twentieth year of the war, the Messenians abandoned Ithômê, which the Lacedæmonians razed to the ground: the rest of the country being speedily conquered, such of the inhabitants as did not flee either to Arcadia or to Eleusis, were reduced to complete submission.

Such is the abridgment of what Pausanias[734] gives as the narrative of the first Messenian war. Most of his details bear the evident stamp of mere late romance; and it will easily be seen that the sequence of events presents no plausible explanation of that which is really indubitable,—the result. The twenty years' war, and the final abandonment of Ithômê, is attested by Tyrtæus beyond all doubt, as well as the harsh treatment of the conquered. "Like asses, worn down by heavy burdens,"[735] says the Spartan poet, "they were compelled to make over to their masters an entire half of the produce of their fields, and to come in the garb of woe to Sparta, themselves and their wives, as mourners at the decease of the kings and principal persons." The revolt of their descendants, against a yoke so oppressive, goes by the name of the second Messenian war.

Had we possessed the account of the first Messenian war as given by Myrôn and Diodorus, it would evidently have been very different from the above, because they included Aristomenês in it, and to him the leading parts would be assigned. As the narrative now stands in Pausanias, we are not introduced to that great Messenian hero,—the Achilles of the epic of Rhianus, [736]—until the second war, in which his gigantic proportions stand prominently forward. He is the great champion of his country in the three battles which are represented as taking place during this war: the first, with indecisive result, at Deræ; the second, a signal victory on the part of the Messenians, at the Boar's Grave; the third, an equally signal defeat, in consequence of the traitorous flight of Aristokratês, king of the Arcadian Orchomenus, who, ostensibly embracing the alliance of the Messenians, had received bribes from Sparta. Thrice did Aristomenês sacrifice to Zeus Ithomatês the sacrifice called Hekatomphonia,[737] reserved for those who had slain with their own hands a hundred enemies in battle. At the head of a chosen band, he carried his incursions more than once into the heart of the Lacedæmonian territory, surprised Amyklæ and Pharis, and even penetrated by night into the unfortified precinct of Sparta itself, where he suspended his shield, as a token of defiance, in the temple of Athênê Chalkiœkus. Thrice was he taken prisoner, but on two occasions marvellously escaped before he could be conveyed to Sparta: the third occasion was more fatal, and he was cast by order of the Spartans into the Keadas, a deep, rocky cavity in Mount Taygetus, into which it was their habit to precipitate criminals. But even in this emergency the divine aid[738] was not withheld from him. While the fifty Messenians who shared his punishment, were all killed by the shock, he alone was both supported by the gods so as to reach the bottom unhurt, and enabled to find an unexpected means of escape. For when, abandoning all hope, he had wrapped himself up in his cloak to die, he perceived a fox creeping about among the dead bodies: waiting until the animal approached him, he grasped its tail, defending himself from its bites as well as he could by means of his cloak; and being thus enabled to find the aperture by which the fox had entered, enlarged it sufficiently for crawling out himself. To the surprise both of friends and enemies, he again appeared, alive and vigorous, at Eira. That fortified mountain on the banks of the river Nedon, and near the Ionian sea, had been occupied by the Messenians, after the battle in which they had been betrayed by Aristokratês, the Arcadian; it was there that they had concentrated their whole force, as in the former war at Ithômê, abandoning the rest of the country. Under the conduct of Aristomenês, assisted by the prophet Theoklus, they maintained this strong position for eleven years. At length, they were compelled to abandon it; but, as in the case of Ithômê, the final determining circumstances are represented to have been, not any superiority of bravery or organization on the part of the Lacedæmonians, but treacherous betrayal and stratagem, seconding the fatal decree of the gods. Unable to maintain Eira longer, Aristomenês, with his sons, and a body of his countrymen, forced his way through the assailants, and quitted the country,— some of them retiring to Arcadia and Elis, and finally migrating to Rhegium. He himself passed the remainder of his days in Rhodes, where he dwelt along with his son-in-law, Damagêtus, the ancestor of the noble Rhodian family, called the Diagorids, celebrated for its numerous Olympic victories.

Such are the main features of what Pausanias calls[739] the second Messenian war, or of what ought rather to be called the Aristomeneïs of the poet Rhianus. That after the foundation of Messênê, and the recall of the exiles by Epameinondas. favor and credence was found for many tales respecting the prowess of the ancient hero whom they invoked[740] in their libations,—tales well calculated to interest the fancy, to vivify the patriotism, and to inflame the anti-Spartan antipathies, of the new inhabitants,—there can be little doubt. And the Messenian maidens of that day may well have sung, in their public processional sacrifices,[741] how "Aristomenês pursued the flying Lacedæmonians down to the mid-plain of Stenyklêrus, and up to the very summit of the mountain." From such stories, *traditions* they ought not to be denominated, Rhianus may doubtless have borrowed; but if proof were wanting to show how completely he looked at his materials from the point of view of the poet, and not from that of the historian, we should find it in the remarkable fact noticed by Pausanias. Rhianus represented Leotychides as having been king of Sparta during the second Messenian war; now Leotychides, as Pausanias observes, did not reign until near a century and a half afterwards, during the Persian invasion.[742]

To the great champion of Messenia, during this war, we may oppose, on the side of Sparta, another remarkable person, less striking as a character of romance, but more interesting, in many ways, to the historian,—I mean, the poet Tyrtæus, a native of Aphidnæ in Attica, an inestimable ally of the Lacedæmonians during most part of this second struggle. According to a story,—which, however, has the air partly of a boast of the later Attic orators, —the Spartans, disheartened at the first successes of the Messenians, consulted the Delphian oracle, and were directed to ask for a leader from Athens. The Athenians complied by sending Tyrtæus, whom Pausanias and Justin represent as a lame man and a schoolmaster, despatched with a view of nominally obeying the oracle, and yet rendering no real assistance.[743] This seems to be a coloring put upon the story by later writers, but the intervention of the Athenians in the matter, in any way, deserves little credit.[744] It seems more probable that the legendary connection of the Dioskuri with Aphidnæ, celebrated at or near that time by the poet Alkman, brought about, through the Delphian oracle, the presence of the Aphidnæan poet at Sparta. Respecting the lameness of Tyrtæus, we can say nothing: but that he was a schoolmaster (if we are constrained to employ an unsuitable term) is highly probable,—for in that day, minstrels, who composed and sung poems, were the only persons from whom the youth received any mental training. Moreover, his sway over the youthful mind is particularly noted in the compliment paid to him, in after-days, by king Leonidas: "Tyrtæus was an adept in tickling the souls of youth."[745] We see enough to satisfy us that he was by birth a stranger, though he became a Spartan by the subsequent recompense of citizenship conferred upon him,—that he was sent through the Delphian oracle,—that he was an impressive and efficacious minstrel, and that he had, moreover, sagacity enough to employ his talents for present purposes and diverse needs; being able, not merely to reanimate the languishing courage of the baffled warrior, but also to soothe the discontents of the mutinous. That his strains, which long maintained undiminished popularity among the Spartans,[746] contributed much to determine the ultimate issue of this war, there is no reason to doubt; nor is his name the only one to attest the susceptibility of the Spartan mind in that day towards music and poetry. The first establishment of the Karneian festival, with its musical competition, at Sparta, falls during the period assigned by Pausanias to the second Messenian war: the Lesbian harper, Terpander, who gained the first recorded prize at this solemnity, is affirmed to have been sent for by the Spartans pursuant to a mandate from the Delphian oracle, and to have been the means of appeasing a sedition. In like manner, the Kretan Thalêtas was invited thither during a pestilence, which his art, as it is pretended, contributed to heal (about 620 B. C.); and Alkman, Xenokritus, Polymnastus, and Sakadas, all foreigners by birth, found favorable reception, and acquired popularity, by their music and poetry. With the exception of Sakadas, who is a little later, all these names fall in the same century as Tyrtæus, between 660 B. C.-610 B. C. The fashion which the Spartan music continued for a long time to maintain, is ascribed chiefly to the genius of Terpander.[747]

The training in which a Spartan passed his life consisted of exercises warlike, social, and religious, blended together. While the individual, strengthened by gymnastics, went through his painful lessons of fatigue, endurance, and aggression,—the citizens collectively were kept in the constant habit of simultaneous and regulated movement in the warlike march, in the religious dance, and in the social procession. Music and song, being constantly employed to direct the measure and keep alive the spirit[748] of these multitudinous movements, became associated with the most powerful feelings which the habitual self-suppression of a Spartan permitted to arise, and especially with those sympathies which are communicated at once to an assembled crowd; indeed, the musician and the minstrel were the only persons who ever addressed themselves to the feelings of a Lacedæmonian assembly. Moreover, the simple music of that early day, though destitute of artistical merit, and superseded afterwards by more complicated combinations, had, nevertheless, a pronounced ethical character; it wrought much more powerfully on the impulses and resolutions of the hearers, though it tickled the ear less gratefully, than the scientific compositions of after-days.

Farther, each particular style of music had its own appropriate mental effect, —the Phrygian mode imparted a wild and maddening stimulus; the Dorian mode created a settled and deliberate resolution, exempt alike from the desponding and from the impetuous sentiments.[749] What is called the Dorian mode, seems to be in reality the old native Greek mode, as contradistinguished from the Phrygian and Lydian,—these being the three primitive modes, subdivided and combined only in later times, with which the first Grecian musicians became conversant. It probably acquired its title of Dorian from the musical celebrity of Sparta and Argos, during the seventh and sixth centuries before the Christian era; but it belonged as much to the Arcadians and Achæans as to the Spartans and Argeians. And the marked ethical effects, produced both by the Dorian and the Phrygian modes in ancient times, are facts perfectly well-attested, however difficult they may be to explain upon any general theory of music.

That the impression produced by Tyrtæus at Sparta, therefore, with his martial music, and emphatic exhortations to bravery in the field, as well as union at home, should have been very considerable, is perfectly consistent with the character both of the age and of the people; especially, as he is represented to have appeared pursuant to the injunction of the Delphian oracle. From the scanty fragments remaining to us of his elegies and anapæsts, however, we can satisfy ourselves only of two facts: first, that the war was long, obstinately contested, and dangerous to Sparta as well as to the Messenians; next, that other parties in Peloponnesus took part on both sides, especially on the side of the Messenians. So frequent and harassing were the aggressions of the latter upon the Spartan territory, that a large portion of the border land was left uncultivated: scarcity ensued, and the proprietors of the deserted farms, driven to despair, pressed for a redivision of the landed property in the state. It was in appeasing these discontents that the poem of Tyrtæus, called Eunomia, "Legal order," was found signally beneficial.[750] It seems certain that a considerable portion of the Arcadians, together with the Pisatæ and the Triphylians, took part with the Messenians; there are also some statements numbering the Eleians among their allies, but this appears not probable. The state of the case rather seems to have been, that the old quarrel between the Eleians and the Pisatæ, respecting the right to preside at the Olympic games, which had already burst forth during the preceding century, in the reign of the Argeian Pheidôn, still continued. Unwilling dependents of Elis, the Pisatæ and Triphylians took part with the subject Messenians, while the masters at Elis and Sparta made common cause, as they had before done against Pheidôn.[751] Pantaleôn, king of Pisa, revolting from Elis, acted as commander of his countrymen in coöperation with the Messenians; and he is farther noted for having, at the period of the 34th Olympiad (644 B. C.), marched a body of troops to Olympia, and thus dispossessed the Eleians, on that occasion, of the presidency: that particular festival,—as well as the 8th Olympiad, in which Pheidôn interfered,—and the 104th Olympiad, in which the Arcadians marched in,—were always marked on the Eleian register as non-Olympiads, or informal celebrations. We may reasonably connect this temporary triumph of the Pisatans with the Messenian war, inasmuch as they were no match for the Eleians single-handed, while the fraternity of Sparta with Elis is in perfect harmony with the scheme of Peloponnesian politics which we have observed as prevalent even before and during the days of Pheidôn.[752] The second Messenian war will thus stand as beginning somewhere about the 33d Olympiad, or 648 B. C., between seventy and eighty years after the close of the first, and lasting, according to Pausanias, seventeen years; according to Plutarch, more than twenty years.[753]

Many of the Messenians who abandoned their country after this second conquest are said to have found shelter and sympathy among the Arcadians, who admitted them to a new home and gave them their daughters in marriage; and who, moreover, punished severely the treason of Aristokratês, king of Orchomenus, in abandoning the Messenians at the battle of the Trench. That perfidious leader was put to death, and his race dethroned, while the crime as well as the punishment was farther commemorated by an inscription, which was to be seen near the altar of Zeus Lykæus, in Arcadia. The inscription doubtless existed in the days of Kallisthenês, in the generation after the restoration of Messênê. But whether it had any existence prior to that event, or what degree of truth there may be in the story of Aristokratês, we are unable to determine:[754] the son of Aristokratês, named Aristodêmus, is alleged in another authority to have reigned afterwards at Orchomenus.[755] That which stands strongly marked is, the sympathy of Arcadians and Messenians against Sparta,—a sentiment which was in its full vigor at the time of the restoration of Messênê.

The second Messenian war was thus terminated by the complete subjugation of the Messenians. Such of them as remained in the country were reduced to a servitude probably not less hard than that which Tyrtæus described them as having endured between the first war and the second. In aftertimes, the whole territory which figures on the map as Messenia,—south of the river Nedon, and westward of the summit of Taygetus,—appears as subject to Sparta, and as forming the western portion of Laconia; distributed, in what proportion we know not, between Periœkic towns and Helot villages. By what steps, or after what degree of farther resistance, the Spartans conquered this country, we have no information; but we are told that they made over Asinê to the expelled Dryopes from the Argolic peninsula and Mothônê to the fugitives from Nauplia.[756] Nor do we hear of any serious revolt from Sparta in this territory until one hundred and fifty years afterwards,[757] subsequent to the Persian invasion,—a revolt which Sparta, after serious efforts, succeeded in crushing. So that the territory remained in her power until her defeat at Leuktra, which led to the foundation of Messênê by Epameinondas. The fertility of the plains,—especially of the central portion near the river Pamisus, so much extolled by observers, modern as well as ancient,—rendered it an acquisition highly valuable. At some time or other, it must of course have been formally partitioned among the Spartans, but it is probable that different and successive allotments were made, according as the various portions of territory, both to the east and to the west of Taygetus, were conquered. Of all this we have no information.[758]

Imperfectly as these two Messenian wars are known to us, we may see enough to warrant us in making two remarks. Both were tedious, protracted, and painful, showing how slowly the results of war were then gathered, and adding one additional illustration to prove how much the rapid and instantaneous conquest of Laconia and Messenia by the Dorians, which the Herakleid legend sets forth, is contradicted by historical analogy. Both were characterized by a similar defensive proceeding on the part of the Messenians, —the occupation of a mountain difficult of access, and the fortification of it for the special purpose and resistance,—Ithômê (which is said to have had already a small town upon it) in the first war, Eira in the second. It is reasonable to infer from hence, that neither their principal town Stenyklêrus, nor any other town in their country, was strongly fortified, so as to be calculated to stand a siege; that there were no walled towns among them analogous to Mykenæ and Tiryns on the eastern portion of Peloponnesus; and that, perhaps, what were called towns were, like Sparta itself, clusters of unfortified villages. The subsequent state of Helotism into which they were reduced is in consistency with this dispersed village residence during their period of freedom.

The relations of Pisa and Elis form a suitable counterpart and sequel to those of Messenia and Sparta. Unwilling subjects themselves, the Pisatans had lent their aid to the Messenians,—and their king, Pantaleôn, one of the leaders of this combined force, had gained so great a temporary success, as to dispossess the Eleians of the agonothesia or administration of the games for one Olympic ceremony, in the 34th Olympiad. Though again reduced to their condition of subjects, they manifested dispositions to renew their revolt at the 48th Olympiad, under Damophôn, the son of Pantaleôn, and the Eleians marched into their country to put them down, but were persuaded to retire by protestations of submission. At length, shortly afterwards, under Pyrrhus, the brother of Damophôn, a serious revolt broke out. The inhabitants of Dyspentium, and the other villages in the Pisatid, assisted by those of

Makistus, Skillus, and the other towns in Triphylia, took up arms to throw off the yoke of Elis; but their strength was inadequate to the undertaking. They were completely conquered; Dyspontium was dismantled, and the inhabitants of it obliged to flee the country, from whence most of them emigrated to the colonies of Epidamnus and Apollonia, in Epirus. The inhabitants of Makistus and Skillus were also chased from their abodes, while the territory became more thoroughly subject to Elis than it had been before. These incidents seem to have occurred about the 50th Olympiad, or B. C. 580; and the dominion of Elis over her Pericekic territory was thus as well assured as that of Sparta.[759] The separate denominations both of Pisa and Triphylia became more and more merged in the sovereign name of Elis: the town of Lepreum alone, in Triphylia, seems to have maintained a separate name and a sort of half-autonomy down to the time of the Peloponnesian war, not without perpetual struggles against the Eleians.[760] But towards the period of the Peloponnesian war, the political interests of Lacedæmon had become considerably changed, and it was to her advantage to maintain the independence of the subordinate states against the superior: accordingly, we find her at that time upholding the autonomy of Lepreum. From what cause the devastation of the Triphylian towns by Elis, which Herodotus mentions as having happened in his time, arose, we do not know; the fact seems to indicate a continual yearning for their original independence, which was still commemorated, down to a much later period, by the ancient Amphiktyony, at Samikum, in Triphylia, in honor of Poseidôn,—a common religious festival frequented by all the Triphylian towns and celebrated by the inhabitants of Makistus, who sent round proclamation of a formal truce for the holy period.[761] The Lacedæmonians, after the close of the Peloponnesian war, had left them undisputed heads of Greece, formally upheld the independence of the Triphylian towns against Elis, and seem to have countenanced their endeavors to attach themselves to the Arcadian aggregate, which, however, was never fully accomplished. Their dependence on Elis became loose and uncertain, but was never wholly shaken off.[762]

# CHAPTER VIII.

## CONQUESTS OF SPARTA TOWARDS ARCADIA AND ARGOLIS.

I HAVE described in the last two chapters, as far as our imperfect evidence permits, how Sparta came into possession both of the southern portion of Laconia along the coast of the Eurotas down to its mouth, and of the Messenian territory westward. Her progress towards Arcadia and Argolis is now to be sketched, so as to conduct her to that position which she occupied during the reign of Peisistratus at Athens, or about 560-540 B. C.,—a time when she had reached the maximum of her territorial possessions, and when she was confessedly the commanding state in Hellas.

The central region of Peloponnesus, called Arcadia, had never received any emigrants from without. Its indigenous inhabitants,—a strong and hardy race of mountaineers, the most numerous Hellenic tribe in the peninsula, and the constant hive for mercenary troops,[763]—were among the rudest and poorest of Greeks, retaining for the longest period their original subdivision into a number of petty hill-villages, each independent of the other; while the union of all who bore the Arcadian name,—though they had some common sacrifices, such as the festival of the Lykæan Zeus, of Despoina, daughter of Poseidôn and Dêmêtêr, and of Artemis Hymnia,[764]—was more loose and ineffective than that of Greeks generally, either in or out of Peloponnesus. The Arcadian villagers were usually denominated by the names of regions, coincident with certain ethnical subdivisions,—the Azānes, the Parrhasii, the Mænalii (adjoining Mount Mænalus), the Eutrêsii, the Ægytæ, the Skiritæ, etc.[765] Some considerable towns, however, there were,—aggregations of villages or demes which had been once autonomous. Of these, the principal were Tegea and Mantineia, bordering on Laconia and Argolis,—Orchomenus, Pheneus, and Stymphalus, towards the north-east, bordering on Achaia and Phlius,—Kleitôr and Heræa, westward, where the country is divided from Elis and Triphylia by the woody mountains of Pholoê and Erymanthus,—and Phigaleia, on the south-western border near to Messenia. The most powerful of all were Tegea and Mantineia,[766]—conterminous towns, nearly equal in force, dividing between them the cold and high plain of Tripolitza, and separated by one of those capricious torrents which only escapes through katabothra. To regulate the efflux of this water was a difficult task, requiring friendly coöperation of both the towns: and when their frequent jealousies brought on a quarrel, the more aggressive of the two inundated the territory of its neighbor as one means of annoyance. The power of Tegea, which had grown up out of nine constituent townships, originally separate,[767] appears to have been more ancient than that of its rival; as we may judge from its splendid heroic pretensions connected with the name of Echemus, and from the post conceded to its hoplites in joint Peloponnesian armaments, which was second in distinction only to that of the Lacedæmonians.[768] If it be correct, as Strabo asserts,[769] that the incorporation of the town of Mantineia, out of its five separate demes, was brought about by the Argeians, we may conjecture that the latter adopted this proceeding as a means of providing some check upon their powerful neighbors of Tegea. The plain common to Tegea and Mantineia was bounded to the west by the wintry heights of Mænalus,[770] beyond which, as far as the boundaries of Laconia, Messenia, and Triphylia, there was nothing in Arcadia but small and unimportant townships, or villages,—without any considerable town, before the important step taken by Epameinondas in founding Megalopolis, a short time after the battle of Leuktra. The mountaineers of these regions, who joined Epameinondas before the battle of Mantineia, at a time when Mantineia and most of the towns of Arcadia were opposed to him, were so inferior to the other Greeks in equipment, that they still carried as their chief weapon, in place of the spear, nothing better than the ancient club.[771]

Both Tegea and Mantineia held several of these smaller Arcadian townships near them in a sort of dependence, and were anxious to extend this empire over others: during the Peloponnesian war, we find the Mantineians establishing and garrisoning a fortress at Kypsela among the Parrhasii, near the site in which Megalopolis was afterwards built.[772] But at this period, Sparta, as the political chief of Hellas,—having a strong interest in keeping all the Grecian towns, small and great, as much isolated from each other as possible, and in checking all schemes for the formation of local confederacies, —stood forward as the protectress of the autonomy of these smaller Arcadians, and drove back the Mantineians within their own limits.[773] At a somewhat later period, during the acmé of her power, a few years before the battle of Leuktra, she even proceeded to the extreme length of breaking up the unity of Mantineia itself, causing the walls to be razed, and the inhabitants to be again parcelled into their five original demes,—a violent arrangement, which the turn of political events very soon reversed.[774] It was not until after the battle of Leuktra and the depression of Sparta that any measures were taken for the formation of an Arcadian political confederacy;[775] and even then, the jealousies of the separate cites rendered it incomplete and short-lived. The great permanent change, the establishment of Megalopolis, was accomplished by the ascendency of Epameinondas. Forty petty Arcadian townships, among those situated to the west of Mount Mænalus, were aggregated into the new city: the jealousies of Tegea, Mantineia, and Kleitôr, were for a while suspended; and œkists came from all of them, as well as from the districts of the Mænalii and Parrhasii, in order to impart to the new establishment a genuine Pan-Arcadian character.[776] It was thus there arose for the first time a powerful city on the borders of Laconia and Messenia, rescuing the Arcadian townships from their dependence on Sparta, and imparting to them political interests of their own, which rendered them, both a check upon their former chief and a support to the reëstablished Messenians.

It has been necessary thus to bring the attention of the reader for one moment to events long posterior in the order of time (Megalopolis was founded in 370 B. C.), in order that he may understand, by contrast, the general course of those incidents of the earlier time, where direct accounts are wanting. The northern boundary of the Spartan territory was formed by some of the many small Arcadian townships or districts, several of which were successively conquered by the Spartans and incorporated with their dominion, though at what precise time we are unable to say. We are told that Charilaus, the reputed nephew and ward of Lykurgus, took Ægys, and that he also invaded the territory of Tegea, but with singular ill-success, for he was defeated and taken prisoner:[777] we also hear that the Spartans took Phigaleia by surprise in the 30th Olympiad, but were driven out again by the neighboring Arcadian Oresthasians.[778] During the second Messenian war, the Arcadians are represented as cordially seconding the Messenians: and it may seem perhaps singular that, while neither Mantineia nor Tegea are mentioned in this war, the more distant town of Orchomenus, with its king Aristokratês, takes the lead. But the facts of the contest come before us with so poetical a coloring, that we cannot venture to draw any positive inference as to the times to which they are referred.

Œnus[779] and Karystus seem to have belonged to the Spartans in the days of Alkman: moreover, the district called Skirîtis bordering on the territory of Tegea,—as well as Belemina and Maleatis to the westward, and Karyæ to the eastward and south-eastward, of Skirîtis,—forming altogether the entire northern frontier of Sparta, and all occupied by Arcadian inhabitants,—had been conquered and made part of the Spartan territory[780] before 600 B. C. And Herodotus tells us, that at this period the Spartan kings Leon and Hegesiklês contemplated nothing less than the conquest of entire Arcadia, and sent to ask from the Delphian oracle a blessing on their enterprise.[781] The priestess dismissed their wishes as extravagant, in reference to the whole of Arcadia, but encouraged them, though with the usual equivocations of language, to try their fortune against Tegea. Flushed with their course of previous success, not less than by the favorable construction which they put upon the words of the oracle, the Lacedæmonians marched against Tegea with such entire confidence of success, as to carry with them chains for the purpose of binding their expected prisoners. But the result was disappointment and defeat. They were repulsed with loss, and the prisoners whom they left behind, bound in the very chains which their own army had brought, were constrained to servile labor on the plain of Tegea,—the words of the oracle being thus literally fulfilled, though in a sense different from that in which the Lacedæmonians had first understood them.[782]

For one whole generation, we are told, they were constantly unsuccessful in their campaigns against the Tegeans, and this strenuous resistance probably prevented them from extending their conquests farther among the petty states of Arcadia.

At length, in the reign of Anaxandridês and Aristô, the successors of Leon and Hegesiklês (about 560 B. C.), the Delphian oracle, in reply to a question from the Spartans,—which of the gods they ought to propitiate in order to become victorious,—enjoined them to find and carry to Sparta the bones of Orestês, son of Agamemnôn. After a vain search, since they did not know where the body of Orestês was to be found, they applied to the oracle for more specific directions, and were told that the son of Agamemnôn was buried at Tegea itself, in a place "where two blasts were blowing under powerful constraint,—where there was stroke and counter-stroke, and destruction upon destruction." These mysterious words were elucidated by a lucky accident. During a truce with Tegea, Lichas, one of the chiefs of the three hundred Spartan chosen youth, who acted as the movable police of the country under the ephors, visited the place, and entered the forge of a blacksmith,—who mentioned to him, in the course of conversation, that, in sinking a well in his outer court, he had recently discovered a coffin containing a body seven cubits long; astounded at the sight, he had left it there undisturbed. It struck Lichas that the gigantic relic of aforetime could be nothing else but the corpse of Orestês, and he felt assured of this, when he reflected how accurately the indications of the oracle were verified; for there were the "two blasts blowing by constraint," in the two bellows of the blacksmith: there was the "stroke and counter-stroke," in his hammer and anvil, as well as the "destruction upon destruction," in the murderous weapons which he was forging. Lichas said nothing, but returned to Sparta with his discovery, which he communicated to the authorities, who, by a concerted scheme, banished him under a pretended criminal accusation. He then returned again to Tegea, under the guise of an exile, prevailed upon the blacksmith to let to him the premises, and when he found himself in possession, dug up and carried off to Sparta the bones of the venerated hero.
[783]

From and after this fortunate acquisition, the character of the contest was changed; the Spartans found themselves constantly victorious over the Tegeans. But it does not seem that these victories led to any positive result, though they might perhaps serve to enforce the practical conviction of Spartan superiority; for the territory of Tegea remained unimpaired, and its autonomy noway restrained. During the Persian invasion, Tegea appears as the willing ally of Lacedæmon, and as the second military power in the Peloponnesus; [784] and we may fairly presume that it was chiefly the strenuous resistance of the Tegeans which prevented the Lacedæmonians from extending their empire over the larger portion of the Arcadian communities. These latter always maintained their independence, though acknowledging Sparta as the presiding power in Peloponnesus, and obeying her orders implicitly as to the disposal of their military force. And the influence which Sparta thus possessed over all Arcadia was one main item in her power, never seriously shaken until the battle of Leuktra; which took away her previous means of insuring success and plunder to her minor followers.[785]

Having thus related the extension of the power of Sparta on her northern or Arcadian frontier, it remains to mention her acquisitions on the eastern and north-eastern side, towards Argos. Originally, as has been before stated, not merely the province of Kynuria and the Thyreātis but also the whole coast down to the promontory of Malea, had either been part of the territory of Argos or belonged to the Argeian confederacy. We learn from Herodotus,[786] that before the time when the embassy from Crœsus, king of Lydia, came to solicit aid in Greece (about 547 B. C.), the whole of this territory had fallen into the power of Sparta; but how long before, or at what precise epoch, we have no information. A considerable victory is said to have been gained by the Argeians over the Spartans in the 27th Olympiad or 669 B. C., at Hysiæ, on the road between Argos and Tegea.[787] At that time it does not seem probable that Kynuria could have been in the possession of the Spartans,—so that we must refer the acquisition to some period in the following century; though Pausanias places it much earlier, during the reign of Theopompus,[788]—and Eusebius connects it with the first establishment of the festival called Gymnopædia at Sparta, in 678 B. C.

About the year 547 B. C., the Argeians made an effort to reconquer Thyrea from Sparta, which led to a combat long memorable in the annals of Grecian heroism. It was agreed between the two powers that the possession of this territory should be determined by a combat of three hundred select champions on each side; the armies of both retiring, in order to leave the field clear. So undaunted and so equal was the valor of these two chosen companies, that the battle terminated by leaving only three of them alive,—Alkênôr and Chromius among the Argeians, Othryadês among the Spartans. The two Argeian warriors hastened home to report their victory, but Othryadês remained on the field, carried off the arms of the enemy's dead into the Spartan camp, and kept his position until he was joined by his countrymen the next morning. Both Argos and Sparta claimed the victory for their respective champions, and the dispute after all was decided by a general conflict, in which the Spartans were the conquerors, though not without much slaughter on both sides. The brave Othryadês, ashamed to return home as the single survivor of the three hundred, fell upon his own sword on the field of battle. [789]

This defeat decided the possession of Thyrea, which did not again pass, until a very late period of Grecian history, under the power of Argos. The preliminary duel of three hundred, with its uncertain issue, though well established as to the general fact, was represented by the Argeians in a manner totally different from the above story, which seems to have been current among the Lacedæmonians.[790] But the most remarkable circumstance is, that more than a century afterwards,—when the two powers were negotiating for a renewal of the then expiring truce, the Argeians, still hankering after this their ancient territory, desired the Lacedæmonians to submit the question to arbitration; which being refused, they next stipulated for the privilege of trying the point in dispute by a duel similar to the former, at any time except during the prevalence of war or of epidemic disease. The historian tells us that the Lacedæmonians acquiesced in this proposition, though they thought it absurd,[791] in consequence of their anxiety to keep their relations with Argos at that time smooth and pacific. But there is no reason to imagine that the real duel, in which Othryadês contended, was considered as absurd at the time when it took place, or during the age immediately succeeding. It fell in with a sort of chivalrous pugnacity which is noticed among the attributes of the early Greeks,[792] and also with various legendary exploits, such as the single combat of Echemus and Hyllus, of Melanthus and Xanthus, of Menelaus and Paris, etc. Moreover, the heroism of Othryadês and his countrymen was a popular theme for poets, not only at the Spartan gymnopædia,[793] but also elsewhere, and appears to have been frequently celebrated. The absurdity attached to this proposition, then, during the Peloponnesian war,—in the minds even of the Spartans, the most old-fashioned and unchanging people in Greece,—is to be ascribed to a change in the Grecian political mind, at and after the Persian war. The habit of political calculation had made such decided progress among them, that the leading states especially had become familiarized with something like a statesmanlike view of their resources, their dangers, and their obligations. How lamentably deficient this sort of sagacity was during the Persian invasion, will appear when we come to describe that imminent crisis of Grecian independence: but the events of those days were well calculated to sharpen it for the future, and the Greeks of the Peloponnesian war had become far more refined political schemers than their forefathers. And thus it happened that the proposition to settle a territorial dispute by a duel of chosen champions, admissible and even becoming a century before, came afterwards to be derided as childish.

The inhabitants of Kynuria are stated by Herodotus to have been Ionians, but completely Dorized through their long subjection to Argos, by whom they were governed as Periœki. Pausanias gives a different account of their race, which he traces to the eponymous hero Kynūrus, son of Perseus: but he does not connect them with the Kynurians whom he mentions in another place as a portion of the inhabitants of Arcadia.[794] It is evident that, even in the time of Herodotus, the traces of their primitive descent were nearly effaced. He says they were "Orneates and Periœki" to Argos; and it appears that the inhabitants of Orneæ also, whom Argos had reduced to the same dependent condition, traced their eponymous hero to an Ionic stock,—Orneus was the son of the Attic Erechtheus.[795] Strabo seems to have conceived the Kynurians as occupying originally, not only the frontier district of Argolis and Laconia, wherein Thyrea is situated, but also the north-western portion of Argolis, under the ridge called Lyrkeium, which separates the latter from the Arcadian territory of Stimphalus.[796] This ridge was near the town of Orneæ, which lay on the border of Argolis near the confines of Phlius; so that Strabo thus helps to confirm the statement of Herodotus, that the Orneates were a portion of Kynurians, held by Argos along with the other Kynurians in the condition of dependent allies and Periœki, and very probably also of Ionian origin.

The conquest of Thyrea (a district valuable to the Lacedæmonians, as we may presume from the large booty which the Argeians got from it during the Peloponnesian war)[797] was the last territorial acquisition made by Sparta. She was now possessed of a continuous dominion, comprising the whole southern portion of the Peloponnesus, from the southern bank of the river Nedon on the western coast, to the northern boundary of Thyreatis on the eastern coast. The area of her territory, including as it did both Laconia and Messenia, was equal to two-fifths of the entire peninsula, all governed from the single city, and for the exclusive purpose and benefit of the citizens of Sparta. Within all this wide area there was not a single community pretending to independent agency. The townships of the Periœki, and the villages of the Helots, were each individually unimportant; nor do we hear of any one of them presuming to treat with a foreign state: both consider themselves as nothing else but subjects of the Spartan ephors and their subordinate officers. They are indeed discontented subjects, hating as well as fearing their masters, and not to be trusted if a favorable opportunity for secure revolt presents itself. But no individual township or district is strong enough to stand up for itself, while combinations among them are prevented by the habitual watchfulness and unscrupulous precautions of the ephors, especially by that jealous secret police called the Krypteia, to which allusion has already been made.

Not only, therefore, was the Spartan territory larger and its population more numerous than that of any other state in Hellas, but its government was also more completely centralized and more strictly obeyed. Its source of weakness was the discontent of its Periœki and Helots, the latter of whom were not—like the slaves of other states—imported barbarians from different countries, and speaking a broken Greek, but genuine Hellens,—of one dialect and lineage, sympathizing with each other, and as much entitled to the protection of Zeus Hellanius as their masters,—from whom, indeed, they stood distinguished by no other line except the perfect training, individual and collective, which was peculiar to the Spartans. During the period on which we are at present dwelling, it does not seem that this discontent comes sensibly into operation; but we shall observe its manifestations very unequivocally after the Persian and during the Peloponnesian war.

To such auxiliary causes of Spartan predominance we must add another,— the excellent military position of Sparta, and the unassailable character of Laconia generally. On three sides that territory is washed by the sea,[798] with a coast remarkably dangerous and destitute of harbors; hence Sparta had nothing to apprehend from this quarter until the Persian invasion and its consequences,—one of the most remarkable of which was, the astonishing development of the Athenian naval force. The city of Sparta, far removed from the sea, was admirably defended by an almost impassable northern frontier, composed of those districts which we have observed above to have been conquered from Arcadia,—Karyātis, Skirītis, Maleātis, and Beleminātis. The difficulty as well as danger of marching into Laconia by these mountain passes, noticed by Euripides, was keenly felt by every enemy of the Lacedæmonians, and has been powerfully stated by a first-rate modern observer, Colonel Leake.[799] No site could be better chosen for holding the key of all the penetrable passes than that of Sparta. This well-protected frontier was a substitute more than sufficient for fortifications to Sparta itself, which always maintained, down to the times of the despot Nabis, its primitive aspect of a group of adjacent hill-villages rather than a regular city.

When, along with such territorial advantages, we contemplate the personal training peculiar to the Spartan citizens, as yet undiminished in their numbers, —combined with the effect of that training upon Grecian sentiment, in inspiring awe and admiration,—we shall not be surprised to find that, during the half-century which elapsed between the year 600 B. C. and the final conquest of Thyreātis from Argos, Sparta had acquired and begun to exercise a recognized ascendency over all the Grecian states. Her military force was at that time superior to that of any of the rest, in a degree much greater than it afterwards came to be; for other states had not yet attained their maximum, and Athens in particular was far short of the height which she afterwards reached. In respect to discipline as well as number, the Spartan military force had even at this early period reached a point which it did not subsequently surpass; while in Athens, Thebes, Argos, Arcadia, and even Elis (as will be hereafter shown), the military training in later days received greater attention, and improved considerably. The Spartans (observes Aristotle)[800] brought to perfection their gymnastic training and their military discipline, at a time when other Greeks neglected both the one and the other: their early superiority was that of the trained men over the untrained, and ceased in after-days, when other states came to subject their citizens to systematic exercises of analogous character or tendency. This fact,—the early period at which Sparta attained her maximum of discipline, power, and territory,—is important to bear in mind, when we are explaining the general acquiescence which her ascendency met with in Greece, and which her subsequent acts would certainly not have enabled her to earn. That acquiescence first began, and became a habit of the Grecian mind, at a time when Sparta had no rival to come near her,—when she had completely shot ahead of Argos,—and when the vigor of the Lykurgean discipline had been manifested in a long series of conquests, made during the stationary period of other states, and ending only, to use the somewhat exaggerated phrase of Herodotus, when she had subdued the greater part of Peloponnesus.[801]

Our accounts of the memorable military organization of Sparta are scanty, and insufficient to place the details of it clearly before us. The arms of the Spartans, as to all material points, were not different from those of other Greek hoplites. But one grand peculiarity is observable from the beginning, as an item in the Lykurgean institutions. That lawgiver established military divisions quite distinct from the civil divisions, whereas in the other states of Greece, until a period much later than that which we have now reached, the two were confounded,—the hoplites or horsemen of the same tribe or ward being marshalled together on the field of battle. Every Lacedæmonian was bound to military service from the age of twenty to sixty, and the ephors, when they sent forth an expedition, called to arms all the men within some given limit of age. Herodotus tells us that Lykurgus established both the syssitia, or public mess, and the enômoties and triākads, or the military subdivisions peculiar to Sparta.[802] The triākads are not mentioned elsewhere, nor can we distinctly make out what they were; but the enômoty was the special characteristic of the system, and the pivot upon which all its arrangements turned. It was a small company of men, the number of whom was variable, being given differently at twenty-five, thirty-two, or thirty-six men,—drilled and practised together in military evolutions, and bound to each other by a common oath.[803] Each enômoty had a separate captain, or enomotarch, the strongest and ablest soldier of the company, who always occupied the front rank, and led the enômoty when it marched in single file, giving the order of march, as well as setting the example. If the enômoty was drawn up in three, or four, or six files, the enomotarch usually occupied the front post on the left, and care was taken that both the front-rank men and the rear-rank men, of each file, should be soldiers of particular merit.[804]

It was upon these small companies that the constant and severe Lacedæmonian drilling was brought to act. They were taught to march in concert, to change rapidly from line to file, to wheel right or left in such manner as that the enomotarch and the other protostates, or front-rank men, should always be the persons immediately opposed to the enemy.[805] Their step was regulated by the fife, which played in martial measures peculiar to Sparta, and was employed in actual battle as well as in military practice; and so perfectly were they habituated to the movements of the enômoty, that, if their order was deranged by any adverse accident, scattered soldiers could spontaneously form themselves into the same order, each man knowing perfectly the duties belonging to the place into which chance had thrown him. [806] Above the enômoty were several larger divisions,—the pentekostys, the lochus, and the mora,[807] of which latter there seem to have been *six* in all. Respecting the number of each division, and the proportion of the larger to the smaller, we find statements altogether different, yet each resting upon good authority,—so that we are driven to suppose that there was no peremptory standard, and that the enômoty comprised twenty-five, thirty-two, or thirty-six men; the pentekostys, two or four enômoties; the lochus, two or four pentekosties, and the mora, four hundred, five hundred, six hundred, or nine hundred men,—at different times, or according to the limits of age which the ephors might prescribe for the men whom they called into the field.[808]

What remains fixed in the system is, first, the small number, though varying within certain limits, of the elementary company called enômoty, trained to act together, and composed of men nearly of the same age,[809] in which every man knew his place; secondly, the scale of divisions and the hierarchy of officers, each rising above the other,—the enômotarch, the pentekontêr, the lochage, and the polemarch, or commander of the mora,— each having the charge of their respective divisions. Orders were transmitted from the king, as commander-in-chief, through the polemarchs to the lochages,—from the lochages to the pentekonters, and then from the latter to the enômotarchs, each of whom caused them to be executed by his enômoty. As all these men had been previously trained to the duties of their respective stations, the Spartan infantry possessed the arrangements and aptitudes of a standing army. Originally, they seem to have had no cavalry at all,[810] and when cavalry was at length introduced into their system, it was of a very inferior character, no provision having been made for it in the Lykurgean training. But the military force of the other cities of Greece, even down to the close of the Peloponnesian war, enjoyed little or no special training, having neither any small company like the enômoty, consisting of particular men drilled to act together,—no fixed and disciplined officers,—nor triple scale of subordination and subdivision. Gymnastics, and the use of arms, made a part of education everywhere, and it is to be presumed that no Grecian hoplite was entirely without some practice of marching in line and military evolutions, inasmuch as the obligation to serve was universal and often enforced. But such practice was casual and unequal, nor had any individual of Argos or Athens a fixed military place and duty. The citizen took arms among his tribe, under a taxiarch, chosen from it for the occasion, and was placed in a rank or line wherein neither his place nor his immediate neighbors were predetermined. The tribe appears to have been the only military classification known to Athens,[811] and the taxiarch the only tribe officer for infantry, as the phylarch was for cavalry, under the general-in-chief. Moreover, orders from the general were proclaimed to the line collectively by a herald of loud voice, not communicated to the taxiarch so as to make him responsible for the proper execution of them by his division. With an arrangement thus perfunctory and unsystematized, we shall be surprised to find how well the military duties were often performed: but every Greek who contrasted it with the symmetrical structure of the Lacedæmonian armed force, and with the laborious preparation of every Spartan for his appropriate duty, felt an internal sentiment of inferiority, which made him willingly accept the headship of "these professional artists in the business of war,"[812] as they are often denominated.

It was through the concurrence of these various circumstances that the willing acknowledgment of Sparta as the leading state of Hellas became a part of Grecian habitual sentiment, during the interval between about 600 B. C. and 547 B. C. During this period too, chiefly, Greece and her colonies were ripening into a sort of recognized and active partnership. The common religious assemblies, which bound the parts together, not only acquired greater formality and more extended development, but also became more numerous and frequent,—while the Pythian, Isthmian, and Nemean games were exalted into a national importance, approaching to that of the Olympic. The recognized superiority of Sparta thus formed part and parcel of the first historical aggregation of the Grecian states. It was about the year 547 B. C., that Crœsus of Lydia, when pressed by Cyrus and the Persians, solicited aid from Greece, addressing himself to the Spartans as confessed presidents of the whole Hellenic body.[813] And the tendencies then at work, towards a certain degree of increased intercourse and coöperation among the dispersed members of the Hellenic name, were doubtless assisted by the existence of a state recognized by all as the first,—a state whose superiority was the more readily acquiesced in, because it was earned by a painful and laborious discipline, which all admired, but none chose to copy.[814]

Whether it be true, as O. Müller and other learned men conceive, that the Homeric mode of fighting was the general practice in Peloponnesus and the rest of Greece anterior to the invasion of the Dorians, and that the latter first introduced the habit of fighting with close ranks and protended spears, is a point which cannot be determined. Throughout all our historical knowledge of Greece, a close rank among the hoplites, charging with spears always in hand, is the prevailing practice; though there are cases of exception, in which the spear is hurled, when troops seem afraid of coming to close quarters.[815] Nor is it by any means certain, that the Homeric manner of fighting ever really prevailed in Peloponnesus, which is a country eminently inconvenient for the use of war-chariots. The descriptions of the bard may perhaps have been founded chiefly upon what he and his auditors witnessed on the coast of Asia Minor, where chariots were more employed, and where the country was much more favorable to them.[816] We have no historical knowledge of any military practice in Peloponnesus anterior to the hoplites with close ranks and protended spears.

One Peloponnesian state there was, and one alone, which disdained to acknowledge the superiority or headship of Lacedæmon. Argos never forgot that she had once been the chief power in the peninsula, and her feeling towards Sparta was that of a jealous, but impotent, competitor. By what steps the decline of her power had taken place, we are unable to make out, nor can we trace the succession of her kings subsequent to Pheidôn. It has been already stated that, about 669 B. C., the Argeians gained a victory over the Spartans at Hysiæ, and that they expelled from the port of Nauplia its preëxisting inhabitants, who found shelter, by favor of the Lacedæmonians, at the port of Mothônê, in Messenia:[817] Damokratidas was then king of Argos. Pausanias tells us that Meltas, the son of Lakidês, was the last descendant of Temenus who succeeded to this dignity; he being condemned and deposed by the people. Plutarch, however, states that the family of the Herakleids died out, and that another king, named Ægôn, was chosen by the people at the indication of the Delphian oracle.[818] Of this story, Pausanias appears to have known nothing. His language implies that the kingly dignity ceased with Meltas,—wherein he is undoubtedly mistaken, since the title existed, though probably with very limited functions, at the time of the Persian war. Moreover, there is some ground for presuming that the king of Argos was even at that time a Herakleid,—since the Spartans offered to him a third part of the command of the Hellenic force, conjointly with their own two kings. [819] The conquest of Thyreātis by the Spartans deprived the Argeians of a valuable portion of their Periœkis, or dependent territory; but Orneæ, and the remaining portion of Kynuria,[820] still continued to belong to them; the plain round their city was very productive; and except Sparta, there was no other power in Peloponnesus superior to them. Mykenæ and Tiryns, nevertheless, seem both to have been independent states at the time of the Persian war, since both sent contingents to the battle of Platæa, at a time when Argos held aloof and rather favored the Persians. At what time Kleônæ became the ally, or dependent, of Argos, we cannot distinctly make out. During the Peloponnesian war, it is numbered in that character along with Orneæ;[821] but it seems not to have lost its autonomy about the year 470 B. C., at which period Pindar represents the Kleonæans as presiding and distributing prizes at the Nemean games.[822] The grove of Nemea was less than two miles from their town, and they were the original presidents of this great festival,—a function of which they were subsequently robbed by the Argeians, in the same manner as the Pisatans had been treated by the Eleians with reference to the Olympic Agôn. The extinction of the autonomy of Kleônæ and the acquisition of the presidency of the Nemean festival by Argos, were doubtless simultaneous, but we are unable to mark the exact time; for the statement of Eusebius, that the Argeians celebrated the Nemean festival as early as the 53d Olympiad, or 568 B. C., is contradicted by the more valuable evidence of Pindar.[823]

Of Corinth and Sikyôn it will be more convenient to speak when we survey what is called the Age of the Tyrants, or Despots; and of the inhabitants of Achaia (who occupied the southern coast of the Corinthian gulf, westward of Sikyôn, as far as Cape Araxus, the north-western point of Peloponnesus), a few words exhaust our whole knowledge, down to the time at which we are arrived. These Achæans are given to us as representing the ante-Dorian inhabitants of Laconia, whom the legend affirms to have retired under Tisamenus to the northern parts of Peloponnesus, from whence they expelled the preëxisting Ionians and occupied the country. The race of their kings is said to have lasted from Tisamenus down to Ogygus,[824]—how long, we do not know. After the death of the latter, the Achæan towns formed each a separate republic, but with periodical festivals and sacrifice at the temple of Zeus Homarius, affording opportunity of settling differences and arranging their common concerns. Of these towns, twelve are known from Herodotus and Strabo,—Pellênê, Ægira, Ægæ, Bura, Helikê, Ægium, Rhypes, Patræ, Pharæ, Olenus, Dymê, Tritæa.[825] But there must originally have been some other autonomous towns besides these twelve; for in the 23d Olympiad, Ikarus of Hyperêsia was proclaimed as victor, and there seems good reason to believe that Hyperêsia, an old town of the Homeric Catalogue, was in Achaia. [826] It is affirmed that, before the Achæan occupation of the country, the Ionians had dwelt in independent villages, several of which were subsequently aggregated into towns: thus Patræ was formed by a coalescence of seven villages, Dymê from eight (one of which was named Teuthea), and Ægium also from seven or eight. But all these towns were small, and some of them underwent a farther junction one with the other; thus Ægæ was joined with Ægeira, and Olenus with Dymê.[827] All the authors seem disposed to recognize twelve cities, and no more, in Achaia; for Polybius, still adhering to that number, substitutes Leontium and Keryneia in place of Ægæ and Rhypes; Pausanias gives Keryneia in place of Patræ.[828] We hear of no facts respecting these Achæan towns until a short time before the Peloponnesian war, and even then their part was inconsiderable.

The greater portion of the territory comprised under the name of Achaia was mountain, forming the northern descent of those high ranges, passable only through very difficult gorges, which separate the country from Arcadia to the south, and which throw out various spurs approaching closely to the gulf of Corinth. A strip of flat land, with white clayey soil, often very fertile, between these mountains and the sea, formed *the plain* of each of the Achæan towns, which were situated for the most part upon steep outlying eminences overhanging it. From the mountains between Achaia and Arcadia, numerous streams flow into the Corinthian gulf, but few of them are perennial, and the whole length of coast is represented as harborless.[829]